HOME

LEANNE TREESE

Moxie Publishing

Leanne Treese/Moxie Publishing, LLC

P.O. Box 5323

Clinton, New Jersey 08809

www.leannetreese.com

Publisher's note: This is a work of fiction. Names, characters, places, and incidents are a product of the author's imagination. Locales and public names are sometimes used for atmospheric purposes. Any resemblance to people, living or dead, or to businesses, companies, events, institutions, or locales is completely coincidental.

Home/Leanne Treese 1st edition

ISBN ebook: 978-1-7358961-9-9

ISBN print: 979-8-9926030-0-2

Cover Design by JRC Designs/Jena R Collins www.jenarcollins.com

MasterOfVectors/Shutterstock.com

Nathapol Kongseang/Shutterstock.com

Kristen Prahl/Shutterstock.com

David Papazian/Shutterstock.com

MARGRIT HIRSCH/Shutterstock.com

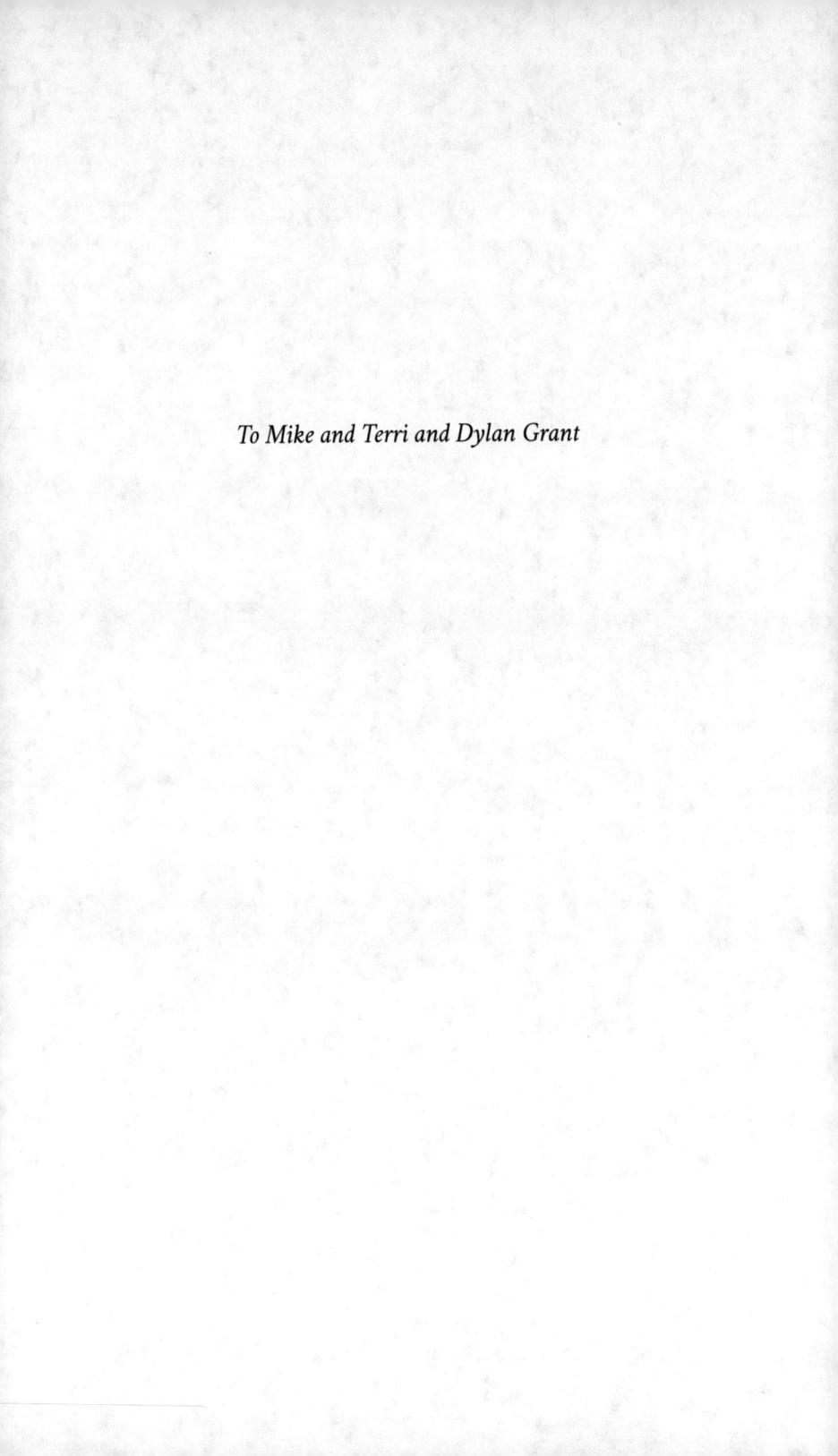

To Mike and Terri and Dylan Grant

CHAPTER 1

Lucas

Mom isn't home yet. She said she'd be "right back" and when Mom says something like that, she usually means it. Right back always means right back. Like fifteen minutes. Maybe twenty. But she's been gone way longer than that. At least an hour. Nate's here—it's not like I'm alone—but still. I'm worried.

It would be easy if I could just call Mom, but I can't. I mean I can, I guess, but it wouldn't help. I can't say words, or at least I can't say the words I want to. I'll think them. I know what I want to say. But somewhere between my brain and my mouth the words get lost and what comes out is gibberish, or worse—jingles and phrases I've said so many times, I can say them at will.

I do have an app on my iPad to help me communicate, but it's for simple things, like "I want pizza." Not feelings. Not, "I'm worried that Mom has been gone for so long."

It sucks, but I've gotten used to being alone inside my head. Half the time I don't even mind, but the other half I really, really do. Like now. Because while I'm sitting on the couch with my attention seemingly fixed on the Back to the Future movie streaming on my iPad, I very much want to call Mom. But I can't, and the movie, with its familiar dialogue and the scenes I've seen dozens of times, is keeping me calm. The movie I can predict. Life, not so much.

There's a knock on the door and Nate, sitting in the chair next to me, hops up and jogs toward it. Before I can see who's there or move or yell out (ha ha, like I could do that anyway), Nate steps outside and closes the door behind him. I stare at it. Who's there? I'd follow outside if I thought whoever was talking to Nate would talk to me. But people usually don't.

Nate doesn't come back inside for the longest time and when he finally does, his face is pale. His eyes are sad. Shocked even. He embraces me in a big bear hug even though it's awkward, with me still stretched out on the couch with my iPad on my lap. He releases me and then starts and stammers, saying things like, "I don't know how to tell you" and "just know everything will be alright" and "I'm so sorry." My eyes are fixed on my tiny screen with Marty McFly flying through Hill Valley on his skateboard, but my mind is frozen. This is bad. I almost know what Nate's going to say before the words come out of his mouth.

And then they do.

"There was a car accident. Your mother died."

CHAPTER 2

Olivia

Still in sweats, I fold my legs over each other on the small kitchen chair in my New York apartment. My body is hunched over my laptop, steaming green tea with a splash of milk on the table next to it. I'm making my monthly goal list. Five entries. First day of the month. I've done this for long as I can remember. Because you can't get where you want to go if you don't have a map. Right?

I scan down the entries.

1. Discuss new admin with William
2. Create spreadsheet to categorize billable hours
3. Find home for Otis
4. Increase fruit and vegetable intake by ten percent
5. Get ahead on Jupiter Rowan case

My eyes snag on the final entry and my heart leaps inside my chest despite knowing that the words are there. Of course they are! I typed them less than thirty seconds ago. Still. The Rowan case is a huge deal, and my involvement is five days new. Jupiter

Rowan has been accused of banking fraud, which ordinarily would seem boring except for, well, Jupiter Rowan. Dubbed the crypto queen by the media and frequently adorned in neon capes and crowns, she's the last person anyone would have expected to make billions off her investments. But she did. Some say illegally. And that's where Bennett Connor comes in. We're the defense. I was put on the team by my boss, William Michaels, as the only non-partner assigned. I glance at the name again—Jupiter Rowan—and silently squeal. It's the most publicized case in Manhattan right now. And I'm smack in the middle of it.

Otis, my foster cat, rubs his gray body across the leg of the chair. I snap the laptop shut, scoop him up, and cradle him against my chest. "Yes, buddy," I say, "I'll tell her no."

The no is for Jess, owner of the Kitty Cat Café, an organization that serves both as a coffee shop and a cat rescue. I'm just fostering Otis—I don't have time for full-time pet ownership—but the candidates for permanent homes have been awful. I interviewed one last night. No way. I'll stop by the café and tell Jess "no" on my way to the office.

I set Otis down, pull my reddish blonde hair into the thinnest of ponytails, and quickly dress in clothes suitable for work on a Saturday. I walk the several blocks from my apartment to the café. Sporadic trees are nestled within the cityscape, giving a pop of color and a rush of nature to what would otherwise be a mass of concrete. Their presence, along with the Rowan case (squeal), buoys my mood. I reach the café and push open the door.

Jess is behind the coffee bar writing the daily specials on a chalkboard that spans the entire back wall, fuchsia-colored chalk gripped in her hand. The café has two floors. Downstairs is the coffee bar, decorated with a menagerie of cat items. Upstairs are the ten to fifteen cats available for adoption. Otis would stay here, but he doesn't get along with other cats.

"Hey, Jess." I cross the space between the door and the bar and slide onto a stool.

"Don't tell me." She finishes writing a special and starts writing a new one. "You don't like the medical student. Ryn, right?"

"I don't."

"Of course, you don't." She turns around. Her face is makeup-free; her shirt has a bunch of cartoon cats doing acrobatics on it. It's classic Jess. The only time I've seen her without at least one cat-related item of apparel was during the short stint where, before she inherited money and opened the Kitty Cat Café, she'd worked in the copy room at Bennett Connor. "What's the issue?"

"She won't have time to care for him," I say. "Plus, he's got that hairball medicine. It must be given regularly, or he'll get hairballs again."

Jess drops the chalk into a container near the board. She turns and looks at me, her eyes wide. "Ryn's in *medical* school. I think she can handle the hairball meds."

"*If* she remembers." I cross and uncross my arms. "I just got a weird vibe is all. Like she was too perfect, you know. She's responsible. She likes cats."

"Are you serious right now?"

"Yes. She's not the one. Not for Otis. Trust me."

Jess leans against the bar. "You know you can adopt him. But if you're not going to, you've got to let him find his forever home."

"I will," I insist.

A smile tugs at the corners of her mouth. "Adopt him?"

"No. Find him his forever home."

She shakes her head. "Come on, Olivia. You've turned down four eligible adoptees. Just admit it. You want Otis. There's nothing wrong with wanting to have someone waiting for you when you get home at the end of the day."

I scoff. I do have someone waiting for me at the end of the day. Jupiter Rowan.

"Protest all you want," Jess continues, "but it's human nature. People need people. Or at least cats."

My phone rings. I'm glad for the interruption because I have nothing left to add to the *people need people* conversation and I DO NOT want Ryn, the perfect-but-not-really-perfect medical student, to adopt Otis. I pull the phone from my pocket and glance at the unknown number. "I should take this."

"Adopt Otis!" Jess yells as I exit.

I shoot her a look at the door and step onto the sidewalk in front of the café. I accept the call. "Hello."

"Hello. Olivia Ellison?" The voice is unfamiliar. Male.

"Speaking."

"Oh. Olivia. Good." The man clears his throat. "I'm Chuck Stockton, an attorney. Stockton and Associates."

I search my brain for the name of the man or the firm and turn up blank.

"You've been named in a will."

"Yeah?" My mind scatters. Whose will could I possibly be named in?

"It's Melanie Moore," Chuck says. "I'm so sorry, but she's passed."

"Melanie Moore," I repeat. Melanie Moore. My father's wife. I pull up her image in my mind. Tall and willowy with long wavy hair down to her mid-back. Always in peasant skirts and loose tees, colorful beaded necklaces and bracelets layered on her neck and wrists. She was, at least back when Dad was alive and I saw her more regularly, a vision of health. "How?"

"It was a car accident. She died at the scene." He pauses. "She wasn't in pain, as I understand it."

I digest the information. I wasn't close to Melanie. I'd always blamed her for the fact that Dad moved from our New Jersey hometown to the middle of Pennsylvania, that I went from seeing him every week to just summers and long holidays. Still. She's gone.

"I'm sorry, Miss Ellison."

"Thank you." I close my eyes and conjure Lucas, my half-brother. It hits me now, how devastated he must be. First our dad died, now his mom. "What about Lucas?"

"That's why I'm calling," Chuck says. "Melanie named you as his guardian."

CHAPTER 3

OLIVIA

Chuck's words ricochet in my mind. *Melanie named you as his guardian.*

Lucas is eighteen years old and nonverbal. He was diagnosed with autism spectrum disorder—ASD—at age three.

"Me?" Adrenaline jolts through my system. "Why?"

"I don't know."

I move to a shady spot on the sidewalk and lean against the building behind me. I scan my brain for legal knowledge about guardianships. None. I have none. My area of expertise is finance law, and now crypto.

"She never mentioned it."

"Oh?" He says the word like a question.

"No."

"Her death was sudden. Maybe she planned to speak to you?"

"She should have asked me first though, right?"

Chuck clears his throat again. "There are no hard and fast rules on this kind of thing, but yes, people generally have a conversation before a guardianship designation."

I puff out a breath. "I live in New York. I have a job here. I don't—I can't—" I try to explain myself without sounding like the type of person who doesn't care about a blood relative—her *brother*—but honestly, what was Melanie thinking? I'm not equipped to care for Lucas. I didn't even fully commit to pet ownership of the world's easiest cat. "Is there someone else?" I blurt.

"You're not required to assume guardianship, Miss Ellison. There are alternate guardians listed in the will."

The summer sun shoots down and I shift to a shadier spot. "I can't do it."

"You don't want to accept guardianship?"

"No. I mean, I don't know." I inhale a breath. "I just heard about this for the first time now. It's—" I pause and try to piece together appropriate words for my emotions. "A lot," I finish lamely.

"I understand." Chuck's voice is kinder now, less lawyerly. "Would it be helpful to come to Greenwillow? You can see Lucas, and I'll make myself available to answer any questions you have."

I know I won't accept the guardianship—I can't, I mean, *no*—but I do need to see Lucas. And I do want to know who the named alternate is in the will. Lucas is my brother. It's the least I can do.

"I think that would be helpful. Can I call you back with a time? I need to check my schedule."

My schedule. That's a joke. I'd looked at it last night, thinking I'd fit the Rowan work into every nook and cranny of free time that I have, including most of this weekend. Blowing a day, possibly two, to go to Greenwillow? It feels impossible. But I can't not go.

I promise to call Chuck back and click off the phone. My mind spins and I stay propped up against the office building. A woman walks by with a big yellow Labrador. A man jogs across the street wearing giant blue headphones. A couple meanders along holding identical Starbucks cups. It's a normal day. That suddenly has nothing normal about it.

Melanie. Gone. How is Lucas handling that?

My mind flashes back to the Christmas after our father died. Lucas was eleven years old, all arms and legs and wearing clothes way too small for his growing frame but among the only he'd deemed acceptable. He was into Transformers back then, toys that turned robots into cars and the reverse. The whole of Christmas morning, all he did was fold his new Transformer from a robot to a car and back. Over and over and over. He'd always been prone to perseverations like this, but the Transformer Christmas was different, like his life depended on the rote actions of transforming the toy.

Obsession with the Transformer was a reaction to our dad's death, I'd assumed. Still, I'd wanted a different one. Dad had been gone less than four weeks, and I was gutted. I wanted Lucas to scream and cry and rail on the unfairness of Dad dying from a heart attack. Didn't he know what death meant? That Dad would never make his special pancakes again, or cheer wildly for the Giants, or hug us so tight that love from his soul poured into our own? There would be no more Dad jokes, no more finding him secretly feeding the barn cats. And here Lucas was, obsessed with a toy.

At Christmas breakfast, Melanie stood at the stove attempting to make Dad's pancakes. Lucas sat at the table with his new transformer, twisting it from a robot to a car and back again. My irritation grew with each transformation until I finally stood, wrestled the toy from his hand and threw it, hard, against the floor.

Lucas was never big on eye contact, but he looked at me then and for an instant I thought I could see it. Sadness and remorse. For Dad? For me? For not being what I needed in that moment? Instantly, I felt awful. I fell to the floor and picked up the errant pieces on my hands and knees. I tried to put the transformer back together. I couldn't; Melanie bought him a new one.

I stop, so out of the present moment that it takes me a second to realize that I'm in the lobby of my apartment building. I've walked the entire way back from the Kitty Cat Café without any recollection of doing so. My phone rings. I stare at it like it's a foreign object. Mom's face is on the screen. I pick up the call.

"Olivia. We missed you last night."

I can't place what she's talking about for a moment. Then I remember. I was supposed to meet Mom and the twins, Shelby and Ellie, my half-sisters, to go over plans for Ellie's bridal shower. I blew it off with a lame work excuse, knowing full well Mom had it planned already. Any input from me would be superfluous.

She launches into an unasked for and detailed description of plans they made. I tune out her words, wanting to tell her, or someone, about Melanie and Lucas and Chuck Stockton's phone call. *She's named you guardian of her son.*

Mom continues to talk.

"Mom."

"We decided lunch is better than brunch," she continues.

"Mom."

"You know, brunch can be so heavy."

"Melanie's dead," I blurt.

The stream of shower-related information stops. "Your father's Melanie?"

"Yes. It was a car accident."

"That's sad. I'm sorry."

I believe she is sorry. Mom had moved on with Adam, her new husband and the twins' father, well before Dad ever met Melanie.

I punch the elevator button. "Melanie named me guardian of Lucas in her will."

"Guardian?" Mom pauses, and I call up her image. Likely dressed to the nines, her makeup heavy but perfect. Frosted blond hair teased into a style. Bulky gold jewelry—necklaces, bracelets, rings, all of it from Adam's chain of jewelry stores. "That's ridiculous," she continues. "You're hardly an adult yourself. You can't be responsible for, well, *Lucas*."

She says his name like he's distasteful. Mother to three neurotypical kids and having no close relatives on the spectrum, Mom's never been all that understanding when it came to him. The few times they crossed paths, judgment always oozed out of her. She thought—and I know this because she outright *said* it— that Lucas's behaviors were a result of poor discipline stemming from Melanie's new age, bohemianish parenting style. A favorite quote: "None of my three ever acted that way."

"I'm not going to accept but still, it's sad. He's lost both his parents. I know you don't like him—"

"I never said that," she interrupts. "And it is sad. But you being guardian? No. Melanie should have never put you in that position. Did she even ask? Did you know?"

"No." I step off the elevator, walk the three doors to my apartment, and unlock the door.

"Of course not," she scoffs. "Figures. It's great to be all loosey goosey like she always was, you know, but this, well—" She pauses. "Please tell me you are not going to do it."

"I already said I'm not going to accept." I step inside my apartment, shut the door, and pick up Otis. "But I feel bad, okay? Like I'm rejecting my brother." Otis wriggles. I set him down and he scurries out of the room. "He is my brother. Same as Ellie and Shelby are my sisters."

"Olivia." Her tone screams condescension. As if Lucas couldn't possibly be a sibling equal to *the twins*.

"He's my brother. Dad's son. Can you just, I don't know, be empathetic or something? His parents died, okay? I'm the closest relative he has left."

Mom pauses a long moment. "I'm sorry that Melanie put you in this untenable position," she says finally. "Adam and I will send some money to whatever cause you think would be helpful."

I pull the phone away from my ear and stare at it, disbelieving that *this* is Mom's big venture into empathy. Money and a backhanded apology. I'm not sure why I'd expected anything different. "Thanks," I say, the word hollow.

I hang up, check my schedule, and call Chuck Stockton back.

CHAPTER 4

LUCAS

Christmas, Age Eleven

Everything is different. Dad is not here. Gone for four weeks.

I'm the one who found him on the day of the heart attack. He was sitting on the couch in his office, his hand on his chest. His breathing was off, his face sweaty. I knew something was wrong and I found Mom outside. She was feeding the animals, her cell phone held against her ear with her shoulder. I tried to tell her something was wrong, but all that came out was gibberish. I hate that nonsense came out of my mouth. I hate that I can't say what I want, not ever, but especially that day. Mom smiled at me because she's kind and tolerant of my verbal stims, but I needed her to move. I tried to say words again, but nothing helpful like "something is wrong with Dad" came out of my mouth. Mom smiled but kept talking. My hands started to flap like they do when my emotions get the better of me, when I'm trying to get control of myself.

I grabbed Mom's arm. "Lucas," she said, scolding. I grabbed her arm again. "I've got to go," she said into the phone. She hugged me, trying to calm me, I guess, but she needed to move. She needed to go to

Dad. She squeezed tighter and I bit her shoulder. "Lucas!" She drew back, and I grabbed her arm again. She followed me inside, and when she reached Dad she screamed. It was too late.

For the past four weeks, all I can do is hate that I couldn't say that something was wrong. That words jam up in my body, unable to express themselves at will. I keep locking and unlocking the pieces of my Transformer. Over and over and over.

Olivia is here and I normally like that. Olivia spends time doing things with me that no one else does, like swimming. And hikes. She takes me to amusement parks too. Just the two of us. And she always talks to me like she'd talk to anyone else, even sharing things like boys she likes and things Ellie and Shelby do that drive her crazy, and I love that. But right now I feel too awful to care that she's here.

I keep at the Transformer all through Christmas morning and all while Mom prepares the pancakes Dad used to make. The Transformer is the only thing, honestly, that's keeping me together, that's making me not have the kind of freak-out that scares people. So I keep doing it. Then Olivia grabs it out of my hand and throws it on the ground. It hits the floor with a smack and scatters into pieces. I look at her.

I am so sorry, Olivia.

CHAPTER 5

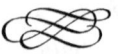

O LIVIA
"For personal reasons," I tell William at work on Monday morning. "Something with my brother."
William raises an eyebrow.

"I'll just be a few days. And I'll work on the Rowan case while I'm there, of course."

He leans back in his chair. He removes the pen from his left ear and taps it against his open palm.

"You can reach me anytime," I continue and it's all I can manage not to add *please don't take me off the Rowan case.*

William springs forward and jabs the pen in my direction. "Okay, Olivia, but remember, I put myself on the line for you. Majorie didn't think you were ready for this."

Marjorie, as in Marjorie Small, senior partner and my secret idol. Marjorie started at Bennett Connor at the same time as my father, and I'd always idolized her - the pretty powerful attorney with an office next to his. William had already told me she didn't think I was ready for such a big case, but I didn't mind. I knew I could prove her wrong. "Yes, of course," I say to William. "And I appreciate it. I won't let you down."

"Okay Olivia. And good luck with your situation." He swivels his chair and looks back at the computer.

It's a dismissal. I step out, go home, and immediately collect Otis. My appointment with the attorney is this afternoon; I don't have a lot of time to spare. I drive—speed, really—the four hours across Pennsylvania to Greenwillow, a suburb outside of Pittsburgh. I go straight to the center of town and park in front of Stockton and Associates. The firm is in a converted house at the end of Main Street, the part where the storefronts end, replaced by row houses with big front porches, rickety steps, and peeling paint. The street is lined with the same kind of trees that dot the New York cityscape and give the area, for this month anyway, the kind of appeal that belies how old and rundown the town is.

Holding Otis's carrier like a purse, I traverse the stairs onto a big porch featuring a collection of half-dead plants. I pull open the door and step inside. It's clear the space was once a home, and I am firmly in what I imagine was a parlor. "Olivia Ellison for Chuck Stockton," I say to the receptionist.

"I'll tell him." Her eyes shift toward the cat carrier.

"He's an emotional support animal," I lie, and the woman averts her eyes. I know I should have gotten a cat sitter to feed him, but Otis doesn't like to be alone overnight. So here he is.

I collapse into a chair in the waiting area and set Otis's carrier on my lap. I'm dressed casually in jeans and a yellow T-shirt, sneakers on my feet. I packed nicer clothes in case I need to go to court to sign off on the guardianship appointment, or whatever it is I need to do, but really I'm hoping everything can be taken care of here. I feel bad enough about stepping aside without having to announce the decision in open court.

Otis meows. "No, O," I whisper. He blinks.

A man with stark white hair and ruddy cheeks pops his head out of a doorway behind the receptionist's desk. "Olivia," he says in my direction. "I'm Chuck." He pushes the door open farther and holds it. He's wearing a red bow tie with navy blue polka dots, old-timey in a way that might seem fashionable on some men, but not Chuck. His navy suit is two different shades of blue, one for the pants, one for the jacket. The fabric is slightly wrinkled and colorful argyle socks peek from the bottom. He looks more like a scatterbrained professor than a lawyer. At least the kind of lawyers I'm used to seeing.

"Third door on the left," Chuck tells me, and I move down the narrow hall, Otis's carrier in hand. I stop at the open door. Chuck stoops down and looks inside the carrier. "And who's this?"

Otis hisses before I can answer, and Chuck stands back. "Feisty."

"His name is Otis, but I'm just fostering him. You know, lack of time due to work and all." I'm not sure why I add this. The preemptive excuse, I guess, for what I'm about to do.

I slide into the chair and set Otis's carrier on the floor. Chuck rounds the desk and flops into a huge swivel chair. The shelves behind him are a hodgepodge of legal books, family photos, and knickknacks. There's a set of golf clubs propped up in the corner, files and boxes stacked on the floor. My brother's file is on the desk, folders and papers spilling from its opening like legal guts.

"So New York City." He leans back and gives a warm smile. "That must be exciting."

"It can be," I say noncommittally.

"I've been there a few times. Saw the ball drop once, been to a few Broadway shows." He grabs a pen and taps it on the edge of the desk. "Phantom. That was one. Ever see it? You know, the guy with the mask."

"Quite a while ago."

"And one about the founding fathers. With the rappers."

"Hamilton?"

"Yes. Wanted to see that. Couldn't get tickets. Imagine it's easier now."

"I think so." There's a pause, but Chuck doesn't fill it. "About Lucas," I prompt.

"Lucas, yes. My wife Susan and Melanie were friends. They ran the farm co-op in town together. And Susan has a gift shop in town. She sold Melanie's jewelry pieces on consignment. Beautiful craftsmanship. And original."

"Sounds like Melanie," I say, and it's true. Making hand-crafted jewelry. Farming local produce. Both are core Melanie Moore activities.

"Lovely person, Melanie. I'm so sorry."

"Thank you." I wait for Chuck to add more, and when he doesn't, I prompt again. "And Lucas?"

"Well"—he pulls a document from those protruding from Lucas's file—"as I told you on the phone, Melanie named you the guardian in her will." He flips the document around and points to a paragraph. My full name—Olivia Lynn Ellison—is right there in black and white.

"You should know Lucas is the beneficiary of a special needs trust that Melanie set up after your father died," Chuck tells me. He pulls a document from the file and pushes it toward me. "There's close to half a million dollars in here. The trust owns the house now too."

I pick up the document and scan it. Half a million dollars is a lot of money, of course, but Lucas is only eighteen with substantial needs. The funds will need to be invested properly if they are going to last his lifetime.

"Lucas gets government benefits too," Chuck continues. "Social security, disability, Medicaid for insurance, some from the State."

"Managed correctly, it seems he should have enough for what he needs," I say emphatically. "I presume the trustee is a bank."

Chuck shakes his head. "No. Melanie set it up so that the guardian is also the trustee. It's unusual but not prohibited. I think she thought it would be easier that way, and she must have trusted the guardian—you—to do what was right with the money without the need for an overseer."

Guilt seers through me. Melanie trusted me with her son *and* his money.

"There is an alternate guardian," Chuck supplies. "Dennis Moore, Melanie's brother."

"Her brother." I grab onto the idea of someone older, a real adult, taking the reins. "I think I remember Melanie mentioning him," I say, but when I peruse my brain for context, I come up short. And though I have no concrete knowledge of Dennis Moore or what he is like, I visualize him as a kind, grandfatherly man. "Why do you think she'd choose me over her brother?"

"I don't know. I've never met Dennis."

"And if Dennis isn't able to take it on?"

"The court will assign a public guardian to make decisions on Lucas's behalf and appoint a conservator to manage the funds."

If Dennis says no, strangers would be making decisions on behalf of my brother.

Chuck whips his glasses off his face and leans forward. "I'm not sure what your relationship with Melanie was like. But I will say I knew her well, and I've seen what a champion she's been for Lucas. She was as dedicated as a mother could be to the well-being of her child. Melanie would not," he continues, "take the guardian designation lightly. She picked you for a reason, Olivia. I think she believed you were the best person to make decisions for *her* child, one she knew firsthand wasn't always the easiest." He folds his hands in front of his desk and nods. "It's about as big a compliment as a person can give."

My heart squeezes. I know all of this. Melanie took Lucas

just as he was, unabashedly accepting every stim, every
outburst, everything different about him. There's no question
she always wanted what was best for him. And she somehow
thought that was me.

"Why didn't she talk to me about it?"

Chuck shakes his head. "I don't know. Like I said on the
phone, I imagine she'd planned to. She probably thought she
had years to go before it would be an issue."

I nod. That makes sense. As devoted a mother as she was,
Melanie was not always the most organized or practical person.
She was always getting to things.

"And if I can't take this on?" I ask. "Do you just contact
Dennis then?"

"Yes. I'd need to notify him and see if he would like the job,
for lack of a better word. Then there's a hearing. The court has
the final say."

He pauses, and I don't know if it's my own guilt or a real
reaction on his part, but the way he looks at me feels different.
Like I'm, I don't know, awful. The kind of person who might
kick a puppy or swindle the elderly out of their life savings.

"Should I reach out to him?" Chuck asks.

I smooth down my T-shirt and tap the top of Otis's carrier
like he is, in fact, an emotional support animal. My mouth goes
dry, and I don't answer. I don't know why. *This,* passing on the
guardianship, is the main reason I'm here. I swallow past a boul-
der-like lump in my throat. "Yes," I say finally, "I think that
would be best."

Chuck nods. "Okay, then. I'll reach out to him. In the meantime, do you plan to see Lucas at Melanie's?"

"Yes."

"Just a heads-up that my nephew is there. Nate. He's worked
extensively with Lucas, and he agreed to stay until all this could
get sorted. I'll let him know you're coming."

"Sure. Thanks."

"Oh, and if you were thinking about services or a funeral . . ." he starts.

For a split second, I don't know what he's talking about. Then I realize it's Melanie. Melanie's funeral. Melanie's services. Concern rises in my chest. Am I in charge of those too?

"Melanie didn't want a service," Chuck says. "It's in her will."

"Nothing?"

"Nothing." He shakes his head. "Church members and friends are taking care of the cremation and burial of the ashes. She'll be at Greenwillow Pines Cemetery."

I nod, grateful that none of this is in my domain. "Thanks for letting me know."

He stands, a signal that the meeting is at an end. I reach down and grab Otis's carrier.

Chuck crosses the room and opens the door. "I'll be in touch, Olivia."

"Thanks," I say, but the word comes out weak. My stomach churns as I walk to my car. *Don't feel bad. Don't feel bad. Don't feel bad.* The phrase repeats itself over and over. *Don't feel bad. Don't feel bad. Don't feel bad.*

I reach the car.

Who am I kidding?

I feel bad.

CHAPTER 6

NATE

Olivia's car pulls up the driveway twenty minutes after I hang up with Uncle Chuck. I'd told Lucas she was coming right after the call. I expected him to retreat to his room, his modus operandi when things are too much, which, since Melanie died, has been just about everything and everyone. But he doesn't. He stays in the family room, iPad on his lap, Animal Planet, a favorite show, beating out of the speakers.

"She's here," I say in his direction.

He doesn't look up or stop the video, but he doesn't move either. Good sign? Maybe.

Olivia gets out of the car and grabs a carrier from the passenger seat. Instead of coming toward the front door, she walks directly to the "farm" area of Melanie's farmette, her tall frame graceful as she moves. She opens the gate, sets the carrier down, and steps to Dusty, the pony in the barn. She strokes his muzzle, and after, she moves past the goat enclosure to the chicken coop and peeks inside. She pets one of the barn cats and returns to the gate. She leans against it a moment, then slides down a fence post and sits on the ground.

A breeze blows at her hair. She's pretty; it's evident from even this far away, not that I didn't know that already. There's a photograph of her and Lucas on the refrigerator. She's all natural in the picture, makeup-free with delicate features. "A natural beauty." That's what Mom would call her. I stare at her for another moment, then, feeling like a voyeur, I step away from the window. She'll come in when she's ready.

I move to the couch, grab my computer, and resume working my résumé. My gaze lands on the gap between college graduation and taking this job two years ago. It's nearly a three-year gap, the reason for which I don't like to think about, let alone explain. I type out a few lines, read, delete. I repeat this process, then again, then one more time. I peer at the cursor blinking over the last deleted letter. This freeze? It's what always happens when I try to move on. I can't get past the empty spots of my life without remembering the events that created them. But this job—caring for Lucas—is over, or will be, and I need to figure something else out.

But not right now.

I slam the laptop shut and move to the kitchen. I retrieve two bottles of water from the fridge. The least I can do is introduce myself to Olivia.

I tell Lucas I'm getting Olivia, step out of the house, and walk toward where she's sitting, her back against the post. "Hey."

She doesn't turn around.

"Hey," I repeat, louder.

Nothing. I can't open the gate because she's leaning against it, so I crouch down and put my mouth near her ear. "Hey," I say a third time.

She vaults into the air.

"I'm sorry," I say at the same time she says, "I was sleeping."

"Sorry," I repeat. "I'm Nate." I hold a water bottle over the fence, and she takes it. Her cheeks are flushed, her eyes the unique shade of brownish green from the fridge picture. I look at them a beat too long.

"I'm Olivia, Lucas's sister. Sorry I'm in here." She gestures around the area. "I came to Greenwillow during the summers as a kid and I always found the animals peaceful. I sat down and, well . . ." She looks around.

"You fell asleep against this super cozy fence post?" I tap the top of the post with an open palm. "Happens more often than you'd think." I open the gate, move inside, and nod at the carrier on the ground, the one she'd brought out of the car. I can tell now that there's an animal inside. "And who's this?"

She picks it up and I peer inside at a behemoth of a gray cat with wideset green eyes.

"This is Otis."

"Nice to meet you, Otis." I bend down and put my face in front of the carrier. Otis swipes a paw in my direction, and I step back by instinct.

"He's been a little rude today," Olivia says. "He's kind of a homebody."

"I get that." I nod and push my ever-present cowlicks down. Not that my appearance matters, but Olivia's managed to look pulled together even after sleeping against a fence post. The least I can do is have hair that doesn't stick up all over.

She smiles again and I open the gate. She walks through, Otis's carrier in her hand.

"So you've been taking care of Lucas?" she asks as we walk toward the house.

"Yeah. I worked for Melanie before she"—I pause—"passed. I'm so sorry, by the way."

"Thanks." She nods. "Me too. How is he? Lucas?"

"He's eating okay, but he's restless and not sleeping all that well." I stop at the doorstep. "You're the guardian?" Uncle Chuck didn't say, but it would make sense. A sister.

An unreadable look crosses her features before she shakes her head. "No. Melanie's brother is guardian."

"Oh." I rack my brain, trying to remember if I'd ever met Melanie's brother. No. I don't even remember her mentioning him.

A cloud crosses over what's left of the evening sun. Olivia takes a step onto the front stoop. She stops suddenly. "Does Lucas know I'm coming?"

"Of course. I told him as soon as I hung up with Uncle Chuck."

"Is he okay about it?" Her gaze drops to the ground. "I haven't been around as much as I should have been since our dad died."

She sounds and looks pained. "I think he's looking forward to seeing you," I say, though I have no idea.

"Really?"

"Yeah." It might be true.

We'll know soon enough.

CHAPTER 7

OLIVIA
    I follow Nate through the front door and into the family room. The space is identical to the last time I was here, same as it was when Dad and Melanie first moved in. The furniture is worn but cozy and the room is connected to the kitchen by a long counter with four stools. Everything in both rooms is some shade of blue, a color Melanie found calming. The navy couches are piled high with pillows and blankets and a large television is centered on the wall across from them. Built-in bookshelves feature stacks of old paperbacks and a hodgepodge of picture frames. An array of plants in an eclectic grouping of pots sit in front of a picture window.

Lucas is on the couch, his iPad on his lap. Even with him sitting down, I can tell he's broader than he was the last time I was here, more muscular. Taller too. His hair is brown and seemingly thicker; he's got the beginnings of a beard on his jaw. His eyes are dark, almost black, like his mother's.

I set Otis down and let him out of the carrier. He darts away, then circles back.

"Hey, Lucas," I say quietly and move next to him on the couch. "I'm so sorry about your mom." I reach my arms around his body and squeeze. He doesn't hug me back; I don't expect him to. I wouldn't hug me either, if I were him.

I release him, not sure what to say or do next. It was always like this for me with Lucas when I'd first come here. Me feeling awkward at his lack of typical responses, taken aback by the stims and the vocalizations and the sometimes tantrums. Then I'd feel guilty that I felt that way. And Dad and Melanie would fall all over themselves trying to foster a connection between the two of us, so much so that it became painful. I'd usually just start talking and hanging with Lucas on my own until I got used to the differences and things felt natural. And I found I liked hanging out with Lu, my nickname for him. Everything we did together had an ease to it, like he was happy just to hang out. And I felt different around him too, less intense. Like lying on a picnic blanket for hours, hiking the small trail by the house, or building with Legos wasn't a big fat waste of time. That I didn't need to prove myself. Just being me was enough. But in the beginning of every summer there was, much like now, a strangeness to our interactions.

Otis jumps onto my lap, and for the first time since I walked in, Lucas averts his eyes from the video. He reaches his hand out for the cat and—ugh—I'm about to tell him not to, that Otis is not in the best mood, but before I can get the words out, Lucas makes contact and strokes his head. Amazingly, Otis doesn't hiss or scratch. He blinks his eyes and settles between us.

"This is Otis, Lu. I think he likes you." I move back on the couch and check the show on his iPad. "Animal Planet. What's this one about? Snakes." I look at him, then back at the video. "Ooh. I've never been much of a snake girl." Lucas doesn't respond but we settle together on the couch, Otis between us, and watch as a giant anaconda slithers across the screen. Yuck. I am really *not* a snake girl.

"Should I get us some dinner?" Nate asks from behind me. "Pizza?"

At the mention of food, I realize I haven't eaten since this morning. I'm starving. "Yes. Pizza would be great." I bump Lucas's shoulder. "You're still a big pizza guy, right?"

"Still a big pizza guy," Nate confirms. "You okay here? I'll be gone twenty minutes or so."

"Sure," I say breezily, though I don't really want Nate to leave. If Lucas needs something more than just sitting on the couch watching Animal Planet, I'm not sure I'm up for it. He can be a lot and I'm out of practice. Then again, it's twenty minutes. Melanie trusted me to care for Lucas his whole life. It would be ridiculous to say no. "Lu and I are all set."

"Great," Nate says. "Be right back."

I return to the video and Animal Planet flips to the next show, one about meerkats. My mind wanders to the Rowan case. I need to work on it at some point, but despite my catnap on the fence post, I'm depleted. Everything today has been so emotionally charged. The meeting with Chuck. Confirming that I don't want guardianship. Seeing Lucas again. Even being in this house is strangely uncomfortable. Like I'm the adult in the room.

I just have to wait until Dennis gets here. Once the baton is passed, my feelings will normalize, and I can get back to work. And once things are set, I can visit more. I can be the sister I should have been the past bunch of years.

No. Not can. Will.

I *will* be the sister I should have been these past years. I'll take Lucas swimming and to zoos. And not just the little zoo near Greenwillow. Big ones with lots of animals. I'll bring him Transformers or whatever today's equivalent is. We'll spend time in nature, skipping stones in the nearby pond, walking on trails, looking for wildlife. We'll set up all the birdfeeders he used to love as a kid. I'll take him out for pizza and ice cream and let him get the big soft serve with rainbow jimmies he always used to love. I can even, especially if I'm a partner at the firm, pay for extra things. Vacations. Therapies. Anything he needs.

Yes. I can do right by Lucas. I might not be able to be guardian, but I can work with Dennis to make sure Lucas is set up for life.

Nate returns with a pizza box and a half-gallon of chocolate ice cream. "Grub's here," he says in a cheerful tone and throws me and Lucas a lopsided grin. He's got a dimple, and his blue eyes crinkle when he smiles. There's a tiny cowlick in the back of his head which sticks up like a little flag. It's cute. I'm not a swoony kind of girl, never boy crazy like the twins had been as teens, but if I *were* that kind of girl, I'd probably be attracted to Nate.

He sets the pizza on the counter that connects the kitchen and the family room and puts the ice cream in the freezer. I spy the Cookie Monster cookie jar and smile. Getting a cookie from the jar was one of the first things I'd do when I came here as a kid. It was always full, always with homemade cookies. I lift the lid and peek inside by instinct, fully expecting it to be empty. It isn't. I pull out a cookie with chocolate chunks and look at Nate.

"Leftover from—" He doesn't finish the sentence.

I stare at the cookie.

"It's fine," Nate prompts. "There's a bunch left."

"Okay." I bite into the cookie. It's just how I remember them.

"Should we play some music?" He stands and gives Lucas a brotherly pat on the shoulder. "Me and Luke love '80s tunes. You?"

"Sure," I say, but the truth is I don't listen to music much these days. Just acoustic stuff while I'm working.

Nate stands, pulls his phone out of his front pocket, and moves to a music dock with a speaker set back on the counter.

A male voice fills the space. Bruce Springsteen. I haven't listened to his music in years.

"So," Nate says once we're assembled around the table, "Uncle Chuck says you're from New York."

"New Jersey originally, but I live in the city now." I pull a slice from the box and set it on my plate. "You?"

"Born and raised in Greenwillow. Most of my family lives here." He takes a bite of pizza and swallows. "Probably seems pretty dull."

I shake my head. "Different, not dull. Like I said, I came here in the summer a bunch of years."

"Did you ever go to Pirate Golf?" he asks.

I jut my chin forward in mock indignation. "Of course. Big Bob's Bowling?"

"Had two birthday parties there. How 'bout Gronsky's Milk House?"

"Been there. I used to love the giant pancake," I admit, thinking of the dinner plate-sized cakes.

"I think the August special pancake is Cinnabon," Nate says. "You liked that last time, right Lucas?"

He pushes playfully at Lucas's shoulder, and my heart surges. I've seen enough people ignore Lucas or talk to him in a way that makes it seem like he's either a small child or doesn't speak the language. Nate's speech is natural.

We finish the meal and clear the plates, both of us still jabbering about our shared Greenwillow experiences. The annual rubber ducky race, the Greenwillow fair, the Treeline Zoo. It turns out that Big Rod's, my favorite sandwich place, is owned by another of Nate's uncles.

"We had to have seen each other," he says, slamming the dishwasher door shut.

"I'm sure we did," I say, but maybe not. Nate is charismatic and friendly enough that it seems like if I'd met him, I'd remember.

"Dessert?"

"Of course," I say, as though I always eat dessert. I don't. Hardly ever.

Nate scoops out ice cream into bowls. He grabs a canister of whipped cream from the fridge and holds it in my direction. "Cream?"

"Yeah. Sure."

He sprays the whipped cream on my scoop. "Say when," he says.

"When."

He continues with the whipped cream.

"When," I say again.

He meets my eyes, smiling, and continues spraying the whipped cream. It tips over on to the counter in a little white blob.

A laugh escapes. "When."

He bugs his eyes out in my direction. "Finally. I thought you were going to use up the whole canister." He shakes it. "Leave some for us next time, will you?"

I shake my head just as the doorbell rings. "I'll get it," Nate says and sets the whipped cream on the counter.

I watch him go, still laughing.

I didn't expect that today.

CHAPTER 8

NATE

I move to the front door, my mind on Olivia. I like that I made her laugh. She gives off a serious vibe, but her smile? It lights up her whole face.

I open the front door, not having given a single thought to who might be on the other side until I open it. A man stands on the step, a cigarette hanging from his lips like an appendage. He's thin and tall, with a thick beard, half gray, half brown, puffy dark circles etched under his eyes. I've lived in Greenwillow my entire life and never seen this guy.

"Can I help you?"

He removes the cigarette and nods toward the house. "This place still Melanie Moore's?"

I take a step back. "Who's asking?"

He thrusts his hand toward mine; I grab it. "Dennis Moore. Melanie's brother. I got a call a couple hours ago from a lawyer about her son."

I drop his hand and squint in his direction. "Chuck Stockton?"

"Yeah, that's the guy. I've been named guardian of Lucas." He takes a quick puff on his cigarette.

"Okay," I say, my mind reeling. I just met this guy, but he doesn't seem like the type of person Melanie would choose as a guardian. But isn't that what Olivia said? That Melanie's brother was the guardian.

Still.

No way.

I hold up my hand. "Just a moment." I duck back inside and text Uncle Chuck. *Dennis Moore? Guardian?*

A single word text comes back. *Yes.*

Yes? Yes. Oh shit. Okay.

I open the door. "Sorry about that."

"This Melanie's place?" he asks again.

"Yeah."

"And this is where Lucas is, right?" He leans forward. "Is he still a little—" He twirls his index finger by his temple.

I narrow my eyes. Did he just do that? Insinuate Lucas was crazy? "He has autism spectrum disorder."

"Right. The spectrum. Okay." He throws his cigarette on the ground and stamps out the glowing ember with the heel of his shoe. "Well, can I see him?"

"Um . . . sure."

Every part of me does not want to facilitate this meeting. But if Melanie picked Dennis to be guardian, he's obviously going to see Lucas.

I push open the door and step inside. Dennis clumps behind me in work boots. Olivia turns around, the bowl of ice cream with whipped cream cascading over the sides still in her hands. I swing my hand in Dennis's direction. "Lucas, Olivia, this is Dennis Moore, Melanie's brother."

Olivia scrunches up her face like I've given her a difficult brain teaser she can't figure out. Lucas remains fixated on his ice cream.

Dennis moves to the table where Lucas is sitting and slaps it with an open palm. "Hey, Lucas. It's Uncle Dennis."

Lucas looks up and seems to register Dennis for the first time. He flaps his hands.

Dennis shakes his head. "Still the same Lucas."

The words could be interpreted as nostalgia, but they don't come across that way. Every nerve ending in my body jolts alive like an alarm. There's no way Melanie would choose this guy as guardian. And it's not like he's been around, like he has a pre-established relationship with Lucas. If he did, I'd have seen him at least once over the past two years.

Olivia sets her uneaten bowl of ice cream on the counter. "I'm sorry for your loss."

A quizzical look crosses Dennis's face.

"Melanie," she prompts.

"Yeah. Mel." He shakes his head. "Amazing she went and I'm still kicking. She was the healthy one, you know. Green beans and yoga and all that."

There's a silence. Long and uncomfortable. Though Dennis stopped smoking, the stench of his clothing fills the room. The clinking of Lucas's spoon against his glass bowl fills the space. Neither Olivia nor I eat, our ice cream melting on the counter.

Lucas finishes his ice cream, gets up, and leaves. Good on him. I'd do the same if I could.

"Do you want some pizza?" Olivia asks finally. She flips the box open.

"Sure. Thanks." Dennis grabs the final slice. He bites into it, bits of grease dribbling down his chin.

Olivia hands him a napkin. "Do you need anything to drink?" she asks.

"Got a beer? It's been a long day." He wipes his chin and consumes the rest of the pizza in one giant bite, like a snake eating a mouse whole.

I pull three Rolling Rocks from the fridge and set them on

the table. I try to catch Olivia's eye, try to figure out if she's thinking what I am, but she doesn't look at me.

Dennis collapses into a kitchen chair, extends his legs out, and grabs a beer. I sit and do the same. Even Olivia, whom I would not have pegged as a beer girl, takes one and twists off the cap.

Olivia, more polite than I am apparently, talks to Dennis. She asks him where he lives (Pittsburgh). She asks him if he's planning to move to Greenwillow to be with Lucas. He says yes (no shit; free lodging). She asks if he's visited Lucas much. He says he has. (Liar.) She asks if they have a good relationship. Yes again. (LIAR)

If that were true, if Lucas trusted him, he would have stuck around like he did when Olivia got here. Plus, I would have seen him before now.

Dennis gulps down the rest of his beer like he's in the desert and this is the first drink he's been offered in days. He smashes the bottle on the table with a loud clank. "Hey, can I crash here? I have that meeting with the lawyer guy at nine tomorrow."

"No," I say, the word an automatic, knee-jerk response.

Dennis stares at me, and for a long moment I think he's going to argue. I don't care. There's no way he's staying here.

Dennis taps the table. "Okay, then," he says standing. "I'll get the paperwork I need from the lawyer." He zips his index finger around the room and makes a square. "This is my house too now."

He leaves without another word, without asking to see Lucas, and a few moments later his car sputters down his drive-way, the brake lights illuminated in the darkening sky.

"What was Melanie thinking?" I spit out. "That guy"—I jerk my thumb toward the window—"no way can he be the guardian."

Olivia bites her lip. "Maybe he's better than we think. A kind of special connection."

"I've been around enough. I've never seen this guy."

"Never?"

"Never. And outside, before we came in, he insinuated Lucas was crazy." I twirl my index finger by my temple in the same way Dennis did. "Did you see how Lucas looked at him?"

Olivia drops her gaze to the floor.

"I'm calling Uncle Chuck." I grab my phone from my pocket.

"Nate, wait." She juts out her hand and puts it over the phone. "Melanie didn't name Dennis as guardian."

I whip my head up. "Wait. What?" She'd said that Melanie's brother was the guardian. So did Chuck.

"She named me first," Olivia says quickly. "I can't handle that kind of responsibility, not with my job and being in New York and all, so I told Chuck to contact the second person on the list. Dennis. I figured he'd be good. You know, an older guy. Melanie's brother." She puffs out a breath. "He might still be okay. We only talked to him a minute."

"You can't be serious."

She crosses her arms across her chest and a long moment passes before she speaks. "And you're involved because?"

My face flushes. It's a fair question. And I get it. This isn't my family; Lucas isn't my brother. But Lucas, Melanie, this job—all of it saved me after what happened. I'll never forget Melanie taking a chance on me. Her trusting me. So I owe it to her and to Lucas to make sure he's okay. Plus, he is like a brother to me now, even if it's not by blood.

These details would explain my reaction, but I can't share them with Olivia without sharing why I needed Melanie to take a chance on me to begin with, and I don't want to do that. "I'm involved because I've been here more," I say instead. The statement feels like an inane version of *because I said so.*

Olivia lifts an eyebrow. "That may be, but it doesn't change my situation. Where I live, the number of hours I work, is not conducive to being Lucas's guardian." She pauses and slides her thumb across the raised letters on the Rolling Rock bottle. Her expression, the mood, is thick with tension.

I open my mouth to apologize. I *should* apologize. This isn't my business, and I just met Olivia. I have no idea what she can and can't do as far as guardianship. But my mouth snaps shut before any apologetic words come out of them. I can't let it seem like Dennis as guardian is a viable option.

"Look," Olivia says finally. "I'm supposed to be at the meeting with Chuck tomorrow too. I'll see what I can find out."

CHAPTER 9

LUCAS

I'm in my room. The Animal Planet video, one about Arctic birds, plays. I stare at it, listening and thinking at the same time. Without the video or some kind of stimulation, my mind races too much. Doing something with my mind or body is the only thing that saves me. Distraction, movement. It's how I keep from going crazy. But it also makes me look crazy. A weird catch-22.

The grief of it, of not having my mom, sits in my stomach like a lead weight. I can't talk about her death or how I'm feeling. I can't express that I miss her. I can't express that I'm scared. I can't ask what happens now? I hate that I'm dependent on other people. That someone's going to have to mind eighteen-year-old me. It sucks for them, and it sucks for me too because, again, it makes me feel awful.

I leave my room and start down the stairs. Olivia and Nate are talking about Dennis. I go still.

"She named me first," Olivia says, and after a few minutes of listening I piece it together. Mom had chosen Olivia to take care of me. Dennis was second choice.

"I'll see what I can find out." Olivia tells Nate about the lawyer meeting, the one where they'll discuss me and my future. A fight not for who gets to take care of me but for who has to. Feels great to be in the middle of that.

Anyway, save yourself. That's what I'd say to Olivia if I could.

But if she did, if she moved here, if she wanted to, it would be a huge relief. I'm pretty sure Uncle Dennis, if he were guardian, would ignore me. Which, of course, I would love at first because what teenager doesn't want to be able to do whatever they want? I could sit in my room all day and stim to my heart's delight. But I'd eventually get lonely and need someone to pull me out. Uncle Dennis won't do that, and I'll get lost inside myself which is a scary place to be day after day after day. I don't want that to happen, but I don't want Olivia to ruin her life for mine.

It's all too much to think about.

I replay the Arctic bird episode of Animal Planet.

CHAPTER 10

OLIVIA
    I stare at the ceiling of my childhood bedroom, twist my head to the side and look at the bright blue digital clock I'd received as a gift for my eleventh birthday. White illuminated numbers stare back at me. 2:17 a.m. Click. One number slides into another. 2:18 a.m.

My computer sits idle on my desk. I tried to review parts of the Rowan file last night and got through a big fat nothing. I lied in an email to William, told him the review was on track. It will be. Soon. Things just need to settle down. Things being Lucas and Dennis and how the heck this situation can all work out.

I fool with the covers, fluff my pillow, and try to get comfortable.

I close my eyes and conjure Dennis with his gray eyes and yellow teeth, smelling like he lives inside a cigarette box. Awful. Really awful. Like a storybook villain almost.

But.

My eyes fly open.

Maybe not? Don't judge a book by its cover (or smell) and all that. Maybe he has a heart of gold. Maybe he shares Lucas's childlike wonder. Maybe he has a relationship with Lucas that Nate doesn't know about. Like he's *fun Uncle Dennis* or *crazy Uncle Dennis* or something like that. There must be a reason Melanie chose him, right? She had to have known I might say no.

Or did she name him as the alternative so I wouldn't say no? She wouldn't.

Would she?

I blow out a breath. I am, as my mother said, in an untenable position. Change up my life and forever dream of being a partner at Bennett Connor, or put Dennis in charge of a vulnerable and nonverbal human being? Or third choice, let the court decide Dennis is awful and appoint a total stranger. No choice is good.

I pull my phone from the nightstand and punch in what feels like the hundredth search about guardianships in Pennsylvania. The results are the same as they were an hour ago, written versions of the information Chuck had already given me during the meeting.

I lay my phone on my stomach and close my eyes. Being in this room—a time capsule of how it looked when I decorated it at age thirteen—brings memories of that initial move. Lucas was three when he was diagnosed with ASD, three when he, Melanie, and Dad moved here as a family unit and broke my heart.

I'd been able to spend a ton of quality time with Lucas when they lived in New Jersey. Blonde and chubby with adoring blue eyes, I'd loved taking care of him. I fed him bottles as an infant, strolled him around the neighborhood block in the oversized stroller, a portable mobile swinging over his head. When he got older, I walked him to the park, his little hand in mine. I'd fix him snacks, read him board books under thick blankets, and push him in the baby swing, his favorite. Unlike the twins who only wanted each other, Lucas wanted me. I felt his love for me from the time he was a baby and that feeling, that knowing, continued well after he started showing signs of autism. I even felt his love today when I got here, not that I'm in any way deserving of it. The people who assume kids with ASD lack feelings and emotion? Dead wrong.

My heart drops at the memories. I have to do better by Lucas than Dennis.

I type another search into my phone. I know I'm looking for a solution which may not exist. It's after three in the morning before I find an idea that I believe might have legs. I bookmark the tab and close my eyes.

As he's been doing since Melanie died, Nate agreed to stay overnight at the house. He sleeps in the guest room, across the hall from mine, which maybe at another time, under a different circumstance, might have been distracting. Nate is disarmingly nice. Which is why the next morning, when I skulk out of the house early, I feel so bad about it. Sneaking out is the ultimate in cowardice, especially as I haven't spoken to Lucas about the situation or said anything more to Nate. But seeing either one of them will muddle my thought process, and I need to be clear-headed for this meeting. After breakfast in town, I pull open the door and step into the parlor-turned-waiting-room at Stockton and Associates.

Dennis is there. He looks entirely different, almost as if a team of style and makeup people descended on him in the night. He's clean-shaven, hair parted and combed. His jeans in need of a wash and old T-shirt have been replaced by khaki pants and a polo, set off by a nice belt. He smells like cologne instead of cigarettes. "Hey, Olivia," he says and smiles in my direction. *This* man is the Dennis I'd imagined. Could this be the real him? Maybe yesterday had been a bad day?

I wave in his direction, check in with the receptionist, and sit down.

"How was Lucas this morning?" he asks.

"Fine. Good," I say, but of course I don't know because I'd snuck out of the house without speaking to him.

"Glad to hear it."

Chuck appears in the doorframe and ushers us both back to his office.

My body is stiff, and I rub my arms. I should be glad Dennis looks good and capable, but it feels fake somehow. Like he's up to something. I shake off the thought. I don't know anything about Dennis; there's no reason to make this assumption. Plus, he wouldn't even be in Greenwillow, wouldn't be talking to Chuck about guardianship or anything else, if it weren't for me.

Dennis and I enter the office and sit in identical chairs across from Chuck's desk. Unlike yesterday, when he'd talked at length about Melanie and New York, he gets right into things.

"I thought it would be good to go over next steps, answer any questions either of you might have about guardianship, the hearing, any of it." He shifts his gaze to Dennis. "As I explained to you on the phone, Melanie named Olivia, Lucas's sister, as guardian. She doesn't feel she'll be able to fulfill that role. You were named as the alternate guardian."

"Sure thing." Dennis's head bobbles up and down. "I'd be happy to care for my nephew. My sister, she dedicated her life to that boy."

"That she did." Chuck leans forward. "You're aware of his special needs, yes?"

"Yes, sir. I've been around Lucas enough. I understand it's a big responsibility. I'm up for the task. I can do it." He hits his chest with a flat hand.

I want to roll my eyes, but really, Dennis is saying everything a good sister—good person, even—would have said yesterday, everything Melanie would have wanted to hear from the individual who would be caring for her son.

Chuck looks in my direction. "And you still have the same

position, Olivia? You still want to decline the guardianship appointment?"

"Well, sort of." My words come out limp, and I will confidence into my voice. "As I understand it, there are two parts of guardianship. Guardianship of the person and guardianship of the property."

Chuck leans back in his chair. "That's right."

"I'm a lawyer, as you know. I work for a big firm and do lots of things with numbers." I pause. "I'm certain I could manage Lucas's assets to ensure they will grow. Make sure there is enough long-term for Lucas's needs." My gaze shifts to Dennis. "Not that you couldn't," I add. "I just thought it might be helpful. You not having to worry about that piece of things."

"So," Chuck starts, "you're proposing split responsibilities. A dual guardianship. You as guardian of the property and Dennis as guardian of the person. Yes?"

"Yes." I let out a relieved breath. Chuck's understanding of my proposal makes it seem more viable. If I'm unable to care for Lucas day-to-day, at least I can ensure he has whatever he needs for as long as he needs. It seemed, at least last night, like an adequate solution.

"The will isn't written that way." Chuck leans forward, grabs a pen, and taps it on the corner of the desk. "But if Dennis is the guardian of the property, nothing would prevent him from appointing you to manage the funds."

The receptionist pokes her head into the room. "Sorry. I wouldn't interrupt a meeting, but Judge Gaynor is on line two. I think you need to take it."

Chuck stands. "Sorry about this." He pulls at his red bow tie and shuffles toward the door. "I'll just be a minute."

The door slams shut behind him, and Dennis whips his head to look at me. "Nice try."

I draw back. "I'm not trying anything. I'm good with money,

I understand trusts, and all the resources are for Lucas anyway. What difference does it make who manages it?"

"If I'm going to be in charge of Lucas, I get the money."

"You don't *get* the money," I quip. "You receive money to pay for Lucas's needs. That's it. As much principal as possible should be invested so the money lasts."

Dennis crosses his arms. "It lasts as long as it lasts."

"It doesn't last as long as it lasts." My heart beats faster; my cheeks heat. "It's not like you spend the money on whatever you want. You need to file accounting documents annually. You know that, right?"

"Yeah. Right." He jabs his index finger in my direction with such force I move backward as though he touched me. "You're going to pilfer off the top. You don't want responsibility for the kid. You just want the money. Funny how that works, isn't it?"

My jaw drops open. "The fact you'd think I'd pilfer even a dime off the top says a lot more about you and what you're thinking than it does about me." I lean forward, my pulse speeding. "And the kid's name," I say, "is Lucas."

I stop. I'm half standing, my voice at full volume. I feel unhinged.

"Excuse me." I stride to the door, step into the hallway, and lean against the wall.

Just then, Chuck emerges from another office. "Can I speak to you?" I whisper. "In there." I nod my chin toward the door of an empty office.

He meets my eyes, then pushes open the door to the vacant room.

I step inside. "He's not fit to be guardian," I hiss. "He's just in it for the money. He doesn't care about Lucas."

Chuck leans against a desk in the space. "Ultimately, a court will decide at a hearing if Dennis is fit. If you have proof of financial misconduct, you can present it."

"It's not just the money. Lucas doesn't like him. He's not good. He's not right. Isn't there another option?"

"Yes." Chuck gently touches my arm. "You."

I shake my head. "Other than me."

"The court will give substantial weight to Dennis as Melanie's choice. But as I said yesterday, if he's unfit, the court will appoint a public guardian."

"Can I interview the guardians?" I blurt. "The public ones?"

"Olivia," Chuck says, standing upright, his tone edged with frustration. "You can accept guardianship, but you don't get to choose who the guardian should be if you decline. The court will." He moves toward the door and puts his hand on the knob.

I look down, my mouth dry.

"Shall we resume the meeting?"

"I need a moment." I look around. I want, I need, more time. "Is there a bathroom?"

Chuck swings open the door. "End of the hall."

I exit the office, hurry down the hall, and step inside the bathroom. I look at myself in the mirror. My face is blotchy red, my nostrils flared. I lean against the sink with straight arms and breathe.

I can't be guardian.

Can I?

I'm smart. Maybe I could figure it out. Accepting guardianship doesn't have to mean giving up my job. I think again about Dennis. Is there any way Lucas would be okay with him at the helm?

I splash water on my face, dab at my skin with a paper towel, and open the door. I step into the hall and toward Chuck's office. The decision, my decision, is seconds away.

And I'm still not sure what I'm going to do.

CHAPTER 11

NATE

Olivia is at the lawyer meeting. Lucas and I circle Stone Pond on the asphalt path. It's his morning walk, an integral component of the summer routine. Despite it being early, it's warm already, and the heat beats down on my skin. Birds chatter; a bright red cardinal flies across the path in front of us. It's Melanie, my mother would say. She's always attributed cardinals to loved ones visiting after they'd passed on.

A pair of ducks eases over the flat surface of the pond, tiny ripples in their wake. Lucas stops to watch a gray squirrel scurry up a tree and disappear into a swath of green foliage. The air is infused with a musty, earthy scent.

I've always enjoyed this walk. Being in nature is a balm to my senses; Lucas's too, I think. A few years back, before I started working with Lucas, Melanie had swapped out most of his therapies for downtime. It was her belief that all the extra activity involved with the treatments stressed Lucas's already overtaxed nervous system and that quiet time and time in nature was more beneficial overall. I didn't know Lucas back then, but the concept of less is more schedule-wise always made sense to me.

I try to picture Dennis on this walk, breathing in fresh air or stopping to watch a toad hop into the pond. I can't. Next, I try to visualize myself staying on if he asked, working for him instead of Melanie, but I can't picture that either.

Maybe Olivia is figuring out a solution at the lawyer meeting. She left early this morning, a sticky note on the fridge. Part of me hopes she'll take on the guardianship. She's good with Lucas; he likes her. And honestly, I do too, the little I know of her.

But I doubt she will.

I put her name into a Google search last night. Salutatorian in her class at Lafayette College, top in her law school class at Rutgers. She's an associate at Bennett Connor, a big law firm in New York city. Not the type of person who would settle in Greenwillow. A person with a big life and a big job, not that far off from what I'd thought my own life would be like way back when.

Lucas stops at a bench at the edge of the pond and sits. He does this sometimes, the only part of the walk that varies from day to day.

I join him on the bench, my feet stretched out in front of me. "So what do you think of your Uncle Dennis, Lu?" The question is a depth charge.

He verbalizes something, a combination of vowels and consonants.

He makes sounds often, but they seldom make a word he hasn't practiced over and over. I wait anyway. Maybe today is the day he'll be able to connect the dots and tell me what he's thinking. My muscles tense with anticipation.

"Nemo! That's a nice name," he spits out.

My shoulders fall; I exhale disappointment. Damn it. The phrase is a verbal stim, a line from *Finding Nemo*. It's one Lucas relies on frequently, a vocalization he finds comforting.

"Nemo! That's a nice name," he says again.

I put my elbows on my knees and stare at the ground. Ants cross the dirt below me in a line, one with a giant crumb on its back.

"Nemo! That's a nice name."

"Come on, Lu," I say, the frustration in my tone unhidden.

I'm used to Lucas's stims, verbal and otherwise. He needs them. He's comforted by them. But even though I get it, I'm now thinking about how they'll seem in Dennis's eyes. Weird. Freaky. Unnatural. I visualize Dennis on the doorstep, index finger twirling around his temple. He's not the type to try to understand.

"Nemo! That's a nice name."

I clamp my mouth shut and stand. I need to move. If I don't, the worry-fueled anxiety teeming inside of me will spill over and I'll say something I regret.

Lucas stands too; he walks ahead of me on the path.

"Nemo! That's a nice name." He flaps his hands.

My muscles tense; my chest tightens. My feelings are unreasonable, I know, but I want the hand flapping and the vocalizations to stop. A few days back, I wouldn't have given them a second thought. But it feels like time has run out. Lucas has spent his life surrounded by people who love and understand him. That won't be the case now. And he's totally unprepared.

He walks ahead of me, his hands flapping in a more vigorous, more noticeable way. A man walking his dog stares and shakes his head. Screw you, guy. Screw you.

"Nemo! That's a nice name."

Hand flapping.

"Nemo! That's a nice name."

Hand flapping.

"Nemo! That's a nice name."

"Goddammit, Lucas," I say, worry bursting out of me like verbal vomit. "Stop it. Stop it already." I stride forward and put my hands over his mid-flap and hold them there. "Stop it."

Lucas pulls his hands away from mine and stands still.

I freeze. Shame overtakes worry and I'm angry at myself for letting my emotions get the best of me. "I'm sorry."

He looks in my direction a long moment, then turns and continues walking toward the house. He doesn't stim, and weirdly, the absence of the hand flapping and the vocalizations make me feel worse than I did before. Like I'd stymied him, shamed him, and joined the tribe of people put off by his normal because it's not mine. Ironically, it's exactly what I'm worried Dennis will do.

Lucas walks a few more strides. The hand flapping resumes, but rather than be frustrated or worried, I'm glad to see it this time.

As we approach the house, I spy Olivia's car in the driveway. I'm hoping she has positive news and that, after today, I'll never have to think about Dennis Moore again.

I push open the front door. Lucas follows and disappears up the stairs. The door to his room opens and shuts.

I find Olivia in the kitchen. She's sitting at the table in dressy, lawyerish clothes, a steaming mug of coffee, still full, between her palms. Otis rubs against her legs.

"Well?"

She lifts her gaze toward me, then looks back at the mug.

"What's happening? Did Chuck have a solution?" My words are fast, frantic, running together like one big line.

She spins the mug around by the handle. The slowness kills me.

"Well. Anything?" I blurt.

"No." She shakes her head. "Sorry. My mind is all over the place."

"I get that." I wait for her to say something more. She doesn't. "So," I start because I can't wait anymore, because I need to know, "is Dennis the guardian?"

She takes a long sip of coffee, sets the mug down, and looks at me. "No," she says. "I am."

CHAPTER 12

LUCAS

I'm in my room after the whole stimfest during the walk this morning. Flapping, saying that stupid line from Finding Nemo. I'd wanted to say something else, but that line was, in the moment, what I could say and, I don't know, saying it made me feel better at first. Then Nate got frustrated, which almost never happens.

So now he and Olivia are in the kitchen. I assume they're talking about the lawyer meeting and whether she or Dennis drew the short straw and has to deal with me for friggin' ever. I hope it's Olivia, but I also hope it isn't because if it is, I'll feel bad for her. She'll need all kinds of help just to make things work. It's like that saying I once heard—"it takes a village." That's how I feel. Like it takes a whole village to meet my needs. At its height, care for me included PTs, OTs, speech therapists, teachers. Now it's mainly Nate. I wish it wasn't like that. I wish my body connected the same way everyone else's does. That it worked. Is that so much to ask? Talk when I want to talk? Move when I want to move? And not to be stuck in this 'no-man's-land where multiple people are needed just to make sure I'm okay.

Ugh. I hate it. Hate it.

I hate it so much.

I hit my head against the wall, and the pain momentarily relieves the anguish I feel inside.

I do it again.

And again.

I feel relief and continue. Bang. I do it, not feeling the pain, just feeling the relief. Bang. Bang. Bang.

Nate's arms are around me, pulling me away. I see Olivia. She looks terrified, horrified.

With every bit of internal strength I have, I force myself to stop flailing and go limp in Nate's arms. I didn't mean to scare Olivia. But, God, sometimes it's too much, you know, dealing with all of this. Sometimes I need an outlet.

And I miss Mom.

I really miss Mom.

CHAPTER 13

OLIVIA

The next day, noon, Lucas and I pull into the parking lot of Include, a resource center for those on the spectrum and their caregivers. The center is a converted two-story house, five blocks away from Greenwillow's Main Street. Like most of the houses around it, it's got a behemoth of a front porch, the kind that beckons rocking chairs and lemonade and ferns.

We exit the car and walk toward the front door. We have an appointment with Dominique, the director and founder. Yesterday, Nate told me she has a daughter on the spectrum, Lucas's age, and a second, older daughter. That's all I remember from the conversation; my brain having been muddled.

Lucas enters the building through a glass door featuring the Include insignia, a large image of a person holding out their arms with lots of smaller people underneath. I follow him inside. There's a small desk with a large version of the insignia behind it. All around the space are framed pictures of kids and adults engaging in a variety of activities. Christmas parties, moon-bounces, hayrides, exercise classes, a dressy dance. I spy

Lucas and Melanie in one at a lake, their faces pink from the sun, arms swung around each other.

A woman at the desk, my age, looks up. Her skin is smooth and brown, her hair long and worn in countless tiny braids, beads at the bottom. "Hey, Lucas." She smiles in his direction before standing and shooting her hand toward me. "I'm Tessa. You're Olivia?"

"Yes. That's me."

"I'll take you back to my mom. Follow me." She stands, waves her hand forward, and I piece together that Tessa is Dominique's older daughter. I follow her just as Lucas strides past both of us and disappears around a corner.

"Lu," I call.

Tessa waves. "He's fine. He knows this place like a second home. I can bet he's going to the Snoezelen room."

"The what?"

"The Snoezelen room. It's a relaxing space designed to reduce anxiety." She meets my eyes. "I can go check on him if you want."

"That would be great," I say, because something happening to Lucas on my first day of being guardian would prove what I already think. What I know. That I'm not up for this job.

Tessa stops at an open door and knocks on it. "Hey, Mom. Olivia's here."

A stunning woman, an older version of Tessa, stands and shakes my hand. "I'm Dominique Williams. Nice to meet you, Olivia." She gestures to a chair. "Please. Sit."

I sit in a chair across from her desk. The office walls are painted a tranquil shade of blue, the furniture worn but comfortable. Behind Dominique's desk are a dozen or so framed photographs of Include events, like those in the waiting room. Two bulletin boards hang on the wall next to the chairs where I'm sitting. One is crammed with notes and cards. The other features flyers of upcoming events at Include or in the community.

"We were all devastated by Melanie's death," Dominique says, sitting. "She was an incredible woman and such a loving person." She reaches out and squeezes my hand. "She'll be greatly missed."

"Thank you," I say, though I'm tired of hearing this. If Melanie was so great and so caring, why didn't she ever speak to me about this appointment? Why would she leave it to chance?

"And you're her stepdaughter. The guardian, right?"

"Yes. Word travels fast."

"In this community it does." She smiles. "You won't find one more caring. Which reminds me." She pulls a large envelope from her desk and hands it to me. "People have been dropping off gift cards and money. There are phone numbers in here too. People that want to help."

I take the envelope from her outstretched hand. It's heavy, laden with contributions and offers for help. So different than what I experienced after my dad died. I'd worked at Bennett Connor that summer. The firm sent me a small fruit basket with a preprinted card: *Sorry for your loss.*

Dominique nods toward the envelope, still gripped in my hand. "Don't be afraid to call people. Include families are, well, a family."

"Thanks." I set the envelope in my lap. "Nate Wilder is at the house now."

"Great. How long can he stay?"

"I'm not sure." In the haze of yesterday, I hadn't asked him. Ridiculously, I hadn't even considered that he might leave. But he would, right? I mean, he'd have to. He must have a life outside of my brother.

At the thought of Nate leaving, the feeling of overwhelm from yesterday creeps into my chest.

Dominque leans forward and meets my eyes. "What can I do for you, Olivia?"

"I don't know what I'm doing," I blurt.

"No one does."

"No," I say, my tone emphatic. "I really don't. Last night, Lucas banged his head on his bedroom wall so hard that the plaster caved in. Nate was there, thank God, but I didn't know what to do. I mean, he could have had a serious injury an hour into me taking this role. And I don't know what I'm going to do about my job. Or the fact that I live in New York." I pause. "I love Lucas. I do. He's my brother and he lost both his parents and this situation is awful. But Melanie never mentioned guardianship to me. If she had, I'd have told her that I'm not equipped to do this." I ball my hands into fists. "I made a mistake to say yes."

Dominque sits still and I wait, expectant.

"You didn't make a mistake," she says finally. "There's a reason Melanie chose you."

Because I'm a chump, I think but don't say. Silence fills the room. I should ask for something, but I don't even know enough to know what.

Dominique breaks the silence. "Olivia, do you like to decorate?"

Do I like to decorate? What? The question is odd and out of context. What difference does it make if I like to decorate or not? My life is literally on fire.

I say nothing; Dominique continues. "Include has a party committee. Tessa's in charge." She gestures toward the front of the building. "I know they're looking for some help." She pauses. "It's a bunch of young people."

"I don't really decorate," I offer, because it's true and because I have no interest in anything other than figuring out how to make this guardianship work without blowing up my life. The party committee? It's not what I need right now. Or ever.

"Well, if you change your mind, call Tessa. Groups can be helpful." She pulls a paper from her desk drawer and slides it across the table. "This is probably what you're looking for."

I take the paper. It's a single-spaced list of agencies and groups, some with phone numbers next to them, some with websites. It's comprehensive, almost overwhelmingly so.

"Lucas gets some services already, I'm sure," she says. "Though Melanie was a big believer in Lucas having downtime."

I nod. That sounds like Melanie. "Do you know which services he gets?"

"No. But Nate will. And the school."

Right. More things I don't know. More things I didn't think about. But in fairness, I had all of one second to make the decision.

"What about out-of-home placements?" I ask. I don't want to pull Lucas from his home, but I may have to. It may be the only way I can make this work.

Dominique takes the paper and puts a star next to an agency. "Call this group," she says. "They'll be able to walk you through that process. As a warning though, it's usually a long wait. Years."

Years? That can't be right.

"And if I need to move Lucas to New York?"

"I'm sure there are wonderful programs in New York," she says noncommittally. "And if you're interested, there are lots of support and activity groups at Include, aside from the party committee, of course."

"Sure," I say, though I have no interest in either. I have a paper full of information sources, which, frankly, is all I need. I can do the rest. Asking for help only slows things down.

CHAPTER 14

N ATE
    While Olivia and Lucas are at the Include meeting, I drive to Big Rod's and order my typical roast beef and cheese on rye. Uncle Rod isn't there, and the counter is manned by a skinny high-school-aged kid I don't recognize. His nametag says Bill.

It bugs me, Bill's presence there. I've worked at Rod's in the past, a bunch, and I've always known everyone. The fact that I don't know Bill shows change. Time is marching on, leaving me and my stuck self behind.

It's a stupid reaction to a sandwich.

But I feel it, nonetheless.

The feeling's not totally out of the blue. I've been restless for a while, predating Melanie's passing. I keep thinking, yes, I can do it now, I'll move on, I'll go back to school, I'll get my life on track. But then I don't. And now here I am, saddened by the fact that a kid named Bill made my sandwich.

I scarf down the food in my truck and drive to my parents' house. My dad said he needed help moving some furniture.

He doesn't.

He's a beloved construction foreman with a loyal crew of guys who'd show up at his house and move anything in a heartbeat. *Moving furniture.* It's code for *we need to talk.*

When I get there, Mom's car is gone, and I find Dad inside. He hugs me tight, then gestures to what looks like the lightest table on earth. "Can you help me move this to the garage?" he asks. I go along, despite that having two people navigate the table makes the task infinitely harder. "Coffee?" he asks after.

"Sure?" He fixes the coffee in the kitchen, and I brace myself for the inevitable future talk. Otherwise known as the *it's been three years and why can't you move on* discussion.

He pours the coffee into mugs and hands me one. We move to the back deck and sit in cushioned chairs around an outdoor table. The space is two-tiered, shady from surrounding woods. My parents' pride and joy.

Dad sips his coffee and leans back in the chair. "How's Lucas?"

I think about yesterday's walk. "He's having a rough time."

"I'm sorry to hear that." Dad sips his coffee slowly, like he's thinking, then sets the mug on the table. "Uncle Chuck says there's a guardian now."

"Yeah. Olivia, his sister. She's . . ." I stop and think about her reluctance to be guardian. "I'm not sure she's up for the task."

"And?"

"And I don't know. I feel bad up and leaving him, especially with someone who doesn't seem to want to be there." I pick up a stray leaf on the table. "Nonverbal doesn't mean non-feeling."

"Of course not," Dad says quickly. "But do you have a choice? Has Olivia asked you to stay on?"

"No." I rip the leaf in half.

"Maybe she's okay with it? Melanie trusted her, right?"

I don't answer. Dad leans forward. "You're not responsible for Lucas, son."

I tip my head back and blow out a breath. "I know that, Dad."

"Do you? Are you sure you haven't been using him, this job, as an excuse to—"

I hold up my palm. "Don't go there."

"It's been three years," he says, ignoring me. "You've done a good job with Lucas; you've seen progress. But it's time for you to move on. Maybe try again for medical school?"

Medical school. The dual words ring in my brain. I got in; I didn't, couldn't go. "Maybe," I say noncommittally.

"Or a job," he says. "A different one. Have you gotten the emails I've been sending?"

"Yes." It's not a lie. I am getting them. I'm just not reading them. I set the coffee mug on the table. "I should go."

"Promise me you'll think about it. Your mother and I are here if you need us."

"I will. Thanks."

I give a hasty goodbye and drive back to Melanie's by rote, the roads I've driven on all my life imprinted on my brain like a map. My conversation with Dad plays in my mind like a loop. Time to move on. Apply to medical school. He's right. I know that. But knowing something and doing something about it are two different things.

I pull into the driveway and park next to Olivia's car. Despite the heat, I spy Lucas out back jumping on the trampoline. Olivia's in the kitchen, pacing, her phone connected to her ear by her shoulder, a paper in her hand. Her computer sits on the kitchen table, open, a legal pad with notes next to it. Otis is curled up on one of the kitchen chairs.

She looks in my direction, then pulls the phone from her ear. "I hate automated attendants." She jabs at the phone, switching it off. "It is too much to ask that real people answer when you call? I mean, honestly. Where is basic customer service these days? If you dial a number, a real honest-to-goodness person should be at the other end. Common courtesy. Right?"

I smirk. Her words sound like something my parents or

grandparents might say and belie how young she looks right now. She's wearing old cutoff shorts and a ratty tee with an owl on the front, the caption: *don't forget to be owlsome*, under it. Her hair is in a haphazard ponytail, and big chunks frame her face. It's cute. Sort of sexy, if I'm honest.

"What?" she barks.

"I'm sorry," I say smiling. "I didn't realize I'd missed your one hundredth birthday."

She says nothing for a beat, then laughs. A deep one, from the belly. "Sorry." She nods toward her computer. "I'm trying to do work and figure out some things out for Lucas." She waves her phone. "And I couldn't get anyone helpful on the line, as I said. Anyway, thanks for the birthday wishes." She winks. "Can't believe I made it to one hundred."

"Me either. Nice shirt."

She looks down, then smiles. "Yes. This beauty. It was in my old room. Part of my teenage owl phase. Pretty sure I've got some owl earrings in there too."

"Well, that's pretty owlsome, if you ask me."

She purses her lips like she's trying to suppress a laugh. "Owls were an important part of my life, Nate. I don't appreciate the snark."

I snort. "I apologize."

My gaze falls to the back window. Lucas is still jumping. His face is reddish, but pale in the middle, his shirt drenched with sweat. "How long has he been out there?"

"Oh, God." She looks at the clock. "Shit. I didn't think, I—" She puts her phone on the table. "I forgot. Shit."

"It's okay. I'm sure he's fine." I open the fridge and grab a water bottle.

"Shit," she repeats.

"Olivia. It's fine. He likes jumping. He's probably having a hoot." I wink in her direction, head out, and step toward the trampoline. "Hey, Lucas," I say, popping my head between the mesh opening. "Take a break?"

He jumps twice more, then stops. He's gasping, and when he moves toward me, he stumbles. I climb in and grab him. His skin is clammy, cold instead of warm.

Olivia jogs toward us. "Is he okay?"

"He's okay. Just got overheated. Right bud?" I step out of the trampoline and assist Lucas in navigating the opening. Once he's on the ground, I hand him the water bottle, and he chugs the contents immediately.

I grab one arm; Olivia grabs the other. Lucas walks two steps, stumbles, then bends over and throws up the water.

Olivia stares at the murky residue on the grass. "Oh, God. I can't believe—"

"He's fine," I interrupt. "He's fine." Lucas senses panic. Olivia freaking out, even mildly, will not be helpful.

"I—" she starts.

I bug my eyes out in her direction. "He's fine," I say and usher him into the house.

Once inside, Lucas sits on the couch. I retrieve another water bottle from the kitchen and hand it to him. "Small sips," I say then direct my attention to Olivia. "Could you get a cold washcloth?"

"Sure. Of course." She bounds out of the room and returns with a damp dish towel. She sets it across Lucas's forehead and stares at him like he'd just survived a war mission.

"He's fine," I say again. "Right?" I bump his shoulder. "You're crazy, man. It's like a hundred degrees out there today." He doesn't move but his breathing calms and his skin color begins to normalize.

Olivia leaves the room without saying anything further, and a moment later I see her outside. She grabs Lucas's shoes, next to the trampoline, and walks back. She stops at a chair on the patio and sits, Lucas's flip-flops on her lap like a prize. Her back is to the window. I can't see her expression, but I hope she isn't beating herself up. Lucas is fine. Things happen.

"Be right back." I tap Lucas's shoulder and head outside.

"Hey." She doesn't turn around and I move to the front of the chair. "Hey. Oh, hey." She's crying, legit crying, not teary. Streams of water pour down her face. I kneel in front of her. "It's alright. Olivia." I put my hand on her knee. "It's alright."

She wipes her cheeks with the back of her hand. "It really isn't," she says, her voice garbled.

"It's fine. He's fine."

"For now." She wipes her face again, black mascara streaking across her skin. "I forgot about him. Forgot. Who does that?"

"It happens."

"It shouldn't. This is day one."

"You're getting used to things."

"And yesterday, with the head banging. If you hadn't been here . . ."

"He rarely does that."

"Still. It's not just me sucking at this and having no business being the guardian of anyone. I'm behind with my work, including the big case I just got assigned, and I haven't talked to my boss about any of this yet. I can't get anyone on the phone about Lucas. It's all call this group or that or I'll connect you and then the call drops. None of its centralized. It feels like no one is in charge." She wipes at her eyes again. "Or I guess I am, right? I'm in charge." She snorts. "How crazy is that?"

"You talked to Dominique?"

"Yes," she exhales. "She suggested I join a committee."

I squint at her. "A committee? Really?"

She blows out a breath. "Yes, but in fairness, I melted down a bit, kind of like now. I think she felt bad for me. Like I needed support." She moves her index fingers like imaginary quotation marks.

"Well, do you?"

"No," she says without a beat. "I can figure things out." She loops a strand of hair around her index finger. "But can I ask you something? Something I probably have no right to."

"You want my first born," I quip. "No. Sorry."

She smiles. "How is it you can make me laugh? I'm upset, damn it."

"Do you want to marry me? No, also. We just met."

She slaps my knee. "Stop it."

"Sex?" I tilt my head.

"Oh my God." She rolls her eyes. "I can see I'm going to regret this, but I was hoping you might be able to stay on for a bit, a few weeks, maybe? Just until I get my feet under me and figure out things." She stops, then adds quickly. "I'll pay you, of course. Whatever Melanie did. More if you need it."

I shift into the chair next to her. I think about the promise I made to my dad less than an hour ago, that I'd take this opportunity to move forward. But Olivia needs help, clearly, and Lucas is still reeling from Melanie's passing. I haven't moved on yet. What's a few more weeks? It's already been three years.

"Sure," I say. "I'd be happy to."

CHAPTER 15

LUCAS

I love to jump. Autism stereotype, I know, but it's true. I can't always feel my body. I bump into things, I trip, I spill. Sometimes I miss my mouth when I'm eating. Seriously! Even toddlers rarely miss their mouths.

But when I jump I know exactly where I am. I feel my body in a way I don't normally. Plus, when I jump I'm not thinking about things like my mom's death or whether Nate will leave or whether Olivia's life might be ruined because of me. I lose myself in the movement, and given all the issues involved with being me, it's nice to get lost for a while.

I jumped too much today. I got too hot, and I didn't realize, and now Olivia is upset. I want to tell her that it's okay, I'm okay, and the jumping was worth getting too hot. I'd like to jump again, but when I get up and start out there, Olivia runs after me and tells me to come back inside. Really? I'm eighteen. I should be able to decide some things on my own. Right? Anyway. Olivia is really upset, and now Nate is outside too, and they're acting like I might die or something if I don't go back inside ASAP. Cool it guys. Honestly.

So I go back in. I didn't want to jump that badly. But really. Being able to make so few decisions bothers me. I can make small ones, like what I'm going to wear or eat, though even those are limited. Mom never let me wear shorts when it got under sixty degrees; she wouldn't let me eat whatever I wanted. I imagine Olivia will be like that also, which I guess makes sense. But wouldn't it make sense too to let me wear shorts in the winter and get cold or eat cookies and get a stomachache? I'd figure what works and what doesn't by trial and error. I'm not an idiot.

If a magic genie swooped down and granted me a bunch of wishes, one of mine would be the right to make mistakes. Weird, I know. But mistakes come from choice. And lack of choice sucks. Trust me.

CHAPTER 16

OLIVIA
Two days after Nate agrees to stay on, I pull open one of the glass doors to the skyscraper which houses Bennett Connor on the top three floors. I step into the elevator and nod at the strangers inside. It's Friday, mid-afternoon, and I have an appointment with William, and later, one to try on bridesmaid dresses with Mom and the twins.

Eyeroll.

I don't want to do either of these things.

The elevator stops at the twenty-eighth floor, and I step off, internally practicing the *I need to work remotely for a period* speech. I don't think William will say no to that. Since COVID, both the firm and the courts are set up for people to work online. It's the Rowan case I'm worried about. All during the four-hour car ride here, I rehearsed all the reasons why he shouldn't reassign the case. I'm ready.

I push open the office door and step inside. The space smells exactly as it always does, like lemon furniture polish. Modern paintings adorn the walls, and the gold carpet has fresh vacuum strips. A professional flower arrangement is centered on a table in the waiting area, neatly arranged couches around it. I've been inside this space hundreds of times since I was a little girl. It never seemed sterile until just now.

Janelle, Bennett Connor's current receptionist, waves from behind the reception desk, an old-fashioned phone hooked under her ear. I wave back and push open the door between the waiting room and the offices. The desks for administrative staff in the center are humming; lawyers bustle around them with files and papers. The atmosphere at Bennett Connor has always teemed with excitement. The action, the movement, the flow of it all. Like big things are happening, right here and right now.

I move inside my office and internally rehearse my speech. Reasons one, two, three to infinity as to why I'll be able to work on the Rowan case remotely. I glance over the cases I'd printed out, ones I think will help with our arguments. My speech, the cases. I puff out a breath. I should be fine.

"Knock. Knock."

I glance up at Todd's gargantuan frame in the door. Todd is my only work friend and I smile broadly as he steps inside. I open my mouth to tell him to close the door so I can fill him in. I assume that's why he's here. To ask me how things are going. But before I get out a word, he sets a file on my desk and puts both of his hands together like he's praying.

"Olivia," he says in a singsong voice.

I squint in his direction. That voice. It usually precedes him requesting that I cover some hearing. But he's not going to ask that today, right? Surely, he's going to ask me where I've been all week.

"Paul got last minute tickets to a concert. And . . ." He untangles his hands and taps on the file. "Could you be a doll and do this appearance for me?" He tips his head and puts his hands back in the prayer position. "I'll owe you one."

I look up. Does he not know I've been out? Or is he aware but just doesn't care enough to ask?

I push the file in his direction. "Sorry. I'm going dress shopping with Mom and the twins."

"Really?" Surprise shoots across his features. "I mean, good on you and all. Dresses."

I can feel he's going to push the issue. Ask *Can't you fit it in? Before you go? Just this once?*

"I've accepted guardianship of my little brother this week," I say preemptively. "I'll be busier than usual for the foreseeable future."

Todd stares at me a moment before his face breaks into a smile. "That's funny, Olivia. Good one. Next, you'll tell me you've gone and adopted Otis." He swipes the file off the desk. "Ciao for now."

He marches out, and I stare at the empty doorframe. I feel like a high schooler who just found out her best friend was using her for her pool or vacation house or something. And the insinuation that I'd joke about something as serious as guardianship? What was that about? Surely, I don't come across as *that* uncaring. Do I? Before I can dwell on Todd's words further, my desk phone buzzes. I swipe it from the base station.

"Olivia," William's assistant says, "he's ready for you now."

"Sure." I gather up my Rowan notes and walk out of my office, toward William's. I pass Todd, joking in the corner with a group. He laughs, loud and gregarious. I purse my lips and continue walking, hating how prim I must look. I shouldn't care if Todd likes me or not, but I do. I thought we were friends.

My cell phone chimes with a text notification. I pull the device out of my suit pocket, fully expecting it to be yet another reminder from Mom about the dress event. But the message is from Nate. A smile tugs at my lips. I click on it and a selfie of Lucas and Nate at Lake Monroe fills the screen. Both are in bathing suits and smiling, arms slung around each other like brothers. *Just checking in. Hope things are going well.*

I stop and fix on the words, touched that Nate would take the time to text me. *All good.*

Three dots appear, and I wait for his response.

Owlsome.

A laugh bursts out of me, and my thumbs fly across the keyboard. *Looks like you guys are having a hoot.*

Not a second later, he responds. *Owl is good.*

I smile again and rack my brain for a good response. A hurried admin bumps into me and I look up, orienting myself to the present. The William meeting. How did I get sidetracked from that? I punch in a quick thumbs-up emoji and head toward his office. When I get there, he's hunched in front of his computer, wire-rimmed glasses on the bridge of his nose. Next to him is an oversized coffee and a half-eaten bagel on a paper plate. An overhead light shines on his balding head.

"Hey."

He looks up. "Olivia. Hello." He smiles a kind of half-smile, like he can't fully commit to the effort. He whips off his glasses and twists his office chair to face me. "So. Rowan? Did you look at the file?"

I'm surprised, honestly, that there are no niceties. No hello or how are things or did anything life-changing happen to you over the past few days. In fairness, I didn't share with anyone the reason for my needing the few days off. Maybe he's trying to respect my privacy?

Yes. That's it, I decide, because that explanation is easier to swallow than *hey, Olivia, no one cares*. I rattle off the holdings of the two cases I'd found.

He leans back, fingers together like a steeple, eyes cast on the ceiling,

I can't tell what he's thinking. I wait, my insides feeling like they might burst. I go through the case holdings in my mind. They're on point, right? I thought so last night. Then again, it was late, really late, and I was tired.

He springs up in his chair like a jack-in-the-box. "I like those. You can derive some good arguments from those holdings. Find more and we'll discuss tomorrow." He twists back toward his computer.

I don't move from the chair. "Umm," I say, softly, passively. "There's something more."

He continues typing a moment, then stops and angles his head toward me, hands still primed at the keyboard.

"You remember my brother?" I ask, though he must. He worked with my dad, and Lucas was the primary reason he left.

"Yes." He shifts toward me. "Lucas, right?"

"His mother, my stepmother, died."

He inhales a quick breath. "Oh. I'm sorry."

"Me too," I say, "but here's the thing." I explain about Lucas and the guardianship and ask to work remotely until the next steps—whatever they are—are in place. I don't say anything about the Rowan case, hoping he won't either.

"Remote work." He nods. "For how long?"

"I don't know yet," I say honestly.

"I'll say yes for now, but I have to take you off Rowan."

No, I scream internally. No. No. No. My mind searches for the words of the speech I'd so diligently practiced in the car ride here. Bits and pieces of nonsensical arguments rise to the surface. Adrenaline shoots through my system; my throat goes dry. I open and close my mouth. Nothing comes out.

"Olivia." A look of pity crosses his features. "You know I need someone here in the office. And you know Marjorie wasn't on board. I had to fight to get you on the team as it is. I can't"—he shakes his head—"I can't make this work. I'm sorry. There will be other partnership track cases."

"But—" I stammer.

He shakes his head. "No. I'm sorry for the situation, and I'm sorry for your loss, but this is a huge case for the firm. The answer is no."

"What if I only need a week? Just one week. Please." I hate how desperate I sound. I hate more how I've given myself a deadline I can't possibly meet. One week? What am I thinking? Before I can retract, or say two weeks, or spit out my eloquent car ride speech with all the reasons I'd be able to work on the case from Greenwillow, he sticks his index finger in the air.

"One week," he says, the two words so emphatic there's not a sliver of room for a but or a maybe or a have you considered this option. I'm stuck with a week.

And I have no idea how I'm going to make that happen.

* * *

I LEAVE the firm and spend the little bit of time I have considering options before the dress shopping event. I lament Melanie's decision not to speak to me about any of this and go on a goose chase of an internet search looking for answers.

By the time I arrive at Perfect Dress, I'm exhausted.

"Olivia!" A petite woman with a pixie haircut and a button nose greets me at the door. "I'm Brooke. Your mom and sisters are back here."

I follow her past displays of ornate gowns and veils and shoes to a dressing room. Mom, the twins, and two girls I vaguely recognize are inside seated on pink puffed couches, champagne glasses in their hands.

"She's here," Mom says in lieu of hello. Or how are you? Or how's that life-changing decision going, yay or nay? It's not like I'd expected her to bring up the guardianship right away, but honestly, it's like we'd never even had the conversation.

"I'm here," I say, the words tired. I go through the obligatory process of hugging everyone in the room, even the women I barely recognize, then fix myself a glass of Coke from the beverage table.

"Okay, girls." Mom claps her hands. "Pick a dress."

Shelby and the other girls scramble for dresses, and I piece together that we're trying them on now, all at the same time. There's stripping and changing and ooing and ahhing. It's total chaos, and I'm not in the mood. My mind is swimming with my issue. How in the heck am I going to reorganize my life to include Lucas in just a week? He has substantial needs. He lives four hours from here. The task seemed impossible when I'd made the offer in William's office. It feels even more so now.

I remain still on the cushion while all the girls bustle around me, snapping photos of themselves in various dresses. I'm hoping I'll go unnoticed, that I can just sit here and melt into the cushion. But Mom grabs a dress from a hanger and thrusts it in my direction. "Olivia," she says, "stop being such a fogy. Join in."

"I really—" I start.

"Your sister only gets married once. Try on the dress."

It's a directive, not a request, and I stand with the heavy garment, too tired to deal with the argument that will ensue if I don't put it on. I pull the dress over my head. It's too large and the material is draped, and the result is that I look like I'm wearing a toga. It doesn't help that the material is the exact color as my skin. I stare at myself in one of the full-length mirrors and it crosses my mind that if Nate were here, he'd tell me the dress looks "owlful" and I'd laugh. But instead, after the William meeting and not knowing how to handle things with Lucas and feeling like the ugly duckling in a roomful of swans, I want to cry.

Mom analyzes me like she's assessing a piece of furniture. "Stand back, honey," she says and puts her finger on her chin, like this dress, this oversized tent-like garment, is actually a possibility. "It's bad, I know."

Mom pokes Ellie's shoulder. "What do you think?"

Both she and Ellie look at me and I want to scream. Actually, I don't. I want to go home, curl up in bed under a fuzzy blanket, and just stay there. After what feels like forever, Ellie suggests

Shelby try the dress on and, poof, the toga becomes adorable. It ends up being *the* dress, no thanks to me.

After the dress is selected, the twins and their friends make plans to go out. I'm invited but it's a half-hearted invite, one with a *we have to ask her* vibe, and I decline. Not that I would have gone even if I had felt wanted. I've got too much to figure out.

The girls leave in a flurry of squeals and screams, and Mom and I walk out together in their wake. She hugs me tight on the sidewalk. It feels momentarily nice to be hugged and cared for and my normally high defenses drop. Nervous energy about the guardianship and the situation with work collide with lack of sleep, and tears slide down my face.

Mom steps back, and a look of alarm crosses her features. "What is it? Are you alright?"

I nod and wipe at the tears.

Mom stands still a moment, then leans forward and asks softly, "Is it Ellie's wedding?" She puts a hand on my shoulder. "You'll find someone soon, dear."

The idea that Mom thinks I'm emotional because I'm not the one getting married immediately stops the tears, overwhelm replaced by anger.

"Really? You think that's what this is about?" I wipe the final tears, streaking the wet across my face. "I tell you Melanie died and named me as Lucas's guardian. You never follow up. You never ask about it. And now you assume I'm emotional because I'm not the one getting married?"

My voice is loud, and passersby look in our direction.

"Olivia," Mom says in a whisper-shout, her tone a seeming admonishment of my unapologetic display of feelings. "We did talk about it. You said you were declining."

"Well, I didn't," I bark back. "I've taken on the role."

Mom's face registers surprise, then dismay, then horror all in the span of a second.

"You didn't."

"I did and I feel good about the decision," I lie.

"Is it too late? Can't you reverse it or something?" She pulls at the pendant on her necklace.

"No," I snarl, though I'm almost positive that's not true. But if I did back out, Dennis would be waiting in the wings, swooping me back to square one. "It's the right thing," I say.

She moves closer to the storefront, away from the stream of people passing by. "Not for you it isn't. What about your career? How will you keep your job and care for Lucas? And if you did meet someone—"

"Mom."

"I'm just saying, it's hard enough to start a relationship when it's just two people. Bringing an adult with Lucas's issues into the mix? No man's going to want to deal with that."

I point at her, my pulse speeding. "You're ridiculous. Sometimes what's right is not what's easy, okay. I'm not worried about getting married or what any fictious future man will or will not want to deal with. I can stand on my own two feet. I don't need anyone. I never have." I step back and puff out a breath. "As for my career, I'm working on it. Everything will be fine."

I don't know this of course, but I won't admit it. Not to her. And not now. "I'll see you, Mom." I spin on my heel and walk down the block. "And thanks for the help."

"Olivia," she calls out, "please reconsider."

I keep walking, my eyes fixed on the sidewalk.

"You're making a huge mistake," she calls.

It's all I can do not to turn around and scream, "I know."

CHAPTER 17

OLIVIA

The morning after the Mom fight, I lie in my bed in my New York apartment, reality not yet crashing through my sleep haze, today seeming an ordinary day. I'll get my standard muffin and large coffee, walk the five blocks to work, and stay for ten hours. After, I'll get take-out and eat standing up in the kitchen, change into sweats, and watch stupid reality TV shows.

My eyes fly open.

Or none of the above.

Instead, I'm going to try again to talk William into letting me work remotely on the Rowan case, using actual words this time. There's no way I can get things settled with Lucas and be back to New York in just one week.

I dress in my favorite power suit, buy William a large coffee from his go-to shop, and wait until there's a gap in his schedule. I find him in his office and march in without asking, shutting the door behind me. I lay out the arguments that I'd practiced in the car. Perfectly. And . . .

"No."

"But—"

"No, Olivia. We talked about this."

I reiterate the points I just made.

William blows out a breath. "Olivia. The answer is no. I'm sorry." He shifts in his seat to face his computer. "I have work to do."

I stand, stunned. I force the new "but" forming on my lips back down my windpipe. There is no but. William was clear. The answer is no.

I stumble out of the office and into the hallway in a fog. Rationally, I know I shouldn't care this deeply about a stupid legal case. But it had felt like I was on my way. That the sacrifices I'd made to get to the point where I'd even be considered for such a case were worth it. I'd be the child Dad would have been proud of, the child Mom would see as an equal to the twins. I'd be an insider in the Bennett Connor legal machine, my home away from home.

I walk in a daze until—boom—I collide hard with someone. I jerk back as papers fall to the floor. "Sorry," I say, bending to pick them up. I scoop the papers into a jumbled pile and lift my head, fully expecting to see the mail clerk or a summer intern. Nope.

It's Marjorie Small. Marjorie, with her perfect gray-blonde bob, signature red lips, and manicured eyebrows.

I jolt up, the haphazard stack of papers—her papers—gripped in my hands. "Here." I shove the pile toward her. "Sorry. I'm so sorry. I was—"

She pulls at the lapel of her gray, fitted pantsuit. "You were talking to William."

"Yes." I'm not sure why, but the statement, combined with her knowledge of where I just came from, feels ominous.

Marjorie neatens the messy pile in her hands. "May I speak to you in my office, Olivia?"

"Sure." I squeak out the word and my mind swirls with

reasons she'd ask to speak to me. I come up with only one. She overheard that I can't be in the office for the foreseeable future and is going to boot me. This is it. From almost partnership to unemployed.

"Sorry again about banging into you," I say because I am sorry but also to fill the agonizingly silent void.

She stops short and her gaze darts in my direction. "Don't over apologize, Olivia. It was an accident." She resumes walking. I fight the urge to apologize for apologizing.

I follow her into her enormous office, a space I've been in only a handful of times. Windows adorn one wall from end to end, New York skyscrapers glistening in the summer sun outside. The desk is massive, intricate carvings cut into the mahogany legs. Neatly arranged legal books sit in size order in floor-to-ceiling shelves behind the desk. A stocked bar cart on wheels sits in the corner behind a conference table adorned with fresh flowers.

She shuts the door. "Olivia, sit."

I sit in a chair by her desk; she takes the seat adjacent to me. For a moment, I think she's done it to make me feel comfortable but quickly realize that this arrangement, being three feet away from a woman who may want to fire me, is way more intimidating.

"I overheard you and William speaking," she says in a clipped tone. "What's this about your need to work remotely?"

My chest tightens; I pull at my jacket. I need to say something, but I can't think, and my heart is pounding, and my face is hot, and this is *Marjorie Small*. "I—" I open my mouth and close it like a human fish.

"Olivia." She leans forward, shortening the already minimal distance between us. "Just spit it out."

"Sorry," I say, and her eyes flare. Irritation, I guess, for me apologizing. "Sorry," I say again (!) and purse my lips. I shake my head, then tell the whole story from the time I got the initial phone call from Chuck Stockton.

When I'm finished, she swivels in her chair, her face impassive. One moment stretches to the next and the next and the next until I'm fairly certain I'll be leaving with my things in a box.

She opens her mouth.

My muscles stiffen. I draw in a breath. This is it.

"I liked how you stood up for yourself with William."

I'm so tense, my body so rigid, I don't comprehend her words.

"You advocated for yourself well, Olivia. I haven't seen that from you before."

"Thank you," I say, though I'm not sure it's a compliment. Like when my soccer coach deigned me "most improved" in first grade, a backhanded way of saying: you sucked before, and now you suck less. Congrats.

Marjorie twists her chair towards mine and leans forward. "May I ask you something?"

I hesitate. It's a question I've always hated because you can't reasonably say no, but what the something is, is unclear. I give the expected answer. "Of course."

"Do you want to be guardian of your brother?"

I don't expect the question; my answer is automatic. "No."

No.

I blink, surprised by the answer, surprised by how quickly it came, how guttural the response. Like I didn't have to think about it. But now that the word—NO—is out in the ether, I'm not sure that it reflects how I feel. At least not totally. The situation is more complicated than that.

Marjorie nods. "I thought maybe not." She reaches out and squeezes my hand. "Like so many women, you've been put in a difficult position when it comes to caretaking. It's not fair. Men are rarely put in this spot." She releases my hand and sits back.

"It's exactly why my children are in boarding school. They enjoy it, and it allows me to do what I love."

"Yes. I understand that." And I do. After just a few days of being guardian, I can feel the crux of that time issue, where career and caregiving collide. And I'm flattered—stunned really —that Marjorie has chosen to confide in me. But I still don't know what it means.

"You're an excellent lawyer, Olivia," Marjorie continues. "A little timid maybe, but getting there." She sits up and points at me with a perfectly manicured finger. "I want to help you with this issue, woman to woman. Help you find a place for your brother. A boarding school, so to speak." She pauses. "That is what you want, right?"

My mouth says "yes," and my mind thinks maybe, then yes. Yes. The word implants firmly in my brain. Yes. That is what I want. A nice out-of-home placement for Lucas would be better than Dennis as guardian. And me, most likely. So yes. Not that Marjorie will be able to help with that. Out-of-home place-ments, boarding schools, so to speak, take years to find, according to Dominique. I'm not sure how she'd get one.

"Thank you," I say. "But I understand it's a long process."

She waves her hand like I've just brought up the most minimal of concerns. "It won't be a problem. I have connec-tions, and the firm does. We'll get this figured out quickly." She reaches out and pats my shoulder. "We need you back on the team pronto."

We. Team. Pronto. My pride swells, each word an affirma-tion. You matter. We care about you. You belong here.

"And I'll talk to William," she says with an eyeroll. "No reason you can't work on the Rowan case remotely while we get this settled."

"Really?"

"Absolutely. We'll get the housing issue sorted in no time. I'll have my admin contact you for whatever information we need about your brother."

She springs out of the chair and ushers me toward the door. "I'll be in touch, Olivia. Keep up the fine work."

* * *

I DRIVE from the firm to Greenwillow, giddy over my conversation with Marjorie. She wants me on the team AND she wants to help find Lucas a fantastic placement, likely near me. It's like she waved a magic wand and, poof, all my concerns evaporated.

When I pull up the drive, it's dusk. Lucas and Nate sit around a lit firepit. Nate holds a long stick with a marshmallow on the end over the fire, and Lucas stuffs the remains of a s'more in his mouth. I walk toward them; their faces are illuminated by flames. Nate erupts into a smile when I step into view. I hadn't expected that, and automatically I smile back.

"Hey, guys," I say and collapse into the Adirondack chair next to Lucas.

"Hey, good to see you," Nate says. "Easy drive?"

"Very much, but I'm starving." I gesture to Lucas's half-eaten s'more. "Any way I could get one of those?"

"You betcha," Nate says. He pulls a marshmallow from the bag. "Any trip highlights?"

"I tried on a tent," I start and recount the hideous dress shopping event. I make it sound funny instead of sad, skipping the fight with Mom. I really exaggerate the awfulness of the dress. "It was the same color as my skin. I looked like Casper the ghost on prom night."

He laughs in a way that makes me wish I had something else funny to say.

"It couldn't have been that bad." He extends a thin paper plate in my direction.

"It was," I say, taking the plate. "Trust me." I hold up the plate, a hot mess of a s'more in its center. "Thank you for this."

"You're welcome." He turns to Lucas. "One more, Lu?"

Lucas is mid-verbal stim, a line from some show I haven't seen, and doesn't respond to the question. "I'll make you one," Nate says without missing a beat and starts to create another chocolate, gooey concoction. "Did you get your work straightened out?" he asks.

I open my mouth, then shut it. During the car ride back, I couldn't wait to share that I'm still on the Rowan case and recount all the flattering things Marjorie had said. But now that I'm here, I find I don't want to talk about any of those things. The case, my ambition. None of it seems to fit here. Like there's a forcefield between that version of myself and this one. "It's all worked out," I say simply. "How were things here?"

"Pretty good." Nate recounts some of the things they did, but I stop listening almost immediately. Because the best-ever chocolatey, gooey, graham cracker taste just exploded in my mouth.

"Oh my God," I interrupt, covering my full mouth with my hand. "This is amazing."

He shrugs. "It's just a s'more."

"It's heaven."

He smiles, big and easy. "I think you haven't lived enough then, Olivia. Make you another?"

"One hundred more, please."

Nate smiles and begins to create another s'more. I stretch out my legs and stare up at the darkening sky, the outline of a white moon in its center. I shoot out my hand and tap Lucas's thigh. "How you doing, Lu?" I know he won't answer, but I wish he could tell me. Melanie hasn't been gone long. He must feel grief about that, even if he can't express it. Then again, after our dad died, he seemed not to feel anything.

"Here," Nate says, extending a plate.

I sit up and take it. "Thank you." I bite the new s'more and shake my head. "Where did you learn to make these?"

He rakes his hair with an open hand. "I was a camp counselor at an overnight camp for years."

"Yeah?" I think a moment. "That fits."

He smiles. "How so?"

"I don't know. I can just see it. You around a campfire with a bunch of kids. You'd be good at that, I think."

"Thanks. And how about you? Ever a camp counselor?"

I pick a crumb from my plate and pop it in my mouth. "I didn't work in the summer because I came here. My dad wanted to spend as much time with me as possible." I recall the long hug he used to give me when I'd get here. "The whole summer with my girl," he'd say. I swallow hard.

Nate's expression turns contemplative. "That must have been hard. Living in two places."

"It wasn't until Dad and Melanie moved here," I say. "Before that, my parents lived just a few minutes apart. I saw them both all the time." I don't expand on the hard parts of that situation. That neither Mom nor Dad wanted to put pressure on me to be with them, so I ended up moving back and forth between their houses constantly, never feeling completely at home in either one. And more so once they each started their own, new families, me the living remnant of their old relationship.

He tells me about his family, an intact unit of four, and how his grandparents, aunts, uncles, and cousins all live in Greenwillow. "Probably sounds dull."

"No. It sounds idyllic," I say, meaning it. The beauty of living in a place where you really belong should never be underestimated.

As I finish the second s'more and a mass of oozy, sticky marshmallow coats my fingers. I hold them up and scan the area for something to wipe them on.

"Here," Nate says. He pulls a Wet One from a container. "I always have these when I make s'mores."

I expect him to hand it to me, but instead he takes one of my hands and gently starts to wipe my fingers. He's close to me now, and I see the beginnings of a five o'clock shadow on his jaw, the deep blue of his eyes. His eyelashes are surprisingly long. He smells like pine. He gently takes my other hand in his and repeats the process. The gesture feels intimate, his closeness more intoxicating than it should be given that I barely know him and my brother is just a few feet away.

I draw back without thinking. Nate's head jerks up. He blinks, and a flush, barely visible in the light of the fire, sweeps across his cheeks. "Sorry." He holds up the wipe. "I was used to doing that for the campers, and Lucas, and, well . . ." He extends the wipe in my direction. "You can do it yourself. Clearly."

"Don't need it," I say, glad his seeming embarrassment will likely detract from the fact I was staring at his facial features and inhaling his scent. I hold up my hands and wiggle my fingers. "You did a good job. All clean. Thank you."

He nods. "You're welcome." He gestures around the space. "Lu and I will clean up. You should go to bed."

"Sure." My back pricks up. Dismissal words for sure. Like he mistakenly made an overture toward friendship and wants to tuck it back inside. No problem. I'm used to that. And given the amount of time I'll be here, it's probably for the best. Being friends with Nate will only complicate things.

CHAPTER 18

N ATE
Olivia sweeps back toward the house, her form disappearing into the darkness.

Shit.

I messed that up. I'd been looking forward to seeing her. I enjoyed our talk, and I like that she can make me laugh. I try to remember the last time a girl made me laugh; I can't think of anyone.

Then I made things weird. Wiping off her hands. Ordering her to bed. Who does that?

Me, I guess.

Whatever.

It's not like I'm ready for a relationship. And it's not like Olivia, if she knew who I really was, what I did, would want to be with a guy like me anyway.

I gather the s'more supplies and place them in a plastic grocery bag. I hand the bag to Lucas and douse the remaining flames in the pit. I turn on my flashlight and Lucas and I follow the little bead of light to the house.

Olivia's not downstairs when we get inside. I help Lucas get ready for bed. He can do most things on his own, but he forgets steps without supervision and prompts. I'll have to go through that routine, all of his routines, with Olivia. Lucas is regimen-oriented, easy enough if you know the drill, but if you don't and you miss a step—whoa—not good. I've been down that road, and I make a mental note to compile a comprehensive list of schedules and rules for Olivia.

I go to bed and when I wake in the morning, it's early. It's a good hour before Lucas will get up, and I head downstairs, not expecting to see anyone. But Olivia's at the kitchen table working, Otis curled up in the chair next to her. She's set up a makeshift office with her computer, a printer, legal pads, and piles of documents. She's wearing wire-rimmed glasses, her hair morning messy, and she's got on pajamas with multi-colored owls all over them. I've seen her in the morning before, but she's always been showered and ready for the day. Seeing her like this feels like a glimpse into the real her. I like it.

"Sorry." She peers at me through her glasses. "The desk in my bedroom is super small, and I always worked in the kitchen in my apartment. I figured there's enough room on the table down there for us to eat and stuff." She nods toward the other end.

"Yeah," I say, staring. It makes sense. It's a big table and she likes working in the kitchen. But she's in Lucas's seat. Otis is in my seat. And she's moved the placements and also the salt, napkin holder, pepper holder that sits in the same place on the table night after night. Half-eaten cereal sits in the singular bowl Lucas likes.

"Is it alright?" she stammers.

"I—" I start, not sure how to say it: you need to move everything ASAP. But if I say nothing, she'll find out why switching things around—multiple things at that—is not a good idea. "Lucas is pretty particular about things being the same. It may sound dumb but—"

"No." She shakes her head. "You're right. I should have remembered that. I'll move this stuff. It's just . . ."

Her voice trails off and I guess that she's trying to think of the best place to set herself up.

"The shed." The word comes out abruptly. "You could set up in the shed."

She lifts an eyebrow.

I realize how ridiculous that suggestion probably sounds. "It's a converted shed. A she-shed. That's where Melanie would make her jewelry and stuff. There's a giant table and couch and rugs and all." I wave my arm toward the door. "I'll show you."

She gets up and follows me. I open the door and catch a glimpse of her feet in bright pink owl slippers. I look at her.

She lifts a foot. "Another find from my junior high things. Owlsome, right?"

"Owlsome indeed."

I open the door and we cross the lawn toward the shed that sits on the edge of the property at the base of the tree line. It's sticky outside, hot despite the early hour. Olivia walks next to me in the ridiculous slippers. "You're up early," I say. "Or should I say, owly."

She slaps my shoulder. "Too early for bad puns."

"You said owlsome," I volley back, glad that things seem normal between us.

"I did. My mistake. No more bad puns until after noon." She stops and shoots out a hand. "Deal?"

"Deal," I say and shake her hand. "But when the clock strikes twelve, owl hell breaks loose."

She snorts a laugh; I do the same. "You're right," I say, still half laughing. "It is too early for this."

We reach the shed. It's small with powder blue siding, a door, and some windows. I haven't been inside it in months, a year maybe, and I hope it's as nice a spot as I'd made it out to be back in the kitchen. Only one way to find out, I guess. I push open the door.

Olivia steps inside and gasps.

The interior is beautiful, more so than I'd remembered. A long wooden table lines the wall opposite the door, an eclectic grouping of frames over it, flowers and foliage Melanie cut and dried inside them. Each of the short walls features white built-in cabinets. One houses books, the other jewelry making supplies. An overstuffed chair with sage green fabric sits in front of the bookshelf, buttressed by a wooden ottoman.

"It's perfect," Olivia says, her head swiveling from one end of the shed interior to the other. "It's the perfect office space."

Her eyes fix on the bookshelf; I track her gaze. The shelf has a few jewelry-making and other crafting books, but the over-whelming majority are books on autism. Titles like *Raising Your Autistic Child, Diet and the Spectrum, Play Theory, ABA and Autism.* A dog-eared book titled *Your Autistic Child Can Be Happy* sits on a painted crate next to the chair.

"She really wanted the best for him," she whispers.

"Yeah," I acknowledge, Melanie clear in my mind. "She did."

Olivia turns her gaze from the shelves to me. "Why me?" she asks. "Why would she pick me? I'm overly driven, I can be self-ish, and I don't make friends easily. I barely even came to visit Lucas after Dad died." She lowers herself onto the ottoman.

I shrug, surprised at Olivia's assessment of herself. "Not sure about the friend bit," I say and sit in the desk chair adjacent to her. "You won *me* over."

"You don't count. You seem like you like everyone."

"Nope," I say. "Not true. There's a teller at the bank that I find very off-putting."

Her mouth splits into a grin.

"Seriously, Olivia. You're good with Lucas. You treat him like a person, not a disability. And he likes you. If I'm Melanie," I say and jut my chin toward the *Your Autistic Child Can Be Happy* book, "that's enough."

A look that I can't decipher crosses her features, and she doesn't speak for a long moment.

"You'll be great at this," I say.

"Okay," she says after a long moment. "Okay," she repeats, like she's made an internal decision and is affirming it to herself. She stands and looks in my direction. "Can you help me move my stuff?"

"Of course." We move the printer, computer, and documents to the shed, and after, return to the kitchen and put the placemats and napkins and everything in its normal order. "I'm going to make Lu some secret waffles before he wakes up. Do you want some?"

"Secret waffles?" she questions. "What are they? Invisible or something?"

"No, but I'll work on that." I pull out waffle ingredients. "They're waffles made with my secret ingredient."

"What's the ingredient?"

"If I told you, it wouldn't be a secret now, would it? Anyway, Lucas loves them. He eats them every morning." I crack an egg into a bowl. "I'll make sure you have the recipe before—" I stop, not sure how to finish the sentence. Before I go. Before you take over. Before you follow through on your undisclosed plans.

"Thanks," she says quickly. "And I'd love a waffle."

I turn back to the bowl and dump in waffle mix. Lucas's feet sound on the stairs. He stumbles into the kitchen, still in his pajamas, hair sticking up all over. "Hey, bud." I plug in the waffle iron. "Just getting these going. Are you excited for the zoo tonight?" We're going to a nighttime event at the Treeline Zoo, a feature they have a few times a summer. Lucas loves it. I always take him, though it occurs to me that Olivia wouldn't know this. That maybe, even, now that she's in charge, I need to ask for her permission. I turn from the waffles. "Is that alright? If we go to the zoo?"

She waves a hand. "Sure. Of course."

"You should come," I say suddenly. As soon as the words come out of my mouth, I realize that I want her to, that the experience would be more fun if she were there. "It'll be fun." I shut the waffle maker.

"Nah." She pulls at a lock of hair. "I'm too far behind. Maybe next time."

CHAPTER 19

OLIVIA

A little before seven, I hear Nate's car rumble down the drive. Feeling extraordinarily lame, I stayed inside the shed as they got ready to go, my *work all night* drinks and snacks in hand. I plan to work on a brief for the Rowan case. Normally, working all night on a legal document wouldn't bother me. I'd enjoy it even. But if I'm honest, I have FOMO about the zoo event. I'd have gone, but this brief is due Monday, and William asked that it be done by tomorrow morning at the latest. He's already a little peeved that Marjorie overruled him about me working on Rowan remotely. I need the brief to be perfect.

I lean forward and scan the facts of a case for the second time. When I'm done, I don't remember what I read. *Come on, Olivia.* I read again, this time electronically highlighting parts. It's better, but when I move on to the legal arguments, my mind blanks.

I lean back in the chair, and my eyes fall on the bookshelf, to the dozens and dozens of books on ASD. I visualize Melanie, or Dad, picking one up at a store and buying it with hope for a better future for Lucas. I blow out a breath, wondering how in the world it is that I'm now in control of that future. Guilt at my plan for an out-of-home placement surges through me, especially as I can see, and feel, how hard they both worked to make a good environment for Lucas here. Right down to hiring Nate, who, besides being understatedly handsome, may be one of the nicest people I've ever met.

I redirect myself to the case on the screen and I try again to read the legal arguments, but my mind keeps trailing away. I try and fail one more time, then snap the computer shut. I'll go to the zoo. It's the least I can do considering how little time I'll have here in Greenwillow. I'll get these feelings of guilt and FOMO out of my system and come back ready to work. I can always get up crazy early and finish.

I return to my room, get out of the comfy clothes I have on, and pull an old, red sundress over my head, a favorite from the teen days. I get to the zoo a little before eight, check in, and receive a bag of complimentary glow items—necklaces, bracelets, and wands. Because it's sensory inclusion night, there are also bags with noise cancelling headphones and fidget toys. Smaller crowds too.

I enter the zoo and text Nate. He doesn't text back, but I make an educated guess that Lucas would want to go to the gorilla enclosure. It was always a favorite. I follow the path to the exhibit, the trees on both sides adorned with bright lights. Gigantic animals made from thousands of colored lights sit all over the park, visible even from the entrance. I take a photo of a huge lion. Additional animals adorn the path every hundred feet or so. I stop and snap photos of a snake and an elephant and a group of zebras.

I reach the gorilla enclosure. It's full of trees and rocks and a tiny pool, half of it inside, half out. I scan the area. A mother and two children stand at the far end near an older couple with an adult child in a wheelchair. There are a pair of large, unmoving gorillas near the edge of the enclosure. A third, smaller gorilla climbs a tree branch. But no Nate and Luke.

I watch the little gorilla scurry across the branch, then leap to a platform nearly hidden in the trees. I stay a moment to see if he'll do anything else, and when he doesn't, I move to the indoor viewing area.

I see Lucas sitting on a bench near the glass of the enclosure directly in front of the large gorillas. Nate is standing a few feet back, engaged in conversation with a woman. She looks about our age from the back with long shapely legs, short shorts, and thick brown hair spilling down her back. My ribs squeeze. A girlfriend? I shake my head. What does it matter? Nate's my roommate, my *employee*, if I want to be technical about it. He's a nice guy and great with Lucas, but we don't have the kind of relationship where I should feel jealous. I mean, I thought there was a little spark there, at the firepit last night and again this morning in the shed, but I could be wrong. I was probably wrong.

The woman slings an arm across Nate's shoulders.

Definitely wrong.

I stare at the pair a moment, feeling all kinds of stupid. I should just turn around and hightail it out of here before they see me. I'll go back to the shed and work on the brief like I should have done to begin with.

As soon as I make the decision, the woman appended to Nate's side turns around.

It's Tessa from Include.

Her face breaks into a smile. "Olivia. Hi." She waves enthusiastically.

Nate turns. "Hey, you made it." He smiles. "Lucas is down there with Avery, Tessa's sister." He gestures to the bench in front of the glass. "You two met, right? The other day at Include?"

"Yeah. Yeah. We met," Tessa supplies. "Mom's trying to

recruit her for the decorating committee." She rolls her eyes, then waves her arm forward. "Come on over, girlfriend. Join us."

I walk toward them, my steps tentative. I've never been easy with people, familiar like the two of them clearly are, and I can't help but feel I'm interrupting their good time by my presence. But I can't go back now. I just got here. I'll stay an hour, tops.

Tessa jerks a thumb toward Avery and Lucas. "Can't drag those two out of here. We've been by the gorillas all night."

I nod. "Lucas was always like that when we'd come here as a family. He'd pick one exhibit and stay. I always wanted to see everything, every exhibit, every animal, even if it was just for a split second. I never saw much of anything, but Melanie and Lu always ended up seeing something amazing."

At that moment, a large gorilla, presumably a mom, walks into the indoor viewing area with a baby riding her back, its arms snug around her neck.

"See?" I say.

We watch the mom and baby in silence.

"You were able to get your work done?" Nate asks finally. It's the kind of boring conversation my presence usually engenders.

"No. Just taking a breather."

"Olivia's a lawyer," Nate tells Tessa. "She's working on a big case."

Rowan is a big case but talking about it seems, somehow, dull in this context. I scramble for something to say that isn't work related. "How long have you two been dating?" I blurt.

Tessa throws her head back and laughs. "That's funny, girl."

Nate's face reddens, and he playfully pushes on her shoulder. "Okay. You don't have to act like it's that crazy." He turns to me. "Tessa and I have been friends since, what, second grade?"

"Second grade," she affirms. "Mrs. Witt's class." She leans forward. "You need any dirt on this guy, you come to me. I got the goods."

Nate rolls his eyes. "This is my employer, Tessa, remember?"

I laugh, feeling part of the group in a way I don't normally.

We move closer to Lucas and Avery and watch the gorillas in congenial silence—or as silent as it can be with Tessa around—until it's time for the nighttime parade. We take our time walking to the route, Lucas stopping at every illuminated animal. Avery struggles with sound, Tessa tells me, so we find spaces in the quiet zone, an area where parade music is lowered or muted as the floats pass by. We sit five in a row on a curb, our legs outstretched. The night is warm with a fullish moon, bright stars peppered across the sky. Zoo employees push kiosks of food, drinks, and souvenirs down the asphalt path.

A feeling of lightness flushes through me. I should have left an hour ago at least to finish the brief, but I haven't wanted to. Every time I think about it, I find an excuse as to why it's okay to stay longer. It's the kind of procrastination I'd normally denigrate.

I spy a kiosk with light-up bubble wands, and in the throes of my good mood, I impulsively hop up and buy five overpriced wands with the zoo insignia on the handle. I pass one out to each of them, then aim mine upward and blast a stream of bubbles into the air.

"Yes, girlfriend," Tessa says. She leaps from the sidewalk, shoots an arm straight up like the Statue of Liberty, and lets loose a cascade of tiny bubbles.

I poke one with my fingertip and it pops. "I love bubbles," I gush and angle my head toward Lucas. "Remember we used to do bubbles all the time, Lu?" I shoot another stream.

"Come on, Lucas," Nate encourages. He slides across the curb so he's next to him and shows him how to shoot the bubbles, hand over hand. "Hold it," he directs. "Press." Bubbles shoot out of Lucas's wand and a rare smile crosses his face. "There you go, Lu." He gives Lucas a friendly shoulder shove, then patiently repeats the process with Avery.

I stare at the interaction, a fluttering in my stomach.

Tessa leans over. "That is a fine man there."

My face heats. I nod instead of speaking, not wanting to give away what feels like a crush. People around us quickly snap up their own bubble blasters and the moment to fess up passes. Soon, the atmosphere around us is a mass of bubbles and light-up wands. Kids and adults run around the space in the middle of what looks like bubble rain. The outdoor lights reflect on the surfaces of the bubbles, and the tiny floating masses look like colored dots in the sky. I stamp on the half-bubbles that land on the asphalt. Lucas does the same, the look on his face pure joy.

I recall what Nate said in the shed about me being guardian. "You'll be great at this." Would I be?

I shake my head and forget the future, the brief, anything but this crazy, spontaneous present moment. The parade starts and the bubbles settle down. Bright animal-themed floats featuring LED versions of hippos, koalas, flamingos, lions, elephants, giraffes, and sea creatures glide by us. The floats are flanked by dozens of costumed dancers all moving in sync. I've seen the parade before, both the regular and sensory versions, but this one seems more spectacular somehow. Like the lights are brighter, the dancers more skilled, the floats bigger. Or maybe it's my mood. Either way, when the final float comes into view, I'm bummed the night is almost over.

Later, I stay up nearly the rest of the night to get the brief done, and when I send it swooshing through cyberspace my heart dips. It isn't my best work. Not the kind of work Marjorie thought I'd be doing when she kept me on Rowan. Tonight was fun, but this, going to zoos, hanging out without a purpose, isn't my life. My life, and possible partnership, are waiting back for me back in New York.

I need to keep my eye on the prize.

CHAPTER 20

LUCAS

Stuck inside a body that doesn't always work the way I want it to, I don't usually describe my days as fun. But today? Today was fun. Nate and I met Avery and Tessa at the night-time zoo event. We spent a long time at the gorilla exhibit because it's Avery's favorite. And I like Avery. A lot. She's pretty with honey-colored skin and green eyes. Her hair is black and wild, but in the best possible way. And we don't talk to each other because, duh, but we've been around each other enough that it's comfortable. Did I mention that I like her?

As for the gorillas, I have mixed feelings about them. I admit that they do interesting things. The mom with the baby tonight? That was cute. The baby ended up sleeping on her chest, and while I wouldn't think I'd want to watch a baby gorilla sleep for a long time, there was something peaceful about it. But I don't know. I feel like those gorillas are thinking things they want us to know and just can't say. Like get me out of this cage or I don't like bananas, bro. Thinking of that makes me feel bad. For obvious reasons.

Olivia came while we were watching them. She's been gone two days. I knew she'd come back but a piece of me was relieved when she returned anyway.

She got to the zoo before the best part of the night—the parade. We got bubble guns before it started. Bubbles were something Olivia and I had been big into during the summers she came. Once she made a special solution and we made crazy giant bubbles, like a couple feet long. We had bubble machines too and we'd set them all off and try to pop as many as we could. Tonight everyone around us got bubble wands and was shooting them all at once—thousands of bubbles. Really cool. I haven't done bubbles in years and years.

Then the parade started. As childish as it might sound, I love nighttime parades. All the lights. The huge floats. I don't mind the music, but Avery does so we sat where it was quiet. I sat next to her, and she put her hand over mine. I think she meant to do it. She kept it there for a while. I opened my mouth to ask her how she liked the parade, so I wouldn't just be sitting there, you know, but nothing that made sense came out. Avery smiled in my direction, so I still felt good about trying. I have to start somewhere.

Anyway, I was bummed when the night was over, but now that I'm lying here, I can think about it. For all my body struggles, my memories work just fine. And today I made some good ones.

CHAPTER 21

OLIVIA

Four days after the nighttime zoo event two major things are scheduled. First, it's meet- the-teacher day for Lucas. Lucas's primary teacher, Lauren Caddell, is the same as last year, but I've never met her, obviously. And though it's possible, likely even, that Lucas won't finish out the school year here, meeting her and seeing where Lucas spends the school day is the kind of thing I need to do as guardian.

Second, it's Melanie's memorial. Not a funeral. She'd put in her will that she didn't want a funeral, that she'd rather the money for it go to Lucas. But people want to say goodbye, and a few close friends put together an informal memorial to take place this afternoon. I discussed it with Nate, and we agreed Lucas needs to be there. It will be hard, but I know from my dad's death that these kinds of events are important for closure.

But first, I follow Lucas into Greenwillow High School, home of the Hornets. The building is super old and looks exactly like what it is: a school built in the 1950s and never updated. Lucas pulls open the front door and we step inside the virtually empty main entrance. A woman sits at a desk, a giant personified hornet painted on the wall behind her. "Good morning, Lucas. You know where to go."

Lucas grabs my hand and pulls me into the hall to a classroom where a stout woman with sprayed black hair and sensible looking clothes stands at the door. Her face lights up when she sees Lucas. "Lucas, honey." She pulls him into a long bear hug. "I'm so happy to see you. So glad you're in my classroom again." She gestures around. "Look around, sweetheart. There are a few new gadgets in the sensory corner." Lauren has a Southern accent and seems incredibly warm.

Lucas moves to the back of the classroom where there are beanbags, a swing, large cubes, and a variety of see-through bins with gadgets inside. A large fish tank sits across one wall. Two other students are there, and Lucas seems comfortable.

Lauren directs her attention to me. "And you're Olivia? Lucas's sister?"

"Yes."

"I'm Lauren Caddell." She pulls me into a hug that would rival the one she gave Lucas. I hate that my body is stiff, that I can't ease into this interaction. But in fairness, spontaneous hugs from strangers are not something I'm accustomed to. I try to picture a single lawyer at Bennett Connor hugging anyone, let alone a stranger, and can't.

If Lauren notices my rigidity, she doesn't let on. She steps back and grabs both my hands in hers. "Aren't you just a doll stepping in for your brother? A pure gem. Lucas is lucky to have you."

My heart twitches. I don't feel like a *pure gem*. I feel like a woman who jumped at the chance to find an out-of-home placement for my brother days into my guardianship reign.

Lauren releases my hands and whispers, "How is he doing, poor sweet thing?"

"I'm not sure," I say honestly.

She looks back at Lucas on a beanbag in the sensory area.

"It's so tough for them, these kids, not to be able to say what's on their minds." She swings her gaze back to me. "But look, he's dressed, he's here, and he looks like he's been eating enough. Sometimes that's all we can ask of ourselves after a tragedy." She pats my shoulder. "I'll keep a good eye on him here during the school day, I promise you that."

"Thank you." My throat constricts, and conflicting feelings ping in my chest. Relief that Lauren is so nice and that Lucas is clearly comfortable here. Guilt about the inevitable move.

An out-of-home placement is better than Dennis and better than a stranger, I tell myself, but the guilt doesn't ease; my mind keeps whirling.

"Are you alright, sugar?" Lauren asks.

I reorient myself to the present. "Yes, I'm fine. Sorry."

Lauren looks back at Lucas and then at me. "He's a sweetheart. I can see how you'd want to do right by him." She gives me a copy of Lucas's most recent IEP—individualized education plan—and a copy of his schedule. I scan the goals, which include things like emotional regulation and increasing vocabulary. I think about the courses I took my senior year of high school. Physics and psychology and AP English literature. I get that Lucas is neurodivergent, but are goals like "consistently recognize numbers one to one hundred" boring to him? It always seemed to me that he had more going on than that.

Lauren turns to welcome other students and their parents. Each student is greeted like a king or queen, each parent like their child is the most important. When we say goodbye, Lauren duplicates the initial bear hugs. She grabs Lucas's hand and squeezes. "See you Monday, doll."

Lucas and I leave the classroom, and I follow him through the corridors back to the front of the building. Once we're in the car, I tell him we're going to the memorial. "We talked about it, remember? People are going to say nice things about your mom. Like they did at Dad's funeral." I glance over at him. He's staring straight ahead, humming in a low octave.

We pull up to the cemetery. It's overcast with thick, dark clouds overhead. The few people who were supposed to come look like several dozen, all crowded around the place where Dad, and now Melanie, are buried. Lucas and I walk toward the crowd, and I hand Lucas a fidget spinner. It's his favorite, per Nate, who suggested the idea. Lucas grips the toy and immediately starts spinning the wheels and vocalizing with a loud and steady hum.

When we reach the group, I recognize Dominique, Tessa, and Chuck in the crowd along with Nate, who's mid-speech. I remain with Lucas in the back, hidden behind a row of people.

"Not that many people would have given me the chance Melanie did," Nate says, his gaze cast downward on a piece of torn notebook paper. "It's another example of how kind she was. Unless you try to cross Lucas," he continues to a smattering of laughter, "then it's game on." He smiles and looks up. "A fierce protector, a loving wife and parent, a good friend, an accomplished artist, a cherished community member. These things are all part of the fabric of Melanie, but more than these things, I think what we'll all remember about Melanie is how she made us feel. For me, it was forgiven." He doesn't move, his eyes fixed on the plot, a fresh mound of dirt on top of the ground. After a long moment, he folds the paper, steps away, and moves into the crowd.

A woman I don't recognize starts to speak but I don't hear her words, my mind trying to puzzle together the meaning behind Nate's. Why would Melanie need to take a chance on him? And why would he need to be forgiven? The sentiment does explain, possibly, why he's so loyal to Lucas and why he opted to stay on when I asked.

The memorial continues. Every person who speaks affirms Melanie's kind and giving nature. Most have examples of the rich life she led here in this small town. One man talks about the two of them chasing—and catching—an errant goat running down the highway. A woman tells about a time she, Melanie, and their kids, babies at the time, accidentally got locked inside a Target. Another talks about her love of glow sticks, at which everyone laughs. Melanie apparently gave them out at every party.

I gather that she tirelessly volunteered at Include and the school and regularly rescued injured animals, paying for vet bills and giving them a home if needed. She bought prom dresses for needy teens and routinely took every leftover angel tree tag of the community Christmas tree. She was funny too, from what I could tell. I hadn't remembered that. Then again, teenage me hadn't tried to get to know Melanie.

I glance at Lucas. I've been so consumed by the speeches that I didn't realize he stopped fidgeting and stands silent instead of vocalizing. His gaze is downcast, his shoulders hunched. I squeeze his hand.

The talks end just as the clouds overhead burst open with thick drops of rain. People hug briefly and scatter; most acknowledge Lucas on their way out. Dominique gives him a long hug. He leans into her and makes a noise so deep and guttural it's painful.

Nate gently takes Lucas's elbow and begins to guide him back toward the car. They walk a step, two, the rain pelting harder now. Without warning, Lucas throws the fidget spinner, wrestles his arm from Nate's light grip, and runs. He barrels over graves, sprints by trees, his mouth open, screams coming out of it. The graveyard is buttressed on two sides by busy highways, Lucas running wildly toward one on them. Nate chases after him, hurdling over gravestones, rain battering his body.

My heart dives into my chest, and my limbs freeze with panic. Rain falls in sheets around me, obscuring my vision. I can barely see Lucas as he careens toward the road. Nate's gaining on him, but not fast enough. "Lucas!" I scream. "Lucas, the road." My voice is drowned out by the rain, but I keep screaming his name, telling him to stop, over and over and over.

He's a few feet from the highway, cars and trucks speeding down it, heavy rain sputtering from the weight of their tires. The vehicles are fast, their visibility limited. The drivers likely won't see a man running into the road; they won't be able to stop in time if even they do.

Oh my God.

Oh my God.

Oh my God.

He's a few feet from the highway when his foot slides from under him on a patch of grass and he falls, flat, on the ground. Nate leaps over his body and blankets it with his own.

Breath pushes out of me, and tears of relief pour out from my eyes in a stream that mixes with the rain. I can't believe that just happened.

CHAPTER 22

LUCAS
I'm in the car now, going back home after the memorial service without Mom.

I hated that service. I loved the nice things people said about Mom, but they don't know the half of how kind she was. Parents to kids like me come in two camps, I think. The "I love you just the way you are camp" and the "why can't you be normal" one. Mom was in the first one, obviously. I always felt loved and understood, even when I was doing things that would seem batshit crazy, things I didn't even under-stand. I always knew she loved me just how I was. And now she's gone, and that service marked the reality of it. No more pretending like she's coming back.

I wasn't ready. I didn't want to leave and when the service ended, I ran. And while it felt good at the time to just run and scream, I have to face the rest of my life without Mom now. I'm not sure how I'll do it. I want to stim and numb myself, disappear inside the repetition of movement or words. But I can't. Mom wouldn't want that. She'd be crushed; I know it. So I'm going to figure out how to live without her. And do it in a way that would make her proud. It may not be easy, and it may not come right away, but I'll figure it out. I have to.

CHAPTER 23

NATE

It's been four weeks since the funeral debacle. I'm not sure Lucas realizes how close he'd been to running onto the highway into fast-moving traffic. That slip on the grass saved him. Thank God. And though Lucas didn't realize the danger he'd been in, Olivia did, and she's beaten herself up in a way I recognize from having done it myself for the past years. But unlike my situation, this one wasn't Olivia's fault. She had no idea Lucas would react like that to Melanie's memorial. Neither of us did.

She's in a good mood today, though. We're at the Elks Lodge decorating for the Include Fall Dance. The theme is Hollywood.

"Tape," I say from the top of a short ladder.

Olivia rips off a piece of tape from the dispenser and holds it up. I grab it, then stick the red and gold streamers to the wall.

Tessa and I cajoled Olivia into joining the Include dance committee a few weeks back, mainly by holding the meetings at Melanie's house. She resisted at first, insisting she had to work, but then we started getting food from Big Rod's, and lighting up the firepit, and sometimes having cocktails, and eventually we wore her down.

The dance committee is rounded out by Tessa's boyfriend, Jared, a local police officer, and Suzanne, a graphic designer. Suzanne is a high school acquaintance of mine and tight with Tessa. Tiny and blonde with a pixie haircut and bright blue eyes, Suzanne is a Disney maniac with an obsession for M&Ms. She likes to brag that she's had all the flavors, even the rare ones like caramel cold brew.

"Tape," I say again.

Olivia rips off another piece and I stick more streamers to the wall. I descend the ladder, move it, and we repeat the process. The task would be mind-bogglingly boring but for the fact that I like hanging out with Olivia. We've gotten into a kind of rhythm the past few weeks. Olivia working like a fiend from early morning until dinner and me doing as I did before. Take Lucas to school, fill in the day with odd jobs, both paying and not, pick up Lucas afterward. If Olivia ever wonders about my haphazard employment, what I do all day while she's toiling away at a real job, she's never let on.

"Tape," I say again, and she hands me another piece. Behind us, Jared and Tessa work on the entry area which includes a long red carpet sectioned off by silver stanchions and velvet ropes. A human-sized inflatable Oscar trophy stands at the end. Suzanne works on table arrangements, and bows, vases, and flowers are spread out on the table in front of her.

We finish at three. Suzanne, Dominique, and Jared agree to get back early for the DJ and last-minute preparations. I grab Lucas from school; Olivia goes home to take a conference call. She and I will come later with Lucas.

Lucas and I change, he into nice pants and a polo and me into a pin-striped three-piece retro suit I got years ago as part of a 1920s gangster costume. We wait for Olivia by the front door. "You ready?" I yell, then move to fix Lucas's collar. Olivia's feet sound on the stairs but I'm fixated on the collar. It's stiff and sticking up in a way that might bother him, I think. "Maybe a different shirt, Lu?" I ask and turn around.

"Whoa." The word escapes from somewhere deep in my throat.

Olivia's cheeks flush and she glances down at her dress, fitted, full-length, and crimson with a slit up one side. Her hair is curled and up; wispy tendrils frame her face. Her makeup is darker, with lipstick the color of her dress.

I shouldn't be surprised. I knew she, Tessa, and Suzanne were getting dressed up. They went to a thrift shop and bought old prom dresses. But I didn't expect, well, this.

"You're stunning," I burst out.

She leans on one foot and puts a hand on her hip. "Really? You're that surprised?" She says it like she's annoyed, but she's laughing so I know I'm okay.

I shake my head. "Sorry. But wow. Wow." My own face heats and we stare at each other like we're actual prom dates. "About twenty minutes ago, I saw you in the kitchen in sweats."

She shrugs. "I work fast." She swivels her head between me and Lucas. "You guys are a handsome duo."

"Thanks." I step back and my eyes fall to her shoes. Thick-soled white sneakers. "Nice."

"My mother would kill me. Formal clothes and sneakers." She puts her hands on her cheeks in mock horror. "But anything goes, right?"

"Absolutely." The rule of Include dances is to have fun and be comfortable, clothing included.

We arrive at the lodge a bit after the dance starts. When we step inside, Tessa, standing in front of the red carpeted entry-way, smiles broadly. "Welcome to Hollywood. Sunglasses?" She holds a basket of plastic sunglasses in our direction. Olivia and I both take some, put them on, and walk the red carpet after Lucas. Jared takes several pictures of us as we go. At the end,

Olivia and I bookend Lucas, our arms swung around his back. Jared snaps the shot, and I know without seeing it that it's going to be one of those great, forever pictures, the kind Melanie used to put on the refrigerator.

There's a fast song playing, and a smattering of kids and adults dance on the makeshift floor. Lucas and Olivia immediately join in. I watch them a moment. They're atrocious dancers, all flailing limbs and no rhythm, but with such huge smiles the whole of it feels perfect. Olivia waves me forward, and I join them. Tessa and Avery join next, and the five of us dance in a circle. I say "do the owl" and move my arms up and down like I'm flying. Olivia laughs, the infectious one I've grown to appreciate. We look like idiots, but no one cares. Include really is an anything goes, come as you are, do as you wish kind of space.

"Next one's coming in dark," the DJ says. It's a warning that overhead lights are going to be replaced by special effects lighting for the next song. It's the best way we could think of to accommodate those who love stimulation and those who avoid it at all costs. At the warning, the configuration of the dance floor immediately changes. Tessa guides Avery, sensory avoidant to her core, to the food and drink tables. Lucas moves to follow her. I pull him back. "It's your favorite part. The lights."

As if on cue, the overhead lights go off and the DJ switches on a disco ball projector. A kaleidoscope of colors immediately fills the space, bouncing off the ceiling, walls, and floor. The song is fast with a strong beat. I dance in between Olivia and Lucas, and colored beads of lights project off our skin and clothes. By the end of the song, we're breathless, and when the lights flip back on, I get the three of us waters.

Olivia takes a long swig of water at the edge of the dance floor. "That was fun. I can't remember the last time I danced like that." She smiles, big, and turns to Lucas. "So fun, Lu. Thanks for including me." She squeezes his shoulder.

A slow song comes on. Olivia takes Lucas's hand. "Dance with me?" She pulls him toward the dance floor. He follows, and the two of them dance. Lucas is clearly comfortable with her in a way he isn't with most people. I wonder if she realizes how unusual that is.

"She's a sweetheart," a voice says behind me.

I turn around. Lauren Caddell is behind me.

"Oh. Hey." I avert my eyes, embarrassed to have been caught staring. "She's good with Lucas."

"Pretty too."

"Sure," I say, not taking the bait. My experience with Lauren is that she's both the nicest and the nosiest person all at once. I don't need her knowing how I feel, or might feel, about Olivia. I haven't even figured that out yet.

The song ends and Lucas and Olivia return to where we're standing. A new slow song starts. Lauren takes her arms and puts them across my shoulder and Olivia's. She pushes us toward each other. "You two young people should dance. I'm going to get some food." She turns to Lucas. "Want to come? There's a slew of cookies back there."

Lucas and Lauren leave, and Olivia faces me. "Well?"

"Do you want to dance?"

"Absolutely."

I lead her to the dance floor and put my arms around her shoulders. Our faces are close to each other. Too close. Like we should stare into each other's eyes or kiss or something. Sensing the awkwardness, I guess, she averts her gaze and instead puts her head on my shoulder. She moves closer to do so, and honestly it's almost as bad as the *faces inches apart* scenario. And by bad, I mean that I like the feel of her body next to mine. Too much so. Olivia's my employer. I don't know how she feels about me. But I appreciate the feel of her body, the smell of her skin, her breath on my shoulder. I close my eyes for a moment and forget that I'm at the Include Fall dance, that there's a dozen other people around us, and that the lights overhead are crazy bright. In this moment it's just me and Olivia.

The song ends and Olivia steps back. "Great dance!" I say with so much enthusiasm even I recognize it to be cringy. Act like you've been there, buddy. That's what Tessa would say.

Olivia doesn't respond and I look at her face for the first time since the dance ended. Her eyes are wet, like she's almost about to cry or just did.

"Oh. Jeez. Olivia. Are you okay?"

She moves her head in a way that makes it seem like she's righting herself. "I'm fine. I just need to use the ladies' room." She marches off, the rubber on her sneakers squeaking on the hard floor.

I watch her go.

Whatever that was, I clearly got it wrong.

CHAPTER 24

OLIVIA

I stand at the sink in the dark-paneled bathroom at the Elks Lodge. My reflection in the mirror looks like a stranger. I don't normally wear makeup like this. Or my hair up. And since I never went to the prom in high school, or had any reason to wear a long, formal gown, I'm not used to seeing myself dressed up.

Plus, the crying. Or almost crying. What kind of insanity was that? One second, I'm dancing with Nate, my head on his shoulder, feeling all kinds of warm and fuzzy. Like how I'm safe in his embrace. How I like the feel of his chest against mine and his arms around me. And most important, how much I low-key *like* him. And then—boom!—I remember I haven't told him or anyone else about my plans to place Lucas, move back to New York, and resume my job and life. That Greenwillow Olivia, the one who doesn't obsess over work and volunteers on committees and has friends and makes stupid puns about owls and spends quality time with her brother, doesn't really exist. She's an illusion. Even if I wanted to, I could never make her last. The real Olivia, the one coursing underneath this small-town version, is way too ambitious and she'll find her way out some-how. It's only a matter of time.

The omission about my plans was easier when the whole thing seemed distant. But today, right after we'd finished deco-rating the space, Marjorie Small called me with "excellent news." The out-of-home placement for Lucas was imminent. She told me to "hang in there" and "keep up the good fight." Solidarity with and support from Marjorie would have rocketed my mood to the moon a few weeks ago, but today our conversation hit me all wrong. First, there's no "fight" nor do I need to "hang in there." And second, it's only been a few weeks. I thought I'd have more time here.

I want more time here.

The door pushes open and Suzanne steps inside. She's wearing a green dress with a flared tulle skirt that I insisted she buy during our thrift store prom shopping spree. She looks exactly like Tinkerbell.

"Hey, chick," she says, stepping into the bathroom space. "I was hoping I'd find you in here. The esteemed Fall dance committee's out on the dance floor and I have working orders from Tessa to 'get your ass out there.'" She makes quotation marks with her fingers, and I smile in spite of the emotions teeming inside me. It's a very Tessa thing to say.

"Sure thing," I say, and for the first time during the interac-tion, Suzanne really looks at me. She leans forward, noticing, I assume, the water still brimming in my eyes, a remnant of the almost cry.

"Are you okay?"

"I'm all good," I lie.

"Are you sure," she tips her head, "because we dance committee members have to look after each other."

"I'm sure," I say, then gush, "I just really like you guys."

I don't know why I say it. The statement is true, but it reeks of a sad kind of desperation that New York Olivia would never have tolerated. I'm crying because I like my friends? This version of me is ridiculous. But before I have a chance to feel even more embarrassed or try to explain myself, Suzanne pulls me into a squeezy hug. "We really like you too, Olivia. You fit right in."

I *fit right in.*

Said no one, ever.

And even if she thinks I fit in now, even if they all do in our group of five, it won't last. The surety of that truth is enough for me to keep it together and not start weeping or bawling or almost crying on Suzanne's Tinkerbell gown. None of this was meant to be forever.

I pull away from Suzanne's embrace, proud to be dry-eyed. "Okay. Let's boogie," I say and push through the door. We join the rest of our committee, Lucas too. They are all dancing, YMCA sounding from the speakers. All of us jump and form the letters with our arms and it's so silly, so fun, that I forget everything else. The DJ plays a bunch of fast dance songs, one after the other. Nate does *the owl* again, and we all follow suit. By the time the set of songs is done and the dance is officially over, I'm sweating like I just worked out and ran a 5K back-to-back.

We stay to clean up and once we're done with the clean-up, Tessa grabs her oversized bag and pulls out a bottle of champagne and a sleeve of plastic cups. We sit at a round brown table, and she pours us each a cup. She holds hers up. "To the first successful event of the Include dance committee."

"Hear, hear," Nate says, and the five of us touch our plastic glasses together. We drink the champagne and laugh about different parts of the night. Nate's owl dance. Jared's subpar photography skills. Tessa's dress ripping during YMCA, something I didn't realize even happened until just now. It's fun and easy, and as pathetic as it might seem, I know this is a night I'll tuck away into that mind folder of happy memories. The kind of memory you take out and treasure when you need it.

Suzanne downs the rest of her champagne and pours more. "Should we put our skills to use toward something else?"

Tessa raises an eyebrow. "Include needs help with the Christmas party," she says, "if you guys are game."

Jared rubs Tessa's back with a flat hand. "You know I'm game, honey."

She shakes her head in his direction in a teasing way. "Yeah. You kind of have to be."

Nate slams his cup down like a gavel; the cheap plastic splinters. "I'm in," he says, "and I meant for that to look much cooler."

"Clearly," Suzanne says. "I'm in too. Not sure what I'd do with my Thursday nights otherwise."

The group shifts their focus to me, the only one who didn't answer. It's the beginning of October, and it's highly unlikely I'll still be here in December. I should fess up my plan right now. I open my mouth, ready to explain, but the words that come out are, "I'm in."

CHAPTER 25

LUCAS

It's after the dance and Avery and I are in the sensory space. Everyone else is cleaning up. I'd help. I wasn't asked. I don't blame anyone for that. Me helping isn't really helpful because I always need assistance. It's rarely a straight shot for me to get a task done. Often, Nate gives me the right support to "help" but it's late and I assume he just wants to clean up and get out of here. Still. It makes me feel lazy watching all of them bustle around. Which is how I end up in the sensory space with Avery. It's a separate room, off the ballroom, and while Ms. Cadell removed all the sensory-themed gear she'd brought for the dance, it's super quiet with a comfy couch. Avery and I sit next to each other on it. She smells good and she's wearing makeup. And I love how she looks in her dress. It's pink and short and she looks really pretty. Maybe she thinks I look good too?

Funny. If we were neurotypical or even so-called higher functioning autistic people instead of nonverbal, I think Olivia and the others might suspect we'd be attracted to each other. That left alone on a couch in a quiet room, we might even make out. Whatever that would be like. I'd love to know. For real.

Because truth.

I'd love to kiss a girl.

Avery moves closer to me and puts her hand over mine, just like she did at the parade, and man, I want to try to kiss her. I move my head toward hers and my heart's hammering in my chest and she's looking at me and, oh man, I'm moving my face toward hers. And . . .

And then I stop. I don't know if it's my stupid nonworking body that makes me unable to move or if I just chickened out like an idiot. All I know is the moment has passed.

CHAPTER 26

NATE

A week after the dance I stop by my parents' house to put up Halloween decorations. My mother is huge into Halloween. She puts up, or directs me to put up, three giant spiders, each eight feet long, on the front of the house. The house is not all that big, so the spiders take up a decent chunk of the facade. I affix fake teeth and eyes to the garage door and line the walkway with light-up pumpkins. Mom hangs ghosts and cobwebs in the trees. A singular blow-up pumpkin is in the center of the lawn. It's a lot, bordering on tacky, but Mom loves it because my sister and I did when we were young. And the kids in the neighborhood still do.

After decorating, Mom and I sit on rockers on the front porch with mugs of her signature tea, chai with milk. "How are you, sweetheart? You haven't been by." She lifts the mug to her lips.

"Sorry. I've been busy," I lie. I've been no busier than I usually am, but ever since I agreed to stay on as a respite worker for Lucas with no end date in site, Dad has ratcheted up the medical school/alternate career conversation. He emails me information about medical school and job opportunities on a near daily basis. The subject line on the emails is always the same: *it's time.*

"How's Lucas?" Mom asks.

"He's good. Better. Took him to the zoo the other day."

"Nice. And Olivia?"

"Doing well. She's working remotely."

I don't elaborate, don't share that Olivia and I have been spending more and more time with each other. We make meals together. She started going with me and Lucas on the daily pond walks. We care for the animals. I tease her about Otis and how he is so not a foster cat. We both love *Who Wants to be a Millionaire* and often watch taped shows over dinner.

It's mundane stuff, all of it, but I don't know, it's somehow fun with Olivia. She makes me feel good and it's been a long time since I felt that way.

I lean back in the rocker. "How's Carly?" Carly, my little sister, is a junior at the University of Pittsburgh.

"Great. She's coming for Sunday dinner at Jenny and Rod's."

Sunday dinner. A once-a-month event where everyone in my entire family within driving distance—and anyone they randomly invite—meets for a potluck. I'd been thinking of skipping this month to avoid further *it's time* conversations with Dad, but if Carly is coming home, I should be there.

Mom sets her mug on the table between us. "Do you want to invite Lucas? And Olivia?"

My first instinct is no. No way. Worlds colliding.

But.

I do like spending time with Olivia. And Lucas always likes it at Jenny's. Plus, their presence will likely deter Dad from bringing up my applying for school or jobs.

"Sure," I say. "I'll ask them."

* * *

"ARE YOU SURE THIS IS ENOUGH?" Olivia squints at the pan of meatloaf on the table. "How many people usually come to Sunday dinner again?"

"It varies," I tell her, and it's true. There've been thirty people and there've been five and any number in between. "And it's not a big deal, I swear. Half the time people literally bring their leftovers from the night before. Once, all we had was cake and pasta. Another time, there wasn't enough food, and we ordered pizza. It's super casual."

She looks at me as if I didn't speak. "Should I bring a hostess gift?"

"Absolutely not." No one, in the history of Wilder Sunday dinners, has ever brought a hostess gift.

She tips her head. "My mother would want me to bring a hostess gift."

She insists. We cover the meatloaf with aluminum foil and on the way the three of us stop at the garden store. Olivia pops in and emerges with a houseplant in a pretty pot. She plunks it into the back seat and pushes her face between the front two, where Lucas and I are sitting. "Do you think this is good?"

"It's perfect, Olivia, honestly." I use my most reassuring voice. Her vibe, since I asked her to the dinner, has been off. Based on her questions, she's going to be sorely disappointed when she sees how haphazard the whole thing is. Like paper plates and lukewarm food that you heat up, one dish at a time, in the microwave kind of haphazard.

When we get there, I push through the unlocked door and move to the kitchen. It's a smallish group with my parents, Carly, Jenny and Rod, and two cousins that belong to my dad's sister. Lucas disappears into their basement, his favorite part of the house. Everyone else is crammed around the large island, a bowl of chips and a plate of carrots and dip in the center.

"Everyone," I say, "this is Olivia Ellison. Olivia Ellison, this is everyone."

There's a smattering of hellos and introductory conversation. Olivia answers questions but she's stiff, the houseplant-hostess gift stuck in her hands like it's glued there.

"So you're the one who's stuck living with Nate," Carly says, slapping me on the back. "Has he made you listen to his terrible '80s playlist yet?"

Olivia smiles, a real one, finally. Her shoulders drop in a way that makes it seem like a whoosh of anxiety released from her body. "He has, as a matter of fact."

"And he sings too, right? When he thinks you can't hear him?"

Olivia busts out a laugh. "Let's just say Madonna's *Like a Virgin* will never quite be the same."

"Come on," I protest. "My Madonna impression is fire." I make a fist and hold it up to my hand like a pretend microphone. "Like a virgin," I sing.

Carly pops her eyes out in my direction. "Please, bro, stop."

The group laughs. My singing talent, or lack thereof, has long been a source of Wilder family humor. I don't mind it, and the conversation seems to put Olivia at ease. She moves toward Jenny and extends the houseplant toward her. "This is for you and Rod."

"It's beautiful. Thank you." She holds it above her head. "See this everyone." She moves the plant around like a preschool teacher showing a picture book to her class. "This is a hostess gift. This," she shakes the pot, "is what normal people do when they come to someone's house." She pulls the plant back down and looks at Olivia. "Thank you. I'm making this the centerpiece in the dining room." She exits with the plant.

Olivia swings her head toward me. "See?" she mouths.

I smile back at her.

"Let's heat up what we got," Rod says. He stuffs a few trays and casserole dishes, including the meatloaf, into a preheated oven. Other items go into the microwave. Nothing looks remotely gourmet.

Once the food is warmed and out, Jenny and Rod put everything on the kitchen table, along with a pile of Halloween-themed paper plates and plastic utensils. Olivia and I get in line to grab food. Olivia's meatloaf is a hit, all of it almost gone before we even get to it.

Lucas emerges from the basement and gets food and the whole group moves to the dining room and sits around the table. Olivia's plant—*the hostess gift*—is smack in the center of it.

Conversation is as usual covering topics like Carly's classes, Dad's new construction project, a new menu idea for Big Rod's. There's a lull, and Mom directs her focus to Olivia. "Are you going to look for a job as a lawyer here?"

Olivia's lasagna-laden fork freezes on the way to her mouth. "I still have my job," she says, setting the fork down. "I'm working remotely."

Mom shakes her head. "All this tech," she says, "it can really be helpful, you know. Your firm is in New York and here you are working in Greenwillow."

Carly whips her head in Olivia's direction. "New York? The city?"

The conversation segues to New York. Olivia answers Carly's questions about Broadway and museums and restaurants and crowds, and it becomes clear how much she loves her current hometown. Something any man who lives with a woman for *two months*, even platonically, should know. Except me, of course. Because I'm an idiot. I assumed she liked Greenwillow and the small routine we carved out for ourselves. Maybe she does. But probably not like I do.

"Will the firm let you keep working from here?" Carly asks. "Don't you need to go to court and all?"

Olivia takes a long sip of water. "Most cases settle," she says, setting down her glass, "so attorneys don't go to court all that often."

The statement is not an answer to either of Carly's questions, but no one presses Olivia, and after, the topic changes to Carly's major and the leads she's following for a summer internship.

There's a lull in the conversation after the internship update. Dad fills it in. "Nate's going back to school," he announces randomly. "A program in Pittsburgh."

The room falls completely silent, the kind that happens right after someone announces big news. A brief moment passes before Jenny lets out an excited yell. Mom presses her open palms against the sides of her face. Carly slaps me on the back. The two cousins, whom I don't even know all that well, high-five me from across the table.

Only Olivia is as quiet as I am. Probably because neither of us know what Dad's talking about. I never mentioned having been in school of any kind to her, let alone *going back*, so she's totally in the dark. As for the program I'm allegedly pursuing, I don't know what it is, what it's for, when it starts, none of it. Information about it is probably in one of Dad's unopened *it's time* emails.

The reactions calm and all eyes are on me, Olivia's too, expectant. I give Dad an angry glance. He shrugs. This is his way of moving me along, I guess. Making me fess up my lack of ambition to the group or just go with it.

I open my mouth, not sure what's going to come out of it, when a hissing sound fills the room. Jenny cries out, pushes back her chair and hops up from the table. A large green insect barrels toward her, and she stumbles back into the credenza, knocking over a vase which crashes to the ground along with picture frames. Rod stands up, then the cousins, the three of them swiping pumpkin-themed napkins at the hissing, airborne bug.

Carly leaps from her chair. "What is that?"

A second bug shoots out of the leaves of Olivia's hostess plant, then a third. It's utter pandemonium now, with everyone up and either running away or shooing the bugs with napkins and plates. They fly high then unexpectedly swoop down to face level, causing another round of chaos. The insects, whatever kind they are, appear to be winning. Decisively.

Mom opens the dining room windows and shoos a bug toward it. Jenny does the same, then Rod, and eventually all of us are running around, shooing the bugs with Halloween-themed napkins. The final insect is a bugger, no pun intended, and it takes quite a while to get it out. When it's gone, Jenny shuts the windows with a start and Rod carries the plant outside lest *more* insects fly out.

"I'm so sorry," Olivia gushes. She moves to the credenza and picks the picture frames from the floor. "I can't believe that happened," she says, gathering pieces of the now broken vase. "I'll get you a new vase," she says.

Jenny moves behind her. "Don't worry about cleaning that up," she directs. "Rod will get it. Rod?"

"Yes, ma'am." He salutes Jenny, and leaves, presumably to get a dustpan.

Olivia stands; she looks shaken.

"You're not upset, are you?" Jenny asks her. "That whole thing was hilarious."

"But your vase."

Jenny waves a hand. "Cheap and replaceable. And worth it. We haven't had such an exciting family dinner since Nate let the crabs loose in the yard."

Olivia shifts her gaze to me.

"I was eight and I was freeing them," I explain.

"What were those anyway?" Jenny asks.

"I have no idea," Mom says.

"We'll call them Natebugs," Carly offers.

"Natebugs? I didn't even bring the plant," I protest.

"Well Olivia's a guest," Jenny says, "so Natebugs it is."

I look to Olivia. She's smiling, the realization, it seems, having finally set in. This is an easy group. No one cares. They think the whole hostess gift/unknown flying insect fiasco is hysterical.

"That's probably the last hostess gift anyone will ever bring," Olivia jokes to a smattering of laughter.

We clean up, talk about the Natebugs, and revisit the dinner where I'd freed the crabs. No one mentions school or Dad's announcement. Except Olivia.

"Going back to school?" she says in the car on the way back.

"Don't want to talk about it." I drive a few blocks. "Your job?" I ask, recalling her dodge of Carly's question about whether the firm will keep letting her work from here.

"Don't want to talk about it," she says.

And that's how we decide. No school talk. No job talk. Fine by me.

CHAPTER 27

OLIVIA

A little over a week after the Sunday dinner, I lean against the wall in the crowded hallway of the Green County Orphans Court, Chuck typing on his phone next to me. Though I accepted guardianship of Lucas months ago, it won't be official-official, meaning I have a signed and sealed court order, until today.

The wait for the case to be heard by the judge is long, over an hour, and I'm glad I didn't insist on Lucas being here. I'd thought he should—it's about him after all—but after the funeral debacle, I'd questioned my judgment. And it's not like the guardianship is a cause for celebration; it's only in place because Melanie died. Ultimately, it seemed better for Lucas to stay in his routine and go to school.

Once Chuck and I are finally in the courtroom, the hearing itself takes only a few minutes, most of the information having been submitted via paperwork. After, we stand in the hall and wait for the final order to be prepared by the judge's clerk and brought outside.

I glance toward the courtroom door and just as I do, it

swings open and a stout woman with a mop of curly black hair strides out. "Here are the orders," she says and thrusts papers in Chuck's direction.

He takes the stack from her hands. "Thank you."

The woman strides back and disappears inside the court-room. Chuck hands me the original and a copy. We walk toward the elevator. And . . .

And nothing.

That's it.

I'm guardian of my brother.

Given how momentous the occasion is for me personally, the entire experience feels anticlimactic. I'm not sure what I'd expected. I'm a lawyer. I've been in crowded court hallways. I've been hurried along by overworked court personnel. I've sat on hearings where the stakes were huge but everyone from the judge to the law clerk to the bailiff looked bored out of their minds. I know how this all goes, but now that it's my life, the humdrum of it seems wrong somehow. It feels like someone should acknowledge the fact that this, this life-altering decision I've taken on, is a big deal.

Chuck and I reach the elevator. "I have another matter," he says and extends his hand.

"Right, of course." I take his hand and stumble over the words, surprised that he's leaving and equally bewildered by my reaction. Of course, he has another matter. My hearing is a small part of his job; I'm just one client of many.

"Thank you." I release his hand.

"You're welcome." He nods toward the court order. "Be sure to keep that original in a safe place. They're a real pain to get replaced, you know."

"Right. Yes." I seem to have lost my ability to say anything but singular, affirmative words. The elevators slide open, and I smush inside, knocking my bag against the door and stumbling forward into a group of people. "Sorry," I say righting myself.

No one responds, and a woman near the door presses the button for lobby.

The elevator descends. My head is light, my breathing off. When it stops and the doors slide open, I step out. I feel weirdly detached from myself, like someone else is controlling my limbs. The words of the people around me are muffled, the lights blindingly white. I spy a bench near the entrance to the courthouse and stumble onto it.

What is wrong with me? I was fine coming here. I was fine during the hearing. It wasn't until Chuck handed me the order, until it dawned on me that it's all official now, that these feelings started. I try to stand, feel lightheaded, and sit back down.

"Olivia?"

I swing my head toward the voice. It's Jared. He strides toward me dressed in his police officer uniform.

"Hey, Jared." I smile and do my best imitation of someone who is *not* a total trainwreck.

"What are you doing here?"

"Guardianship." I hold up the order. "It's official."

"Wow. Good on you." He claps my shoulder. "That's badass."

Badass. Not the word I was thinking, but Jared saying it makes me sit up tall.

"You going to Include for the Fab Five meeting tonight?"

Fab Five. It's what we started calling ourselves, the name—Christmas party planning committee—having gotten too long to say.

"Yes," I say. "I'll be there." We're meeting at Include instead of Melanie's house to assess the space for the Christmas party.

He points a finger gun in my direction and shoots. "See you there, BA." He winks and moves along the corridor.

BA? It takes me a moment to decipher the meaning. BA. Badass. I smile.

Badass.

I like that.

The boost of confidence the nickname gives me is enough to catapult my psyche out of the bout of derealization or whatever that was, and I navigate my way to Melanie's from the courthouse just fine. Just Otis is there when I arrive. I scoop him up and we retreat to my childhood bedroom. I put the court order in the top drawer of my pink and white child-sized desk. The paper sits on top of old smencils (pencils that smell), erasers shaped like animals, and a hodgepodge of markers, paperclips, and rubber bands. My desk drawer is not the kind of *safe place* Chuck Stockton envisioned, I'm sure.

I shut the drawer, head to the shed, pull up emails on my computer. I scan down the line of subjects, nothing unusual, until my eyes snag on words: brother's placement. I glance at the sender. Marjorie Small. I realize, just now, that I don't know what I'm hoping the email will say. That there is a placement. That there's not. That there's a waitlist. My emotions are indecipherable. I inhale a breath, click, and read.

We found placement for your brother pending approval. He can move in ASAP. Paperwork to be sent via separate email. Attached is information about the facility. Thrilled for you and to have you back in the office soon.

I exhale.

Okay. I read the words a second time. Okay. There is a placement. That's good, right? I mean, less than an hour ago I was low-key wigged out about the guardianship being official. I should be thrilled.

Thrilled.

Yes.

I am thrilled.

I think.

Right?

I click on the attachment about the facility. There's a picture of a house on the first page. It's a beautiful, two-story colonial, with white siding, red shutters, and a red door. The lot is spacious with a big lawn and flowering trees. I read about the home. Were Lucas to live there, he'd have his own room and bathroom. Four other men live in the home, along with two attendants. And it's in Parksburg, only an hour and a half drive from Greenwillow. *Also, an hour and a half farther from New York.* I let that thought slide through me. I stare at the photograph and seize on the placement like it's the holy grail of placements. Lucas will be happy here. I feel it. And I can still see him. And we can still come back to Greenwillow. Being at the placement is kind of like boarding school or college. Kids his age do leave home. Why shouldn't he have the opportunity?

A knock sounds on the door of the shed. "Olivia. You in there?" Nate.

"Sure." I flip down the computer.

He pushes open the door and steps inside. He's wearing a navy sweater with jeans, a hint of stubble on his face. He looks good. Like *that's* what's important right now.

"You ready? It's time for the Fab Five meeting."

"Oh," I say, then add, "yes" with a big smile to mask my disappointment. Of all people, I thought Nate would have remembered the guardianship hearing today. But it's clear he doesn't. More proof that the impact of today encompasses only a circle of two: me and Lucas. Everyone else's life goes on as is. All the more reason for me to make this decision and move on with my own life.

I stand and brush nonexistent lint off my pants. "I'm good."

We take Nate's car to Include, Lucas in the passenger seat, me in the back. But for the songs on the radio, it's quiet. I'm the talker normally, but this day has drained me in a way I didn't expect.

Once we're inside the Include building, Lucas immediately heads for the Snoezelen room. I know enough now to just let him go. Nate strides toward the back room, where all the big events are held.

I stop at the conference room, put my hand on the knob. "They'll probably want to meet in here."

"Nope. I don't think so." He waves toward the back room, pushes open the door, and stands aside. I step through. The room is full. Not just with the Fab Five. They're there but also a dozen or more people. Dominique, Lauren Caddell, Nate's parents, Chuck Stockton, Rod and Jenny, and a slew of people I don't even remember meeting. I stand still, not sure how to react. I want to think that this, whatever it is, isn't about me, but everyone is looking in my direction, including Nate, so it feels very much like it is.

I lift a hand. "Hello."

"Olivia," Dominique says in her commanding, take-charge tone, "we know the guardianship is official today. We also know the circumstances surrounding you becoming guardian, the loss of Melanie, are tragic. So this isn't a celebration, but it is a welcome. And an outreach of support." She smiles. "If you and Lucas need anything, anything at all, we are here for you. We want you to know that. All of us." She opens her arms in an expansive gesture.

I look around at everyone in stunned silence. "Wow," I say finally. "This is, wow." I pause and attempt to quell the emotions rising inside me before they turn into another cryfest. Or before my thoughts snag upon the placement for Lucas that I just, less than an hour ago, was looking at.

"Thank you," I say, calming myself. "Thank you so much."

CHAPTER 28

NATE

Olivia pulls a slice of cold pizza from a box on the table and bites into it. It's just the Fab Five and Lucas now, the official party having ended a half hour ago. All six of us are sitting at a round table, picking at leftovers and sharing a bottle of wine.

"High," Tessa says, referring to high-low, the game where you state the best and worst part of your day. Tessa asked for a high-low at one of the first committee meetings, and since then it's become a regular thing.

"For me," Tessa adds, "it's finding these sweet earrings on sale." She bumps at a dangling earring shaped like a parrot.

Suzanne tells us her high is her new graphic design client, and Jared's is the meatball sandwich he had at lunch, both of which track. I say my high is my fastest five-mile run to date, which is a total lie. I didn't even run today. My actual high? Seeing Olivia's face light up when we walked in here.

"This," Olivia volunteers, spreading her arms out around the room. "My high is definitely this. All the people, all the support." Her voice wavers. "It's so nice. Thank you so much."

We go through lows, which historically range from ridiculous to sad. Tonight's ridiculous goes to Jared, who's low was finishing the meatball sandwich. The sad low was Suzanne's; her family's cat was diagnosed with feline leukemia. Tessa and I say ours, neither of which is noteworthy. Olivia's strangely quiet; her eyes are cast downward.

"Your low, Olivia?" I prompt. I wouldn't normally push, but her mood has clearly shifted, and I want to know why.

"This," she says.

I take in the word. This. This, right now, is her high *and* her low. I open my mouth to ask what she means by that, but before I get the question out, a cherry tomato flies by my face and hits Olivia on the head.

Olivia touches her head where the tomato hit, sits up, and laughs. And just like that, the melancholy disappears, her typical countenance returned. "Wait," she says, recovering, "I changed my mind. My low is being hit in the head by a vegetable." She picks up the tomato and throws it back at Jared. He catches it mid-air.

"They're fruit," Jared says and throws the tomato at Tessa. It explodes onto her shirt. She looks down at the stain and back up at Jared. "We doing this, J?"

He throws a baby carrot at her.

She waits a long moment, then swipes a slice of cake from a plate with her bare hand, stands up, and smushes it on Jared's head. He rubs his hand in the icing and smears it on her face. Suzanne throws a piece of apple pie in my direction. I pick up a bowl of chips and dump them on Olivia, next to me. Olivia throws cake. Tessa grabs watermelon pieces and hurls them across the table. Jared takes a piece she threw and puts it down her back.

And it's on. Whatever leftover food there is flies in every direction, on every person, save Lucas, who is watching the whole thing unfold like a movie. It's complete chaos and a complete mess. Wasteful, yes, but ridiculously fun.

We stop once the throwable, messiest food is gone, all of us covered in sauces and icing and dips, remnants of solid food all over the room.

Tessa scans the space. "Ah, shit."

"We'll clean it." Suzanne bounces out of her seat. "I'll get supplies."

She returns with reams of paper towels, trash bags, and a vacuum. I grab a bunch of towels, wad them up, and wipe at the salsa, dip, and icing that covers my face and arms. Olivia does the same. She looks in my direction. "Did I get everything?"

She still has icing on her face and a bit on her nose. I point at the spot on her face where the icing is; she wipes and misses. "Yeah?"

"No. I'll get it." I rip off a paper towel and wet it with water from a water bottle. I step forward and gently wipe at the parts of her face still covered with food fight residue. Tiny freckles I'd never noticed before span her nose. I step back. "All set." I force my eyes downward.

"You're the worst food fight competitor ever," she says.

I whip my face up. "Ever?" I grab a trash bag, open it, and hold it out. "That's a pretty bold statement, Olivia. What's your data?"

"Just calling it the way I see it." She throws a watermelon rind in the bag.

"I had some good shots. I'm pretty sure your shirt would agree."

Her gaze falls to her shirt, bits of salsa and chocolate cake on the front of it. "Maybe."

"So you'll retract that statement?"

She puts her hands on her chin like she's thinking really, really hard. "Nah," she says finally. "The statement stands."

I swipe a cracker from the table and throw it at her.

Tessa points at me. "Don't get started again. We have enough to clean up."

"Fine."

"Worst ever," she whispers. She pushes her face toward me and gives what I think is supposed to be an intimidating look. It's super cute instead.

We finish cleaning as a group, our efforts so efficient that the room looks better than it did when we got there.

Jared grabs some leftover cleaning supplies. "I feel like we just cleaned up after a high-school party to cover the evidence."

"We kind of did," Tessa says. "I mean, Mom would be none too pleased that we had a food fight at Include."

Suzanne rakes her hair, and a tortilla chip falls out. She swipes it from the floor. "No one has to know," she says. "What happens with the Fab Five stays with the Fab Five."

"Agreed," I say at the same time as Olivia.

"Jinx," we say in unison, then laugh at the stupid coincidence.

I push at her shoulder. "I said it first."

She stumbles slightly, rights herself, then pokes me in the stomach with her index finger. "No way."

"Jose." We sit at the same time again and start laughing.

"Oh my God, you two." Tessa puts her hands on her hips. "Get a room already."

Our laughter abates so fast, it's almost like Tessa threw a bucket of cold water at us. I sneak a peek at Olivia. Her cheeks are pink; I'm not sure what to glean from that. That she's interested? Or the opposite?

"Good one, Tessa" I say, finally. "Olivia has better taste than to be with me."

She doesn't deny the statement. The omission tells me what I need to know.

CHAPTER 29

LUCAS
No one asked me to play at the post-party game of high-low, but here it is:

Today
High: stimming
Low: stimming
Yesterday
High: stimming
Low: stimming
The day before yesterday
High: stimming
Low: stimming
Yesterdays, ad infinitum
High: stimming
Low: stimming
Future, ad infinitum
High: stimming
Low: stimming
Stop the stim! It's like stop the steal, right? Donald Trump? 2020?
Anyway, my life is a stimfest, which is why every single day stimming

is my high and my low. I stim to make myself feel better, because I'm bored, because I'm upset, or sometimes because it's just plain fun. Spinning, jumping, flapping, banging, repeating words. All good. Until I realize how stupid I look or how much time I just wasted or that I've upset someone who loves me by not being able to stop stims on demand. Then I get upset, and then, yup, I want to stim to make myself feel better.

I am, right now, trying very hard not to flap my hands. It is hard work. Because I really, really want to flap them. And honestly, hand flapping and other stims aren't that bad. It's not like I'm abusing alcohol or drugs or something. I'm not a criminal or a warlord. I mean, it's just a hand flap! Calm down, people. Still. People who don't stim (most people) rule the world, and they don't get why I like to do it. And I can't explain it to them. So if I'm going to make my way in this world as it exists now, I'm going to need to get my stimming under control.

It's really hard.

CHAPTER 30

OLIVIA

Nate puts kindling on the logs in the fireplace at Melanie's, ignites a lighter, and sets it.

It's post-party, and both of us are showered and wearing warm sweats. Lucas is on the couch, iPad set on his lap. I break out wine and pour glasses for me and Nate. I don't mean for the mood to be romantic. But it starts to snow. And almost as soon as we sit down with the wine, Lucas leaves the room, his heavy footsteps falling on the stairs. And boom. The mood instantly switches from platonic, the three of us in sweats, to me and Nate alone in front of a roaring fire.

He moves back, his face illuminated by the flames. "Can I ask you something?" He sits on the far end of the couch, Otis curled up between us on the center cushion like a chaperone.

"Sure." I brace myself for the question I'm sure he's going to ask: what are my plans?

"What did you mean when you said the party was your low?"

I process the unexpected question.

"And don't say you were just kidding."

I was going to say that, a knee-jerk reaction. Scary how he knew.

I sip my wine, and in the moment it takes for me to swallow, I decide not to hold back. I may not be in Nate's orbit much longer, and we may as well enjoy the time we have left. "Promise you won't think I'm pathetic."

"Olivia."

Warmth flushes through me. His tone and the sentiment behind it—that he would never see me as pathetic—gives me a sense of security, the kind I haven't felt since my dad died.

"Other than with my dad," I start, "I never had close relationships growing up. I don't know why. I was always a third wheel with the twins and my mother's least favorite daughter. When I came here in the summers, I didn't know anyone except my family. Plus, when I first started coming, Lucas had just been diagnosed. Dad and Melanie were trying to figure everything out. They did a good job with him, as you know, but there wasn't a lot left for me." I scrunch up my face. I probably sound spoiled. "I didn't mean—" I start.

He shakes his head. "No. I get it."

I shift my gaze downward. "When I got to college and law school, I was all about proving myself, being the best of the best at everything, which didn't leave much time for anything else, including relationships. And Bennett Connor is about as competitive as it gets in the legal world. My colleagues are nice on the surface, but there's always an angle, you know." I orient my gaze toward the fire. "You guys, the Fab Five, hanging out and just doing dumb stuff, like the food fight"—I pause and meet his eyes—"it feels like what I'd missed out on all those years."

Nate tips his head. "Why is that bad?"

I blow out a breath. "Because it's not going to last."

"You don't know that."

"I do."

It's the perfect time to tell him about the placement and the deal with my job and the fact that I never intended to stay in Greenwillow.

"Olivia." He says my name like it's a gift and gives me a look so tender my entire body tingles. "I don't know what happened in your past, what was wrong with the people in your life back then, but we all love you. And we're not going anywhere."

The words are affirming and lovely and perfect. A feeling of lightness whooshes through me, and I lose all motivation to say anything about the move. It can wait. This moment can't.

Nate looks at me warmly, his hair still damp from the shower, the smell of his soap fresh on his skin. I recall how his body felt pressed up against mine when we danced. And all the nights we sat side by side on the couch, thighs touching, pats on the arm if one of us knew a *Who Wants to Be a Millionaire* answer that the other one didn't. I picture him patiently helping Lucas. I love his awful singing and his equally awful favorite songs and visualize him dancing around the kitchen as he cooks. I love that he gives Otis secret pieces of chicken and tuna when he thinks I'm not looking. And I love that sometimes, when he looks at me, it feels like he thinks I'm a woman to be desired.

I swing my head up and he meets my eyes and smiles in a way that reaches deep into my heart and the thought of doing anything other than kissing this man leaves my mind. Without thinking, at least not with my brain, I catapult forward on the couch, Otis scurrying off with my movement. I put my hands on either side of his jaw, his scratchy stubble underneath my fingertips. I pull his face forward, part my lips, and put my mouth on his and . . .

He doesn't kiss me back.

At all.

I fly back on the couch. "I'm so sorry," I blurt. My face is on fire, my stomach hardens. "I thought, I—" I stand up.

He grabs my hand. "Olivia."

"I'm sorry. I misread the situation. I'm—"

"Olivia," he repeats, but I'm tittering on, talking over him, embarrassment coursing through my system like a life force.

"Olivia," he says, louder. "Olivia." He squeezes my hand and finally I stop talking. "You didn't misread anything." He shakes his head. "Believe me, you didn't."

I angle my face toward his. His eyes reflect back at me.

"There is nothing I'd rather do than kiss you right now." He rakes his hair.

I squint in his direction. I try to read his expression, try to understand his reaction to the kiss he says he wanted. It hits me then, something I stupidly had never considered. "You have a girlfriend." I say it like a declaration, then more panicked, "A wife?"

"No. No. That's not it."

"So..."

"Olivia, if you knew the true me, if you knew about my past, you wouldn't want me. It's not fair to start something when you don't know everything."

I sit back. Whatever everything is, it can't possibly be that bad. Nate is as kind as they come. I visualize him and Lucas taking their daily pond walks. I picture him with his family. I recall the look on his face when I walked into the surprise party tonight, like something that made me happy was a gift for him instead. "Tell me everything then."

"I don't want to."

"Nate?" I put my hand on his thigh, his name a question in my mouth.

"Olivia," he says after a long moment, his voice strangled. "I killed someone."

CHAPTER 31

NATE

Olivia's mouth drops open; she covers it with her palm. Her eyes widen, the look in them a combination of shock and horror.

"I know. I know." I tilt my head up and look at the ceiling, thinking about how to best tell her. I swing my head down and look in her direction but fix my gaze on the wall behind her. Because looking right at her, seeing the expression on her face as this story unfolds, is not something I want to do.

"I'll give you the short version. Senior year of college, the week after graduation. I was at a party, part of senior week. I was drinking and it was raining, and like an asshole, I got in the car and drove."

She grips her hand tighter around her mouth.

"The road was slick, and I should have pulled over or slowed down or something. But I kept going, feeling invincible and all that, and I hydroplaned headfirst into the car in the other lane. The driver died on impact. His name was Mark Carney."

"Oh." The word is a gasp.

"But I," I hit my chest with an open palm, "in some mass injustice, walked away, completely unscathed." I drop my gaze to the floor. "I still picture him, the driver. The look of horror on his face as my car came barreling towards his. He was fifty-seven and on his way to meet his wife for dinner."

"Nate." She says my name like an exhale, pushes her hand out to cover mine. "I'm so sorry."

I move my hand from under hers. "Don't feel sorry for me," I say, meaning it. "Be sorry for Mark and his family." I hold up two fingers. "Two kids. He had two kids. I saw pictures of the family in the paper after the accident. I'll never get that photograph out of my head." I picture it now. It was one of those beach shots where everyone is in khaki pants and a white T-shirt. Mark and his wife were in the back, a child in front of each, one daughter, one son, all of them smiling and tanned by the sun.

She moves closer to me on the couch. "Nate."

The atmosphere around us feels choked, full of regret and remorse and guilt, and I move back, as if to protect her from the toxicity.

"It was an accident," she says.

"No." I say the word forcefully because that's what everyone says, the line that's supposed to magically make it okay that I killed someone. "An accident is something that can't be helped. I could have prevented this."

"But—"

"No." I cut her off. "Sorry. But I can guess what you're going to say. That the accident might have happened anyway. Or that I should forgive myself."

Her head bobs in a slight nod.

"That's what everyone says. My parents, Carly, the useless therapist I saw after it happened." I pause. "I won't let myself off the hook that easily. The accident, Mark's death, it pulses under everything I do. I can never forget." I pick at a piece of lint on the couch. "Not that I don't deserve that. It's my penance, you know." The year I spent in jail. Two years of probation. A two-year loss of my driver's license. None of those so-called punishments compare to the hell of my own memory.

We sit in silence. It's a situation that can't be made better with words and I'm grateful Olivia doesn't say anything. She leans against me, our shoulders touching. The fire crackles in fits and starts; snowflakes fall in big clumps outside and blanket the ground. I listen to the sound of Olivia's breathing, feel the rise and fall of her chest. We sit in stillness for a long time until my eyelids droop and close, open again, then droop and close in a pattern that finally ends in sleep.

When I wake, I'm on one end of the couch covered in one of Melanie's blankets. I vaguely remember Olivia putting it on me last night. I slept more deeply than I normally do, and I feel the brightness in the room even without opening my eyes. It's morning.

I open my eyes. The sun shines bright outside, rays hitting the layer of white, untouched snow, ice glistening on its surface.

"You're awake."

I sit up and see Olivia on the chair, a mug of coffee gripped between her palms. The truth of what I told her last night sits in my stomach like a lead weight. My normal method of coping is never to talk about the accident. Last night was the opposite of that.

"Nate," she says, her tone empathetic. "About what you told me last night. I'm so sorry."

"Thank you." I sit up further on the couch, push the blanket to the ground. "Let's not talk about it."

"You don't think it would help? It has to weigh on you."

"It does weigh on me." I shift. "But I've been to therapy and support groups and all they do is dredge up the memories. The memories get stuck in my mind, and I can't get them out."

"It seems like you're holding on to it."

"I am. And I will." I stand up, irritation sliding down my gut like slime. *This* is why I hate talking about the accident. People mean well, but they never leave the subject alone. As if one good conversation is all I need to forget about *killing someone*. "I'm going to make waffles."

I move to the kitchen, find the waffle maker, and plug it in. I grab ingredients from the pantry.

Olivia enters the kitchen and walks toward me. "I'm sorry," she says, her voice soft. "I won't bring it up again unless you do. I appreciate you telling me."

"Thanks." I exhale, relieved that the subject, for now, is over. "School's cancelled right?"

"Yup."

"You a snow person?"

"If by a snow person you mean a person who sits in front of a fire inside with hot chocolate and watches the flakes fall from a distance, then yes."

I dump waffle mix into a bowl. "Really? Not a skier?"

"Definitely not."

"Snow angels? Snowmen?" I prompt.

"No and no. Lucas hates snow too."

Just as she says it, Lucas's feet sound on the stairs. He plops down in his chair at the kitchen table.

"I happen to know," I say, "that Lucas loves snow." I look at him. "Right, Lu?"

"No way," Olivia says. She bumps Lucas on the shoulder. "You always hated it, bud."

"He did. Now he doesn't." I hold up my hands. "What can I say? I'm a snow master."

Olivia laughs, and the tension in the room dissipates with the sound. She raises an eyebrow. "What does it take to be a snow master anyway?"

I crack an egg and dump water into the bowl with the mix. "I'm just good at snow."

"Good at snow?"

"Yes. Good at snow. You'll see." I pour the first bit of batter into the preheated iron. "I'll show you after breakfast."

CHAPTER 32

LUCAS

Nate told Olivia he was "good at snow" and he's right. He's the one who got me to like it. As a kid, I hated it. But in fairness, when you're a kid, no one warns you about it. It's white and it's everywhere and it looks cool from inside your house where it's warm. You're looking at the white out the window and next thing you know, you're being stuffed inside puffy, itchy clothes and plopped in the middle of it. And bam! It's cold and wet and clumps of flakes get inside your coat sleeves and your pants and freeze your bare skin. It's a surprise in the worst possible way. So if you're someone like me who hates even good surprises, snow is not the best.

Besides the surprise element, my senses are overpowering. A bit of cold is like ice. A bright light is blinding. Same with noise (LOUD), and smell (yuck), and texture (ouch). All the senses. Mine are too much, all of them going at full blast all the time. Like, give it a rest already. Really, body. Give it a rest.

Anyway, to get me more comfortable in the snow, Nate gave me a hat that pulled over my face so just my eyes peeked out. It wasn't even wool, like most winter hats, which was a bonus. Then he duct-taped my coat sleeves to my gloves and my snow pants to my boots. I had a major tantrum over that. But Nate told me I'd be glad, and he was right. NO snow got on my skin, plus I knew what to expect so there were no ultra-crazy reactions in my body. I've been good with snow since.

So snow days, for me, are great. They're fun but also a reminder that things can change. Things I hate might become things I love. Things I can't do can become things I can. Maybe things I can't even imagine. Like talking. Or living on my own. Or having a job. Or a girlfriend. Or all of it. I just need to keep the faith.

CHAPTER 33

OLIVIA

Once breakfast is over and the dishes are done, Nate seems to believe that I'm going to spend the day in the snow. But I need to work. I have a pre-trial motion due on the Rowan case in two days and several other projects I haven't even started. I'd planned to work yesterday after the hearing, but then there was the party and the almost-kiss and Nate's confession, and I couldn't concentrate.

That talk was—ugh—heavy and mournful. Sadness and guilt emanated from Nate's soul, seeping into the atmosphere around us. And now that I know, I see him differently. Not in a bad way. It's just that *before* I didn't know enough to look for his brokenness; now I can see it. I see it in the way he pauses and looks straight ahead like he's forgotten what he's doing. I see it in his excess energy, his need to be constantly upbeat. And I see it in his eyes. And while I know he thinks his story will repel me, that his brokenness makes him unlovable, the opposite is true. I still like him, more so even. Still. I don't know if the feeling is reciprocated, romantically anyway. He said he wanted to kiss me last night. I understand that what he had to tell me took over and wiped out the mood. But I don't normally throw myself at men, and, well, every time I think about it—me catapulting across the couch like that—ugh. It's embarrassing.

"Okay," Nate says, "Lucas knows this, but for the snow newbie, rule number one is wardrobe. You can't have fun in the snow if you're cold. Lucas and I have stuff, but let's check out the closet for you." He takes a step toward the closet.

"I can't go," I blurt. "I have to work."

He stops mid-step. "You can't play in the snow?"

The way he says the question is so earnest, so childlike, that I almost tease him. But I can't. And it strikes me that maybe it's important that I go, to show him that what he told me doesn't change the way I see him. I mentally assess my to-dos. I can take an hour or two. "You know, I've changed my mind. I'm in."

I move to the front closet and throw on every article of winter outdoor gear I can find, none of them matching, but all of it warm. Nate smirks when he sees me. "Nice. Did you forget the kitchen sink?"

I stamp my foot. "You said to dress warm. Rule number one, right?"

He stifles a laugh. "You're right, you're right. My bad."

We all walk to the front door, swishy and slow, like a group of Michelin men. Lucas opens the door, and we step outside. The fresh snow glistens in the sunlight, drifts of it around the trees, big clumps on the branches. Sun rays peek out from under fat clouds, warming my face.

Nate grabs a toboggan he must have set outside for this purpose. He looks genuinely happy, so different from the grief-stricken man of last night that I'm relieved on his behalf. Maybe he's right. Maybe talking about the accident doesn't work for him.

"Onward," he says and begins dragging the long sled across the snow. Lucas and I follow, walking in the light tracks of the sled, our boots crunching on the snow, footprints behind us like a trail. At the edge of the property, we step onto a snow-covered path that leads into the woods. Once we're farther in, the houses and roads fall out of view, the only evidence of them billows of smoke from distant chimneys and the occasional bark of a dog. My skin warms with the effort of walking, my breath steady puffs in the cold. Our boots hit the snow-covered path in a rhythmic, collective pattern.

A cardinal flies past, a bright spot against the snow-covered trees. Under a bush, there's a squirrel nibbling on a nut. Deer tracks etched in fresh snow lead into the woods, and branches adorned with bright red berries buttress the path. I breathe in; appreciation for the ordinary fills my senses.

We reach our destination—Hale's Christmas tree farm. There's a hill behind it, one I've never sledded on, though I did come here once with Lucas, then eight years old. I'd had a big plan to take him sledding, but as soon as we got here, he wailed and threw himself on the ground. We left before we even reached the hill.

I look back at Lucas now. At ease and comfortable.

We reach the back of the farm and the top of Hale's hill. It's wide, long, and steep, with few trees. Not surprisingly, there are other sledders here already and an array of colorful jackets, hats, and sleds dot the white expanse of the hill. Nate sets the toboggan down. "I'll go first. Lucas likes to be on the end." He angles his head toward me. "You good for the middle?"

I'm suddenly distracted by the way he fills out his jacket. The bits of hair that peek out from under his hat like a frame for his face. His ruddy cheeks, full lips. Eyes that are amazingly the exact color blue of the sky. And incredibly kind.

"Olivia?"

I snap to attention, heat blasting my cheeks. "In the middle," I say quickly. "Sure."

We get into line on the sled, and I ease behind Nate, my legs cast out in front of his torso on either side.

"Scooch forward, and put your arms around me," he directs.

I do as he instructs, every part of my body pressed up against his. I feel his muscles, the hardness of his body, and my own tingles with the contact. Warmth flushes through me despite the cold; my heart flutters in my chest. I shake my head. What is wrong with me? We're sledding with dozens of other people and my brother. Plus, if last night proved anything, it's that he probably doesn't—likely doesn't—feel any kind of attraction toward me.

Lucas situates himself behind me on the sled, and I swish back into normal friend-sister mode.

"Lean forward," Nate directs. "On three. One." He places his hands down flat on the snow on either side. "Two," he says, and a giddy kind of excitement shoots through me, like I'm about to sled down one of the Swiss alps instead of the hill behind Hale's Christmas tree farm. "Three."

Nate pushes with his hands, and we all lean forward. The toboggan starts to move slowly, slowly, slowly, and then whoosh—we're flying down the hill. Wind and bits of snow whip at my face as the sled gains momentum. We keep moving, faster and faster, until we get to the bottom, deep flat snow stopping the course of the sled on a dime. We tumble off, me on top of Nate, our faces close to each other.

"You like it?" Nate asks, his face incredibly close to my own.

"Yes." I scuttle sideways so I'm no longer on top of him and collapse into the snow. "That was a blast."

He winks. "Told ya."

"Hey, all!" A woman waves from the top of the hill with one whole arm, a snow tube gripped in the other. It's Tessa. Jared and Avery stand next to her with their own tubes. We scramble up the hill and spend the next hour sledding with them. It's fun, similar to the stupid food fight.

My phone pings with William's ringtone. I want to let the call go to voicemail, but I can't. It might be important. And besides, I spent way more time out here than I anticipated already.

I step away from the group and accept the call. I grip the phone against one ear, cover the other with my hand.

"Olivia," William barks. "Where are you?"

"Outside."

"Did you get my email? About the Order to Show Cause?"

Adrenaline shoots through me. The cases I handle normally proceed at a snail's pace, each side dumping enough paper and discovery requests on the other to keep things going for years. But Orders to Show Cause need to be answered the day they are filed. "I didn't see it."

"Well, you would have if you were here."

"I—" I start, but I don't have a comeback. He's right. I'm sledding and salivating over my housemate instead of doing my job.

"Never mind. Look at it and get back to me, yes?"

"Yes. Of course."

I find Nate. "I've got to go back," I say and hold up my phone. "Work emergency."

He eyes widen. "Oh. I'm sorry." He looks at the bottom of the hill where Lucas stands with Tessa and Avery. "Do you know how to get back? Though the woods and all?"

I hesitate. Do I?

Before I answer, Nate does. "I'll go with you. Lucas can stay here with Tessa and them."

In what feels like an instant, he runs down the hill, communicates the situation, and is back by my side. "Ready?"

"You don't have to—" I start.

"I want to make sure you get back okay."

I don't fight it. I can't afford to get lost. "Thanks."

We walk back, fast, and I don't appreciate any of the things I did on the way out here. No birds or deer tracks or sun on my face. I don't even swoon over Nate.

When we walk inside the house, I head straight for my

room. I moved my computer up there from the shed yesterday. "Thank you," I call and race up the stairs.

Still bundled in all my now damp gear, I collapse into my desk chair, pull up William's email, and scan the document. The plaintiffs are trying to enjoin Jupiter Rowan from making any further crypto trades pending the trial. I read through it. Arguments form in my mind. My heart steadies, and by the time I call William back I have a good defensive strategy, one I can put together quickly and file with the court. I share it with him and almost feel his smile through the phone. "Perfect, Olivia. Get it filed."

CHAPTER 34

NATE

I glance at Lucas, asleep on the couch. He stayed out in the snow with Tessa and the others for at least another hour after I came back with Olivia. I haven't seen her since she disappeared inside her room, over three hours ago. And given how panicked she'd looked when she got that call, I'm a little worried.

I pour a glass of milk and put a few cookies on a plate to bring to her room. A nice gesture.

And an excuse to see her.

I didn't fully appreciate her making the first romantic move last night. I was honest when I said I wanted to kiss her, but in the throes of sharing the details of "the incident," I doused the mood. I don't regret it; she needed to know. But now I can't help but wonder: does she still like me like that? Now that she knows?

I walk up the stairs, stop at her closed door, and knock. "Proof of life check."

She laughs and a moment later the door swings open. "Affirmative." She eyes the cookies and milk, and her face splits into a wide smile. "Snacks. Nate Wilder, you are the best." She pushes the door open wider and gestures me in.

I step inside. She's shed her outer gear and stands in jeans and a tight thermal top, the thick wool socks on her feet pulled up to her mid-calf. Her cheeks are sunburned, her hair a mess around her face in a way that's sexy instead of sloppy.

I set down the glass and cookies on her dresser, the surface of it covered with awards and knickknacks from earlier days. I pick up one, a certificate in a black frame. "The perfect attendance award?"

She shakes her head. "My dad framed everything. Saved everything too." She swipes a cookie from the plate. "Whatever you do, don't look in my top dresser drawer."

I lift an eyebrow.

"My baby teeth are in there."

"Lots of uses for those, I'd imagine."

"Use them all the time." She gestures around the room. "Anyway, sit."

The only place to sit beside her desk chair is the bed.

"I don't want to bug you," I say, still standing. "I just wanted to make sure you were okay. Did you get that matter done? The emergency one?"

"Yeah, done. Working on some other things now."

"Right." My gaze falls to her desk and the reams of papers and notes surrounding it. Reality snaps in. Olivia has legitimate things to do. She's not sitting in here, pining away for me, wishing I would come by with milk and cookies. I'm ridiculous. "Well, I'll let you go."

She shakes her head. "You don't just swing by with snacks and not keep me company for a bit."

"Are you sure?"

She pushes the door shut with her foot. "Absolutely."

I move farther inside, feeling like a teenager alone in a bedroom with a girl for the first time. Probably because this room hasn't changed since Olivia's high school days. Among the plethora of awards and trophies is a picture of Kate Middleton and Prince William on their wedding day, a stack of Twilight books, a bottle of perfume from PINK, and piles and piles of old spiral notebooks. Taped to the wall is a small poster of Supreme Court Justice Sandra Day O'Connor next to one of a bunch of kittens in a basket. Stuffed animals sit across a shelf by her window.

She sits on the edge of the bed. "It's crazy in here, I know."

"I love it."

She pats the space next to her and I sit.

"I can tell a lot about high school Olivia from this room. Like that." I point to the picture of Princess Kate and Prince William. "You're a fan of the royals."

"Obsessed. Or was, at least." She takes a bite of cookie. "Not so much now."

"What's in the notebooks?" I nod toward a stack in the corner.

"Old notes, mainly. I was always afraid I'd need something later."

"That tracks. And you probably never needed them, right?"

She smiles. "Right. Never." She pops the rest of the cookie in her mouth, chews, and swallows. "How's Lucas? I heard him come in."

"Asleep on the couch."

"Good on you for getting him to like the snow." She puts her hand on my thigh.

"Thanks." She removes her hand but its short stint there, along with the closed door, makes me hyper aware of her proximity. I try to think of something to say but I can't. All I can think of is what she started last night.

Silence envelops the space around us, normal at first, then growing awkward. "About last night—" I start.

She says the same thing. At the same time.

"You first," I offer.

She nods. "I know you don't want to talk about what you told me," she says, "and that's okay. I just want you to know that what you said doesn't change the way I feel about you. You're a good person, Nate. A mistake you made years ago doesn't change that."

"Thanks," I manage. Relief washes through me. Olivia is the first woman I've had any interest in since the incident, the first person outside my family and inner circle I've told about it. Her acceptance of what happened? It's huge. Hope surges through me. Maybe there could be something between us. Maybe she doesn't regret what she started last night.

"But," she continues.

I stop short, and my head snaps up to meet her eyes. And I can tell. This isn't a *let's give this a try* moment but rather a *thank God we dodged that bullet* one.

"I think last night was a mistake," she blurts, grabbing a lock of hair and twisting it around her finger. "I shouldn't have kissed you. I'm sorry."

A snort-laugh escapes from my lips. "Sorry? Olivia, I wanted to kiss you. I meant what I said last night." I take her hand. "Believe me, I wanted to kiss you. From the first night you arrived."

Her brow furrows, and I can practically see her mind running through our first meeting. "When I fell asleep on the fence post? Really?"

"Yes, really. Yellow shirt and jeans. Sneakers. Hair pulled back with wisps around your face. I remember."

Her lips upturn into a small smile. "Gray shirt and black shorts," she says after a moment.

"No. It was a yellow shirt," I insist.

She shakes her head. "That's what you had on. A gray T-shirt and black shorts. And you smelled like pine." She hesitates. "I remember too. But—"

I inch closer to her. "No buts."

"But the future is uncertain and everything is complicated and—" She stops. "And I don't know. I like you, but—"

"Olivia." I take one of her hands in one of mine. "I like you too. There doesn't have to be a but."

"But."

I lean in and touch her face. "No buts."

"But," she says again but with a laugh that feels like an invitation. I pull her toward me and give her a moment to say no, or but really, or something, and when she doesn't, I press my lips against hers. She responds, opening her mouth and moving closer, her body pressed up against mine. I skim my hands over her breasts and down her waist, and she lets out a soft moan.

I pull back and trail her cheek with my thumb. "You are so beautiful, Olivia." I stare at her a moment, her full lips, wide eyes, the rise and fall of her chest. "So beautiful," I repeat and lean in. She puts her hands around my head and pulls me toward her. She kisses me, deeply, her fingers clawing at my hair, her tongue inside my mouth. And in the next moment, she swings one leg over my body, straddling me on the bed, and we're a tangle of hands and mouths, her pelvis rocking against mine.

I respond and pull her closer. "God, Olivia," I say, and she pushes herself off me and pulls off my shirt. She kisses my chest, her hands sliding inside my jeans.

The phone rings. And the computer.

"Don't get it," I murmur.

She pulls off her shirt, a pink lacy bra underneath.

"Olivia," a woman's voice says, and God, it sounds like she's in the room with us, her face on the computer screen.

Olivia flies off me, and both of us shift toward the noise.

I jerk up. What is happening? Is this live?

"Video voicemail. She can't see us," Olivia says, grabbing for her shirt.

"We've secured the placement," the woman continues.

"But—" I start.

Her shirt still off, Olivia dives across the bed and grabs her phone from the nightstand. "I've got to take this," she hisses. Her eyes flare and she puts the phone to her ear. "Hey, Marjorie." Her voice is normal, businesslike even. Like she wasn't on top of me a moment ago.

She waves her arm toward the door in a shooing motion, and I stand shirtless in her childhood bedroom, the aftermath of our interlude a bulk in my pants. I'm not sure I've ever felt more stupid during a romantic encounter. She covers the receiver of the phone and mouths, "I need to take this."

I stand corrected.

I feel more stupid now.

I grab my shirt and pull it over my body. I step out of the room and lean against the wall. The sequence of events is fresh in my mind, replaying on a loop, right up to when a half-naked Olivia got up to take a work call. *A work call.* I mean, I get it, I guess. Maybe she *had* to take that call.

Still. I can't help but wonder if this how it would be, to be involved with Olivia. For everything—*everything*—to take a backseat to her job? Or was this a rare occurrence, spawned by the emergency that took place earlier?

Really, it doesn't matter.

Because either way, I'm in too deep not to find out.

CHAPTER 35

OLIVIA
Nate shuts the door, and I grip my cell closer to my ear. Marjorie is speaking, but only every few words filter through, the rest of the space in my brain taken up with images of Nate. His dark, rumpled bedhead hair. His mouth on mine. His pine scent. His voice. "Olivia, you are so beautiful."

God. What must he think? One second, I'm all over him, and the next I'm diving across the bed to take a call. But the video message feature would have kept going and he would have heard about Lucas's placement. Not that he won't find out about it. But that moment? The wrong time to tell him. Obviously.

"The matter is time sensitive," Marjorie says, and boom, my mind swings from Nate back to this conversation.

"Time sensitive?" I repeat the words like a question. How can the matter be time sensitive? This is Lucas's life. Finding a placement shouldn't be rushed.

Except I rushed it.

This phone call is the culmination of the ball *I* set in motion after I'd just gotten here. Before I reconnected with Lucas.

Before I'd been anointed as part of the Fab Five. And before I had feelings for Nate. He's no longer just a guy who's nice to my brother. I *like* him.

"Time sensitive. These placements are hard to get." She pauses before asking, "So you can go? You'll see the placement tomorrow?"

Blood rushes to my head; my mind goes fuzzy. Tomorrow. *Tomorrow*. It's too soon.

"Olivia?"

"Yes," I blurt.

"The information about the facility is in the attachment to the email my admin sent a few weeks ago," she continues.

"Yes. I saw." I call up the house. A white colonial and red shutters on an expansive, tree-filled lot. Pretty. Perfect even.

"And Olivia."

"Yes."

"We need you back in person at the office ASAP. Things are heating up on Rowan and your remote work, well, it hasn't been strong. Your billables are way down."

I swallow. I knew both of those things, but I hoped they'd slip by unnoticed.

"I see your father's brilliance in you," Marjorie continues. "Your talent, your drive." She pauses. "Don't let it slip away."

I squeeze my eyes shut, an image of Dad when he worked for Bennett Connor clear in my mind. That version of him? It's what I'd emulated since I was a little girl. "I won't."

"Good. Talk to you." She hangs up.

A heaviness falls over my body. It's difficult to imagine that less than five minutes ago I was on the precipice of having sex with Nate, every nerve ending in my body thrumming with passion. That earlier today, I was sledding with my brother and friends, and despite being the most snow-hating person on earth, loving it. After, I plowed through an emergency motion like it was nothing. I felt invincible. But those emotions are muted now, reality rearing its ugly head. The fractured truth I created the past several months is about to come crashing down.

I leave my room and thump down the stairs in search of Nate. I peek at Lucas, still asleep on the couch, the same small snores I remember as a child escaping from an open mouth. Nate's not here or in the kitchen. I look around and catch a glimpse of a black coat outside shoveling snow off the walk. His movements are solid and strong. Capable.

I swipe an old coat from the coat closet, take a step for the door, and put my hand on the doorknob. I need to explain myself. I twist the knob and stop, my mind running with all the things I could possibly say:

Sorry I took a call when we were about to have sex.

I'm seeing a time-sensitive out-of-home placement for Lucas *tomorrow*.

I never planned to stay in Greenwillow.

Yeah.

No.

Despite that every single one of those statements reflects the truth, I don't want to say any of them.

I ease out of my coat and stuff it back in the closet. Later. All this can wait until later. Maybe by then the exact right words will sweep into my brain, and I'll find a way to tell Nate everything and not have him hate me.

I skulk back to my bedroom, pull up the email from Marjorie's admin, and look again at the pretty colonial house with the red door. I stare at the image and try to visualize Lucas there and can't. I snap the computer shut. I just need to see it first.

I move to my bed and lie back. The outline of glow-in-the-dark constellation stickers are visible on my ceiling. Dad put them there during a short-lived astronomy phase. He'd agree with my choice regarding Lucas and the placement, I think.

He'd want me to succeed in my career. It was different for him when he left Bennett Connor. He'd already had his success. He'd done what he set out to. Me? I'm just at the start of things.

A knock sounds on the door, and I jolt up in bed. "Who's there?" I ask. It's a stupid question; I know who it is. Lucas doesn't knock.

"It's Nate."

I push myself off the bed and pull open the door. And he's there in the frame, all six foot two of him, his face ruddy from the cold, his chest and shoulders filling out a thermal top. My face heats.

"Hey," he says. "Sorry to interrupt, but I just"—his gaze falls to the floor—"I just don't want things to be weird between us." He puffs out a breath and angles his head up, blue eyes meeting mine. "I don't trust a lot of people with what I told you. About the accident. It's—" He stops. "You're important to me, Olivia," he spits out.

My heart lifts. "You're important to me too, Nate."

"I know. Which is why I shouldn't have pushed things earlier. You said the kiss yesterday was a mistake and I kept pushing and, well," he takes a step back, "I don't want to mess this up."

I nod, digesting his words, fairly certain about the direction this conversation going. He's thinking like I am: we should try this.

He pushes his hand in my direction. "So friends?"

Friends? My gaze drops to his outstretched hand. Friends. He wants to be friends, nothing more. And I should want that. Yes. It's the best I'll be able to hope for once I share the news about moving. But agreeing to it feels like a loss somehow.

Nate looks up and meets my eyes, and I realize I've left him standing there with his hand outstretched. I take it. "Friends," I agree.

We hold on to each other's hand much longer than is necessary for a handshake, and when he finally drops mine, he says, "So are you up for a movie and chili?"

A movie and chili. We're definitely in the friend zone now. "Sure," I say brightly.

Later, Nate makes chili and the three of us watch *Back to the Future*. I've seen it at least a dozen times, we all have, but it's one of Lucas's favorites so we're watching it again. I know the plot so well I can even repeat some of the dialogue verbatim, which does not help as far as distraction from the placement issue. My mind keeps going back to the picture of the house, and frankly, the fact that we are watching this movie *again* makes me think that a change of scene would be good for Lucas.

Change might just be the best thing.

CHAPTER 36

LUCAS

Tonight me, Nate, and Olivia are watching Back to the Future. *I've seen it before. Lots and lots of times, but I like to watch the same movie over and over and over. It's a control thing. Knowing what's going to happen in a movie right down to the next line of dialogue is a huge comfort for someone who can't control anything else. Sameness. It's boring for most people, but I need it. It keeps me sane.*

Marty McFly is the best. I love how he goes back in time in a DeLorean. I'd do that in a heartbeat if I could prevent myself from having ASD. What would non-ASD Lucas Ellison be like? I think about that sometimes. I'd be an athlete, probably soccer or maybe a skier since I like sledding now. Avery would definitely be my girlfriend. I'd go to college to study the brain and figure out once and for all what the deal is with ASD. I mean, I gotta hand it to the condition, it's super strange across the board. Some of us are literally geniuses. Some of us learn to talk and blend and seem to do pretty well. Then there's some of us—ME—who can talk but barely, who need help out the wazoo with basically everything. The short end of the ASD stick for sure.

I'd also like to understand the social part of ASD. That's really screwed up. Many of those on the spectrum who can speak state they have trouble reading social cues. So now people assume none of us can. That reading emotions is hard for us. It isn't. Not for me, anyway. I can tell, right now, that Olivia is annoyed that we are watching Back to the Future, *again*. She's looking at her phone, or at the wall, everywhere but the television. And she's sighed like ten gazillion times.

I don't blame her. I probably should have gotten up and switched the movie off. Bam. Done. Goodbye Marty McFly and Doc and Biff and George and Lorraine. Goodbye Hill Valley. I thought about doing it. But I didn't, and the movie ended the same way it always does.

Maybe next time.

There's always a next time to do better, right?

CHAPTER 37

NATE

I park in front of my parents' house. It's Saturday, two days after the snow day, the day of the friendship pact. Theoretically, our relationship should revert to the way it was before. Easy, fun, light. But it doesn't. Because the things I like about Olivia—the way her eyes crinkle when she laughs, how she bites her bottom lip when she's thinking, the way she says my name—have only intensified since the kiss.

So I'm glad for today, a chance to get out and clear my head. It's snowfest, an annual event in my parents' neighborhood the Saturday after the first snowfall. A day where everyone helps everyone else with their shoveling. There's always hot apple cider, homemade baked treats, and music. At night, there's a potluck at someone's house.

I grab my shovel from the trunk of my car, make my way up the walkway, and push open the door. "Knock, knock. It's me."

No answer.

"Hello?"

Mom rushes out of the dining room area. She's dressed

nicely, *not* in shoveling clothes. "Nate," she says, like she's surprised to see me. "You're here early."

"Mom?"

"This way, sweetheart, this way." She flutters her hand.

I squint in her direction, none of this seeming right. "Mom? What's going on?"

"Please, honey, just come." She flutters her hand again.

I follow her into the dining room, the snow shovel still in my hand. A smattering of my relatives are crammed around the table. Mom, Dad, Carly, Jenny, Rod, and Chuck.

"Hello, Nate." It's a super deep voice, one I recognize but can't place. I look in the direction it came from and see Dr. Alan Short—Dr. Alan, he likes to be called—at the head of the table, a pitcher of water and plastic cups in front him. I blink in his direction, piecing together what is happening just as he says it.

"Nate. This is an intervention."

"Really?" I look around the table. This is about me *moving on.* No way. Not now. Olivia needs me and so does Lucas. I turn around and take a step toward the door.

Carly grips my forearm. "Just hear us out."

"We care about you Nate," Mom says. "So much." Her tone is anxious.

Fine.

I set the shovel against the wall, turn back around, and remove my coat. Worried gazes meet mine. Like I'm an addict or am engaging in destructive behavior instead of caring for a kid with ASD. Honestly.

"Nate, please sit." Dr. Alan gestures to the only empty seat.

As an aside, I do not like Dr. Alan. A so-called trauma specialist, I was supposed to see him long-term once I got out of jail. He didn't help me at all, and I ditched after three sessions. I lied to my parents about it for months. Week after week, I told them I was still going and went to the park instead. I don't know that they ever found out the truth.

I sit in the empty chair.

"Does anyone want to start?" Dr. Alan asks.

I raise my hand, and he nods in my direction. "Nate."

"I thought it was snowfest."

No one laughs.

"When are you moving on with your life?" Dad barks, ever the diplomat.

Mom gives him a wide-eyed *I can't believe you just said that* look and puts her hand over his. "What Dad meant," she interjects, "is that you've never moved past the accident. What can we do to help you heal so you can move on?"

"He's had plenty of time to heal."

"John," Mom hisses.

It's silent. I pick at a hangnail. I could say something, but I don't. I will not try to save this trainwreck of an intervention.

Dr. Alan taps a pen on the table. "Why don't we go around and each say what our concerns are?" he suggests and points at Jenny with a pen. He is almost as bad at this as he was at therapy.

Without hesitation, Jenny says, "I'm concerned that you're stuck, Nate."

Rod puts a hand on her shoulder. "Me too. You seem to be, I don't know, adrift."

"You can't live in Melanie's house forever," Chuck adds. "I mean, is that the long-term plan, to just live there with Lucas and Olivia?"

I cross my arms across my chest. This feels less like what I'd imagine an intervention to be and more like *let's take jabs at Nate's choices* hour.

Dr. Alan angles the pen in my direction. It's a cheap one, with bite marks on the bottom. "Nate, do you have any thoughts about what has been said so far?"

"No." I tighten my arms around myself. "It's pretty clear how everyone feels."

"Show him," Carly whispers to Mom.

Mom pushes a paper across the table. "Your father emailed this to you."

"And you didn't bother to open it," Dad finishes.

I glance at him but say nothing because he's right. I scan down the paper which details a program sponsored by DSI, the doctor shortage initiative. It lists schools that hold spots for prospective applicants who are willing to go into needed specialties in underserved areas. One of the schools listed is the Oakland School of Medicine, where, but for the accident, I would have started four years ago.

"What do you think about the program, Nate?" Dr. Alan asks.

I slide the paper back across the table. "I think it has nothing to do with me."

"But if it did," Mom says, her voice hopeful.

"It doesn't."

She wrings her hands together, her expression a combination of excitement and concern.

"They're giving interviews to anyone interested in DSI," Dad says.

"So you've got an interview if you want one." Mom clasps her hands together like this is the greatest news ever. "If you got in, you'd start in the fall. It would be like—" She stops midsentence.

"Like it never happened? Is that what you were going to say?"

Her face falls. "Honey."

"It did happen," I say. "And I'm sure Mark's family hasn't forgotten. It's not like any of them can just pick up where they left off." I don't add the rest. My debilitating fear is that in a role like a doctor, I might miss something. The concern is not one I'd had when I'd applied the first go around. But since the accident, whenever I consider becoming a doctor, I just know I'll make a mistake. I'll hurt or kill someone else. Just like Mark Carney.

Dad grabs the DSI paper and shakes it. "If not this, then what? You're throwing your life away. You made a mistake; you paid for it. You need to move on. It doesn't need to be medical school, but it has to be something."

"I am doing something."

"Helping with Lucas? That's not a career, Nate. It's babysitting."

"Babysitting," I repeat.

"Yes, babysitting." He shifts his body away from me.

I push up the sleeves of my sweatshirt and shake my head. "Don't hold back, Dad. Tell me how you really feel."

The tension in the room, already thick, becomes almost unbearable. Mom looks on the verge of tears. Carly appears stunned. Everyone else looks massively uncomfortable, like they'd rather be anywhere else.

Except Dr. Alan. He looks completely relaxed. Kind of like a man who gets paid no matter what happens. He grabs the water pitcher, pours himself a glass, and drinks down the whole thing with loud, obnoxious gulping noises. He says "ahhh" when he's done and slams the cup down like he just finished a beer. "What do you think about what your dad just said, Nate?"

"I think it sucks."

Dr. Alan leans forward, and I can practically see him thinking, "Now we're getting somewhere." Part of me wants to shut down, not give him the satisfaction of engaging, but my emotions are too surface level for that. "Why, Nate?" he asks. "Why does it suck?"

"Why does it suck that my dad—my family"—I circle my finger around the table —"felt a need to hold an intervention for me, the general consensus seeming to be that I'm wasting my life? I think the reason that sucks is pretty obvious, no?"

"And how do you feel?" Dr. Alan prompts.

"I feel like helping Lucas make his way in a world that doesn't understand him is a whole lot more than babysitting. Olivia and I get along well, and she needs me right now." I pause. "I'm in a better place. Isn't that what you all wanted?"

"So this is about the girl?" Dad says.

"What? No."

"You work for Olivia," Chuck adds. "It could get complicated to date her."

Carly, next to me, puts her hand over mine. "And she never directly answered my question about whether the firm will let her continue to work remotely. What would happen if she had to go back?"

I shut my eyes.

"She's a lawyer at a big, prestigious firm," Dad says. "You think she's going to date her brother's minder long-term? Or are you just a fun sidepiece while she's in Greenwillow?"

I slam my hand on the table. "Sidepiece? Jeez, Dad."

He pushes up from the table and meets my eyes. "You could be so much more."

He walks out and my body tenses, every nerve on alert. In the span of five minutes, Dad just gave voice to a real fear I had about my relationship with Olivia, about the trajectory of my life. Can I be, as Dad said, *so much more*? Does Olivia really care about me or am I someone to pass the time with on her way to greater things? Will she become resentful that I work for her? Will I?

"Nate," Dr. Alan says, "what are your thoughts?"

I swing my head in his direction, incredulous that he's continuing.

"I think," I say finally, "that this intervention is over."

CHAPTER 38

OLIVIA
I put my foot on the gas. I'm on my way to see the placement for Lucas but my mind is fixed on the conversation I just had with Nate. First fight? Or maybe he was just off or in a bad mood for some reason. I don't know. He's been quiet since he got back from the snowfest yesterday.

He made breakfast for himself and Lucas, waffles as usual. He always makes one for me too, so when I got downstairs, I said jokingly, *where are my waffles, man?* I added on to the comment, teasing about how I couldn't depend on him to do something as simple as making a waffle. I was kidding. *Kidding.* But instead of laughing or saying something funny-insulting back like he normally would, he slammed the waffle maker shut and said, "I think everyone here can make their own food." Right after, he left to take Lucas to school. I waited for him to get back so I could air things out or apologize or whatever. But he didn't return, and I had to leave. So here I am, driving like a maniac, my mind on Nate instead of Lucas.

I pull into a gas station, fill up my tank, then park and scroll through my texts. None from Nate. I start and stop a text message to him five times at least. I imagine him watching the dots on his phone reappear and disappear over and over because the sender—me—is an idiot. The wimpy *does he still like me* mantra flies through my mind, even though we're supposed to be friends and nothing more. Ugh.

I throw the phone on to the passenger seat, start the car, and merge onto the highway. I push this morning's conversation with Nate aside and conjure the placement. I've visualized the home at least a dozen times since yesterday and each time it becomes even more ideal. A spacious house on lots of land with a few animals that roam the property, maybe a house cat or two. Kind attendants and nice housemates, all around Lucas's age, with at least one who also likes Animal Planet. There would be daily activities and enrichment and field trips on the weekend. I'd take him back to Greenwillow for vacations and holidays.

It's ideal, so much so that when I get to the placement, I drive right past the home despite the GPS woman telling me that "the destination is on the right." I realize the error, circle back, and park a bit away from the house. Hmm.

Okay. It's nice. Not exactly as great as it seemed in the picture—or my mind—but nice. The landscaping is trimmed back; there's a basketball hoop in the driveway, along with a white van. A yellow plastic figure at the edge of the property warns drivers to "slow down."

The front door swings open. An older man wearing a baseball hat, fifties maybe, guides a similarly aged man, very heavyset, out of the house by his elbow. The second man seems to be on the spectrum and he's saying something; I can't tell what. They walk slowly toward the van, and the baseball hat man is patient enough with the other, not urging him on or expressing any annoyance. But there's something off. I watch the pair, my mind comparing them to how Nate and Lucas might act in the same scenario. Nate would be patient too. But his countenance would be different. Happy, energized. He'd be talking to Lucas as they walked. Like they're friends. In contrast, this man, the one in the baseball hat, looks miserable.

They get in the van and the two of them drive off. I lean back in the car seat and replay the interaction. The baseball hat man's objective was clear: keeping the other man safe. But second man was obviously a means to an end, not a person he cared about.

I puff out a breath.

Okay.

Okay. The baseball hat man is one person, and what I observed was one interaction. I don't really know anything. Maybe the man was having a bad day. And maybe the other attendant is great, and the other housemates closer to Lucas's age. I can't make a judgment after just a few minutes.

I get out of the car, shove my phone in my pocket, and traverse the street. Lots of traffic. I push these negatives from my mind as I make my way to the front door. I lift my hand to knock, but before I do it swings open. A skinny man with glasses stands in the doorframe. He's my age as best I can tell and seems more energetic than the baseball cap man.

"Olivia?"

"Yes."

He shoots out a hand. "I'm Jay."

I shake his hand, and he looks at the space around me.

"No Lucas?"

"Not today." I open my mouth to add that I didn't bring him because he'd be upset at the disruption to his routine, then shut it, realizing how ridiculous that would sound. If just visiting would upset him, how could he possibly *live* here? It's *the* question, obviously, but not the one for today.

Jay swings the door open, and I step into the house. He shows me all the rooms on the first floor: the kitchen, the dining room, the family room, the laundry. No one is in any of them; I'm unsure where the residents are. Every room is clean, almost too much so, with a strong smell of antiseptic that reminds me of a hospital. The furnishings are new enough but blocky and uncomfortable looking. Framed pictures of generic flower arrangements hang on the walls. There are no throw pillows, quilts, plants, or photographs. No silly magnets on the fridge. No Cookie Monster cookie jar on the counter. No pet dishes on the floor.

"Are pets allowed?"

Jay smiles broadly. "We've got fish, if that counts." He gestures toward the stairway with his entire arm. "Come on, I'll show you." He bounds up the stairs and stops at a small fish tank that centers the window in the landing area. He taps hard on the glass—which I'm pretty sure you're not supposed to do—and a group of generic orange and white fish scatter. "There's a big one at the bottom." He points at the tank. "See it? See it there?"

I don't care about the fish, but Jay keeps pointing and asking if I see it, so I angle my head and look in the tank. Yup, it's big and kind of cool looking but a sad substitute for horses, chickens, and cats. Blocky uncomfortable furniture is not the same as cushiony ones that smell like home. The sound of cars whizzing by pales in comparison to the sound of crickets and birds and owls.

Jay rights himself, taps on the fish tank again, and continues the tour. I follow and try to visualize Lucas here. I try to see him in the small bedroom that would be his, in his bright white bathroom, in the kitchen area filled with typewritten notes about food allergies and taste preferences for the residents. I picture him outside in the yard enclosed by a chain link fence, sitting in the dining room surrounded by a group of strangers. I see him feeding the fish—his pets now—once or twice a week as per the schedule. One image locks into the next and the next and the next until the conclusion becomes rock solid: Lucas would hate it here.

He would. I know it. But he's not the only person involved.

If I don't take the placement, if I don't at least have him give it a try, what then? Out-of-home placements are almost impossible to get. There won't be another opening any time soon, and this one, this house, is so close to Greenwillow. It *could* work.

Jay leads me back to the foyer. "Any questions?"

I have a ton of questions, but I can't formulate any of them right now. "It's a lot to take in," I say honestly. All I want to do at this moment is get out of here and think. "Can I call or email you?"

"Sure thing. You've got my contact information."

"Yes."

He opens the door, and I hustle across the busy street to my car. As soon as I get inside, there's a text from Marjorie. "All settled with the placement?"

I stare at the words. I just left the tour. How could things be settled already? It's not like I'm dropping Lucas off for a week of sleep-away camp or taking a pet to a kennel. I toss my phone on the passenger seat but the fact that Marjorie sent it at all is unsettling. She's the senior partner; I'm just an associate. The fact that she wants this all wrapped up and done *today* tells me one thing: I'm out of time.

The entire ride home, my thoughts ping back and forth in the extreme:

Definitely yes, definitely no.

One hundred percent yes, 100 percent no.

Absolutely yes, absolutely no.

The back and forth goes on and on, each decision seeming right for about two seconds until all the reasons it isn't rear their ugly heads. And in between the yeses and the nos, I think about Nate and what was up this morning. The mental ping-pong is emotionally exhausting, and by the time I get back to Greenwillow, all I want is a Big Rod's sandwich and a nap. In that order.

I pull into the parking lot of Big Rod's and step out of my car.

"Olivia?"

Crap. I don't want to talk to anyone right now. But I can't very well get back into my car and drive away without addressing whoever this is. I turn my head. Carly, Nate's sister, waves in my direction.

"Hey, Carly."

"Hey."

I met Carly just once, at the dinner with the Natebugs, but she seemed pretty cheerful. Her demeanor is different today.

"I guess," she starts, her voice just above a whisper, "Nate told you about the intervention."

I go still, and a flush of adrenaline tingles through me.

"Do know where his head's at?" Carly asks. "Do you think he has any intention of going back to med school? Did he mention the interview at Oakland Med?"

"I don't know where his head is," I say, not sure that a truer statement has ever been spoken. Intervention? Med school? I had no idea about either of those things. All I know about Nate career-wise is that he majored in biology at Pitt and worked for Melanie after the accident. There'd been that comment by his dad about him going back to school, but I'd never followed up on it, per our deal—no school or work talk. In truth, I'd forgotten about it.

Carly leans against her car. "I mean, this job with you, helping with Lucas, it's not permanent, right?"

I drop open my mouth, but nothing comes out. Considering I was just looking at an out-of-home placement for Lucas, I can't very well say the position is lock solid. "I don't know," I say finally.

"Yeah." She nods. "I thought maybe you'd have to move back to New York." She looks down, kicks at a stray stone, and looks back up at me. "Do you think you could talk to him? Try and convince him to at least take the interview. He's so guilt ridden about the accident." Her eyes widen. "You know about that right?"

"Yes." Finally, something I know.

"Anyway, he just won't let himself be happy. Self-sabotage and all. We think—me, my parents, our relatives—that Nate going back to school would be the best way for him to get out of this funk."

Funk. The word hits me wrong. Because if his current situation is a funk, then I'm part of that. Part of the funk. The idea doesn't feel the best.

"You'll talk to him?" Carly asks, oblivious.

"Yes." I nod. "I definitely will."

CHAPTER 39

NATE

Olivia steps inside the family room from wherever she's been. I look up from the couch and smile at her. She tips her head in an acknowledgment but doesn't smile back. I don't blame her. I've been a jerk.

She hangs up her coat and moves purposely in my direction, her expression serious. "Why didn't you tell me about medical school?"

Adrenaline hits my bloodstream, and I sit up straight. Medical school. Shit. I thought she was going to give me crap about not making her a waffle. I'm unprepared for this.

"I had no idea you wanted to be doctor."

"Wanted. Past tense. That's the key. I didn't tell you because it's not relevant."

"Well, Carly says you have an interview at Oakland Med, so you must have applied."

I lean back and blow out a breath. Carly. I guess Olivia saw her somewhere and she spilled the beans.

"I didn't apply. It's a program where they're giving automatic interviews."

Otis hops up onto the side of the couch and she strokes his fur a long moment before continuing. "But you want to go, right?" She looks at me like I should want to go, like not wanting to be a doctor, not wanting other people's lives in my hands, would be crazy.

"Not right now. Maybe sometime."

Otis starts to knead the couch with his claws, and she sets him down on the floor. "What would you do instead?"

"I don't know, Olivia. I thought I *was* doing something. You of all people should know that." Frustration boils up inside me. The rational part of my brain knows she means well; the rest of me feels like screaming. What is it with everyone? Why is my current choice not enough?

She squeezes her eyes shut. "I'm only asking," she says, opening them, "because I might have an out-of-home placement for Lucas."

"What?" I ask, though I understand perfectly what she said.

"Actually, I do have an out-of-home placement for Lucas."

A cloud crosses over the sun outside, darkening the room in a way that feels like foreshadowing. "I thought you liked working remotely. I thought the firm was okay with it."

"I do and the firm was good with it for the short term. Staying was never the permanent plan. I need to go back to New York."

Staying was never the permanent plan. The words ricochet in my head.

She puts her hand on my shoulder. "I'm sorry. I'm so sorry. I didn't know if it was going to work out and, well, I saw it . . ."

"You *saw* it?" I stand up, effectively removing her hand from my shoulder.

"I did."

"Why didn't you tell me?"

"Because I didn't know anything. It might not have been

relevant." She puffs out a breath. "Kind of like you and medical school."

"That's not at all the same." I shake my head vigorously. "Medical school was in the past. This, the placement for Lucas, is happening right now." I want to add that I'll miss her if she goes. And also, that caring for Lucas has been *my job* for the past two years, a position I'll no longer have once he moves. But, of course, I don't say either of these things. Both are too pathetic.

"I'm sorry," she says again. "But, please, I need your input. I don't know what to do about the placement. It's close, but I don't think Lucas will like it." She twists a lock of her hair. "I know he won't."

From what I've seen, Olivia's not a crier, but right now she looks on the verge of it. I soften a little, then everything my family said comes flying back at me. I'm Lucas's babysitter. Olivia's using me. I'm lost. I'm adrift. I'm a man whose choices caused my family to stage an intervention, the last person who should be giving advice.

"Nate?"

"Look, I get that you want my opinion, but where Lucas lives and who cares for him isn't my decision. I mean, I had no idea you were even considering moving him from Greenwillow. I haven't seen the placement. I don't know what I could possibly say."

"Maybe you could see it with me? Maybe we could—"

"Olivia," I say firmly, "I'm not going to weigh in on this. It has nothing to do with me. Clearly." I glance at my watch. "I've got to get Lucas from school."

I walk out and drive to the school feeling completely blind-sided. I thought there might have been something between us, that Olivia had at least a sliver of real feelings for me. Obviously not. She had no intention of staying here. Ever.

I park at the school and go inside to get Lucas. He's waiting at the entrance with the other students from Ms. Caddell's class.

She's standing with them, poking at her phone with a red-nailed finger.

She glances up. "Hey, Nate."

"Hey."

She squints her eyes in my direction. "What's up? You look lower than a snake's belly in a wagon rut."

It's a ridiculous phrase, and if I didn't feel lower than a snake's belly in a wagon rut, I would laugh. I force a smile instead. The last thing I need is for Lauren Caddell to be on the scent of something amiss. "All good on my end," I lie and turn my focus to Lucas. "All ready, bud?"

Lucas picks up his backpack and follows me to the car. I drive him back to Melanie's in silence. I normally talk on the way, ask him about his day and tell him about mine. He doesn't answer, but I've always felt like he was listening, that he appreciated my efforts to keep up conversation despite his inability to participate in it. I know I should say something, keep the routine, keep things the same, but, honestly, what's the use?

Everything's going to change for Lucas soon enough.

He may as well get used to it.

CHAPTER 40

LUCAS
    I'm in the car with Nate and he's not talking. At all. Not about how he spent his day. Not mentioning what Ms. Caddell told him I did and acting like the information came from me. He doesn't have music on. He's not humming or beating his hands on the steering wheel. He's not talking about what's for dinner. It's freaky. I don't like it.

We pull up to the house. Nate gets out of the car, still not talking. He and I walk inside. He calls to Olivia that he's going out. And then he leaves. Like, that's it. That's never *happened before. And here I am standing in the foyer with my backpack still on my back with both straps. I feel frozen in place. The differentness of today as compared to every other day is alarming and I don't move.*

Olivia comes into the space and puts her hands on the straps of my backpack. It's enough to jolt me back into normalcy—at least normalcy for me—and I remove the pack and follow her into the kitchen. She pulls cookies out of the Cookie Monster jar and grabs two plastic cups from the cabinet, presumably for milk. I'd be relieved that she's here, doing all the things Nate normally does, except it's still different and she seems off too. Too cheerful.

My heart drops. Something is going to happen. And not a good something. I feel it, just like I did when Mom didn't come back right away. An innate sense that something is wrong. And that I'm helpless to change it.

CHAPTER 41

OLIVIA
Forty-eight hours after seeing the placement for Lucas, I'm on a bench near Bennett Connor, my fingers flying over my phone. *I won't be back until tomorrow.*

Nate's response is instantaneous. *Okay.*

I stare at the word. Our relationship since the placement conversation has changed from light to transactional. He put in what he called a *loose notice*; essentially, he'll stay on as long as I need him, unless he gets another opportunity first. He didn't share what types of opportunities he was looking at. School, job, I don't know. Both nights, he stayed at his parents' house instead of at Melanie's, and the one time I brought up the subject he said he didn't want to talk about it.

It's weird and it's lonely. I saw a change in Lucas the first night Nate didn't stay over. And me? I miss him. Every part. His lopsided grin. The way his face looked when I walked into the room. I miss watching *Who Wants to Be a Millionaire* together, eating the bad food we made for dinner, neither of us being skilled chefs. I miss his '80s playlists, his laugh. How he always looked disheveled in the best possible way. I miss that, for the first time in as long as I can remember, I had not one but two people waiting on the other side of the door when I walked into a room.

And I'm not willing to give that up.

Not without trying like heck to save it.

I check my watch. Five minutes until my appointment with Marjorie and William about the Rowan case. Part one of my four-part plan.

I navigate through the firm's corridors to William's office, and when I reach it, it honestly feels like Groundhog Day. It's exactly the same as it was the last time I was here. William wearing the same light blue dress shirt, typing at the computer in the same furious manner, his eyes fixed on the keyboard like they're glued to it. A half-eaten bagel sits on a paper wrapper on his desk, which I hope for his sake is *not* the same.

"Hey, William." I ease into the office.

He lifts his head and glances in my direction. "Olivia."

I sit in one of the chairs in front of his desk.

"Marjorie's not coming." He twists his chair around to face me. "She got called into court. Huge case." He raps his fingers on the desk. "Did you see the new Rowan discovery online?"

"I saw it."

He whips his glasses off and furrows his brow. "Then you understand how essential it is that you're here in the office then."

"I do."

"Things are all set with your brother?"

"They are," I say and pause before spitting out the rest of it, "but I'm not taking the placement."

He tips his head. "Why? We've been through this. The remote work . . . that was just a temporary thing."

"I know. I—"

"Then what is it?" he interrupts, a bad habit I realize now is supremely annoying. It's one he and Marjorie share, neither one of them having enough patience to wait for someone else to finish a thought.

"Thank you so much for your help," I start again, "but I'm moving Lucas with me to New York."

He nods, like he's trying to understand my words but can't quite do it. "But you have a placement."

"It isn't right for Lucas. I've been doing research and New York City has all the services he needs. Better than what he gets right now." *Any* service would be better since Melanie didn't believe in therapy. "New York will be great for him," I continue, "and I can still work at the firm in person."

He scrunches up his face. "Are you sure? You know what the job is, Olivia. Late nights, weekends. Your work in Greenwillow, well—"

He stops before finishing the sentence, but I get the memo: no more shoddy work.

"It won't be like that."

"Okay, okay." He nods like he's trying to make sense of the decision. "When can we expect you back?"

"I'll be in a week from Monday."

One week. It's soon, but if I'm going to do this, I need to do it. No more wringing my hands. No more going back and forth. This or that, this or that, this or that. I need to act.

"Alright, then. I'll let Marjorie know."

I say goodbye and leave the office. I walk several blocks to the Autism Center for Education (ACE). In the past forty-eight hours, I've had video calls with the director, Lucas's would-be teacher, the activities coordinator, and a parent who is head of the Parent Teacher Organization. The premise at ACE—teach up not down—is rooted in the philosophy that autistic individuals are capable of more than traditional education models give them credit for. They assume understanding and intelligence in all students, even those who can't verbalize it.

It's the opposite of Lauren Caddell's childish classroom with its cartoon reminders and progress sticker charts. Also contrary to Melanie's insistence, per Nate, that Lucas's downtime be idle. And while I know both women meant the best, after immersing myself in the ACE philosophy, I'm convinced their approach is better.

I'm not normally impulsive, but I signed Lucas up for ACE sight unseen yesterday. I e-signed the contract and put the hefty deposit on my credit card, the rush engendered in part from my fear that, if I didn't commit, I'd chicken out and remain inside the awful bubble I'd been in since the placement visit. Should I? Shouldn't I? Should I? Shouldn't I? Enough already. Let's go.

I swing open the door to ACE and step inside. The space is just as bright and modern as it was in the photographs. The backdrop is white and peppered with words like ACHIEVE and VISION and INSPIRE in a blocky black font. A half-circle reception desk sits in the center, a perfectly made-up woman dressed in a suit behind it. Behind her is a sleek granite wall, a stream of water running from the top over the word ACE and the ACE logo, an up arrow.

"I'm Olivia Ellison," I say.

"Ms. Ellison," she says, her voice professional. "I'm Amelia. I've got your orientation and school materials here." She holds out a spiral bound packet of materials with a plastic shield cover. I take it from her, the weight of it heavy in my hands.

"Thank you."

She nods. "We'll see you and Lucas Monday, then."

I crane my neck, hoping to see more of the school, something that will confirm that this is, as I thought, the right place for Lucas. But this isn't Include or Lauren Caddell's class; it's not the kind of place where you just pop in and walk around.

"Anything else I can do for you, Miss Ellison?" Amelia asks, but it's clear she wants the answer to be no.

I shake my head. "I'm all set."

I walk out, the thick book of materials gripped in my hand. Two of four.

Next, I take the bus to the Manhattan School of Medicine, ManMed for short. The school was on the doctor shortage initiative list Carly had told me about and they're still accepting applications. I take pictures of every building from the outside, join an ongoing tour, and get pictures of labs and classrooms, including one with dummies that simulate different medical issues. After, I walk back to my apartment and take pictures of everything in New York I think Nate would love. Delis and bakeries and landmarks like the Rockefeller Center. And that's just what I pass.

I get my favorite Thai take-out, something they don't have in Greenwillow, and eat it in my apartment. I take a long bubble bath, and after I go to bed, the silky sheets and memory foam mattress are a treat compared to my lumpy childhood bed. I close my eyes and will myself to fall asleep. I'll need it. The hardest and final step of my plan is tomorrow.

CHAPTER 42

NATE

Mid-afternoon on Saturday, Olivia's car rattles up the drive. Reflexively, my heart lifts; I tamp it down and internally repeat my mantra:

Olivia is your employer.

Olivia is moving to New York.

Olivia does not feel about you the way you feel about her.

Stupid that I need to repeat those truths to myself as often as I do. But in fairness, Olivia is full of mixed messages. Sometimes she barely notices me, seeming preoccupied. Like she's thinking, planning, and strategizing about who knows what? But then, just as much, I'll catch her looking at me in that soft way of hers and I feel like there's still something there. And maybe there is. But it doesn't matter. Even if our connection is real, it's not strong enough to tip the scales in favor of her staying. She's made that clear.

She parks the car, and immediately after my phone pings with a text: *can you meet me in the barn?*

I stare at the message. Meet her in the barn? I lift my head and see her out the window, already walking, the hood on her coat obscuring her face.

I grab a coat and gloves and tell Lucas I'll be right back. I head to the barn and find Olivia inside, her cheeks flushed pink from the cold. She looks cute—kissable—in a way I wish she didn't.

"Sorry for meeting out here," she says. "I didn't want Lucas to know about this yet."

I nod, assuming she wants to talk about the out-of-home placement. I don't. I've been working hard to extricate myself from this decision, one that seems already set in stone.

"I'm not taking the placement."

My heart stutters. I look up. Olivia's eyes are on me.

"But I'm not staying in Greenwillow," she says immediately. "I'm moving Lucas to New York." She shoves her hands in her coat pockets. "I want you to come with us."

I stand dumbly, taking way too long to unpack the statement. "Move with you to New York?" I ask finally.

"Yes, New York. I could keep my job and there's a great school for Lucas and—" she pauses. "And you could go back to school. There's a program at Manhattan Medical and they're still accepting applications. Same deal as Oakland, automatic interviews."

She moves next to me and takes her phone from her pocket. She pulls up a picture of a modern-looking building, the ManMed logo on the door. She scrolls to another one, then another and another, words of explanation flying fast out of her mouth. The last photo is the view from her apartment window at night, a stunning panoramic of the nearby buildings, all lit up like it's Christmas. She glances up at me, her expression hopeful. "What do you think?"

I kick at a hay pile on the ground. "It's a lot. I mean, up until a few days ago I thought you and Lucas were staying in Greenwillow. Then there was the placement. And now moving to

New York?" I look around the barn. "And what about the animals? What about the house?"

"It's a lot, I know. I'm planning to talk to the vet about the pony and animals; I'll line up care." She loops a strand of hair around her finger. "Look, I know it will be a lot for Lucas. But sometimes you have to act."

Sometimes you have to act. Her words slice through me. Whether or not she intended them to, they feel like a cut. That she, like my parents and family, thinks I'm wasting my life.

"And your decision is for me to live in New York and go back to school?" I quip.

She orients her body so she's facing me. "Don't say it like that, Nate. New York is a great opportunity for all three of us. You, me, and Lucas. There's an amazing school for him. He can get tons of services to help with his communication, motor skills, socialization. You name it. And school for you. A chance. And maybe." She pauses. "And maybe if we're living together in a way that isn't temporary, we could try to"—she bites her lower lip, a hopeful expression on her features—"pick up where we left off."

"Pick up where we left off," I repeat. "But only if I'm living in New York and going to medical school."

The hopeful look vanishes from her face. "That isn't what I meant."

"What did you mean, then? Because it sounds like you've planned things out for me."

"It's a way to move forward, Nate."

"And if I don't want to move forward?" I ask, leaving the real questions unsaid. What if I can't? What if I'm too afraid? What if I don't want to?

Olivia keeps her eyes trained on mine with the intensity of a little kid in a staring contest.

"No," I say finally.

"No?" Her eyes widen. "That's it? You don't even want to talk about it?"

"I don't. And while you didn't ask me—because why would you ask the opinion of the person who spends the most time with him? —I don't think moving to New York is best for Lucas. The city, the school, it's the opposite of everything Melanie tried to cultivate here in Greenwillow. Familiarity, controlled sensory experiences, that's what works for him. A new school in New York City won't provide that." I cross my arms. "Not that my opinion matters."

"I never said your opinion didn't matter." She kicks at the hay. "And for what it's worth, I think Melanie's approach was wrong. Lucas is capable of much more."

I scoff. "And you know this from the two months you've spent with him."

"And from my summers here. And my research. Melanie was great, but she didn't research things. She was always too flighty."

"Flighty? She was caring, Olivia."

"She was shortsighted." She angles her head toward the open barn door, then shifts her gaze back to me. "Sometimes you have to act, Nate."

Sometimes you have to act. Those words again, echoing the unwanted sentiments of my parents. Anger flushes through me; my body heats.

"Lucas and I are moving to New York this weekend," she continues. "Are you in or out?"

My eyes widen. "This weekend?" A sarcastic laugh escapes from inside of me. "Well, good luck with that. I'm out."

"Fine," she says, the thoughtful expression from earlier now one of disdain. "Will you at least finish the week?"

The bombshell that Olivia and Lucas are moving in a few days collides with the one about the placement earlier in the week, and every frivolous, small, and petty part of me wants to tell her no. But I can't do that to Lucas.

"I'll finish the week."

CHAPTER 43

LUCAS

"I think it will be great, Lu," Olivia concludes. She angles her face toward mine. I don't look at her and instead keep fiddling with the magnet balls on my bed, acting like the stupid pattern I'm making is the be-all and end-all of everything. Like Olivia didn't just tell me that she and I will be moving to New York in five days. Nate will stay here. Nate. One of the few people I'm truly comfortable around will—BOOM—be out of my life. Along with Avery. And everyone else I know except Olivia. Just like Mom and Dad. And I have nothing to say about it.

We're not taking the animals. Obviously. Olivia told me that Nate is going to care for them, then a vet tech, but I'll miss them. I'm used to seeing them every day. Otis is coming, so that's good at least, but I still can't help but think this whole move will be a disaster.

I mean, how can it not be a disaster? New everything for the person who can't get used to anything? And my senses—overloaded in my normal environment—how will they react to one of the busiest, most stimulating cities in the world? Plus, it took me eighteen years to make just one friend—Avery. Will I make any more? I doubt it. Especially because I'll likely be overwhelmed and freaked out and stimming like crazy, which is not the most appealing introduction in the world. Hi, friend. Let me flap my hands or repeat phrases or completely flip out in unpredictable and scary ways.

Olivia pats my shoulder. "It'll be alright, Lu. An adjustment, but it'll be alright."

"Will it?" I'd ask if I could. How can changing every part of my life end up being "alright?" It won't. That's the answer. I don't love my life, but I am comfortable in it.

I shift away from her, picking at the beads at a more rapid pace, losing myself in the color, the texture, and the movement. The repetitive action is soothing. I feel myself disappearing from the present, fading away to the space inside myself where I always know what's going to happen. And where it's always safe.

CHAPTER 44

OLIVIA
From the cabinet in my New York apartment, I pull out one of the dishes Lucas likes from Greenwillow. I plop my best replica of a Nate waffle on top of it. He gave me the recipe the day before I left. Also, on that final day, he helped me pack up items he thought might help Lucas with the transition. He seemed less angry, so much so that right up until the last minute I thought he might change his mind. I sat in the car, Lucas in the passenger seat with Otis's carrier on his lap, and waited for the words: "Olivia, wait."

He didn't say them, or anything, and when the atmosphere grew awkward, I finally pulled out of the drive, my eyes fixed on the rearview mirror image of Nate in pajama bottoms and socked feet. My heart skittered in my chest; doubt pulsed through my body. The positivity I felt when I made the decision to move evaporated, an empty shell of uncertainty in its place.

Now Lucas and I are two and a half days into living in New York. I can't gauge how it's going. Lucas spends most of his time in a chair that overlooks the street playing with an old set of magnetic balls. No stimming. No repetition of words and phrases. The constant sound of Animal Planet or other videos is muted. And as much as I'd been internally frustrated by those things in the past, I miss them now. The parts of Lucas that hummed in the background like white noise were, I realize, the behaviors I'd relied upon as signals that he was okay. Without them, I don't know.

I set the plate with the waffle on the table in front of Lucas. "Eat up, Lu. First day of the new school."

When he's done eating, I take a picture of him in front of the apartment door, then a selfie of the two of us. The latter one is cute; it almost looks like Lucas is smiling. I stare at it a moment, then impulsively text the photo to Nate with the caption "first day at ACE!!!!" It's a flex and totally unnecessary.

Immediately, there's a ping back and I jolt at the sound of it. I stare at the little text bubble, a thumbs-up emoji in the center of it. It seems insultingly spartan. Not that I expected confetti, but maybe a good luck or have a great day. Whatever. I click off the text and shove the phone in my pocket.

We wait for an empty elevator—Lucas does not like riding with people, I've found—and take it to the first floor. We spill out onto the street and walk in crowds sparse by New York standards but massively busy for Greenwillow. Lucas stiffens; I take his elbow. "Just a few blocks," I say. I blabber on about the school and his teacher, Mrs. Walsh, and Daniel, the onsite care worker who'll be with him a few hours before and after the school day. I make it seem like he's going to love them, but the truth is I'm not so sure.

I met them both on Zoom and again yesterday afternoon with Lucas. Mrs. Walsh, an older woman with sprayed black hair and a stripe of red lipstick, had few words. She did not hug me or Lucas. Nor was there a big sensory area in the back of her classroom for breaks, colorful pictures on the walls, or desks mashed together as tables. Daniel was the opposite of her, almost too nice, a waifish kid, the kind I could picture getting stuffed in a locker in high school.

"It's going to be great," I say, too cheerily. "You're going to learn so much."

When we reach ACE and step inside, Amelia, the receptionist, is behind the desk. "Hello, Lucas, Miss Ellison." She nods twice. One for each of us, I guess.

Lucas and I stand still at the edge of the desk, his expression flat. Unlike Greenwillow, where caregivers were encouraged to drop off and pick up in the classroom, ACE protocol is for students to go back on their own. I loved the concept in theory, but now that I'm here, I want to make sure Lucas is settled in his classroom before I leave.

"I have a question for Mrs. Walsh," I lie. "Okay if I go back a moment?"

Amelia swings her head toward me. "Any questions for Mrs. Walsh can be posted in the portal, Miss Ellison."

Right. I remind myself that this type of professionalism is the reason I was drawn to ACE to begin with. I no longer wanted to correspond through handwritten notes on the back of old worksheets. Or to have my meetings with Ms. Caddell interrupted by whomever happened to be in the classroom. I didn't want Lucas to be babied with easy material or sticker incentives or stuck in a classroom where the weather was still featured on the wall. *This*—the structure and the independence and the adherence to rules—is why we are here.

I blow out a breath and force any hesitation, any traces of regret or doubt, out of my system. I let go of Lucas's arm and tap his shoulder. "Okay, Lu. Classroom is straight back and on the left. I'll see you at dinnertime."

I step away from Lucas and move outside the building. I don't look back. I wait on the sidewalk for what feels like a full minute before circling back, pulling the door open a crack, and peering at the spot where Lucas had been standing. He's no longer there, and I step fully inside. I crane my neck toward the hallway just in time to see Lucas's tall form disappear inside Mrs. Walsh's classroom.

After, I skulk into work, feeling like I'm late even though it's not even 9:00 a.m. When I get in my office, there's a pile of files with a sticky from William on top that reads "welcome back" in nearly illegible scrawl. Nice. I push the stack aside, open the Rowan portal on my computer, and pull up the list of discovery entries I've been assigned to review. There are thousands of documents, the sheer number designed to intimidate and obscure any incriminating information. Most lawyers hate this type of needle-in-the-haystack work; I thrive on it. A legal version of Where's Waldo.

I pull up the first document, a bank statement, and scan down the long list of numbers. I read their corresponding entries, but before I can comprehend even one, a vision of Nate at the top of the driveway in his socked feet materializes in my mind. I wonder what he's doing or if he'll call tonight to find out about Lucas's first day. At the thought of Lucas, my mind wanders to him and what he might be doing in school. I conjure his schedule, then realize I'm way off track. I refocus on the bank statements and get through a few before the same thing happens again. My typically laser-focused mind feels like it's been hijacked.

Mom's ringtone, a blaring horn, blasts from my phone speaker. I stare at her image on the screen, and after the second horn blast, pick up. I'll get back on track with work after this call.

As soon as I answer, her voice fills the airspace. "Are you coming for Thanksgiving?"

I shake my head. Honestly. No questions about me. Just straight to her point. "I'm fine, Mom," I say, sarcasm oozing in the statement. "You?"

"Sorry. Ellie invited Hunter's parents for Thanksgiving. We

haven't met them, as you know, and I just need everything to be perfect."

"And my presence will enhance the perfection? Or hinder it?"

Her exasperated sigh fills the space in my office like hot air escaping from a balloon. "I'm trying to get a head count, Olivia."

Nate's Aunt Jenny invited me to the Wilder Thanksgiving potluck, and I planned to go. But that was before. It would be weird for me to go now, if I'm even still welcome. But spending Thanksgiving in the apartment alone with Lucas seems so pathetically lonely that I'd actually rather go to Mom's. "I'll be there," I say, then add, "with Lucas."

The long stretch of silence that follows those two words says volumes, and I know what Mom's thinking. That Lucas and a picture-perfect Thanksgiving aren't exactly like peas and carrots.

"He's my brother," I say finally.

"I understand that," Mom huffs out. "I'm still not sure why you took him in, Olivia."

"He's not a stray dog," I spit out. "I was asked to care for him in a legal document, there are no other suitable guardians, and I love him. He is my brother, and he's been through enough."

A second exasperated sigh sounds through the phone and I'm about to end the call when she says, "I'll put you down for two, Olivia, but..."

She lets the sentence trail off; I fill it in. "Can I take him home if he's behavioral?" I let the question hang, then continue. "Of course. It's not like Lucas would want to be there in that case anyway."

She exhales. "Thanks, Olivia. I'll be in touch." She hangs up, and her face disappears from the tiny phone screen. Anger flushes through me, and the need to vent builds up inside me like water in front of a dam. I pull up my phone contacts and my thumb hovers over Nate's name, then I see it. The clinical thumbs-up icon in response to my "first day at ACE!!!!" text. I put the phone down. I'd call someone else in the Fab Five, but like Aunt Jenny, where I stand with them is unclear. They're Nate's friends, not mine.

I shut my eyes. I breathe until the angry feelings fade enough that I can resume working. Sort of. A sporadic parade of inter-ruptions fills the rest of my day. From Marjorie. From William. From phone calls and emails and further Thanksgiving-related texts from Mom. And, of course, from the Nate and Lucas based mind-wandering that digs in anytime my mind veers from the task at hand. I wonder if Lucas is having a good day. If he's made any friends. If behind the scenes, Mrs. Walsh is a bit warmer than she seemed. And I wonder what Nate is doing. If he's applying to school or looking for jobs. I wonder about stupid things like if he's getting Big Rod's for lunch or if he still walks around the pond or if he's wearing that blue sweatshirt that brings out the color of his eyes. By the time I leave to get Lucas, I have almost nothing to show for my time here.

I do not get to speak to Mrs. Walsh when I pick up Lucas but am instead directed to look at "the portal" for updates. I knew this was the protocol, but this being his first day I thought . . . well, I thought wrong. And also, no other parent or caregiver said hello or aren't you new or anything to acknowledge either one of us. For a moment, I thought a man waved and I waved back only to realize he'd just spilled soda on his hand.

Once I have Lucas, we fight the New York crowds to get to the pizza shop, me gripping his upper arm. He gives nothing away about his day, verbally or otherwise, and a look at the portal in the pizza shop line reveals only three words: "good first day."

Ugh. I get home, feed Otis, and scarf down the pizza at the table with Lucas. I babble on to Lucas about my day the way I did in Greenwillow, but without Nate, the exercise feels useless. He's not answering, not giving me any clue as to how he's feeling, and right after dinner he returns to the big chair by the window, swipes the magnetic balls from the side table, and manipulates them.

I move to the kitchen chair and sit, squeezing my eyes shut as a torrent of frustration and loneliness bubbles up inside me. My eyes well and I resist a moment before I allow the silent streams of wet to streak down my face.

CHAPTER 45

NATE

It's been two weeks since Olivia and Lucas moved to New York, and I've heard from her exactly twice. First was a text selfie of the two of them on Lucas's first day at ACE. They both looked incredibly happy, even Lucas who was low-key smiling, a thing that happens almost never. The second communication, also via text, was a question: "what sock brands does Lucas like best?" No other context. That one was a gut punch.

I pull open the cupboard at Melanie's, note all the missing Lucas-favorite dishes, and grab a glass. I made the mistake of saying I'd stay here to watch the animals and take care of the house until I found something else to do and someplace else to live. At the time, the arrangement seemed a win-win.

It isn't.

The house is so infused with memories of Lucas and Olivia that I can't walk two steps without being confronted by one of them. Case-in-point, the missing dishes. Lucas's now empty trampoline in the yard. The back deck perch where Olivia drank her morning coffee. The scented soaps she put in all the bathrooms. Lucas's last class picture on the fridge. The place we made smores. The spot each of them would sit on the couch. Otis's bowl, left behind.

Olivia was here a few months, and nothing is the same.

I fill my glass with milk and chocolate sauce—an after school treat I used to make for Lucas—and stir it with a spoon.

I should have gone with them.

This singular regret reverberates through my mind dozens of times every day. I should have gone with them. I should have just submitted the application to ManMed, accepted the automatic interview, and gone with them. I don't think I'll get in, and I'm not even sure a medical career is what I want anymore, but at least it would have been a path forward. I'd be living my life with two people I care about instead of in a house inhabited by their ghosts.

Last week, the regret loomed so large inside me that I grabbed my phone and pulled up Olivia's number. The picture of her and Lucas on his first day of school, their heads together, broad smiles across their faces, flashed on my screen and I put the device down. If a picture is worth a thousand words, that one tells a simple story: they don't need me.

I slam down the milk, put the empty glass in the sink, and pull up the first day image on my phone again.

They don't need me.

A text flashes and my heart lifts. For a split second, while I read the words, I think it's Olivia. It isn't. It's Tessa. *You coming, bro?*

I look at the time on my phone. I was supposed be at Tessa's twenty minutes ago to help her hang bookshelves. Crap. I have nothing solid to do today but this, and I forgot about it. That's the thing about free time with no tethers; as endless and as easy as it seems, it gets away from you. And while I should be spending part of the day applying for schools and jobs or both, each time I try I end up getting stuck on the one question most people overlook as a no-brainer: have you ever been convicted of or pled guilty to a felony?

I text Tessa that I'm on my way. A few minutes later I pull into the spot in front of her townhouse, grab my toolbox, and let myself inside.

"Nate," she calls from her sitting area, "check this out."

I step into the room, the television on a network news show. An older man stands outside a courthouse with a woman dressed head to toe in hot pink spandex. Behind him, to the left, is Olivia in a fitted black suit and a tastefully made-up face, her hair blown out straight. Her expression is serious. She looks beautiful but different from the woman who wore cutoff shorts around the house, her hair in haphazard ponytails. Different from the woman who sat with her brother and watched mini marathons of Animal Planet. Different from the woman who used to smile at me so widely I felt like royalty.

Is she different, this New York version of her?

I set my toolbox down. I don't catch anything that's said about the case; I'm too riveted on Olivia's image. When the segment ends, I'm still staring at the place on the screen where she'd been. Tessa catapults from the couch and slaps me on the shoulder. "That's your girl," she says.

"She's not my girl. We're friends. Or we were."

She angles her face so it's in front of mine and rolls her eyes. "Stop it with the drama, Nate. Friends, more than friends, you like Olivia. I saw that way back when we went to the zoo and you were like all moon eyes and shit."

"I was not all moon eyes." A laugh escapes. "What does that even mean?"

"You like her, that's what it means. You liked her then; you like her now. You were happy with Olivia around. Admit it. And, clearly, Olivia likes you too or she wouldn't have gone to all that trouble to convince you to go to New York, taking pictures and all. Friends or more, she didn't have to do that."

"I know," I say, because I do know. I think about that. All the effort she made and how I quickly blew it off that night in the barn. I've been so busy being angry, assuming she was deciding a path for me in the way my parents had been doing, that I haven't considered her perspective. She doesn't want to give up her legal career at Bennett Connor. She wants to do right by her brother. She doesn't want to just walk away from our relationship. None of it is terrible, really. It's very rational, not that I should be surprised.

"You know I'd miss you like crazy," she says, "but I think you should go."

"I'm not sure if she still wants me there."

Through the thick fog of indecision in my brain, I'm not sure if I say these words out loud.

But then Tessa answers.

"There's only one way to find out."

CHAPTER 46

LUCAS

It's morning, and in my mind I'm in my bed in Green-willow. When I open my eyes, I'll look outside my bedroom window and see Dusty and the chickens and the goats and the giant tree with the tire swing. I'll get on the bus to school and Miss Alyssa, the driver, will give me a high five. I'll go to room 41 and Ms. Caddell will say, "Good morning" and flash a bright smile, and the day will start with her going over things I already know like the weather and the date. And I'll see Avery and everyone else I'm used to seeing every day.

I open my eyes.

I'm not in Greenwillow.

I'm in New York.

My bedroom is different, though Olivia tried to make it the same by bringing things from home. Like my Star Wars comforter—I got it when I was eight, don't judge—and the baby jungle animal poster—also from when I was eight. My clothes are all the same, along with toothpaste and food and shampoo and soap and some throw pillows and blankets and my preferred plates and glasses and silverware. Basically, anything that could be easily transported was transported. And I appreciate that. And I know I'm not the only one in this situation, so I'm trying not to be a big homesick baby.

But I don't like it here. I miss my house and my animals and my friends and the pond—everything familiar. And I miss Nate, how he just kind of seemed to get me as I was, no questions asked. And, of course, I miss Avery.

Anyway, with all the stimulation in New York and my perch on the apartment chair looking down on it all, I should probably like it here more. I should probably like, too, the fact that at ACE they don't go over elementary level things but instead teach at or near grade level. Their philosophy, according to Olivia, is "to teach to the expected intellect of their students rather than assume it matches the physical manifestation of ASD." Head scratch. I think it means that just because we're nonverbal doesn't mean we're dummies. So, yeah, good concept. One I should love, right? And sometimes I do, but most of the time what I'm dealing with in my body and with my emotions is enough, and I just want to be presented with information I know like the back of my hand. Stupid, right?

I know. Boo-hoo. Pity party. I'll stop whining. Time to put on my big boy pants. Today is Thanksgiving and we're going to Olivia's Mom's house. It's my first Thanksgiving without my own mom. I'd rather go back to Greenwillow.

CHAPTER 47

OLIVIA

"They're nice. Salt-of-the-earth people, right?" Mom's voice is a whisper. We're in her kitchen putting the Thanksgiving appetizers she bought at the store and is passing off as her own on silver trays.

"Yes, definitely." I stifle a laugh. Mom and Adam's obsession with meeting "the Cushings," my sister Ellie's fiancé's parents, spiraled to new heights as Thanksgiving neared. I received email instructions about what to wear and subjects to talk about as well as a directive to bring pumpkin pies from a deli in Brooklyn that Mom heard were "the best." I almost considered bailing, but I still haven't heard from Nate. I thought he would reach out by now, at least to find out about Lucas, if not me. But he hasn't, and the lack of contact makes me feel like what I felt in Greenwillow and what he felt were on entirely different stratospheres. I was willing to take a chance on our relationship in New York; he didn't even consider it. And now, he appears not to want to stay in contact at all. The whole *he's not that into you* has been a slow-release realization, the effect a deep sense of loneliness. It's the main reason I opted to come to Mom and Adam's Thanksgiving shitshow.

I'm so glad I did.

Because woven into her Thanksgiving texts, emails, and phone calls, Mom has an image of Hunter's parents, Sloane and Beau Cushing. She's assumed that the Cushings are the type that would think nothing of wearing pastel clothing with tiny whales stitched all over them or who would frequent lunch in tennis whites. Vacations in the Vineyard, anniversaries at Montauk.

Anyway . . .

They're hippies.

Yup. Hippies. And not like, hey, we're a little bohemian-leaning, Melanieish kind of hippies. They look like they came in a portal straight from the '70s. Long hair, beads, bright Baja hoodies, harem pants. Sloane brought tofu shaped like a turkey because neither she nor Beau eat animals or animal products. Beau brought a ukulele to play after dinner. And Mom and Adam are falling all over themselves to make it seem as if the Cushings are exactly who they expected to walk through the door.

It's glorious.

Because the energy for Mom to get over the mismatch of what she expected, with the reality of what is in relation to the Cushings, is so massive there's none left to make a big deal about me moving to New York with Lucas. Or about my being his guardian and how that's the worst thing ever. Or to ask about my love life. For Mom and Adam, it's all hands on deck with Operation *the Cushings are lovely, right?*

"I'll bring these out," Mom says. She picks up the tray of hors d'oeuvres. "Can you bring the champagne flutes?"

"Sure." I grab the tray of drinks and follow Mom out to the living room. The group is spread around, Ellie and Hunter together on one couch, Lucas and Shelby in chairs, and Adam and Sloane on the other couch. Beau is on the floor with his legs crossed.

"Beau," Mom says, her voice shrill, "we can get you a chair." She flails her hand toward Adam. "Honey, get him a chair."

Beau holds out a hand. "No worries, Deborah. I prefer the floor. Much better for posture and blood flow. All the bodily functions, really." He slaps the side of his rear end with an open palm. "Since I started my floor sits, my bowels have never been so regular. They're like clockwork. Nine, three, and seven, every day. You could put money on it."

Sloane rolls her eyes with affection. "No one's going to put money on your bowels, Beau."

Mom opens her mouth. I'm positive she's trying to conjure a comment and just can't think of anything. Bowel talk? At Thanksgiving dinner?

Adam nods. "We could all use some more regularity in that area, am I right? I'll join you." He moves, sits on the floor next to Beau, then contorts himself into a criss-cross-applesauce pose that I'm pretty sure his body hasn't done since elementary school. He shakes his hands out. "Feels good. Blood flowing better already. Try it, Deborah."

"Oh." Mom grabs the pendant on her necklace and moves it back and forth across the chain.

"I could use some more regular bowels," I pipe up. I stand, remove my shoes, and sit down next to Adam.

Hunter, Shelby, and Ellie get up and move to the floor in turn. Lucas remains in his chair, sitting up straight, being quiet, looping his fingers around a fidget toy. He's the *only* one acting in accordance with Mom's dinner party standards. Who would have thought?

Mom grabs the tray of appetizers and a pile of napkins that say Give Thanks! in fancy script on the front. She walks around the edge of the circle, dipping in at each person so they can take a few apps from the tray. She repeats the same sequence with the champagne flutes, the whole scenario looking like an adult version of the game duck-duck-goose.

Sloane takes a flute and angles her head toward Mom. "It's a tradition in our family to do a Thanksgiving meditation. May we lead one here?"

Mom's mouth drops open and she pauses for a beat too long. Adam answers for her. "Of course."

"Beau?" Sloane looks in his direction.

Beau closes his eyes, takes several deep breaths, then says, "May I be happy. May I be well. May I be safe. May I be peaceful and free from suffering." He repeats these phrases about a dozen times then says the same thing but substituting *you* for *I*. "May you be happy. May you be well. May you be safe. May you be peaceful and free from suffering."

When Beau started the meditation, I thought it was going to be ridiculous, right up there with the bowel comments. But it isn't. Instead of silly, the phrases are healing somehow. Like the universe and this group of people are rooting for me to be happy and well and free of pain. And me, them.

"Namaste," Beau says in conclusion.

I open my eyes. I might be imagining it, but the group looks collectively more peaceful. The energy in the room is changed too. Serene instead of stiff. I feel different. Like the mental weight I'd carried in here, the renewed loneliness, the sadness over the effective end of my relationship with Nate has been lessened somehow.

"That was beautiful, Beau," Mom says. I think she means it.

The day goes on with champagne and wine flowing freely. Mom lets go of the need for everything—or anything—to be perfect. She sets out the tofu turkey. She throws extra veggies on a regular plate, not matching and not china (gasp!), to fill in the meal gaps from the Cushings' surprise *we don't eat animals or animal products* revelation. She heats up the pizza I brought for Lucas without an eyeroll. And when Shelby spills red wine on her dress and changes into sweats, she doesn't urge her to go back and choose something more suitable.

I get a new appreciation for the Cushings during the dinner conversation. They both work for a nonprofit which focuses on worldwide access to clean drinking water. Beau shares that he not only plays the ukulele but the guitar, the piano, the recorder, and the harp. Sloane runs a free meditation class for pregnant teens on Saturdays. And despite Lucas's inability to reciprocate in kind, both Sloane and Beau include him in every conversation. They may not be what Adam and Mom expected, but I imagine that the Cushings are as impressive as any guests they've ever had.

After dinner, Mom, Adam, Hunter, and the Cushings have a drink on the patio, and I clear the plates with Ellie and Shelby. Lucas hangs out with us in the kitchen. The mood is light, the entire day being more fun than I expected. "Remember the shows?" Shelby asks.

"The ones we used to put on after Thanksgiving when we were little?" I laugh and pick up a dish to dry. "They were awful."

"We thought they were so great," Ellie chimes in.

I smile. I did love putting on those shows, as bad as they were. "Remember the dress-up box?" I ask. "With all those hats and dresses and the high-heeled shoes."

"And the boas," Shelby says.

"The boas!" I say, remembering. The hot pink boas Mom had gotten from New Orleans were our favorite. They came apart little by little each year, the bright feathers flying across the yard and eventually becoming part of birds' nests.

The doorbell rings and I throw a turkey-themed dish towel on the counter. "I'll get it." I half jog to the door, thinking about pink boas and silly kid shows. For the first time in as long as I can remember, I feel part of my immediate family. I'm not thinking about Nate at all.

Until I pull open the front door.

CHAPTER 48

NATE

Olivia's mouth drops open. "Nate?" she says just as Lucas rounds the corner and smashes into my chest.

I toss the bouquet I'm holding to Olivia and envelop him in a tight squeeze. He likes this type of physical contact, but he doesn't often initiate it. This is new. I step back and look at him. "Lucas. Good to see you, man." I shift my gaze back to Olivia. "Hey."

"Hey."

There's a long silence which I know I should fill—I'm the surprise here—but I can't.

"What are you doing here?" she blurts, the flowers gripped in her hands. "I mean, you haven't called. Not even Lucas."

"I know." I lift my eyes to meet hers.

"And now you're here?"

She says it like a question. I get it. I pushed off her offer and now, weeks later, here I am. Surprise!

She gestures for me to come in and shuts the door behind me. At least that's good. I'm in the door.

I step inside the two-story foyer, a sparkly chandelier overhead. Everything looks breakable, and by habit, I shoot a look at Lucas. He's leaning against the door. Fine.

"I came to apologize. I thought you were happy and that maybe me not coming with you guys was a relief. And I didn't hear from you, so I assumed all was good. But I should have called."

"So that's it? You traveled four hours on Thanksgiving to say you're sorry?" She shakes her head. "How did you even find us?"

"I guessed."

"You guessed?"

I nod. "You mentioned the town you grew up in and I knew your mom and Adam's last name." I shrug. "Their address was easy to find."

She grips the flowers tighter, her face softening for the first time since I got here. "But what if you'd been wrong? Wycoff is four hours from Greenwillow."

"Four hours of driving? It's nothing. I really wanted to see you and Lucas." I look down and back up again. "I missed you guys. A lot."

A blush creeps across her pale features. I've been so busy thinking about my speech, so full of nerves about how she and Lucas would react to my being here, that it takes until this moment to really take her in. She's wearing a hunter green sweater dress and tall brown boots, pieces of her hair pulled back in a barrette, the rest of it long. She looks pretty, understatedly beautiful, really.

"Plus," I continue, "someone really smart once told me sometimes you have to act." I pause. "I applied to ManMed."

Her face blooms into a smile. "Really?"

"Yup." I tap my foot. I know why I'm here. I know what I want to ask. I just need a moment to gather courage.

"That's great, Nate," she says.

Footsteps sound in the hall and I know the perfect time to

ask is going to run out. "Is your offer from the barn still open?" I rush out the words.

Understanding cascades across her features and any doubt I had that she didn't want me to come after all fades in its brightness. "New York? You're willing to move?"

I tip my head. "I'll move if you're still willing to have me."

The same broad smile from earlier stretches across her face and she flings herself at me. "Of course we're still willing to have you." She throws her arms around my neck and pulls me to her, her body slammed up against my own. She lets go almost as quickly, I think realizing at the same time as I do that, by agreement, we're just friends and that this full-body hug is way too intense.

"Oh my gosh," she gushes. "You won't regret it. I'll make sure you taking this chance is worth it, I promise. There's so much to see in New York. Right, Lu?" She bumps Lucas's arm. "In fact, we're planning to see the Rockefeller tree tomorrow. You could come!"

She's beaming, so clearly thrilled with my decision to move that I kick myself for not saying yes to begin with.

She tips her head up at me, and she looks so adorably happy that I hope she meant what she said in the barn about us picking up where we left off. But even if she didn't, even if she's changed her mind and wants to just be friends, I'll take New York with Olivia and Lucas in it over Greenwillow without them.

"So yes? You'll come?"

"I'll come."

How could I say no?

* * *

THE NEXT MORNING we're in front of the Rockefeller tree at 5:00 a.m. It's the least crowded time to see the tree, so the best time for Lucas.

"You know this tree has something like 50,000 lights and five miles of wire," Olivia tells me. She adjusts her hat, blue with a giant pom-pom on top.

I take a step back, angle my phone camera at the tree, and shoot. The tree is majestic. I understand now why so many people are drawn to it, how it's part of the New York experience, like the Rockettes and Madison Square Garden and Broadway.

I sling an arm around Lucas. "What do you think, Lu?"

He doesn't respond with body language or otherwise, his eyes fixed on the tree. He looks happy. Maybe I've been wrong, and New York has been good for him. Maybe ACE is just what he needed.

Olivia grabs Lucas's hand. "Do you want to see the window displays?" she asks. "Before it gets busy?"

"I think we have to," I pipe in. "It is New York at Christmastime."

"Good answer." She loops her free arm through mine and the three of us walk down the sidewalk. We walk slowly, Lucas—and me—enjoying the sites of Manhattan for the first time. It's nice. Different in the best possible way.

Olivia directs us onto Sixth Street and Lucas stops at a window with a moving Ferris wheel. We step back from him, and Olivia squeezes my arm with a gloved hand. "I'm so glad you decided to come."

I angle my face down at her. "Me too."

CHAPTER 49

LUCAS

Nate's here. He showed up at Olivia's mom's yesterday out of the blue. He stayed the night last night in the apartment, with me in the other twin bed in my room. He's getting his stuff from Greenwillow this week and moving in. Right!?

Normally, I wouldn't want to share my bedroom, but I'm okay if it's Nate. And—yes!—no more Daniel in the mornings and afternoons. He was a nice enough guy, but way intense. There was never a time to just hang out. It was drill, drill, drill, all the time, each one of them designed to work on my myriad of deficits. I get it. There's a lot to work on when it comes to me. But let me live a little too, okay?

Anyway, as if Nate being here wasn't enough, we just saw the Rockefeller tree. I've seen it on television and it's cool, but not like it is in person. It's ginormous, and Olivia said there were 50,000 lights, which, of course, me being a light fanatic, I loved. No one much was around, and I got a clear view. I couldn't help but think how much Avery would have liked the tree and how I wish I could take her here to see it. Just the tree, not all of New York. New York is way too crazy and loud for Avery.

Maybe someday. I imagine Avery and me at the tree together and think on the vision so hard that it becomes almost real. I wish it were.

CHAPTER 50

OLIVIA
"Are you ready for tonight?" I ask.

Nate looks up from where he's sitting on the couch. "For the surprise? You bet."

Nate has been here for two weeks. It's been great and Lucas is noticeably peppier, but I can't say it's been the experience I promised. The Rowan trial, scheduled for March, has required massive amounts of additional work. I've been busy and haven't taken Nate to anything cool since the Rockefeller tree. He says it's fine, he doesn't need his hand held, and I know that's true. But I wanted to experience the city with him, in the same way he showed me Greenwillow. Never too late, so I've carved out tonight and planned something I think he'll love.

The doorbell rings. I answer and Shelby and Ellie tumble inside, bits of snow flurries on their bright colored ski hats. Shelby has a pizza box in her hand. Ellie holds up a grocery bag. "Ice cream."

A bonus since Thanksgiving is that Shelby, Ellie, and I have become closer. When I told them about my plan tonight, they offered to come over and hang with Lucas. Nate and I eat pizza with them, and after, we stuff ourselves in massive amounts of warm outerwear per my instructions. We say our goodbyes and waddle out of the apartment and down the hall. Once we're in the elevator, I press the button for the lobby. The doors slide shut, and Nate and I are alone for the first time since he moved in.

So far, I've been the most exceptional friend ever. I don't venture too close to him when we're in the same room; I don't bring up the taboo topic of *more*. It hasn't been that hard. I'm busy, Nate's been getting used to things, and Lucas is almost always around. It's easy to keep the sexual tension at bay.

It's harder now.

And as soon as the elevator door slides shut, the tension rachets up inside me. My nostrils fill with the woodsy scent of his aftershave, and though we're a foot apart, I feel his presence like I'm touching him. I wonder briefly if he's having thoughts like this about me, if his pulse is faster, if his body is flooded with warmth.

Probably not.

The elevator slides open, and we spill out into the lobby and make our way to the sidewalk. "No hints?" he asks.

"Why would I give you a hint?"

"To be nice."

I push open the door. "Well, I'm not nice."

A broad smile stretches across his features. "Now's the time to tell me."

"We'll get there by car. There's a hint." I raise my hand, and a cab zooms to the sidewalk. I pull a note from my pocket and hand it to the driver.

"Wow. You really want this to be a secret."

"I do." I lean back and puff out a breath. "I haven't shown you much of New York. I wanted tonight to be special. And surprises are special."

He lifts an eyebrow. "I hadn't pegged you as a surprise girl."

"I love surprises," I tell him, and it's true. I love wrapped gifts and surprise parties and secret events. I even like the mystery-flavored Dum-Dums lollipops. "Now close your eyes."

"Really?"

"Yup."

He closes his eyes, and while this wasn't my intention, it gives me a chance to really look at him without feeling self-conscious. I angle myself on the seat and look in his direction. Probably something to do with the layers he's wearing, but he looks exceptionally muscular. His eyelashes are long and jet black, and his hands have the nicks and cuts that come with the work he's always doing for others.

The cab makes its way through the streets of midtown, stopping and starting at traffic lights in the haphazard pattern every New Yorker gets used to. I avert my gaze from Nate and look out the window at the pedestrians hurrying along and the signs of Christmas that adorn each window. I puff out a breath. I do love it here.

When the cab comes to a stop, I tell Nate to keep his eyes closed.

"Really?"

"Yes. Really." I pay the driver via app and help Nate out of the cab. I guide him forward until we reach part one of our destination. "Okay. Open them."

His eyes fly open. We're standing on a pathway lined with huge elm trees sprinkled with light snow, the middle of them forming an arch. Cast-iron lampposts with globes on top sit in front of the trees, illuminating the space. Benches pepper the walkway, all of them covered with a light dusting of snow. Giant skyscrapers peek through the trees in the distance.

I hold out my hands. "Ta da."

"Central Park."

I smile. "You haven't been yet, right?"

"No." He looks around. "But I've been wanting to come. It's on the list."

The list. We made it together at my apartment kitchen table the night of Thanksgiving. All the places Nate wanted to see; all the places he didn't know about that I promised to take him. I made a show of putting it on the fridge with a magnet. I'm glad we are finally doing something on it.

I grab his hand. "Come on. There's more to the surprise." I pull him down the walk, our boots making footprints on the snow. It's crowded—Central Park always is—but it still feels like we're alone somehow. Together in a city of strangers.

I should let go of his hand. He's on the path and he doesn't need me guiding him. But I like the feel of it, the feel of him near me. And friends hold hands all the time. Right? I angle my head toward his. "What are you thinking?"

"I'm thinking about how nice this is," he says. "It's like something out of a movie."

"It is the most filmed public park in the world."

"Yeah?"

"Yup. Over 500 films were shot here."

"How do you know that?"

"My dad told me. He loved New York and was full of little snippets of information he'd pass on to me."

"Like?"

"Like New York is home to the first pizzeria. The Empire State building has its own zip code. More than 800 languages are spoken here. Anyway, ta da." I let go of his hand and gesture to the ice-skating rink in Central Park. The iconic rink is surrounded by cone-shaped Christmas trees of various sizes illuminated with thousands of tiny white lights. Skyscrapers dot the landscape in the background, their lights brightening the darkening sky. A myriad of ice skaters in colorful winter gear glide across the man-made pond. "Have you ever ice-skated?"

He snorts. "Of course. Every winter. You?"

"Once when I was a kid. I was terrible, but I think I'll be better now."

"Probably, but I can teach you if you need help."

We check in and get our skates. I stuff my feet into them and Nate smirks in my direction. My face flushes from his attention. "What?"

"You're doing it wrong."

I lift a foot. "I'm just tying them."

"You're tying them wrong." He bends down. "Let me." He gently takes a foot and puts it on one of his thighs. He looks into my eyes. "You need to lace them tight. Helps with stability."

There's nothing remotely sexy, remotely romantic about those statements but my body responds as if he just declared his undying love. A flush of warmth washes through me; every sense in my body tingles as if on high alert. I touch his arm. "Thank you."

"Of course." He pulls the laces tighter on one skate, then the other, before directing his gaze back at me for the second time. "You should be all set now." He taps on the skate and sets it on the ground.

The bit of contact with the earth pulls me back to reality. We weren't just having "a moment." Nate was fixing my skate.

"You ready?" I ask.

"Ready when you are."

We move to the entry point for the rink. It's crowded, and we need to wait for a break in the skaters to step onto the ice. Nate goes first and extends his hands out to me. I take them both, step out, and . . . plop. I slip and fall onto the ice. "Whoops."

"Happens to the best of us," Nate says and helps me up. Whoosh. I fall again. We repeat the sequence a third time and we both fall, skidding across the ice like cartoon characters.

"Sorry." I slide to the wall and pull myself up using it as a support. "Man, I still suck at this."

Nate shakes his head. "You'll get it. Let's go around the edge of the rink to warm up." He slides over, next to me. "I should have suggested that first."

We move around the edge, me hanging on to the wall like it's a piece of life support. I get a bit more comfortable after one lap, even more after two. Still holding on to the wall, I look back at Nate. He's looking in my direction with a gaze so tender I want to bottle it up.

"Do you think you're ready?" he asks.

"I think so."

He moves away from the wall and holds out his hand. I take it. "Small steps," he says. "Once you do those for a bit, you can glide."

I take some tentative steps, Nate next to me. I take more steps, easier.

"Good. Try to glide."

I do. One step, a second, a third. Soon Nate and I are making our way around the rink, his hand in mine, *Holly Jolly Christmas* piping through speakers. I love the feel of him close, and I wish we were here on a real date instead of a friendship outing. We move around the rink again. I'm not as fast or as pretty as the other skaters, but I'm doing it.

"You're getting it, Liv. Good job."

Liv. He hasn't called me that before. I like it, like the feeling of familiarity it imbues. I look in his direction, but the tiny change in movement causes me to lose my balance. I start to flail. Nate reaches his arms around me and pulls me upright. He makes sure I've regained my balance before letting go. "You're okay. I got you." He grabs my hands. "I got you."

His words pierce through a layer of protective emotional armor. How long has it been since someone "got me"? Since I didn't feel like I was on an island of one? I don't want to be *just friends* with Nate. I want more. I think he does too. Maybe? He guides me to the nearest wall for a break.

"I really like you, Nate."

"I like you too."

I shake my head, ready to go for this whether it's a good idea or not. "No. I really like you." I move closer to him, my heart pounding, my pulse racing. "And I don't want to be just friends." Before I can talk myself out of it, I pull his face to mine and kiss him.

CHAPTER 51

NATE

Olivia pulls back from the kiss and tilts her head up. "Did I just ruin things?"

"Ruin things? Are you kidding?" He shakes his head. "Being just friends with you has been the bane of my existence. You made things infinitely better by making the first move. Thank you."

She kisses me again. "This is okay?"

"Umm. Yes."

She kisses me again. "And this."

"That too."

I move so that I'm in front of her, her back against the rink wall, my hand on either side of her. "How's this?" I tip her face up toward mine, lean down, and kiss her. She pulls me toward her and all the want that's been built up for months explodes into this moment, this kiss. We stay locked together and the distractions of the bright lights, the hundreds of people, and the Christmas tunes piping out of a nearby speaker fade away. A teenage boy yells "get a room" as he skates by and Olivia and I both smile, our teeth knocking together.

I pull back and kiss the side of her head, inhaling her scent. I put my mouth by her ear. "Do you want to get out of here?"

She inclines her head up and meets my eyes. "Yes."

I keep my gaze on her a long moment, noticing things about her face I haven't before. Her eyelashes, dark at the bottom, light at the tips. The black flecks in her otherwise green-brown eyes. How one side of her lip curls up more than the other when she smiles. I kiss that spot, then step back. "Let's get out of here, then." I pull Olivia from the wall, wrap my arms around her shoulders, and guide her with small steps to the exit. Once we're out of the rink, she sits on the bleachers by the skate rentals. I kneel on one knee in front of her. "I'll do it."

She smiles. "Very chivalrous, Nate, but I can get it."

I shake my head. "I know you can get it, but I want to take care of you. You deserve that." She doesn't move and I gently put her foot on my thigh, untie the laces, and loosen them. I repeat the process on the other side. The entire experience feels way more erotic than it should considering we're bundled in layers, there are two crying children next to us, and hundreds of ice skaters just feet away.

She kisses the top of my head, her lips lingering there a long moment. "Thank you."

"Always."

The entire way back, from Central Park to the apartment building, we touch each other. I put my hand on the small of her back as we walk toward the sidewalk. She puts her hand on my thigh in the back of the cab. In the back seat, I kiss her hand, her neck, her forehead. She smooths back my hair, touches my jawline. When the cab stops, I help her out. She grabs my waist and leads me inside the apartment building. In the elevator, I pull her to me in what's meant as a chaste kiss that quickly turns to more. When the elevator doors slide open, she grabs my hand, and we tumble toward the apartment door like little kids.

When we're standing in front of the apartment, she drops my hand. "We should stop."

My body goes still. I don't want to stop. This is the relationship I've been waiting for, the one I didn't think I'd deserved. "What?"

She stands on her tiptoes and whispers in my ear, her lips brushing my skin. "Just until Ellie and Shelby leave. And Lucas goes to bed."

"Right." I exhale. "Makes sense."

She puts her hand on the doorknob.

I shake my hands and jog in place.

Her mouth curves into a smile. "You good there, Nate?"

"Yeah. Just shaking out the romance."

She snorts out a laugh. "Shaking out the romance," she repeats.

I'm about to explain further when the door swings open, Ellie in its frame. "You're back, early," she exclaims. "We thought we heard someone out here. It's just Olivia and Nate," she calls out and pushes the door open farther. We step inside, take off our outer gear, and set it in the closet.

Lucas is sitting on his favorite spot on the couch, *Back to the Future* blaring on the television screen. Empty ice cream bowls sit on the coffee table. Olivia talks to her sisters in the kitchen. I sit next to Lucas, and bits of their conversation waft over to me. It's so normal, so mundane, that I almost feel like I've fictionalized what just happened between us.

Everything is exactly the same. As physically charged and as emotionally changed as I feel right now, the universe of Apartment 4B remains unaltered.

She ushers Ellie and Shelby out after a few minutes, and we sit on either side of Lucas and watch the end of *Back to the Future*. I'm not usually bothered by the repeat movies. But right now, all I can think about is Olivia and what we started, and all I want is for this movie to end before either of us has the bright revelation that this—living together and dating—is a horrifically bad idea.

The movie inches along, scene by scene by scene. God. Was it always this long? I steal glances and Olivia, as far as I can tell, is engrossed in this millionth retelling. When we finally reach the end, the scene where Doc is on the clock and Marty's in the DeLorean, I catch Olivia's eye.

And she yawns.

Not a little *hand over my mouth* one, but a big gaping *I am going to fall asleep standing up one*. But then, her eyes still on mine, she winks.

I smile and blow out a breath. Once the movie is over, she and I jump up from the couch like it's on fire. We hurry Lucas along, both of us helping him with bed-related tasks he normally does on his own. He doesn't seem to notice or care, and within twenty minutes he's settled in his room. I shut his door, swing around, and see Olivia behind me. I grab her waist and shimmy her toward her own bedroom door. I brush her hair back from her face with my hand. "Do you still want to be friends?" I mean the question earnestly, but my voice is husky, my want clear.

Olivia takes my hand. "Nate," she says as she pulls me through her bedroom door. "I can honestly say I never want to be friends with you again."

I widen my eyes in mock surprise. "Never?"

She shakes her head. "Never." She shuts the door, and I draw her face toward mine and kiss her. My hands skim down her body and she lets out a soft moan. I respond immediately. "You're not going to take a phone call, are you?" I ask through the kiss.

I feel her smile. "Not this time, Nate."

CHAPTER 52

LUCAS

Nate just came into the room and slid under the covers like he's been here all night. I'd give a big fat eyeroll if I could manage it. Not because he and Olivia hooked up, but because they think I didn't notice their attraction. Hello! I live with you both. I could tell how much you liked each other way back in Greenwillow.

Nate was always nice, but I could feel his sadness, you know. His sadness lifted when Olivia moved in. And Olivia. When Nate's around, she's relaxed in a way she'd never been growing up and definitely not in the pre-Nate time here. That time was rough. She tried, but she was always hurried. I could feel her stress even if she never used that word.

I'm glad for them. Jealous even. Not because it's Olivia—my sister, gross—but because they have each other. Finding that person you can share things with? It's golden, you know. For me, that person would be Avery. I want to share my messed up, supersensitive, not-quite-working self with her. I don't care that she's equally messed up, supersensitive, and not quite working. I'd love her just as she is.

I think I already do.

CHAPTER 53

OLIVIA
Two months later
I stand before William. "Today's the day I need to leave early."

He looks up from a conference table littered with discovery and briefs and trial binders, a paper carton of food and half-empty cup of coffee next to him. "What?"

"It's four," I say. "Nate's taking me out. Remember?" I don't add that it's Friday and that I've been working around the clock. I don't say that I'm tired and overworked and have pushed just about all of the care of Lucas onto Nate for weeks. I don't explain how I feel mired in guilt, how the stupid New York list on the fridge haunts me, or how Nate and I rarely have sex anymore because I don't have the energy. I don't say these things, but all of them teem in my mind as I wait for William's response.

He whips off his glasses, squints, and puts his thumb and forefinger on either side of the bridge on his nose. His eyes are red, etched with deep, dark circles. "The trial is in less than two weeks."

"I know."

Had he asked me, I would have told Nate that this weekend wasn't a good time for a date. But he didn't ask. He just announced that he had something special planned for tonight and tomorrow. A surprise. I would have said no, but I've been such a grade-A sucky girlfriend, I didn't feel like I could. Being unavailable to work for part of one weekend? It shouldn't be a problem.

William blows out a long breath. "It's really not a good time, Olivia." He circles his hand around the conference room. "It's all hands on deck here since the new discovery."

"I know." The new discovery blew up our theory of the case, and months of strategy-work became moot. The team has been working on new angles.

He picks up a paper coffee cup, drains it, and throws it toward a waste bin. The cup bounces off the rim and falls to the floor. He stares at it a moment, then swings his head back to me. "Can't this thing with Nate wait until after the trial? I mean, we all have lives, but this is it. The end. It's not like we can go back for a redo once it's over."

I open my mouth to say no, but I can't get the word out. William's not wrong. Everyone here has something they'd rather be doing. Plus, I don't even know what this surprise is. For all I know, it's dinner and a movie at home. "Let me call Nate."

I step out of the conference room, pull out my phone, and punch in Nate's contact. The conference room walls are glass and everyone on Team Rowan—from William, to the admins, to the intern who started *this* week—is around that table pouring through case law and discovery and endless legal briefs. It wouldn't be right to leave.

Nate answers, his voice upbeat. "Hey, Liv. You on your way?"

He sounds like a man excited about a surprise.

Shit.

I grip the phone to my ear. "Any chance you can you tell me what we're doing?"

He scoffs. "Nice try. No. It's a *surprise*."

The way he says surprise tugs at my heart.

I keep my voice light. "But is it the kind of surprise we can do anytime?"

No response.

"Nate?"

"Can you not make it?"

The disappointment in his tone guts me. "It's not the best time."

"It's a good surprise."

The pit in my gut intensifies, and I swing my head back to the conference room. Everyone is there. I can't leave. "I'm sorry," I blow out. "There's a lot of work still and everyone is strapped in. It seems wrong to leave. Like missing one of the last practices before the big game, that kind of thing."

"I can get the idea without the sports analogy, Olivia."

"Sorry." I pause. "I just"—I start, then blurt—"I can go tomorrow."

Tomorrow is the second part of the surprise, and though Team Rowan will be strapped in then too, the atmosphere on weekends is more open-ended. I'll be able to come into the office around whatever Nate has planned.

"Okay."

"Really?"

"Really. Do what you need to do. The main part of the surprise is tomorrow." He pauses. "I'll see you later, Liv."

He disconnects before I can say anything else. I return to the conference room, the sliver of guilt in my gut like an infected splinter. I lean into the camaraderie of working with colleagues. William orders pizza, wings, mozzarella sticks, and salad from a nearby Italian joint. One of the newer associates gets a case of cheap beer. When the food arrives, the conference room smells like fresh bread, tomato sauce, and melted cheese. We work and talk while we eat from thin paper plates and drink beer from the bottles. Jokes emerge, either new installments of old jests or entirely new inside humor. Work gets done in haphazard fashion, but the overall feel is one of a team. Win or lose, we're in this together.

It's nearly ten o'clock and I'm well past the point of exhaustion when I pull myself down the hall toward the apartment, my briefcase-purse slung across my body like a work sash. Party noise blasts from somewhere in the hall. Though it is Friday night and not all that late by normal standards, irritation coats my nerves. Is someone seriously having a party? All I want is to tumble into bed, snuggle under the covers, and sleep like it's a sport.

When I'm directly in front of my own apartment door, it sounds, for a second, like the noise is coming from inside. I step back. No. Right? No. Nate hardly knows anyone in New York. And he wouldn't throw a party. Not with Lucas here. The noise must be coming from somewhere else.

I slide my key into the lock and push open the door. When I walk inside, I'm assaulted by whoops and screams, Tessa and Suzanne barreling toward me with their arms open. "Surprise!" They wrap their limbs around me and squeeze, and I realize that *this*—these people, our friends, being in New York—is Nate's surprise. When the hug huddle ends, I stand back. Jared and Nate stand behind the women. Lucas and Avery are sitting at a series of card tables pushed together in front of the kitchen space. Crepe streamers are looped around the light fixture over them; balloons are tied to foldable chairs.

"Oh my gosh," I say, the words inadequate.

"Happy birthday." Jared lunges forward and slaps me on the shoulder.

I'm about to protest that it's not my birthday, not for six months, when Nate says, "Half-birthday."

Half-birthday. These four people travelled hours to New York to celebrate an event that no one ever celebrates. And I blew them off. I blew this off. Nate's surprise. The realization lodges in my gut like a stone.

"I know you've been stressed," Nate says. "And how much you love surprises. So"— he gestures toward the group—"surprise." He bridges the small space between us and kisses my cheek.

"Thank you." I lean toward him. "You should have told me the Fab Five was here," I whisper.

He cocks his head. "Would it have made a difference?" He doesn't look angry, but the question carries an edge, the meaning clear: it would have been okay to blow off him but no one else.

I step out of my heels. "Of course not," I say, recovering. "I just feel bad for being late."

Suzanne holds her wine glass straight up in the air. "Well, we started without you, so no worries. And Nate took us to the M&M store."

"The M&M store?" The two-story megastore in Times Square was one of the first places I'd put on "the list." But, of course, we haven't been there yet.

"You should sit down," Nate interjects. He ushers me toward the assembly of card tables in a way that's reminiscent of our Central Park ice-skating experience, when I needed to lean on him just to say upright. He steers me to a chair, and I collapse into it. A round chocolate birthday cake with gooey icing sits on a plate in front of me.

Tessa thrusts a glass of wine in my direction "Happy half-birthday, girl."

I take the wine, gulp down a long sip, and hold my glass up. "Here's to twenty-eight and a half."

"Here's to that," Suzanne says.

Our glasses meet in the center. Nate pulls a matchbook from his pocket and holds it up. "Ready for cake?"

"Who wouldn't be ready for cake?" I say, trying to be light.

"Here goes nothing, then." He lights each candle, and when he's finished a raucous and off-key version of *Happy Half-Birthday* rings out in the apartment.

"Make a wish," Tessa insists.

"Of course," I say, but as I blow at the candles, I can't think of any wish other than to do better. I don't know even know at what. Everything. *Do better, Olivia. Do better.*

We eat huge slices of cake and catch up. The group shares typical things that, had I kept in touch better, I would have known already. Suzanne has a new graphic design client, and Jared is up for a promotion. Tessa is still in the same job and helping her mom at Include in her spare time.

"So how are you doing, legal superstar?" Jared asks.

"Legal superstar?" I scoff. "Hardly."

"Don't be modest." Tessa points her fork in my direction. "That case is always on the news. It's a big deal."

I tip my head. "It's going well," I lie. I'm not about to share that Team Rowan is on the precipice of losing one of the biggest cases the firm has ever had.

"Fantastic," Tessa says. "And Nate," she shifts her head in his direction. "How's the med school stuff going?"

He takes a long swig of beer. "Pretty good. I have an interview at ManMed next week."

My mouth drops open, surprise at this statement hitting my bloodstream like a shot. Nate has been waiting for the interview date since he moved here. He got it? Why didn't he tell me? "They scheduled it? When?"

He shifts in his seat. "Couple days back."

Couple days back? Couple days back and he didn't tell me. I want to demand why, but not in front of our friends.

"Doctor in the house!" Jared says and holds his hand up.

Nate smacks Jared's hand with his own. "Not yet, not yet. Have to get in first."

"You will, buddy. You got it."

There's a smattering of congratulations before the conversation digresses toward events I didn't partake in and people I don't know. Which makes sense. They're the friends; I'm the newcomer.

I listen, but fatigue overtakes me, and my eyelids get heavy. I try to stay awake, but my eyes keep shutting. Nate's hand cups my shoulder. "Liv," he whispers, "you're tired. Why don't you go to bed?"

"No. No. I'm good."

"Go to bed, hon," Suzanne says. "We'll all still be here tomorrow."

"I can stay up," I say, but after a minute the whole open-closed eyelid sequence starts again. I can't do it. I'm too drained. "I'm sorry guys," I say. I get up and go to bed. I'm probably the first person to ever sleep through her own surprise party.

CHAPTER 54

NATE

I wake up in bed next to Olivia, her body curled next to mine, Otis at our feet. Her eyes flicker open, and as she's the early riser between the two of us, I know she's been awake for a while. She props herself up and kisses my cheek. "Thanks for last night."

"Sure. Sorry for the timing. It was hard to coordinate schedules and all."

She falls back onto the pillow. "Don't be sorry. I'm the asshole in this scenario."

It would seem the right thing to say is that she isn't, that I get it, the work thing and all. And I do, but more and more it feels like I'm in the way. Like my being here is a hassle instead of help.

"Why didn't you tell me about the ManMed interview?" she asks softly.

I stare at the ceiling, wishing I had an answer for her. I planned to tell her, then I just didn't. Just like I didn't tell her about the job interview I had at a blood bank two weeks ago. I took it on a whim, a safeguard in case ManMed didn't work out, and botched it royally.

"It's not a big deal." I fix my gaze on the ceiling. "It's just the date."

She slides her hand under my T-shirt. "It is a big deal," she says, her voice quiet. "The interview, ManMed. It's the reason you came here to New York."

I want to say the reason was her, but the admission feels pathetic. "I'm sorry." I smile. "The next time I get a medical school interview, I'll tell you."

She lets out a soft chuckle, and for a snapshot of time things seem light before silence fills the space between us again. In Greenwillow and when I first got to New York, stretches of silence like these were nice, a tribute to how comfortable we were with each other. The quiet feels charged now, like unsaid things course beneath the calm.

Olivia brushes a lock of hair off her face. "Do you like it here?"

Do I like it here? I shut my eyes. It isn't a question that can be answered with a yes or no. "Sometimes."

"And sometimes not?"

I open my eyes and angle my body so we're facing each other, our heads on our respective pillows, our noses inches apart. "Sometimes I miss Greenwillow."

She nods and after a moment speaks again. "Is it because I'm not around? Is Lucas too much?"

My jaw clenches. "Lucas is fine. And you've got Rowan coming up." I sit up in bed. "I'm just at a crossroads right now. I'm not sure what I'll do if I don't get into ManMed." Or if I even want to go if I do.

She sits up and puts a hand on my shoulder. "Can I do anything to help with the interview? Ask you questions?"

I pull back. "No. I'm good." I pause. "But could you be standby for Lucas this Wednesday?"

"Of course." She slaps my shoulder. "You don't have to ask that. I'm his sister."

She says it indignantly, but I honestly don't know how easy Olivia would be to contact during the week. I don't typically call her.

Our conversation is interrupted by a double rap on the door. "You lovebirds decent?" Tessa asks.

I look down. I'm in boxers; Olivia is wearing my old Pirates T-shirt. "All clear," I say.

Tessa charges in, fully dressed and ready for the day. "Jared and I are going in search of New York bagels. You want anything?"

"I can get them," I offer.

"I'm not waiting on bagels for *this*"—she draws a finger line across my body in the air—"to be ready to go."

"Fair enough. I'd try Bagelicious on Fifth."

"Sure."

Tessa and Jared set out, and when they return, we eat bagels around the family room, remnants of last night's party strewn across the table behind us. After breakfast, we take two Ubers to Chelsea Piers, the launch site for the Lady Liberty Experience. I picked Lady Liberty because the boats are yachts, much smaller than the big cruise lines and less stimulating for Avery and Lucas. They also have assigned tables inside and they serve food.

We board the yacht, settle in at our eight-person table, Lucas and Avery by the window. It's a sunny day, cold but with a bright blue sky, and for the first time in as long as I can remember, Olivia looks relaxed. Her shoulders are slack, her posture normal.

We order drinks and the yacht starts cruising up the Hudson, the New York skyline edging slowly by us as we pass. Olivia points out landmarks like the Empire State Building and Millionaire's Row. Tessa snaps pictures for the group. We cruise

under the George Washington Bridge and past the Grand
Palisade Cliffs and Olivia gives more of the facts she learned
from her dad. The cliffs were formed 200 million years ago and
are about 800 feet above sea level. She tells us that the New
Jersey town behind them, Weehawken, is based on the Native
American word Wee-Awk-En, meaning rocks that look like
trees.

"Wow, Olivia, you're like a tour guide," Jared says.

She shifts away from the window. "I love New York. I want
you guys to love it too."

Tessa swings an arm around Olivia. "We love it because
you're here."

"And there's an M&M store," Suzanne adds.

I hold up my glass. "To New York and to M&Ms."

"Here, here," Jared says, and we clink our glasses in the
table's center.

Lunch is served. Bright green salad and savory chicken with
fresh bread. I don't know if it's the company or the atmosphere
or the fact that Olivia is so relaxed, but I'm infused with a sense
of well-being.

Kind of like everything is going to work out.

CHAPTER 55

L UCAS
   I love the cruise. It's slow and it's pretty and I'm surrounded by people I trust. And Avery. Biggest bonus of all. I didn't know she was coming. Avery and I are sitting next to each other. Tessa takes a picture of the two of us, our heads together, the skyline in the background. It's one of those cameras where the picture shoots out the bottom and she gives Avery and me each a photo. I stuff it in my bag. No way am I losing it. It's the only photo of Avery that I have.

   Avery looks like she's enjoying the cruise. The landscape changes from skyscrapers to smaller buildings to cliffs. Having lived in the city for four months, I've seen my share of big buildings and been inside a bunch. And though Olivia and Nate try to minimize stimulation by keeping pedestrian outings to a minimum, I've had my fill of it all. Of the crowded sidewalks and busy streets and loud noises and weird smells. But looking at the buildings from a distance, I can appreciate the city. From out here, the skyscrapers look cool.

   I wonder what Avery thinks of them? There are a lot of questions I'd ask Avery if I could. Like how are things going at school? Is Randolph still having those crazy tantrums because the lights are too bright? Has Ms. Caddell figured out that that is the problem yet? Have you been to any events at Include? How's the weather and have you seen my horse and goats and chickens? Do you know if they're doing okay? What do you think of it here? Do you miss me?

That last one is important. Because I miss Avery very much.

CHAPTER 56

OLIVIA
Wednesday. Interview day. I kiss Nate goodbye, wish him luck, and leave for work. I'm excited for him, and for us. Everything since Saturday has felt different. I don't know if it's the infusion of time with friends or the relaxing cruise or the renewed sense of closeness with Nate—probably all three—but I feel happy, like if I were a Disney character, animated birds would fly around me kind of happy.

I swing open the door to Bennett Connor and smile wide at Janelle. "Good morning."

"Olivia, you're here," she says, her voice rushed. "William's looking for you."

My mood dips at the stressed sound of her words. I take a step toward the desk and crane my neck toward her. "Do you know why?"

"I don't. But it seems urgent."

"Okay. I'll find him."

I walk into the office space and check my watch. It's not even eight o'clock in the morning. I left here late. What could possibly have happened overnight that's so urgent William's searching for me?

I find him in his office and step inside. "Janelle said you were looking for me."

"Yes. Yes. Olivia," he looks up, a thick document in his hand.

He pauses. I wait.

"We need you for an appearance at a hearing."

I digest the words; William waves his hand. "Not a big deal. It's the Centerton trial, Rick's civil case, and he just came down with COVID. He's fine. The case is mild, but he can't go to court. All you need to do is get an adjournment. Rick knows the judge, Higgins. He said it should be fine. He let the client know and he'll be on standby, but again, it should all be good."

"Right." I stand dumbly. I don't want to go. It's the one day I agreed to do something for Nate, and while there's little chance ACE will call, I want to be available if they do.

"Can't we just call the judge?"

"Not with Higgins, you can't. The firm needs to send a body."

A body. Me. Great. "And Rick doesn't have an associate? Someone who knows the file?"

"Not who can go this morning." He sets down the document. "Look, Olivia. You know how things are right now. You're good on your feet and you're good with judges. Just tell the judge Rick has COVID. It's fine. I trust you."

"So I should get the adjournment, then?"

He leans back in his chair. "It's a simple matter, Olivia."

Simple matter. Right. He's right. Adjournments are routine. Judges have more than one case scheduled each day for situations just like this. And the chances of ACE calling in the hour or so I'm in court is infinitesimally small. It's fine. I'm being stupid.

"Sure. I got it."

I get the Centerton file from Rick's admin, walk to the courthouse, and find Judge Higgins's courtroom. I check in with the court officer outside. "You can go in and set up," he tells me.

"No need. It's just an adjournment request," I say, breeze in, and sit at the defense table. Two lawyers and a man who I assume to be the client sit on the plaintiff's side, files stacked in neat rows in front of them. No one clued them in about Rick's COVID situation, it would appear.

The judge's clerk comes out of the door behind the bench. "All rise for the Honorable June Higgins."

We stand and the judge, a tiny woman with a round face and straight black bob, enters the courtroom.

"Please be seated."

We sit, and she puts the case on the record, name and docket number, and asks us to make our appearances.

"Olivia Ellison of Bennett Connor for the defense, Centerton Cinemas." I pause. "We have a request, Your Honor." I tell her the situation: Rick's sick, this is his case, and we need the date changed.

"Request denied."

I move to pick up the file before the statement hits me. I look up.

"Request denied, Miss Ellison," she repeats.

"But Rick Byer is the trial attorney on this matter."

"So you've told me."

"And—"

"And you are here. Are you not a member of the bar?"

"Yes, but—"

"Yes. That's all." She nods to the plaintiff's attorneys. "You may begin."

The trial begins. The plaintiff's attorneys waive the opening argument, and because they present their case first, all I do is take copious notes for Rick. Judge Higgins adjourns for a recess. In the hallway outside the courtroom, I pull up the messages on my phone. I don't expect to see anything.

But there are two messages from ACE.

My eyes widen. I play the message and put the phone to my ear: "Olivia, it's Amelia from ACE. Lucas hit another student. The student is fine, and so is Lucas, but we don't adhere to violence at ACE. You need to come and get him. Call me."

Lucas hit another student? I need to get him. What? I pull the phone away from my ear and look at the time the call was made. 9:17 a.m. Almost two hours ago. There's a second message from ACE five minutes after.

I press on the message from the second call. "Olivia. Amelia from ACE again. I was able to reach Nate. He's on his way to get Lucas. No worries. Call if you need me."

Shit. No. I bang the wall of the room with the side of my fist. I pull out my phone and dial Nate's number. When there's no answer, I look at the location finder on my phone. He and Lucas are at the apartment.

The court officer calls to resume the case. I type out a quick text to Nate: SORRY. *Will explain.*

When court adjourns after 4:00 p.m., I go directly home instead of to the office. As soon as I walk into the apartment, the lights go off. Then on. Then off. On. Off.

"That's enough," Nate says. His tone is irritable, the beacon of patience he normally has with Lucas frayed by whatever has been going on.

I slide off my heels by the door and peek around the corner into the main room. Lucas is in his chair. He claps his hands, and the lights go off. Clap. On. Clap. Off. Clap. On.

Clap-on lighting, a smart feature for the apartment that I didn't even remember I had.

"I'm so sorry," I say as enter the room. "There was an emergency trial. I tried to get out of it and—"

"Do you know how to turn off this whole clap thing?" he interrupts. "He's been doing it since we got back."

I look at the lights. "I don't know. I've never used that

feature." I set my bag down and move to the foyer, where the switch is, but there's nothing on it that tells how to turn off the clapping mechanism. "I'll call the front desk." I make the call. The front desk clerk doesn't know how to switch it off—no one has ever asked apparently—but he assures me that he'll find out. I shove the phone in my pocket. "They're going to call back."

On.

"Lucas," I say and move toward him, "can you please stop? Please stop with the lights."

Off.

"I've tried everything," Nate says. "He's not going to stop. He's in full-out stim mode now."

On.

"Did his teacher say anything?"

Off.

"She was busy, so I didn't get a lot of details. Just that he was off, and the kid he hit had something he wanted. He flipped out."

On.

"And you? Did you get to do the interview?"

Off.

"Yes."

On

"Yes." Relief pours out of me. "Thank God. Tell me about it."

Off.

"It was fine."

On.

Fine. It's never a good answer. "Any details?"

Off.

"Look, Liv, I can't talk right now. Not with this going on. I'm going to get some air."

On.

He grabs his coat from the rack. I pull on his forearm. I want to talk to him, hug him, tell him I'm sorry, find out how his thing went.

Off.

"Olivia," he shakes his head. "I need some air."

On.

I let him go.

Off.

CHAPTER 57

LUCAS

Clap. On. Clap. Off. Clap. On. Clap. Off.

I keep doing it. On. Off. On. Off. On. Off. The lights going on and off is the best thing, the most consistent thing, and doing it makes me forget temporarily that I hit Michael and the piercing sound of his wail and the fact that I feel sick. Right now the lights are saving me, and I can't stop. Even though Nate is telling me to.

I didn't feel well this morning. My stomach was churning, the lights brighter than usual. Nate typically takes me to school, but Olivia was in charge this morning, and when I didn't eat my waffle, she got agitated. I didn't eat it because, again, I felt sick, but she didn't know that. She urged me to eat like the fate of the world depended on it. So I ate it and we left and started the few blocks to school. I normally like the walk but like everything else this morning, it was all wrong. Olivia's steps were faster than Nate's, and she didn't tell me everything she was doing for the day, the way he usually does. Plus, I was extra cold, and I still felt sick, and I honestly just wanted to lie down in bed. I'm pretty sure I would have slept for the whole day. I started to think about how good that would feel, and I grabbed Olivia's hand and pulled her toward the apartment.

She pulled back. "Come on, Lu. You have school today and I have work. Sucks, but that's how it is."

I tried again and Olivia lost it a little, yelling that I had what I needed and we had to go.

So I dropped her hand. Getting what I wanted—to go home and lie down—was not going to happen. Plus, a day off for me would be a day off for her, and given her vibe, there was no way she wasn't going into the office.

When I got into the classroom, the desks were rearranged into a U shape. Ms. Hughes changes the configuration of the room every month or so. Most times it's fine, but in this arrangement, I was next to Michael, my least favorite person in the class. If Michael were allowed out into the world unsupervised, I'm 100 percent positive he'd be a shoplifter. He's always taking things, usually from Ms. Hughes, who seems unaware of the pens, bookmarks, paperclips, index cards, and other random stuff of hers that he has stuffed into his desk. He's taken things from other students as well. I think it's a compulsion. Like me and lights.

Anyway, we sat in our new seats and Ms. Hughes led us in the morning activities. I was tired and cold, and my stomach still didn't feel right. Michael tapped his pen on his desk. Tap. Tap. Tap. The sound probably wasn't loud, but it felt loud to me, and it kept going. And it wasn't in rhythm. Not really tap, tap, tap, but more like tap, pause, pause, tap, pause, tap, pause, pause, pause, pause, tap. The noise and erratic beat irritated me enough that I got up to sharpen a pencil.

When I got back to my seat, I spied the picture of Avery and me from the cruise in Michael's desk. Thief! I grabbed at the picture; he hit my hand. I grabbed for it again and got it. I stuffed it in my desk and not a second elapsed before Michael's hand was in there again. This time he took the pencil I just sharpened. Normally, I wouldn't care. But I did today because I didn't feel well, and he took my only picture of Avery and me, and I was tired of his nonrhythmic tapping and of him and school and of being here in New York instead of in Greenwillow.

I let him have the pencil but then he reached inside my desk again and it was too much. I made a fist, pulled my arm back, and punched him, hard, right in the jaw. I'd never punched anyone, and when he fell off his chair I was as surprised as he was. He looked at me a moment, a what the hell man look, before he started to wail. The room aide grabbed me and led me out. And then Michael really started to scream, and I felt bad, and the tension in the room was way high. I sat in the office in the front, and they called Olivia and then Nate and then Olivia, and my stomach was really roiling by then. I wished I had been able to stay home, but that didn't happen, and Nate arrived a while later, seeming frustrated, probably because of me.

It was too much, and when I got to the apartment I clapped once. I don't know why. But that was when the lights started. On. Off. On. Off. On. Off.

I can't stop doing it.

CHAPTER 58

NATE
I step out onto the street and stomp away from the apartment. The disastrous interview, Lucas hitting a kid, the incessant on-off of the lights for what felt like forever. All of it has me on edge. And Olivia. I get it, I guess. But it was just *one* day. How hard is it to say no? No, I can't do the emergency trial. Or no, I need Friday night off. Or no, I can't work until eight or ten or any other unreasonable hour.

Then again, I'm the loser, pushover, guy-that-killed-a-guy, the one who blows everything. Like Midas, but instead of gold everything I touch turns to shit. So maybe I shouldn't judge Olivia. Maybe I shouldn't even be with her, given my track record of tainting things.

After a few blocks, I step into one of the zillion coffee shops that pepper the Manhattan streets. I order a large coffee and find a table in the back with a bench against the wall. It's crowded and loud and I know no one. It's all the things I dislike about New York. I'm grateful for them now. I want to lose myself in this mass of humanity.

I lean against the wall and flash back to the interview. I

cried. Cried. Like question, answer, pause . . . me crying. There I was, interviewing to be *a doctor*, and I couldn't answer a basic question without becoming an emotional wreck. The question that threw me into a tailspin: what accomplishment are you the most proud of? It's an ordinary interview question, one I should have had a ready answer for. But I didn't, and when Dr. Hyle, my interviewer, asked it, my mind went completely blank. I couldn't think of a thing. Not a single accomplishment, let alone one I was proud of. And then Mark Carney, aka *the guy I killed*, popped in my head, and I started to think about him and the accomplishments he probably had or would have had if it hadn't been for me. And it seemed like such a waste that he was gone, and I was here. A lump formed in my throat, and I knew I had all of one second to get myself together before I fell apart. But then it was too late, and I was crying, not a floodgate, thank God, but still obvious to the point where Dr. Hyle shoved a box of Kleenex across the desk. After I calmed down, he asked a few more questions, but it was clear the interview was over.

So ManMed is a no. Which leaves me with exactly nothing. I knew getting back into medical school wouldn't be easy, but it had been the plan, and absent the isolated blood bank interview, I'd held on to it. Now, poof, the potential opportunity is gone.

I take a long swig of coffee. My phone pings with a text, Olivia's name on the screen. I pull up the message. *Light situation fixed. Ordered pizza. Celebrate your interview?* There's a long pause, then a second text. *And sorry again about today.*

I stare at the words. Crap. She shouldn't be sorry. The phone call from ACE isn't what flubbed the interview; that was all me. I didn't even get the call until it was over. And given that I'm surely not going to medical school, and I don't have another job, making sure Lucas has what he needs *is* my job right now. I type back a message. *Sure. Be right there.*

When I walk into the apartment, Olivia is lighting a candle on the kitchen table, wine glasses are out, and a box of pizza from my favorite place sits on the counter. Otis saunters toward me and I bend down to pet him. Lucas isn't there. In his room, I imagine.

Olivia looks up at me, and her face lights up so bright it makes my heart hurt. She could do so much better.

She strides toward me, gives me a kiss on the mouth, and a squeezy hug. She lets go and shakes my shoulders. "So how was it? How was the interview?"

"It was good," I lie.

"Yeah?" She walks back to the table, pours two glasses of wine, and hands me one. "What kinds of things did they ask? Tell me about it."

"Usual stuff. You know, why I wanted to get into medicine and all that." I take a sip of wine.

"So you think it went well? You think maybe . . ."

She lets the thought trail off, and I finish the sentence in my mind: do I think maybe I got in?

Not a snowflake's chance in hell.

"I think maybe," I say instead.

She squeals, a high-pitched noise I'm not sure I've ever heard her make. Then she grabs her wine glass and holds it up. "To the future Dr. Nathan Wilder."

"Let's not get carried away."

"Whatever you say, *doctor*."

I clink my class to hers. She smiles wide, and I wish what she was smiling about was true instead of a big hunk of bull.

She turns around, pulls a slice of pizza from the box, puts it on my plate, then repeats the process with hers.

"How's Lucas?" I ask.

She sits across from me and picks up her slice. "Tired." She takes a bite and swallows. "And you didn't get an idea of what happened with the kid he hit?"

I set down my glass. "The teacher said she'd send it in the portal."

"Okay. Good. It doesn't seem like Lucas to hit someone. I'll bet that kid provoked him or something."

I take a sip of wine. "Or maybe he was just sick of things." I blurt out the statement, thinking more of me than of Lucas.

"You think he's sick of things?"

"No," I say, not wanting to tip off my own internal state. "I just . . . I don't know why I said that."

She exhales. "Alright, good. Because I thought things were going pretty well." She pauses. "Absent today, of course."

"Today was not the best."

We finish our pizza and wine and settle on the couch. Both of us have our legs stretched out on the coffee table, computers on our laps. We sit like this for a while. I'd normally seek more interaction in the little bit of time we have together, but right now I'm glad for the lack of it. The day has taken its toll, and I doze off. I feel pressure on my shoulder, then shaking, and open my eyes. Olivia's face is over mine.

"Lucas's teacher is suspending him for ten days."

It takes me a moment to process. "Ten days? What?" I shift next to her, and she orients her computer so I can see. In a nutshell, the altercation with Michael, the other child, was unprovoked, and in light of the school's "up not down" policy, they are disciplining Lucas in the same manner as any neurotypical school would. He doesn't get treated differently for being on the spectrum; they assume he understands what he did was wrong.

"Well, that sucks," she says, and leans back, eyes fixed on the portal entry. "I'd really like to know more about the incident, why they think it's unprovoked."

"I know. It doesn't sound like him."

"Ten days. That's a lot of school."

I pick a piece of lint from my pants. "Maybe I could take him back to Greenwillow for a few days."

Olivia sets her computer on the coffee table. "I couldn't ask you to do that."

"It's fine. I've been meaning to visit my parents anyway. And you have the trial next week. You can have the whole apartment to yourself to prepare." The more I talk about it, the more the idea makes sense. "It's the best possible solution, I think. Lucas would be miserable in the apartment all day, and like I said, you can work on the trial without us under your feet."

She tips her head. "Are you sure?"

"I am. It'll be good for Lucas to have a change of scene." And me, I think but don't say.

"Thanks so much." She leans over and kisses my cheek. "I don't know what I'll do once you start school."

I smile weakly. She's not going to have to worry about it.

CHAPTER 59

OLIVIA
The evening after Lucas is suspended, he and Nate are gone when I get home. Otis greets me at the door. I set my bag of Thai take-out on the kitchen table, bend down, and pat his square head.

Walking in the door with no one here, just Otis, feels strange, and I hate to say it, but it feels good too. That under-current of guilt I have almost always? Amazingly absent. I know Nate and Lucas never set out to make me feel bad, quite the opposite, but most of the time I can't help but think that I made them both come to New York and I'm not doing any of the things I'd said we would. Them in Greenwillow for ten days? It's freeing.

I open the food container, inhale the aroma, and eat standing while scrolling through my phone. It's the ultimate single-person-dining-alone move, and right now it feels decadent rather than lonely.

After dinner, I move to the bathroom, fill the tub with steamy hot water and bubbles, and remove my work clothes. I submerge myself in the water—toe, foot, ankle, shin, and so on—until each part of me acclimates to the heat. Once submerged, I slide down the tub's edge, bubbles up to my chin. The tight muscles in my neck and shoulders unfurl; my eyelids droop with exhaustion. I stay under the curtain of bubbles until my skin beings to prune and the water begins to cool, and I finally step out and dry myself off with a fluffy towel. I slip into my favorite robe, the owl one I had as a teen and brought back from Greenwillow because it cracked Nate up.

My phone rings. A FaceTime from Nate. The guilt—I'm here luxuriating after a bath while he's taking care of my brother— immediately surges, and while I could remind myself that Lucas's care is technically Nate's job, I don't. The move to New York was never supposed to be a continuation of the status quo. It was meant to be a good change for all of us and it's just that Nate's piece—medical school—hasn't started yet. I wish into the ether for good news from ManMed and pick up the call. "Hey, you," I say as soon as his face appears on the screen.

"Hey, yourself. You got the owl robe going." He smiles. "Clearly, I'm missing out."

"Yeah. It's a real hoot here," I say, but the joke feels hollow. Old. "How are things?"

"Good. Got sandwiches at Big Rod's."

"Nooo," I say, though honestly, I was happy with my stand-alone dinner.

"Lu was really excited to see all the animals. We did the pond walk earlier."

"That's great." I recall the three of us doing that walk back in the fall, the bright sky, the border of crimson, yellow, and orange leaves on the trees, the brisk weather. Nostalgia surges through me, but at the same time, the idea of strolling around a small neighborhood pond for fun seems foreign now that I'm back in New York.

We talk a little more, about their drive out there, about the animals, about the weather, of all mundane things. And it's weird, like this brief separation has somehow caused a chasm between us. Not an insurmountable divide, but a distance. A little fracture. One that could, if we're not careful, turn into a break.

Or maybe I'm imagining it.

"I should get going," I say after the weather conversation goes on too long. "Talk soon?"

"Talk soon."

With the trial starting Monday, I work at the office with William and the team all weekend. William references my dad a bunch, how proud he'd be of me and how he might handle this or that. I'm not sure why he does it, but it has the result of making me feel even more jacked up and nervous than I was before. Like anything less than perfection would let my dad down.

I keep so busy that it isn't until late Sunday night when I realize I haven't called Nate. In fairness, he hasn't called me either. He's probably busy seeing his parents and our friends and doing things with Lucas. And I'm in the midst of trial prep, which has left me with little interesting to talk about. But that same worry I've had since he left creeps back inside me: that this is how it happens; this is how people grow apart.

I think about it a moment, my life before Nate and Lucas were in it. Do I want that? Work, work, work? Achieve, achieve, achieve. Maybe? No. NO. Of course not.

I grab my phone and FaceTime Nate. His image immediately materializes inside the rectangle of my phone screen. He's smiling and sitting in the family room.

"Liv, hey. I didn't want to call. I figured you're busy with the trial. Lucas is here too."

He angles the phone and Lucas appears on my screen, stretched out on the couch. He looks more relaxed, and his coloring is better.

Nate angles the phone back to himself. "So how are things? You and William ready for the big day tomorrow?"

"Ready as we'll ever be." I pause. "And you guys? Things there are good?"

"Fantastic."

He smiles brightly, the way I used to love. He doesn't smile like that as much in New York. Or at all. "What kinds of things have you been doing?"

He tells me, in more detail than I need, all the activities they've been doing. The Treeline Zoo, dinner at his parents, a visit from Tessa and Avery. They ran into Ms. Caddell and she invited Lucas to spend a day in the old classroom.

His cadence is way cheerful, and it shouldn't bother me, but it does. I should be happy he's happy, and Lucas is happy, and they're having a jolly good time reconnecting with the Greenwillow peeps and all. And I know he misses home. Still. Nate's thrilled attitude makes me feel like a failure. By any measure, New York City beats Greenwillow. Central Park vs. Monroe Pond. The Brooklyn Zoo vs. the Treeline Zoo. Broadway vs. the high school play. World-renowned restaurants vs. Big Rod's. Art, music, sports—any of it, all of it—Greenwillow comes up short. And yet it's clear from the huge smile on Nate's face and the tone of his voice and his relaxed posture that I've failed to make NYC a better place to live than a tiny town in the middle of Pennsylvania. What was supposed to be a nice call, an *are we okay* sanity check, is now a source of indignation. Greenwillow? Over New York City? My muscles tense; my temples start to throb. Irritation coats my nerves.

"Do you ever miss it here?" he asks.

It's the wrong question to ask and it rachets up my irritation to anger. "What would I miss about it?" I snap.

"I don't know. Nature? The people?"

"Nature? I can find that in Central Park or at the New York Botanical Gardens. Or Bryant Park or Liberty Park or Hudson

River Park. And countless other places. There's plenty of nature in New York, Nate. Just because it's not in the middle of nowhere here doesn't mean there isn't nature."

He says nothing; I continue on my rampage.

"And people? Over eight million people live in New York City. I'm sure at least a few of them are as interesting as the people you've known forever. New York is the center of the world. Greenwillow is the center of nothing."

I finish, breathless. Nate stays silent and my anger starts to dissipate. Slowly, the realization that I have just overreacted in a very substantial and insulting way creeps into my psyche, inching further and further until the anger is gone and all I'm left with is tirade-embarrassment. The words I just said ricochet through my mind, all the tiny barbs and innuendos that seem completely uncalled for now. "I'm sorry. I'm not sure where that came from."

He shuts his eyes and opens them, his lips sealed together. If I had to guess, I'd say he was centering himself before saying something mean or shortsighted or that he'd regret.

Like I just did.

"It's fine," he says finally. "I'm sure you're tired from all the trial prep."

"I am but . . . I'm still sorry."

"Let's talk later, Liv," he says, every feature on his face conveying that he's done with me and this conversation. "Good luck tomorrow."

"Sure, thanks," I say, disappointed that I railroaded the check-in conversation toward this unsatisfying end. "We'll talk this week."

"Sounds good."

He clicks off and his face disappears, and I'm left with a heart-heavy, unsettled feeling of wrong. The heaviness lodges in my chest and stays there until I arrive at the courthouse the next morning. I'm pulled out of my melancholy by the zoo of

humanity in front of me. The normally empty courthouse steps
are jammed with reporters with giant microphones; two news
trucks are parked out front. I'm low enough on the totem pole
at Bennett Connor to escape notice and I quickly slide into the
building. I wait in line at security, pass through, and find the
courtroom. William and James, a second Bennett Connor partner, are there, along with Jupiter Rowan, the latter with rhine-
stone studded nails and a hot pink newsboy cap on her head,
her long dusty blond hair spilling down her back in waves. She's
wearing a suit—black with pink pinstripes—and the highest
heels I have ever seen.

I say brief hellos; the tension at the table and around the
courtroom won't allow for any more. I take my place on the end
of the counsel table next to William. Exhibits are my primary
job, and despite the fact that the defense won't be going right
away, I double-check to make sure they're all in a row. After, I
glance over at the plaintiff's table. Just two women. The client
and her attorney, neither of which look terribly intimidating,
and it feels a little silly to be stacked with so many lawyers on
our side.

Twenty minutes later, the judge emerges from her chambers
and calls the case. And immediately, I'm caught up in all of it,
everything and everyone else forgotten.

CHAPTER 60

N ATE

"So how about Olivia's trial?" Mom asks. "I keep seeing things about it on the news."

It's Sunday dinner and everyone who's usually there is smushed around the dining room table at Jenny's house.

"Lots of coverage," I acknowledge. Lots is an understatement. Every news outlet is covering the trial of New York's self-described crypto queen. I never asked Olivia about the case figuring she'd want a break from it at home. I didn't fully realize what a big deal it was until this week. I didn't realize either that the defendant, Jupiter Rowan, is accused of defrauding clients out of millions of dollars.

Jenny opens a bottle of wine. "How's she doing? She managing it all okay?"

"She's doing fine," I say, but the truth is I haven't talked to her since our conversation about Greenwillow. I don't have much to say—not in comparison to being in the middle of a newsworthy trial—so I don't call, and she doesn't, and that's how it's become a week since we've spoken.

"Does she know Jupiter Rowan?" Carly asks, starstruck.

"I don't know," I admit. "I assume so."

"How about ManMed?" Dad asks. "Any news?"

"Not yet." It's technically true. I haven't heard anything. The fact that I'm 99.99 percent sure of the answer—NO—is beside the point.

The conversation moves away from me and Olivia and on to the Pittsburgh Pirates and what kind of year they might have. I'm glad the spotlight is off. When dinner is over, I help Mom clear the dishes. I'm piling plates near the sink and see a stack of business cards for Dr. Alan pushed back amidst the hodgepodge of stuff on the counters. The intervention was months ago; I'm surprised they're still here.

"You can throw those out," Mom says, and I turn and see her looking in my direction. "Seems things are on the right track now." She pats my shoulder.

"Sure." I swallow hard, not wanting her or anyone to know that things are most likely *not* on the right track. I open the lid to the trash can and drop in the stack save one, which I shove into my pocket. I don't know why I do it. In my mind, the chances of me calling Dr. Alan are slimmer than those of me getting into ManMed. Still, it seems right to have his contact information. Just in case.

I finish up with the dishes, talk a bit more, then find Lucas and head home. I type out "goodnight Olivia" in a text. The message is transactional and boring, and I add a gif of a cat sleeping before sending it. Olivia loves the image. She's awake; I don't call. She doesn't either.

The next few days are similar to the last few with visits to friends and familiar places and Lucas spending a full day in his old classroom per the insistence of Ms. Caddell. I'm early to get him and waiting in the parking lot of the school when I click on my phone and see the news. Jupiter Rowan's case has wrapped up. The news isn't a big deal. There's no verdict yet, because judges in civil trials take cases under advisement. But there's a video clip of William Sterling outside the courthouse. I click on it. He talks about how they're confident justice will prevail and blah, blah, blah. The video pans back and I see Olivia in the background. Her hair is pulled severely away from her face, her makeup heavy instead of light. It reminds me very much of the clip I saw of her months ago at Tessa's house, before I came to New York. Her physical appearance then was different in the same way, but her expression had been more resigned. This Olivia has a vibe of noteworthiness in her posture. Like the defense of a woman who calls herself a queen and who frequently adorns herself in crowns and capes—one who likely defrauded innocent Americans—is of critical importance. I pause the video and stare at her image. It's like looking at a stranger.

I glance at Olivia's impression one more time, then turn off my phone and go into the school. I'm the first to the classroom and Lauren immediately greets me. "Nate!" She gives me a hug so squeezy I almost feel a need to move away. "Are you able to stay a bit?'" she asks. "I'd like to talk to you a minute if you've got one."

"Sure," I say, and she gestures for me to come inside the classroom. I lean against the wall and spy Lucas in the back of the room with two classmates, all of them playing with slime.

"Gotta love slime!" Lauren says. "There are all kinds of scents, and some have sensory bits inside. The kids love it."

I nod, watching Lucas and the others immersed in this side-by-side activity. I'm fairly certain slime would not be an approved activity at ACE, and none of the instructors there would ever call Lucas, an eighteen-year-old, a kid. I glance again at the boys in the back, and they all look pretty darn happy. So maybe all's well with how they do it here at Green-willow High.

Parents and caregivers come to pick up students who don't take the bus home. I know all of them, and five different times I go through how everything in New York is going just so gosh-darned great. And yes, I have seen news about the trial and Olivia on television and all of that. Finally, when it's just Lucas left, Lauren motions for me to step into the hall.

"So how's it going?" she whispers.

"Fine. Why?"

"Well," she says, craning her neck forward. "Lucas was fine all day, really happy, I'd say. Anyway, when the other kids went to recreational classes, it was just him and me in the classroom and I asked him how he liked New York." She stops.

"And?"

"And his reaction was strange. Like he'd gone inside himself or something. He'd been swinging and he just stopped, and his face got all slack, and it was like he was no longer getting information. He was like that for long enough that it concerned me."

I say nothing, digesting the information, and Lauren waves a hand. "It's probably nothing, but when kids are nonverbal and they can't tell us what they're thinking, it's important to decipher, you know, as best you can. And I've never seen Lucas react to anything in that way."

"Thank you," I say. "That's good information." I step inside the classroom and glance back at her, still in the hall. "And thanks for having Lucas today. I'm sure he enjoyed seeing you and his friends. You're a special teacher, Lauren."

A blush blooms across her cheeks. "Well, what I lack in technology and gadgets and whatnot, I try to make up for with caring. And I care about Lucas, that's for sure."

"I feel that. Thank you." And I do. There's a warmth in this space that ACE just doesn't have.

After not one but two squeezy hugs, Lucas and I leave the school. He seems melancholy during the car ride home and I stop to get food at Big Rod's. We take the food home and set it up at the kitchen table.

"Let's call Olivia." Maybe seeing her would cheer him up. I'd also like to get the image of her in the posttrial video out of my mind. The woman in that clip does not seem at all like the woman I fell in love with.

I FaceTime Olivia. It rings once, twice, five times before I disconnect. Almost immediately after I do, she calls me. "Nate. Is everything all right?"

"Yeah. Fine. I just saw the case was over and I—" My train of thought is interrupted by the sound of background voices and music. Oh. "Are you out? I didn't mean to—"

"Yeah. We're at Bistro to celebrate. Everyone thinks we nailed the trial."

I open my mouth, willing myself to think of something positive to say about an outcome where Jupiter Rowan gets away with defrauding her own investors. I don't, can't, and then someone yells "cheers" on Olivia's end and there's general reverie and clinking glasses.

"You should go," I say. "Celebrate."

"Okay. Yeah. Talk later?"

"Actually, we'll be home tomorrow."

"Oh. Right. Right, of course." She pauses a long moment. "Can't wait to see you."

"Yeah," I say, my voice hollow, "me either."

CHAPTER 61

LUCAS

It's the final day before I go back to ACE, and Nate and I are back in the New York apartment eating pizza with Olivia. Greenwillow was great. I saw Avery, Tessa, Dominique, Ms. Cadell—everyone, really. And my animals. All of them. I slept in my bed, ate pizza from Big Rod's, and walked around Monroe Pond. I appreciated my home more the past ten days than I ever did when I lived there full-time. Funny how that works.

There are some things I like about New York and even ACE. I like not being talked down to, ever, and I like some of the lessons, the ones I can get, which is not all of them because the school skipped like a gazillion years between where I was at Greenwillow and where they expect me to be now. But some of the classes are good. I like history.

But a history class doesn't beat Greenwillow and the way being in that town makes me feel. The sense of comfort and belonging and familiarity. It's not something I often get. So I'll trade ACE and New York and all the bells and whistles for plain, boring, learn the same thing every day, home.

I think Nate feels the same way. I think he wants to go back. And I need him to convince Olivia because I can't. So I'm kind of, sort of, very much hoping he's going to bring it up.

Olivia's blabbering on about her trial. Nate is not responding. He looks sad and his shoulders are hunched, and I can't believe Olivia's not picking up on any of this but is instead continuing with her monologue. When she finally stops talking, a big fat wall of silence covers the room, and oh, man, is it tense. So much so that I slip away and lie on the couch in the family room.

"Is something wrong?" Olivia asks finally, FINALLY, and I brace myself. This is the moment. Come on Nate. Do it. Do it for us both.

CHAPTER 62

OLIVIA

"Is something wrong?" I ask Nate. He's been off. I haven't seen him for ten days and all his answers are one word. He's acting as if my retelling of the trial—the most newsworthy event in New York right now—is not quite as interesting as watching paint dry.

"No." He rubs the back of his neck. "Not really."

"What do you mean not really?" I press.

He pulls a piece of cardboard from the pizza box and folds it in half. "This isn't the time, Olivia. You're celebrating your case and all."

I narrow my eyes. "Isn't the time for what?"

Lucas leaves the table without eating.

"Isn't the time for what, Nate?" I repeat. "Just tell me."

"I don't think New York is the best place for Lucas," he spits out.

I drop the pizza slice. The statement was not what I expected him to say.

"I've been thinking it for a while now. The trip to Greenwillow confirmed it."

I cross my arms across my chest. "How do you mean? Because here, except for the lights, which was just one time, he doesn't stim all the time. He likes it here. He has his favorite chair." I scour my mind for additional examples of things Lucas likes, but I've been so caught up at work that I don't know. "This move has been good for Lucas," I say definitively and without proof.

"I don't know." He gestures to the window. "He sits and looks out that window and I know we thought that was good, but I think he's depressed. Stimming isn't always a sign of agitation. Sometimes it can be a sign of happiness. Just sitting and doing nothing? It seems like a red flag."

"That's ridiculous," I snap. "He stims when he's upset. I've seen it over and over." Probably not as many times as Nate, but I will not be dissuaded from the idea that Lucas is doing well here. That I did the right thing moving him.

Nate shrugs. "I disagree. He's not himself here or at ACE."

"He is absolutely himself," I insist. "He's making a ton of progress."

"Is he?"

"Yes. Check the portal."

He pushes back his chair, and the legs screech across the hardwood floor. "Maybe I don't want to check the portal, Olivia. Maybe I'd rather talk to an actual human, his teacher, than correspond in cyberspace. For all we know, she's generating the notes with AI."

"That's ridiculous."

"Is it? Who knows? I pick him up and drop him off every day and I've never once spoken to her. At least in Greenwillow, you get to talk to Lauren Caddell. You know she cares. Lucas is happier in there."

He makes the statement like it's an absolute, like measuring happiness is an exact science. "I disagree."

"I was just there with him. You weren't."

The statement feels like a dig. "Yes, I know I wasn't there, Nate, this time. But New York is good for him. His chance to enhance his communication skills are way better at ACE."

Nate opens his mouth, closes it.

My face flushes. "He likes it here," I proclaim. "He likes ACE."

"He hit a kid!"

"Once. One time. And he's been disciplined like any other student would be. I like that kind of accountability. I would think you would too." I push back my chair and stand up. He does the same.

"ACE is impersonal."

I stamp my foot. "Impersonal or professional? Miss Lauren treats her high school students like they're five. Would you want to be eighteen and treated like a five-year-old? Lucas has a chance to make real progress at ACE. Why would you want to take that away from him?" Anger courses through me. "Actually, you can't. I'm the guardian." Ridiculously, I point to myself. "I decide." I pick up the dishes and pile them on top of each other, hard. I move to the sink. Nate follows, half-full glasses in his hands.

"We both care about Lucas," he says. "I'm just trying to tell you what I observed. He's happier in Greenwillow."

"And you know this because"—I pause a moment—"because he got to feed chickens, go to the zoo, and spend a day with Miss Lauren."

"Yes. It's the value of community, of relationships that span decades. Of being surrounded by people that care about you instead of a bunch of strangers, professional as they may be." He sets the glasses in the sink. "Not everyone measures success by achievement whether it's whatever's in the portal or helping crypto queens get away with fraud. Some people are just happy being around the people they love."

Every emotion I've held back since we moved comes barreling to the surface. "Really!?" I scream the word, then lower my voice to a menacing whisper. "You know what I think? I think this isn't about Lucas at all. This is about you. What about ManMed? You interviewed there. Are you just going to forget about it? I think you want to. You don't want to move on." My words are hurtful; I can't stop them. They keep coming in a tsunami of unbridled emotion. "Bad enough that you've given up," I continue, "but now you're trying to drag Lucas down with you. You use him, your job as a caretaker, as a shield, you know."

He stares at me, hurt fixed in his eyes. The impact, the offensiveness, of everything I just said begins to pierce through my anger.

My phone buzzes. I swipe it off the counter and see William's number. The Rowan decision. He must have gotten it. My body thrums with anticipation and I click to accept the call even as Nate is still staring at me and even as I know what a terrible message me taking a work call sends at this moment. But I have to know. I put the phone to my ear and simultaneously hold up an index finger to Nate as a signal to wait. He looks at me a long moment before waving his hand dismissively and disappearing down the hall. I'll apologize later. Right now, I need to know the decision. "Hey, did you get it?" I bark into the phone.

"Olivia?"

It's a woman's voice, not William's.

"Yes?"

"It's Adrienne," she says. "William's daughter."

"Adrienne. Is everything alright?"

"My dad's dead," she spits out.

I press the phone to my ear. "What?"

"It was a heart attack."

"Oh my God. I'm so sorry." I fix my eyes on the floor, head spinning, words flying out of my mouth. "I can't believe it. I'm so sorry."

"Thanks. It's alright." Her tone is factual and without emotion. "We weren't close."

"But still," I start. Still, she has to care. Still, he's her dad. Still, William was living and breathing yesterday and now he's dead. "It still has to be hard," I finish.

"Haven't spoken to him in over a year," she says. "He hasn't remembered my birthday in three." A chewing sound emits through the phone line. "He was married to his work, Olivia. You know that. Anyway, services are going to be Thursday at Grace Cathedral. I was hoping you would speak."

"Me? I'm sure there's—"

"There's no one better," she interrupts. "We're looking for people."

"Sure," I say, still unclear how there couldn't be other, better people to speak at William's funeral. I write down the information about the service, the whole conversation feeling detached from reality. William is dead. I just saw him yesterday.

CHAPTER 63

OLIVIA
Neither Nate nor I revisit the argument after I tell him about William. At least not out loud. Still, the things we each said percolate under the surface of our interactions, the unaired insults manifesting in the banal small talk, in how far we sit apart, in the sound of utensils scratching on plates during dinner.

Work is crazy with news of William's death and the redistribution of cases because of it. By habit, I allow the new briefs and cases to serve as an elixir and an excuse. I don't bring up the topic of Lucas being better off in Greenwillow. I don't apologize to Nate for the things I said. I let everything wrong just sit there and hope it will go away.

The day of William's funeral, four days after I received the news of his death, Nate stands at the stovetop with a spatula in his hand. He flips an omelet onto a plate and glances in my direction. "Do you want eggs?"

"No, thanks." I fix myself a cup of coffee.

Nate leans against the counter, plate in his hand, and spoons a bite of omelet into his mouth. "I'm not sure I can do this anymore."

I stop drinking mid-sip and set my mug on the counter. "This?"

"Living here. In New York. I know I said I thought it wasn't good for Lucas, and I don't, but I don't think it's good for me either." He blows out a breath. "I don't belong here."

His admission shouldn't be a surprise, but the words still fly through me, the possibility of him leaving crashing full force into my mind. "Nate, no." I pull the plate from his hand and set it on the counter. "You do belong here. Things have been weird and busy and I'm sorry. But Rowan is over and as soon as we get things adjusted with William's caseload, it'll be way less crazy. Plus, you're still waiting to hear from ManMed." I wrap my arms around his neck. "Just give it some more time. Please."

He doesn't put his arms around me, and I stand awkwardly in the unreciprocated hug a long moment before letting go.

"I don't know," he says.

I check my watch. "Look. I need to get to the funeral, but can we talk about this when we get back? Please."

"Sure," he says, but the word feels halfhearted.

I grab my purse. "Things will be fine." I say it to Nate, but the words are just as much for me. It will be fine, I tell myself. We'll work things out. This is just a rough patch.

I take an Uber to the church. During the ride, I scan the notecards for my speech, and the reality of William being dead slides over me like gooey, ugly slime. I've spent the past several days racking my brain for funny stories or touching moments for my eulogy. I have plenty to say about William, but all of it is related to work and I can't help but compare what's on my notecards to the things people said about Melanie during the impromptu Greenwillow service. How kind she was. How much she gave back to others. How much she cared for her son.

The Uber drops me off and I move inside the cathedral. The

ceiling is tall, at least twenty-five feet, with stained glass on the sides and front. Ornate arches line the outside of the pews; the ceiling is painted with angels and cherubs and clouds. People stand near the front by the framed picture of William and his closed casket. The photograph of him is the same as on the Bennett Connor legal brochures.

I walk toward the front of the church, toward the who's who in the legal community gathered there. I'm pretty certain that, but for the fact that he's dead, William would have been pleased to have drawn such an impressive crowd. Bits of conversation reach me as I navigate through people, just about all of it centered on Rowan and what the judge might decide. The underlying legal buzz feels wrong, and I slip into a front pew without getting roped into a conversation.

It takes a while for people to settle, the entire atmosphere feeling more like a networking event than a funeral. The service, when it does start, is formal and long. The sermon stretches on well after the time anyone is interested, and phones start to appear in the pews. By the time the speakers are asked to come forward, I'm pretty sure no one is listening anymore.

William's brother and only sibling speaks first. He details a few funny stories but each with an edge, the picture of William emerging as a hyper-competitive child with a win-at-all-costs mentality. Clyde Allen, a senior partner at the firm, centers his recollections on William's need to be the best. Other partners pick up the baton and talk about what a driven lawyer William was. One of them relates the amount of business William drove to the firm like that's his legacy. Maybe it is.

When it's my turn, I walk to the pulpit. The crowd is bigger than I realized, employees of Bennett Connor peppered through the pews in the same dark suits they wear to the office daily. I place my notecards on the lectern and scan the boring, unin- spired words. All about work and the firm, just like the others. Although legal prominence may have been what drove William, it doesn't feel right that it's the only topic at his funeral. But I don't know much else about him. The William behind the lawyer.

In an unexpected move for a planner like me, I turn the note cards over, clear my throat, and talk from the heart.

"William was my boss," I start. "He encouraged me and mentored me and looked for opportunities for me to expand my legal knowledge. I'm grateful for that. And I know things about William. Like he's a morning person, that he's a proud Penn State alum, that he liked to cycle in the little bit of free time he had. But honestly, I wish I knew him better. That's my loss. I wish I knew the kinds of things that would make him laugh so hard he'd cry or what his favorite movie was or what Olympic event he looked forward to watching every four years. I'd like to know where he spent his most favorite vacation, his first memory, and if he's a roller coaster guy or the kind who holds the coats. I'd like to know his favorite flavor of ice cream, what his first job was as a teen, and what New York City tradition he just can't miss each year. And for real, I'd like to have known if he ever ate anything other than bagels with cream cheese for breakfast."

There's a smattering of laughter at that.

"And I wish I'd told him more things about myself. Like how I was obsessed with owls as a kid. How I love brushing my brother, Lucas's, horse. That sunsets in the morning in the country give me a sense of peace. I'd share that my iPhone playlist now reveals an unhealthy obsession with '80s rock and that I have a foster cat I haven't officially adopted, but he's mine in every sense of the word. If I were brave, I might share my struggles with friendships or I might just leave it at I used to like owls. Either way, I'd have revealed a little bit more of myself and hoped to have seen more snapshots of the man behind the brilliance in return.

"I'll remember William fondly as a phenomenal lawyer and a

dedicated mentor. But in his memory, I'm going to let people in more. And I hope, by doing so, I'll get to understand and appreciate the essence of those around me. The way I wish I had with William."

I pick up the pile of unread notecards and I step away from the pulpit. A sick feeling sits in the pit of my stomach, like I just bared my soul to a group of colleagues.

I walk back to my pew in what feels like slow motion; I don't make eye contact with anyone, hoping people were too bored to listen, that my unprompted confessional went unnoticed. I slide into my seat. The elderly woman next to me pats my shoulder. "That was lovely, darling," she whispers.

"Thank you," I whisper back.

The man behind me cranes his neck forward. "Very nice. And I've known William to enjoy a good diner omelet."

A vision of William at a diner materializes in my mind and I smile. There's a reception at a restaurant after, and I learn more snippets about William. Adrienne tells me her dad was so competitive that he never let her win any games, even Candy Land. His old neighbor shares that he used to wipe the snow off her car in the winter. Fred, one of the partners at the firm, tells me that he was a bourbon drinker. I learn that he liked to watch race car driving on television and documentaries of all kinds. That he had a penchant for Big Macs. That after he divorced from his second wife, he kept up with her rose bushes anyway. All the pieces I learn fill in what I already knew and create a three-dimensional memory from one that had been almost flat.

After about an hour, the crowd starts to dwindle. Fatigue hits me, a culmination of the funeral, my speech, and the ongoing tension with Nate. I don't think he meant what he said, that he didn't belong here, but I don't know. I've been so busy, I haven't made it my business to.

I hand my ticket to the coat-check woman. I yawn without

meaning to and just as my mouth is agape, a voice sounds in my ear. "Olivia."

I snap my lips shut and spin around. Marjorie Small is behind me, coat-check ticket in hand. I'd seen her in passing a few times today, but we hadn't spoken. "Hey, Marjorie."

"Beautiful eulogy."

"Thank you."

She leans forward. "I happen to know William's first job was as a cashier in a supermarket."

The woman in the coat check holds out my coat. I take it, and Marjorie extends her ticket.

"And my first job was as a parade dancer."

I pivot in her direction. "Really?"

"Yes. At Sesame Place. I followed the float with Big Bird."

"That's awesome." I file the tidbit of information away, an unexpected, almost extraordinary, piece of Marjorie. "I worked at Bennett Connor in high school. As you know."

She takes her coat and slips into it. "Of course. You've been a staple at this firm for as long as I can remember."

"Yeah," I say, and it does feel like that. That I've been a part of Bennett Connor for most of my life, the steady connection akin to that of a family. I put on my coat and hold open an ornate door for Marjorie. She steps through and we stand together on the top landing of the steps.

"You should know," she leans toward me, her voice a whisper, "that everyone was quite impressed with your work on the Rowan case." She looks around like she's trying to make sure no one is in earshot. "There's been some talk of partnership. Not the track. Now."

Marjorie's words cascade through my psyche. Partnership. Now. The little girl who'd sat in empty lawyer offices on Saturdays; the teen who'd worked the mailroom; the law college and law student who'd given up social opportunities to study—all those versions of me had been dreaming of this moment.

"You're young," Marjorie continues, "but you're a strong advocate, and you're dedicated to Bennett Connor in the way we need from our partners." She shakes her head. "Anyway, I didn't want you to be taken by surprise when the opportunity comes up. It'll be hard work and long hours, but if you're willing to handle it, partnership is all but yours. I'll make sure of it."

CHAPTER 64

NATE

"So, partnership," I repeat.

Olivia leans against the kitchen counter in the apartment, still in the black suit she'd worn to the funeral. "It was a shock. I didn't expect to be partner for a few years, at least." She dips down, removes her high heels, and holds them in her hand. "I know things haven't been the best recently." She pauses. "What do you think?"

The question comes out neutral, but I can tell she's excited. Bennett Connor has been a mainstay in her life, partnership a North Star. I couldn't possibly tell her not to go for it. I won't stand in her way, especially as my own North Star is so dull I can't even see it anymore. "I think you should take it."

"Really!?" She sets her heels on the counter, lunges in my direction, and swings her arms around me so hard I'm temporarily taken off balance. I embrace her back, holding her body tight against my own. I make an imprint of how she feels, how she smells, how she sounds. One that will last. Because while I do think she should take this opportunity, my affirmation doesn't mean what she clearly thinks it does.

"Olivia," I say into her ear, the word, her name, catching in my throat.

She releases her arms, steps back, and grabs my hands. "What?"

"I'm leaving."

Her face falls.

"It's not because of you getting partnership or our disagreement about what's best for Lucas." I let go of her hands. "I'm making this decision for me."

"Nate, no." She leans against the counter. "Things could be good here. Partnership is a lot, but—"

"It's not the partnership," I interrupt. "I'm thrilled for you about that, really. You deserve it and I'd never, ever ask you to turn down an opportunity like that." I cross my arms. "But Olivia, you fit here. You know what you want, and you know what you need to do to get it. I'm just—" I pause. "I'm lost. I thought coming here, applying again to medical school, was the answer, but everything I'd run from just followed me here."

Her eyes go soft. "Nate."

"You deserve someone who has it together."

"Stop it," she says, then more quietly asks, "what if you get into ManMed?"

"I won't," I say honestly. "And I need some time that's not"—I look around the space—"here."

* * *

A WEEK LATER, I fold Olivia into an embrace at the door. Neither of us have made a big deal about my moving out, both treating it like a break instead of a breakup. Maybe it will end up that way, but I doubt it. Olivia's on a good path; she doesn't need me.

She steps back and meets my gaze. "You're good with telling Lucas on your own? You don't want me to stay?"

I shake my head. "No. I'm okay." I'm not, really. I've been

dropping hints about leaving and moving on all week, but I've been putting off telling Lucas for real.

Olivia gives me a peck on the lips and puts her hand on the doorknob. "You'll call, right?"

"Of course, I'll call."

She slips out the door without looking back. I stand still in the foyer a long time. I have to do this. I puff out a breath and go to Lucas's room. He's awake and dressed. "Waffles, bud?"

He makes a verbal assent and follows me into the kitchen. I fix waffles in the same way I have hundreds of times before and slide into a seat at the table across from him.

"Hey, Lu. I have something to tell you."

He takes a bite of waffle.

"I'm moving out," I say, the word feeling like a Band-Aid ripped off. "I know it's sudden. I'm sorry for that."

He chews and swallows the waffle and takes another bite. I don't feel that I'm getting through. "It has nothing to do with you or Olivia," I continue, doing my best to gauge what he might be thinking. "I just need to figure some things out for myself."

He finishes the waffle.

"Olivia will make sure you have everything you need, obviously, and I'll come visit and all." I shift in my seat. "You'll be okay," I say, ostensibly to Lucas, but to myself too. "ACE has everything you need." I put my hand on his shoulder. "Keep at it. They have a lot of good resources there." I pause. "And remember Olivia wants what's best for you. She's a smart woman. She's never failed at anything in her life. You can't go wrong following her lead." I swallow, worried I'm talking too much, trying too hard, but wanting Lucas to feel taken care of all the same.

Lucas gets up and puts his dish in the sink. I viscerally want to know that he understood what I said. I want him to tell me he'll be alright. Or that he won't. Something. I want to know what he's feeling, what he's thinking, how I can help. But he's not giving anything away emotion-wise, not even with his body language.

He grabs his backpack, and we walk out of the apartment and the few blocks to his school. The walk is bittersweet, and I hug Lucas outside his classroom. He hugs me back in a way that makes me feel like maybe he understands. I finally let go. "See ya, buddy." I rap him on the back, and he disappears behind the classroom door.

I forcefully put the image of Olivia this morning and of Lucas right now out of my mind. I hail a cab, get in, and spend the rest of the day traveling. Cab to train to airplane to rental car. It's night before I reach my destination, the one I've told only my parents about.

I park the rental car, step out, and grab my duffel from the back. I walk toward the main building. It's night and it's dark but the path and building are illuminated. The main structure is an impressive two stories, made from log and stone, nearly the entire front constructed of windows. It's too dark to see now, but I know from the online pictures that there are mountains behind it.

I stop short at the front door and wish I were here with Olivia instead of on my own. We'd spend our days kayaking and hiking and visiting iconic places. We'd eat at cool restaurants and no matter how full she was she'd always want dessert anyway. We'd make love and sleep late, and she'd wake up and drink coffee in one those thick hotel robes. I picture her in one, skin sun-touched, hair spilling out around her shoulders. The image becomes so vivid I almost forget why I'm here. And that there's no me and Olivia anymore.

I stand still, staring at the thick wood door, duffel across my back.

I don't want to do this. It won't work. It was a stupid idea spawned from a single phone call with Dr. Alan.

I don't have to do it.

I can leave. I can go back to Greenwillow or New York. I can get a flight tomorrow.

I take a step back and just as I do the door swings open and a man who looks like he should be on the cover of American Cowboy stands in its frame. Cowboy hat, boots with spurs, a belt with a fat silver buckle in the center. I stare. This—he—is not what I expected.

The cowboy juts out a hand. "Nate Wilder?"

I grab his hand. "Yes."

"Tristan Boone. Welcome."

CHAPTER 65

L UCAS
I sit at my desk after Nate dropped me off. He's not
coming back. My stomach feels like lead is piled up on the
bottom. My movements are slow. Everything around me—sounds,
people, images—feel muffled and distant.

I'm sad, but I'm mad too. I get mad at myself a lot, but not usually
at others. Never at Nate. But I'm pretty sure he went to Greenwillow
without me. And I wanted more than anything for him to take me with
him. He's not the only one who misses it there.

I blow out a breath and pull a pencil out of my desk. Okay, I get
that he's not the guardian. He doesn't get to decide. But I'm still mad.
The whole thing is unfair. Nate gets to choose what he wants to do,
where he wants to live. I don't. I have to do what others decide is best. I
hate that.

But . . .

I could act out here at ACE. I could punch Michael again. I could
flip a desk. I could scream or pound my fists or throw the lunch bin
across the room. If my behavior was bad enough, ACE would expel me.
I'd never have to come back here again. Right?

Right.

One moment passes into the next and I very much want to be disruptive. Hugely so. I want to get kicked out of ACE. For once, I want my actions to bring about the result I'm looking for, not what someone else thinks is best. Disturbance = Expulsion. It's that easy.

But me doing that, me getting kicked out, wouldn't necessarily mean I would go back to Greenwillow. My behavior wouldn't bring Nate back. Or Mom or Dad. All me getting expelled would do is cause issues for Olivia, the only immediate family member I have left, the sister who reorganized her life to fit me into it, who saved me from Dennis. I care about Olivia. I can't, won't, do that to her. So I'm stuck.

CHAPTER 66

OLIVIA

Two weeks and three days after Nate left, I review the partnership agreement on my computer. I'm to e-sign it. That's it. Somehow, I thought there'd be a bigger hoopla surrounding the occasion. Like I'd sign the agreement in the big conference room with a Montblanc pen, surrounded by my fellow partners, all raising a toast with exclusive champagne served in cut crystal glasses. Instead, I'm at my kitchen table eating a bowl of Lucky Charms for dinner, an episode of Animal Planet about penguins blaring from Lucas's iPad in the next room, Otis curled up by his side.

I sign the agreement, or rather click on the e-sign button, and stare at the computer after.

I'm not sure what I expect will happen. That confetti will shoot out of the screen. That Marjorie will call on the spot with an impromptu celebratory invite. That I'll suddenly feel whole in the way I always thought I would.

None of it happens. I feel roughly the same as I did before I signed the agreement.

I dial Nate's number after, thinking maybe he'll answer this

time. He doesn't. There's not even a voicemail. Just a bunch of
rings that connect to nothing apparently. I remember what he
said at the door—"of course, I'll call." But he hasn't. And he
hasn't answered any of mine.

I reached out to Tessa and learned that he didn't move back
to Greenwillow either. She spoke to his parents who assured
her he was fine. But that's it. She doesn't know any more than I
do. Where he is, what he's doing. Why he's dropped off the face
of the earth. But knowing that he was "fine" per his parents
makes the lack of contact worse. He hasn't been kidnapped. He's
not sick. He's not lost. He's "fine." And a fine person can call.
He's just choosing not to.

I squeeze my eyes shut, willing myself to be as excited about
this moment as I'd always dreamed I would be. Partnership
anywhere is a big deal. At a firm like Bennett Connor, it's huge.

Enough, Olivia.

I open my eyes and pull a gallon of Rocky Road ice cream
out of the freezer. I gather the sundae items Nate stocked the
apartment with and take down bowls. I fix obscenely large
sundaes, complete with Nate-style whipped cream towers. I
carry them into the family room and when he sees me, Lucas
puts down his iPad. I hand him a bowl and clink my spoon
against his.

I sit crisscross applesauce on the sofa across from Lucas,
Otis centered between us. I spoon a bite of ice cream in my
mouth. "I'm a partner at Bennett Connor now," I tell him. "Like
Dad was. I'm kind of intimidated by the senior partner, though.
Marjorie. I miss William, my old boss. He's the one who died a
few weeks back. And Todd, my old work friend, still ignores me
since I don't do his cases anymore." I confide in Lucas how
much that hurts my feelings. In the absence of Nate, having no
friends at work and no mentor like William has been really
hard.

Lucas spoons ice cream into his mouth.

"I've been following your progress on the ACE portal. You're really killing it, Lu." I reach out and squeeze his hand. "I'm proud of you. I know this move has been hard in a lot of ways. I'm sorry for that."

We finish our ice cream in congenial silence, penguin facts blaring out of the iPad like pleasant background noise. It feels like we're bonding in the way we had during those Greenwillow summers.

The next morning is beautiful with a bright blue sky and the kind of temperature that makes me crave fresh air. I peel open a few windows in the apartment, take my time getting ready, and walk with Lucas to school at a leisurely pace instead of my normal hurried one. After, I take the long way to work, soaking in the feeling of a major life goal—partnership—achieved. The role will be challenging, but I'm convinced I can handle the job.

I can't handle the job.

Not at first. I struggle with time, with supervision of other lawyers, with the competition between partners for news-worthy cases and department billables. The pressure to network at evening events and bring in clients with big dollars. The fear of being the dreaded department with a slow quarter. Just doing a good job isn't enough anymore.

* * *

TWO MONTHS IN, I'm fully indoctrinated into the Bennett Connor grind. I thrive on the adrenaline of it all in the same way I always have, but it's more intense now. The more accolades I get, the more clients I bring in, the more money my department makes, the more I internally thrive. Strive and thrive. It's a saying among the partners. I say it to Lucas too. Strive and thrive, Lu. I've loaded him up with so many tutors and activities and extra school time that he's almost as busy as I am. Both of us too busy to miss Nate or wonder if he'll ever call.

Too busy to keep up with the Greenwillow gang. My fault, that one. I declined offers to visit, stopped returning calls and texts. And as much as I want the two worlds to be like a Venn diagram, where they can and do intersect, they don't. And they won't. I've chosen New York. It's best for me, and it's best for Lucas.

Right now, Lucas is at school and I'm at the Kitty Cat Café.

"Are you sure?" Jess shoves her hands into a cotton jumper with cat faces on it.

"He's a foster cat." I set Otis's carrier on the bar. "And you said you had a forever home."

She tips her head. "Yes, but there have been adoptees before. You've never been willing to let him go." She peeks inside the carrier. "What's changed?"

"Me. My life." The words sound flippant but they're true. My life looks nothing like it did pre-Lucas, pre-Nate, and pre-partnership. The landscape has completely changed, and I have no time for a pet. He gets fed after midnight lots of days, or he's holed up in my bedroom for hours because one of Lucas's tutors/caregivers is afraid of him and another is allergic. He's escaped into the hallway more than once. He deserves better and this forever home is on a farm.

I glance at the carrier. *You'll love it*, I say in my head, hoping the thought will teleport into his psyche. I pivot my gaze away. "He loved living in the country when I was in Greenwillow," I tell Jess. "And he'll like being part of a family who's around more. Lucas and I just aren't." I tap on the carrier. "It's time to let him have a real home."

"Okay." Jess picks up the carrier. "If you're sure."

"I'm sure," I manage, the word a lump in my throat that feels the size of a boulder. "Don't forget to give them his supplies," I squeak out and nod toward the giant box I brought with Otis's bed, favorite toys, food dishes, and blanket. "And make sure you tell them he only likes paté cat food, not minced. Stella and

Chewy. The cans are purple." I point to the box. "I left a note in there."

"Sure." She starts toward the stairs, Otis's head visible through the gray mesh. His yellow eyes stare at me, betrayed.

"He doesn't like to be handled," I yell after Jess. "Cuddled, but on his terms, you know. Can you tell them that?"

"I will."

"I don't want him getting overstimulated."

Jess stops short at the bottom of the stairs and swings her head in my direction. "You don't have to do this." She holds up the carrier. "Take him home, Olivia."

In that snapshot of a moment, I see myself striding across the room, grabbing the carrier, and hightailing it back to the apartment, Otis in tow. But I can't. I have a court appearance after this, a full day of work, and a networking event in between getting Lucas from school to his tutoring session to home. I'll be flying from thing to thing, and I know I'll forget about Otis somewhere in the mix. Living on a farm with a family will make him happy.

I've got to let him go.

"Take care, O," I say in his direction and walk out the door.

CHAPTER 67

LUCAS

"Come on, Lucas." Olivia is standing by the apartment door, key in her hand. She's shaking it. "We've got to go."

I don't even know where we're going, to be honest. Olivia has me doing the exact same gazillion therapies Mom cut out of my schedule right before Nate came on so I could have time to" just be." I'd really appreciated that at the time, and more so now, in the absence of it. The constant going, even if I do have multiple "deficits" to work on, is no way to live. I step to the door.

"Okay, let's go. We need to get to OT."

OT. Occupational therapy. At least that's good. I like OT. My OT, Miss Cassidy, is super nice, and she lets me pick the activities as much as she can. But other than OT, everything is a drag, though I am "improving." I can say more words. My muscle tone is better. I control stims better. But these improvements are incremental, and the tiny bits of progress don't make me "normal" in the sense most people use the word. It's not like I can say something like "let's move back to Green-willow" or "where is Nate?" or "why are you hardly ever here anymore?"

If I could say these kinds of things, it would make all the work *worth it. But all I can do now is say more phrases like "help with iPad" and frankly, holding up the iPad was working just fine. Plus, no matter how much inflection I try to infuse into my voice, the words always come out monotone. Plus, Olivia's barely around and not engaged with me if she is. So, careful what you wish for and all. Because as much as I'd wished for Olivia to take on the guardianship after Mom died, I wonder if I might not have been better off with Uncle Dennis in the end. At least I'd still be at home.*

CHAPTER 68

O LIVIA
"You can do it?" Marjorie asks.

I pull at my pajama top and shift on the couch. I should say no. It's Saturday, the first one I've taken off in forever, and I have tickets for Lucas and me to see the autism-friendly matinee version of Mary Poppins on Broadway. I've been talking up the show for weeks. There are plenty of partners who could take this last-minute meeting at the firm with Hank Lenkins of Zapple, a multi-million-dollar beverage company looking for new legal counsel.

Marjorie just spent the past several minutes detailing why our chance of getting the job is minimal. I guess that's why she's comfortable sending me, the least experienced, least senior partner at the firm, in her stead.

"Yes?" she prompts.

If I keep the meeting to less than an hour, we'll have enough time to make the show. "Of course." I spew out the words. It's not like I have enough guts to say no to Marjorie anyway. Despite being a partner, I still feel like that little girl working with her dad on Saturday mornings, Marjorie the glamorous woman attorney with an office next door.

"Thanks, Olivia," she blows out, like I just agreed to get her a glass of water instead of taking on a big meeting at the last moment.

She disconnects the call, and my mind runs through people I could call to hang with Lucas during the meeting. If I were in Greenwillow, there would be a ton of options; here, I'm down to two. Mom or the twins, neither of whom live close enough. I could call one of Lucas's tutors or caregivers, but they're usually booked way in advance, and I don't have time to waste on a bunch of calls and texts likely to yield nothing.

I glance at Lucas on the other side of the couch, already dressed, and make a snap decision to bring him along. I'll set him up in my office with a video. It'll be fine.

I rush through a shower and pull on the first dress clothes I see. I hurry Lucas along to the firm and we take the elevator up to the Bennett Connor main floor. Once in the office, I quickly show Lucas the library, the kitchen, and where Dad used to sit. I show him the conference room where I'll be meeting Hank Lenkins, and lead him to my office. He sits at my desk and leans forward in the direction of the three framed photographs. One is of Lucas in front of the tree at Rockefeller Center. The second is Otis in a sunny spot. And the third is a selfie of me and Nate in Central Park. I'd like to say I'd forgotten the Nate and Otis pictures were there, but I hadn't. I'd put the Nate picture in my desk drawer after it became clear he would remain MIA, but I'd missed seeing his face, in person and in the photo. So I took the photograph back out.

Lucas's gaze remains fixed on the pictures, and I finally say, "I miss them too." The acknowledgment seems to be enough to switch his focus, and he turns on his iPad. I sit in the chair opposite him and make a few meeting notes based on the bare-bones email Marjorie had sent about Zapple. When it's time for the meeting, I remind Lucas what conference room I'll be in, walk out to the reception area, and introduce myself to Hank.

The meeting goes fast, too fast for me to feel it's a success, but given how little Marjorie seemed to care about Zapple as a client, I don't worry about the "failure to convert" in the way I normally would. It's not like I had any time to prepare, and I brought in plenty of business in my short tenure as a partner. This can't possibly be used as an invisible strike against me, the unspoken but well-accounted for tally of partner failures.

I clear Hank Lenkins and Zapple and the super quick meeting from my mind and walk back to my office. I let out a sigh of relief when I find Lucas there. Not that I really thought he'd go anywhere; still, I shouldn't have left him alone. If he had gotten up for some reason, if he'd left, if he was missing? I'm not sure what I'd do.

I coax him to get up and look at my watch. "Believe it or not, we have plenty of time," I tell him. "Let's stop at the Times Square Krispy Kreme. You're not going to believe how big it is."

CHAPTER 69

LUCAS

We're in the cab, having just left the meeting at the firm. I liked Olivia's office. There's a picture of me in it. And one of Otis. And Nate. I was surprised by the last two. She doesn't mention either of them much anymore, but she did say, today, that she missed them. I do too.

Anyway, we're on our way to what Olivia said is the biggest Krispy Kreme in the world. We'll stop there and go to the show after. I'm good with that. I love Krispy Kreme. But the farther we go, the crazier the scene outside the cab gets. More cars. More people. Horses pull carriages; bike riders pull people behind them in carts. There are giant red busses with people riding on top. A person in a gorilla costume walks down the street. I'm not sure anymore about going to Krispy Kreme. Doesn't seem worth it.

I push my back into the cushions of the cab. I remind myself that I'm safe inside this space, separate from whatever craziness is happening outside. Surely, Olivia must think it's nuts too. She'll want to get dropped off right in front of the theatre.

But the cab stops, and Olivia opens the door into the middle of the craziness and waves me forward. I move back, but she urges me to "come on" and it's clear I'm to get out. Since I can't just stay in the cab or tell the driver to take me somewhere, literally anywhere else, I step into the chaos. My heartbeat accelerates, my hands flap. I want to verbalize "no" but I make nonsensical noises instead. No one seems to care or take notice; everyone just pushes by. A bonus, I guess, of the insanity.

Olivia grabs my arm and tells me Krispy Kreme is just two blocks ahead. Not that I could possibly miss it. It's huge. We forge through the crowd like we're joined at the hip. I feel safer then, and when we finally reach the Krispy Kreme, I realize I need to go to the bathroom.

I had to go at the firm, but I hadn't known where the bathrooms were, and once I was in the cab, everything was all so crazy. So now I've waited too long, and I really need to go. I spy the telltale bathroom signs and pull Olivia towards them. She realizes what I need, and I know she won't want me to go into the men's room at the Krispy Kreme by myself. She's taken me into the ladies' room with her in the past, and the looks of shock or pity or both at the grown-ass man in the bathroom is the worst. I don't want to go through that. Plus, the ladies' room has a line out the door and I really have to go. So I slip into the men's room before Olivia can suggest anything else and she calls out that she'll be right outside.

But the thing is, when I get out, she isn't.

CHAPTER 70

OLIVIA

"Lu, wait," I yell, but he slips into the men's room before I can stop him. Public restrooms were easy when Nate was around, but I hate them for this very reason. Something about a nonverbal autistic man in a public bathroom makes me nervous.

I lean against the wall across from the bathroom and blow out a breath. It'll be fine. I'm just being paranoid.

My phone buzzes. I pull it out of my pocket, see its Marjorie, and answer.

"What did you say to Hank Lenkins?" she asks in lieu of hello.

I pull the phone closer to my ear. "What? Nothing."

"I just spoke to him. He's not interested in Bennett Connor as firm counsel. At all."

I blink. "But that's what you thought, right? That it was unlikely he'd be interested." I walk in a circle and run through the conversation we'd had this morning. Minimal chance. Those were her exact words.

"Unlikely, yes. But it was up to you to convince him, Olivia."

She goes on to tell me that she's set up a second meeting with Hank on Monday and she'd like me to be there.

"Of course."

Marjorie gives a terse goodbye and disconnects the call.

My body heat rises, my thoughts frozen on Marjorie's words and how she sounded when she said them. Like I disappointed her. She's always been a big advocate for me, from making sure I stayed on the Rowan case to pushing for partnership. This is the first time I felt like I didn't live up to one of her expectations. It's weird. My own mother is perpetually disappointed in me, and I don't care. But Marjorie's dissatisfaction? It's a gut punch.

I cross my arms, disgrace washing over me like a wave. I did a bad job. As hard as I tried to do everything perfectly, I messed up. I fixate on the meeting, going through it frame by frame, until it finally dawns on me: Lucas has been in the bathroom for a long time.

A sliver of nervousness pings in my chest. "Lucas," I call into the void of the men's room door. "Lucas."

There's no answer, not that I expected one, but I hope me yelling his name will spur him along. I move closer to the entrance, like a sentry on guard. A portly man with an I heart New York T-shirt on comes out, then a young guy in a Knicks jersey. No Lucas. A third man emerges, a fatherly type, and I touch his arm.

"I'm sorry," I say, "but my brother is autistic and he went into the rest room and . . ."

"Want me to check for him?" the man asks, and I smile.

"Please," I say. "He's tall, brown hair. He has on a yellow shirt."

The man steps into the rest room and comes out almost immediately. "He's not in there."

My stomach flutters. "Are you sure? I've been standing here, and he hasn't come out."

The man shakes his head. "There are only two people in there and neither of them sound like the way you described your brother." He moves his index finger in the air. "Maybe look around here."

"But—" I start. Adrenaline shoots through me. I was right here the whole time. Right? Yes? Yes, but I was distracted. Maybe he slipped out when I was talking to Marjorie. I punch at my phone to check the air tag Lucas always has in his pocket. I put it in there. Right? No? Shit. The icon is there. At the apartment. I was in such a rush to get to the last-minute meeting with Hank Lenkins, I forgot all about it.

Panic slices through me. "Lucas? Lu?" I call again, frantic enough now that people around me stare. "Lucas!" I stride into the bathroom. A man's at a sink, another at a urinal. I kick open the door to the only bathroom stall with my foot. "Lucas?" No one. I whip around and look at the men, the urinal man pulling up his pants. "Did you see a tall man, brown hair?" I blurt out, my speech rushed. "Yellow shirt. He came in here a while ago."

The men exchange glances and shrug. "No."

"He was here. He came in here."

There's no window and I kick open the stall again as if might have missed him the first time. "Oh my God. Oh my God."

I fly out of the bathroom and step onto a chair in the middle of the Krispy Kreme store. "Lucas," I yell. "Lucas." My eyes dart around the space, willing Lucas to come into view, his head above everyone else's. Please. Please. Please, Lu. Please be here. Please.

No Lucas. Missing person stories flash in my mind.

"Did anyone see a tall man?" I yell. "Brown hair. Yellow shirt."

The crowd quiets, everyone now staring in my direction. "A man," I say again. "Eighteen. Brown hair. Tall. Yellow shirt."

I press a palm against my chest. "He's autistic," I blurt. "Help.

I need help. Did anyone see a tall man, brown hair? He was in the restroom. His name is Lucas. Lucas! Lucas."

There's pressure on my leg.

Lucas! It's Lucas.

Relief floods my body, and I drop my head. But in a flash, my mind registers that the person pulling on my leg is not Lucas. It's a woman in a Krispy Kreme polo.

"Ma'am," she says, "ma'am. You need to get down. We'll try to help you."

I ignore her and whip my head around, looking for Lucas, frenzied and uncontrolled. "Lucas!"

"Ma'am. Please."

I step down. "He's gone," I say. "I lost my brother."

CHAPTER 71

LUCAS

I'm outside the Krispy Kreme, hurrying toward the woman who I thought was Olivia but now I'm not sure. I don't know what else to do so I keep following her. Smells and sounds and the push of people shoving past me assault my senses from all sides and I lose track of the woman who might be Olivia. I keep walking, panic beating at my chest. I reach the end of the sidewalk, but I don't think to stop—I'm not thinking at all—and I keep walking. A car stops just short of hitting me. The driver beeps, loud and long, like the entire force of his body is on his steering wheel, and I freeze. My mind says "move" but I don't move, I just stand there. Shock and fear lock my arms and legs in place. I start to yell, and more cars beep, and drivers open their windows and scream. I ball up where I am in the middle of the road. A man from the sidewalk runs forward and tries to move me. He puts his hands under my armpits, and I don't know him and he's touching me and I want him to let go.

And then time skips. Red and blue lights flash in the periphery of my vision and two police officers get out of a car and head toward me. The man who had been pushing shouts to the officers that I assaulted him. He holds up his arm and there are bite marks and blood. The man says I bit and hit and kicked him and that I'm crazy. And I want to say no, that I didn't and that I'm not and where is my sister, but honestly, there's a space between when he touched me in the road and this moment, and I don't know what happened.

The two policemen stand on either side of me and start to push me toward their vehicle. I struggle against them, not wanting to get into their car, wanting to stay here and wait for Olivia, but they overpower me. I start to laugh, high-pitched and wild, and I try to stop, but it happens again and again, crazy sounds with a life of their own.

My face is pinned against the police car window and handcuffs are being clamped around my hands. I'm shoved inside the car, arms twisted and behind my back. I'm still laugh-screaming; the cops shake their heads at each other. Maybe I am crazy.

CHAPTER 72

OLIVIA
    "Ma'am, I'm sure—" the woman in the Krispy Kreme polo starts.

"You don't get it," I yell. "He can't speak. He's autistic. He's not familiar with the city. He won't know where he is." The concept that he's not lost, but taken, flashes in my mind. One horrific image after another after another burst into my mind, a mental parade of monstrosities. My breath shortens. I drop my head into my hands, tears streaming down my face. "Oh my God. I can't believe this is happening."

A man near me leans closer. "I just called the police."

I look up and wipe the tears and snot on my face with my bare arm. My heart is still racing, my breath still short, but the thought that the police are coming stalls the panic from accelerating further. There are things that can be done to find him. Lucas is somewhere. He didn't just vanish into thin air.

My gaze falls on the glass windows that line the entire façade of the store and the throng of people on the sidewalk outside of it. Lucas could be out there. He could be waiting for me.

"Wait for the police," I yell and stride to the glass door. I step out onto the sidewalk.

"Lucas," I call. "Lucas." I cup my hands around my mouth for volume. "Lucas. Lucas. Has anyone seen a tall man, brown hair, in a yellow shirt?" No one stops. "Has anyone seen a tall man, brown hair, in a yellow shirt?" I repeat. Nothing. It's like I'm yelling into a void.

A police car pulls up in front of the Krispy Kreme. An officer emerges from the vehicle; I push through the crowd. "Are you here about the missing autistic man?" I spit out. He doesn't answer and words continue to fly from my mouth. "My brother. He's autistic." I race through the scenario, how Lucas went into the bathroom and now he's gone. "I was right there," I say. "Outside the bathroom."

"Officer Ty Anders," he says, gesturing toward his police car like I didn't even speak. "I'd like to get some information."

"We need to look for him. He can't have gone far." I look around, wild. "Can't you blow a horn or something, stop everyone so we can just find him?" I stand on my toes and look over the throngs of people. "Do something," I yell. "The longer he's gone, the harder it will be to find him."

"Ma'am," Officer Anders says, "I need to you to listen."

His calmness—like my nonverbal autistic brother being missing is no big deal—frays my already battered nerves. "Lucas," I yell. "Lucas." I shove past people, hurtling down the sidewalk, the act of doing something, anything, the only way to manage my rising hysteria.

Officer Anders catches up and puts his hand on my upper arm. "Ma'am," he says with force, "you need to calm down."

I give a final, frenetic look around the crowded Times Square streets. No dark head of hair sticks out above the crowd. No yellow shirt. No flapping hands from overstimulation. He's gone.

"Ma'am," Officer Anders prompts and I follow him to his vehicle and slide into the passenger seat.

Officer Anders asks a variety of simple questions. My name. Lucas's name. Lucas's age. What he was wearing. A physical description. What happened. With each question, I get more and more riled up. We need to do something. We need to look for Lucas.

Officer Anders pulls a giant phone from a holster on his hip. "I'm going to give his description to dispatch. See if anyone fitting his physical characteristics has been picked up."

He makes the call and describes Lucas by the traits I'd given him. Brown hair, 6'1", brown eyes, yellow shirt, autistic, nonverbal. The portrayal is correct. Still, it strikes me how much more there is to my brother than this six-attribute description and the fact that he's autistic. The quiet part of him. His seldom given full-faced smiles. His love of animals. The joy he gets jumping on the trampoline. The morning waffles he can't do without. His favorite clothes, worn over and over. The contemplative walks around the pond that he loves. And the way he's always made me feel, like one minute could slide into the next and the next and the next and we didn't have to *do* anything. Just being with me was enough.

My phone rings and my heart leaps. Lucas. This has to do with Lucas. I'm certain of it. I grab the phone inside my suit jacket and see Marjorie's face on the screen. Anger pings inside me. She's seriously calling? Again? I shove the phone back inside my suit jacket.

"Nothing yet." Officer Anders stands. "I'll get a report filed and we'll get a search started." He meets my eyes. "Can I bring you somewhere in the meantime? Home?"

"No." There's no way I'm leaving this area.

"Is there anyone I can call?"

I open my mouth. I want to say Nate. Call Nate. He's who I need right now. He'd know what to do. But of course, any call to

Nate will just end up the way it always does. With endless rings. Because wherever Nate is, he doesn't want to be reached. I think a moment, then utter words I never thought I would in relation to Lucas. "Could you call my mother?"

Officer Anders calls Mom and arranges for her to go to my apartment in the unlikely event Lucas finds his way back there. He punches what I gather is the police report into a giant iPad. I pivot my head toward the masses outside, dozens of people streaming through every second. "Should we be doing something right now?"

"I've got to get the report into the system."

I stare at him. His index fingers punch at the keyboard. It's slow. Agonizingly so. Like the man has never seen a keyboard. "I can type." I reach for the device. "I can do it."

He stops typing, left index finger poised over the keyboard. "No thank you."

I watch him another moment. Adrenaline shoots through my system; I feel dizzy. I've got to move. "I'm going to look for him." I push open the car door and step into the mass of humanity outside. The intense crowds, the tall skyscrapers, the gigantic electronic billboards that flash and change every few seconds—all pieces of the Times Square slice of New York City I'd once found so exciting—are nightmarish now. I push through throngs of people toward the West Riding Theatre where Lucas and I were going to see Mary Poppins. Maybe he remembers? Maybe he'll be there? Waiting for me? My eyes scan the crowd as I walk and my gaze shoots toward glimpses of yellow like Lucas's shirt. Purses, sweatshirts, shoes. Never Lucas.

I reach the theatre and stop short. No one is at the ticket kiosk. No one behind the red felt ropes. No Lucas. I stare at the building. But for my ill-timed and completely unnecessary work-related distraction, we'd be in there right now.

Overwhelm pulses through my veins; tears prick at my eyes. How did I let this happen?

CHAPTER 73

OLIVIA
    I remain still in front of the theatre as people stream past. My phone rings in my suit jacket pocket. I pull it out, no longer expecting it to be about Lucas. Probably Marjorie. Again.

"Hello."

"Olivia. Officer Anders."

My body straightens. "Yes? Anything?"

"Someone with Lucas's description is in police custody."

"Really?" Relief floods my system.

"He was agitated and may have sprained his arm," he explains. "They've taken him to Presby on 71st. I assume you'll go. Verify it's him."

"Yes. I'll go right now."

I catch a cab, take it to Presby, and find out what room Lucas is in at the front desk. I shoot through the halls, on to the elevator, and race toward the room. A police officer is stationed in a folding chair by the front door like a guard. I stride past her and make a beeline for the bed. I need to know that it's really Lucas in there. I reach the bed, breath escaping from my body, the tension in my muscles easing. It's him. He's there. Lucas. Asleep, but safe. Thank God.

My feet root to the floor.

"Are you the sister?"

I look up. The police officer from the folding chair is in the room. A tall woman with sleek black hair pulled away from her face in a bun. Her eyes are tired. Lipstick feathers around the wrinkles in her mouth.

"Officer Anders called me." She juts her hand out in my direction. "I'm Officer Danielle Clark."

She grips my hand and lets it go. "What happened?" I ask.

Danielle explains the scene. I visualize it easily. Lucas balled up in the road, interfering with traffic. Lucas bit the man who tried to move him and later bit Danielle's partner. Biting would seem out of character, but not if Lucas were stressed or scared or both.

"What happens next?"

"If you're the guardian, I can release custody of Lucas to you, and you can work out with the hospital when he can go home. But he'll have to appear in court. The district attorney will decide whether to file formal charges."

My mouth drops open. "Seriously?" I get that Lucas was obstructing traffic, that he *bit* two people, but he was also lost, scared, and he's autistic. Context matters. "Don't you think he's been traumatized enough?"

"I do," she says. "The DA won't charge him, I don't think."

"But they might."

"It's not up to me. If I were you, I'd retain a lawyer."

"I am a lawyer," I say automatically.

Surprise crosses her features, and I realize how ridiculous the statement sounds given how little I seem to know. My legal knowledge does not extend to situations where an average person might need advice, apparently. It seems, suddenly, a waste. Of my education. Of my career. Of my life even. What good is it to be an attorney if I can't help people when it matters?

"Well, you'll be all set then," Danielle says. "I'll document the release of custody to you and get going."

"Thanks."

I scan my mind for attorneys I know that might be able to help. Probably because she'd just called, my mind fixes on Marjorie. She doesn't do criminal law, but she'd know who to call. She probably has a connection to the DA even. She could make sure charges against Lucas are never brought. The more I think about it, the more the idea has legs. Marjorie was able to get an almost impossible to find out-of-home placement for Lucas in a matter of weeks. Surely, getting the DA to drop a bogus case would be easier than that.

"I'll be right back," I say to Danielle and walk to the nearest bathroom. I pull open the door and step inside. A giant mirror reflects a woman I barely recognize. One with stress lines in her forehead, dark circles under her eyes, and frazzled, uncombed hair. I turn away from my image, one of a stranger, and dial Marjorie. She answers on the first ring.

"Olivia. Good. I've been trying to reach you."

"Yes," I start.

"There's a rumor the Rowan decision is ready to be released. Scuttlebutt is that it's good. I need you to call Jupiter and—"

"I can't right now. My brother is in the hospital. He's been arrested." I pause and wait for her to affirm that she's heard me. When she doesn't, I continue. "I need your help."

"I'm sorry your brother is in the hospital."

I exhale. "Thank you."

"But Bennett Connor doesn't handle petty criminal cases, Olivia. You should know that."

Petty. The word hits my gut, there seeming nothing petty about this situation. My brother, so scared out of his mind that he balled up in the center of New York Times and bit the people trying to help him? There's nothing petty about that.

"There's no case yet," I say. "Just an arrest. I was hoping you might know someone in the District Attorney's office. That maybe you could see to it that no charges are brought."

"I'd love to help, but I have no idea what he's done. If he's guilty. If he hurt someone. I can't put the firm's name on the line like that."

"He didn't do anything," I quip. "He was lost and resisted the people trying to help. Things got out of hand."

"I'm sorry," she says. "It just isn't a good mix, you know, personal life and firm life."

Her comments hit my gut, all of them contradictory. The firm helps guilty people all the time, like Jupiter Rowan. And personal and firm life is already inextricably mixed. Wills provided, advice dispensed, phone calls made behind closed doors to help our own. The out-of-home placement she secured. Marjorie can help. She doesn't want to.

"Maybe call Brian Lawlor," she suggests.

My eyes widen. Brian Lawlor? That's a joke. He represents celebrities. Not Joe Shmo's like Lucas.

"I'll deal with the Jupiter thing," she says. "Good luck with your brother."

She clicks off, and her words—good luck with your brother—reverberate inside me. Good luck? What, like he's taking a trip? Or moving? I'm flooded with the realization that Marjorie Small, outstanding lawyer she may be, is not in my corner in the way I'd always thought.

I shove my cell inside my pocket and walk down the hall to Lucas's room. Danielle is gone and I walk past her empty chair and move to one next to Lucas's bed. I collapse into it, and the emotions of the day swarm inside me, pelting from the inside. I fall asleep upright in the chair. When I rouse, Lucas is awake.

CHAPTER 74

LUCAS
When I open my eyes and see Olivia sitting there, my heart bursts open. Thank God. I would hug her if I could, but I'm stuck in a hospital bed. She's sleeping anyway. After a few minutes, she opens her eyes, and they meet mine. I'm not usually comfortable with eye contact, but right now it's all good. I'm so relieved.

She stands up and gives me the hug I wanted to give her but couldn't. She apologizes for what happened over and over. I want to tell her not to worry. If I weren't, well ME, it never would have been an issue to begin with. I wouldn't have needed to be minded and us getting separated would not have led to the giantic friggin' breakdown that I still don't entirely remember. I remember getting lost and being in the road and the man trying to move me. I felt anger at the man, explosive, crazy, heated anger, but then . . . nothing. I don't remember the rest. But whatever I did must have been bad because there was a police officer in my hospital room. That can't be what normally happens, right? Maybe it's a New York thing? I don't know. But I hope I didn't hurt that man. Now that I'm calm and safe and not lost in *what felt like the center of sensory hell, I understand that he was just trying to help me.*

CHAPTER 75

OLIVIA

I sit with Lucas until visiting hours are over, and after, I take a cab to my apartment. When I reach the door, a voice sounds from inside—my mother. I forgot she'd be here, forgot Officer Anders's call to her. It all seems so long ago.

Under most circumstances, and especially ones that involve Lucas, I wouldn't want her here. But right now, I do. I want her to hug me tight, to tell me all the mistakes I've made will end up okay in the end. That I'm doing all right. That I'm on course. That I am not, right now, utterly, and completely alone.

I push open the unlocked door and step inside. Mom hurries toward me, high heels clicking across the hardwood, arms outstretched. She envelops me in a tight squeeze and the emotions I've been holding back release all at once. I close my eyes, but tears stream from them anyway and my breath goes ragged.

"It's okay, sweetheart," she says in my ear. "It's okay."

I pull back and wipe the tears. It's then that I see everyone. Ellie and Shelby. Tessa, Dominique, Suzanne, and Avery. My eyes widen. "What are you all doing here?"

Dominique answers. "Your mom called us."

I scan other parts of the room for Nate; he's not here.

"Lucas has been found," I say, realizing that they must think he is still missing, that this is an emergency. "He's in the hospital."

Mom nods. "We know. Officer Anders called me."

My brows furrow.

"We're here for you, dummy," Tessa says. "To help."

I look around the adjoining family room and kitchen, the scent of lasagna and freshly baked bread now evident. Containers of food with handwritten labels on masking tape line the counter. Two freshly folded baskets of laundry sit on the floor. Vacuum marks are evident on the area rug, and new throw pillows and plants adorn the room, along with an array of fresh magazines. Light piano music plays softly from a portable speaker, and a lit candle sits in the center of the table. It looks and smells like a home instead of the pit stop I'd been using it as.

"We figured you've been through a lot today," Dominque says, pulling out a chair. "You'll take care of Lucas, we know that, but someone has to look out for you."

I blink. It's the absolute perfect thing to say, a salve to my psyche. I haven't felt like someone was looking out for me since Nate left. I didn't realize I missed the feeling until now. My throat constricts. "Thank you."

"Come eat something." Shelby sets a plate of lasagna on the table with a flourish. "Ta da. I made this from scratch, if you can believe it."

"I can't believe it," I joke and collapse into a chair at the table. I shovel a bite of food into my mouth. "It's delicious." It may be that I haven't eaten since this morning, but this lasagna tastes, in this moment, like the best food I've ever had, and I'm touched Shelby would go to the trouble to make it. "So good," I say in her direction.

"Glad you like it. There's another one in your freezer."

All of them gradually assemble around the table, around me, and I tell them the whole story. From the apparently fruitless meeting with Hank Lenkins of Zapple, to Lucas running into the bathroom, to scouring Times Square, to the final conversation with Marjorie at the hospital, where she wished me "good luck."

Tessa slaps the table with an open palm. "Are you shitting me right now? That's what she said? Good luck with your brother?"

I nod. The statement, repeated, still stings but there's an edge of humor to it now. Like the remark is so objectively awful as to be absurd. I spoon the last piece of lasagna into my mouth and swallow. "Problem is, I don't know anything about criminal law or any good lawyers who specialize in it that would have reasonable fees."

"Chuck Stockton," Dominique says without hesitation. "He used to be a public defender. He'll help you."

"He'd help? Really?" I barely know Chuck. Given that Marjorie, whom I've known nearly my entire life, won't help me, I can't imagine that he'd want to.

"Of course. I'll call him right now."

During a two-minute conversation, Chuck agrees to conference with me tomorrow, and also to reach out to some contacts who may know someone who knows someone and all that. With my stomach full of homecooked food, a band of people to support me, and a solid plan, I feel infinitely better than I did just a few hours ago.

"We've got to go." Dominque yawns and my gaze shifts to the clock. It's ten at night.

"You're not going home." My mind turns to how all six of the women here, seven including myself, can fit comfortably in my apartment to sleep.

"Of course not." She puts her hand on my shoulder. "We have a hotel room. We'll be back tomorrow."

"I can give you a ride," Shelby offers. She pulls out her keys, and in the next few moments, after a swell of hugs and good-byes and get some rest, it's just me and Mom.

"I'll stay if you want me to, sweetheart," Mom says. "It's no problem."

"Thanks. I'd like that."

She sweeps my used plate off the table and brings it into the kitchen. I follow her and lean against the counter. "Thank you for all this," I say. "For coming, for calling everyone. You didn't have to do that."

"Nonsense," she says and pulls on a pair of thick rubber gloves I didn't even know I owned. She fills the sink with water and dishwashing liquid and proceeds to clean the plate so thoroughly you'd think royalty might eat off it next.

I hand her a dish towel. "I needed you here, Mom. Really. Thank you for coming."

She dries off the plate and sets it and the towel on the counter. "I haven't been very supportive of your decision to care for Lucas," she says, turning to face me.

I inhale a breath. The statement is true, clearly, but Mom's never admitted it before.

She pushes a frosted lock of hair behind her ear. "As your mother, I was worried for you and how taking on such a big responsibility would impact your life."

I release my breath and brace myself, the cascade of *I told you so's* feeling imminent.

"Caring for Lucas," she continues, "it's a good thing you've done. One most people would never have been brave enough to try. I wouldn't have been. Not now. And certainly not when I was twenty-eight." She steps forward and grazes her hand across my cheek. "I'm so proud of you, Olivia. Of the character you've shown. Of the woman you've become. Your father would be too. And he'd be so grateful to you, for looking out for his son." Her voice catches on the last words, and I fall into her arms, her unexpected approval lodging in my mind.

"Thanks, Mom," I whisper.

"It's nothing." She pulls back and grabs the dish towel from the counter and flicks it in my direction. "Get to bed now. You look like death, and we can't have that. There's only so much eye cream can do, you know."

A smile tugs at my mouth at the Mom-like statement, endearing in this context. "Yes, Mother." I kiss her cheek.

I get ready for bed and lie down. Despite this being the worst day and the fact that this nightmare isn't over, I feel better than I have in months.

CHAPTER 76

OLIVIA

The district attorney does not drop the case in advance, and right now Lucas stands next to me at the courthouse, pulling at the sleeves of a suit I bought off of Amazon last week. Dominique, who agreed to stay through this hearing, stands on the other side of him. We flank him, our arms entwined in his. It's loud and bright and smells like a combination of sweat, mold, and perfume. I glance at Lucas and wish I hadn't insisted he wear the suit. The sensory experience of just being in court is enough without the addition of itchy clothes.

I scan the hallway outside the courtroom for John, the DA I was told was handling Lucas's matter. I spot a wiry, bald man with a stack of manila folders, a line of people in front of him. I assume he's John. I watch the interaction between John and a presumed defendant, amazed at the informality. Like nothing is at stake. You know, just a clean record or freedom or both. No problem to talk about the cases in a public hallway a few minutes before the hearing.

We move as a trio and stand at the end of the line. I listen to

John and try to glean something about his lawyer personality. He scoffs at a youngish man representing himself, yells "next" when he's in mid-sentence. He tells the lawyer who's after him to "just forget it." His arms are crossed. His talks too fast. His attitude screams "get off my lawn." Shit. This guy is a jerk.

At my turn, I let go of Lucas's arm, step up to John, and inhale the scent of his too strong, too spicy aftershave. My heart thrums in my chest like a motor and I pull at Mom's pendant, one she let me borrow for good luck. "State of New York v. Ellison. Olivia Ellison, attorney."

John glances at me, then thumbs through the stack of files. He pulls out a thin manila folder with Lucas's name scrawled across the top in pen. He extracts papers from the folder and scans them.

Lucas, next to me, flaps his hands.

"My brother is autistic," I say preemptively. "The defendant," I clarify.

"Disability isn't a defense per se, counselor," John says without looking up.

"But there were extenuating circumstances—" I start.

"Polar bears have black skin," Lucas says, his voice crystal clear in a way it isn't normally. He flaps his hands. "Polar bears have black skin," he says again.

People behind him snicker and my defenses rachet up on his behalf. "Lucas," I whisper.

"Shh."

"Polar bears have black skin."

John looks up from the paper. "Assault by biting?"

"He was under duress."

"Polar bears have black skin." Lucas laughs after saying the phrase this time, high and crazy.

I move to touch his arm, to do something to stave off this verbal stim, when I catch Dominique's eye. "Let it go," she mouths.

Understanding rushes through me. Lucas's behavior is his best defense.

"Polar bears have black skin."

John shifts his posture. "Is he going to keep saying that?"

I cross my arms. "It's a verbal stim. He's autistic, like I said."

"Polar bears have black skin."

I say nothing, letting the repeated phrase fill the space between us.

"Bring him into court if you want," I say finally. "I think it will be hard to prove competency."

"Polar bears have black skin."

"He'll need some accommodations, allowed by the ADA, of course," I add.

John's expression changes. His eyes fix toward the line of people behind me. He moves his stack of files like he's weighing them in his hand.

"Polar bears have black skin."

"All the extenuating circumstances surrounding crime will be hard to get around. The crowds, the fact he was lost. He put himself in harm's way, he was so confused."

"Polar bears have black skin."

John scans the document in his hand, pulls another from the file. "I see he has no prior record."

I keep my face neutral. "That's right."

"Polar bears have black skin."

John says nothing. Lucas lets out a high-pitched squeal.

"Okay," John says in a way that makes it seem like he's reluctantly admitting defeat. "I'll drop the charges, given . . ." he looks to Lucas, "everything."

"Thank you. I assume we don't need to stay."

John shakes his head like us staying is the last thing he would want. "No."

"Okay, then." I take Lucas's hand; Dominique takes the other one. We walk toward the elevator door. My heart explodes in my chest, and I have to force myself not to run. I want, I need, for us to get out of here before John changes his mind.

The elevator door slides open.

"Miss Ellison," John calls, his voice loud in the hallway.

For a moment, I consider pulling Lucas into the elevator and just escaping already, but in the next, I realize that wouldn't do anything. The charges haven't been dropped yet. I turn around and meet John's eyes.

"Good luck with your brother."

CHAPTER 77

L UCAS
 *Polar bears have black skin. I can't believe that ridicu-
lous verbal stim is what saved me. But here's a big secret.*
You ready?

I did that on purpose.

*Me. Lucas Ellison. Figuring out how to use ASD to help myself at
last. And as is fair in this particular situation. I didn't mean to hurt
the man. I don't even remember doing it!*

*At first, the phrase popped out without my meaning it to. It's not
one I've ever said in the past and it felt good, you know, to say something different. And calming. Because I was way nervous. And overstimulated. The courthouse was loud with weird smells and overhead
lighting that was about as bright as it could be outside of being inside
the sun. Plus, I didn't know what was happening.*

*Anyway, once I said it, I said it again. "Polar bears have black
skin." Then I said it a third time. I flapped my hands after. People
around me started to stare and the man Olivia was talking to, the DA,
looked at me with intense irritation. Like I was saying it on purpose to
annoy him, which at that point, I wasn't. He asked Oliva if I was
going to keep saying the phrase and the whole thing clicked. This*

phrase, the hand flapping, the whole autistic persona I was giving off was making this guy, the DA, think. How could he press charges against me? All I could say is "polar bears have black skin"?

So I said it more. And faster. People around us looked and stared; a few laughed. I kept saying the phrase, even as the DA was trying to talk, and even after I could have stopped, if I wanted to. "Polar bears have black skin." "Polar bears have black skin." "Polar bears have black skin" I said it over and over. And then it happened.

The DA dropped the charges. And while I don't advocate manipulating people, it felt so good that something I did had the intended effect. That hardly ever happens. Stim for the win!

CHAPTER 78

OLIVIA
 Days after the charges are dropped, after Dominique returns to Greenwillow, after Mom, Ellie, and Shelby resume their normal lives, after Lucas goes back to ACE, I make a slow trek to the Bennett Connor offices. This walk I once loved feels different now, the concrete landscape harsher, the air more polluted, the crowds pushier. I'm different now too, I guess. The past few days have changed me.

I take the elevator up to the 28th floor and commit details like the gold doors, the marble floor, and the whooshing sound as the boxcar ascends to memory. The elevator stops and I step across the plush red hallway rug, my shoes making prints in the fibers. I inhale the familiar scent of lemon furniture polish and glance around the lobby space that for so long felt like a second home. I say hi to Janelle and she waves, phone to her ear. I touch a petal on the giant vase of fresh flowers on her desk, and after, stride to Marjorie's office. I haven't spoken to her since our conversation about Lucas in the hospital.

I don't have an appointment, but I peek my head in the open door anyway. Marjorie's at her desk, papers strewn across it.

She swings her head up and I wait for her to ask how things went with Lucas. "Yes?" she says instead, her voice tone tinged with irritation.

Her attitude, the tone, the lack of concern about me or my brother bolsters my resolve. What I'm about to do, whatever comes of it, has to be done. "Got a minute?"

She whips her glasses off her face. "One," she says curtly.

I step into the office and shut the door.

"Olivia, really. I'm in the middle of trial prep." She gestures around the papers on her desk.

"You've given me a minute." I stand across from her desk. "I'm not sure if you know this," I start, "but I've admired, almost idolized you, since I was a little girl. The beautiful, powerful, female attorney with the office next to my dad's. And for as long as I can remember, I aspired to be just like you. Capable. Unflappable. The kind of person and lawyer that people respect." I pause and swallow. "And you are amazing. At law. At running this office."

A hint of blush appears on her cheekbones, and her mouth widens into a smile. "Thank you, Olivia. That's very kind."

I hold up my palm. "I'm not finished."

She rolls back in her office chair, a single eyebrow raised.

I press my fingertips against her desk, the wood grounding me. "When my dad left here, I could never figure out why he did it," I start. "Why would he leave a firm like Bennett Connor, where he could be in the center of some of the most exciting cases in New York, if not the country? When I'd ask him, all he'd say was one day you'll understand. But for the longest time I didn't."

A sigh escapes from her lips. "Is this about your brother? That thing over the weekend?"

"That thing?" Anger shoots through me. "My autistic brother being arrested and in the hospital is not *a thing*. And yes, this is about that, but only in that it showed me what this firm—what you—are really about."

"Be careful, Olivia." She stands.

I meet her eyes, and any hesitation I had about this decision evaporates. "Bennett Connor isn't a family," I continue. "And that conversation we had months back, about us needing to stick together as women, was total bullshit. You'll help me only if it serves you. Whether or not I, or my brother, actually needs the help is irrelevant."

I reach into my purse, pull out the envelope, and hold it in my hands. "Like I said, I've always admired you. I was willing to give the firm everything, all of me, just like you've done. But I don't want to do that anymore." I drop the envelope on her desk. "My resignation, effective immediately."

She shakes her head. "You can't be serious. You're a *partner*, Olivia. And before age thirty. Do you know how extraordinary that is? How many lawyers would trade places with you?" She walks in front of her desk and puts a hand on my shoulder, her eyes meeting mine. "You have the chance to be one of the few women to break through the ceiling at this firm," she says, her voice softer. "I know you, Olivia. I *was* you at your age. And you can be me, at mine. Don't break. Don't let your personal life cloud your judgment. Those issues can be dealt with. But an opportunity like this? It's once in a lifetime." She sweeps the envelope off her desk and extends it toward me.

I stare at the paper, and for a moment I consider taking it back. I've made the proverbial legal dream team, and even after telling Marjorie off in a way I'd never dreamed of, she's giving me a second chance. Kind of like you'd get from a family. Right? Yes?

"Olivia?" Marjorie prompts.

"No." The word emanates from deep inside my gut. From the place where I know defending guilty crypto criminals and chasing the latest big client in a cutthroat partnership race is not the life I want to lead, no matter how much I thought I did. I don't want to be like William, remembered only for his job. "No," I say again, more forcefully. "Thank you. My resignation stands."

"Honestly. I'm saving you from yourself." She waves the letter. "Last chance."

"No. Thank you for the once-in-a-lifetime opportunity, but I have one life to live, and I don't want to spend it here. I appreciate the opportunity you've given me, I do. It's just not what I want anymore." I extend my hand in her direction.

She ignores the overture and strides back to her desk. "You're just like your father." She collapses into the swivel chair. It moves with the force of her weight, putting her off balance in a way I've rarely seen. She rights herself. "You'll regret leaving here, Olivia. You walk out, you don't come back."

Her words have an air of desperation, and I catch her eyes. In that moment, she doesn't look steely or strong or confident. She just looks tired.

"Thanks for everything, Marjorie," I say and walk out.

I return to my office and grab the few framed pictures off the desk. I leave the firm. I say goodbye to Janelle on the way out but don't look for anyone else.

I spill out onto the sidewalk in front of the firm, adrenaline rushing through me. I fight the urge to run, jump, and squeal; the feeling is comparable to leaving school for summer vacation.

I stride toward the Kitty Cat Café and swing open the door. There's a smattering of customers around the coffee bar. I slide onto a stool and wait for Jess to finish up with the existing customers.

"Look what the cat dragged in," she says when she's done. She grabs a mug, pours a cup of coffee, and slides it across the bar in my direction. "How's partnership?"

I cup the warm drink between my palms. "I quit."

"What?"

"Yup, quit," I affirm. "But that's not why I'm here. I wanted to check on Otis. See how he's making out with his new family."

She tips her head. "Not too well, actually."

"No?"

She shakes her head. "He meowed all the time. Scratched the toddler. Spent most of his time hiding," they said.

My belly flutters. "What are they going to do?"

"They gave him back," she says.

I cover my mouth with my hand.

"He's available," she says, an air of levity in her tone. "For a forever home." She widens her eyes in my direction. "Not a foster."

My mouth splits into a grin. "And if I were to apply?"

Jess shakes her head. "He's your cat, Olivia. You know that."

"So?"

She waves her arm forward. "Come on. Let's go get your little man."

CHAPTER 79

OLIVIA

Three weeks later

Chuck Stockton gestures around the office space in Greenwillow. "It's a little rundown." His tone is apologetic.

I glance around the office, Lucas next to me. Deep rivets and obvious scratches scuff the hardwood floor. Paint peels around a window which looks out onto the main street, an old rooster-themed valance over it. The furniture is pocked and mismatched and has '80s vibes. Old law books line a bookshelf in the back, pushed against the edge of it by an empty glass vase. On the top of the shelf is a small, framed handstitched quote: Love is Everything. This office is, in every way, the opposite of my sleek and modern space at Bennett Connor.

"It's perfect."

"Yeah? So you'll start Monday?"

"Absolutely."

Chuck ushers Lucas and me out of the office. We've been back in Greenwillow for less than two weeks, but things have fallen into place so quickly it's like we were meant to come back. Chuck is looking to retire in a few years. I'm going to work under him and learn how to handle the kind of matters that help ordinary people, with the eventual goal for me to take over the practice. Lucas is reenrolled at Greenwillow High School, his class filled with all the same students he's grown up with, including Avery. He seems happy about it, so I am too.

Lucas and I file into my car, and I drive back to Melanie's. Otis is sitting in the window as we pull up, an array of potted plants around him. He blinks at us as we make our way up the walkway. I push open the front door, never locked—because, Greenwillow—and we tumble inside. Like my new office at Stockton and Associates, this house has none of the sophistication of my NYC apartment. No clap on lighting (thank God) or 500 thread count sheets. The appliances are old, not stainless steel, and the kitchen countertops are Formica instead of granite. The furniture is cushy instead of streamlined, the space cluttered rather than minimalistic. But despite handpicking everything in my apartment, this space feels more like home than that one ever did. There are still remnants of Nate, but even those are lessening the longer I'm here. He seems less real now. Like a helpful ghost who appeared in my life and disappeared from it just as quickly.

Lucas and I take the walk around Monroe pond, and after, I drive to Big Rod's. We order a pizza to share, and I place the box and paper plate stack on one of the painted blue picnic tables out back. I slide onto the attached bench. Lucas does the same. I pull out a slice and bite into it. It isn't NYC Neapolitan, but it's good enough.

"Olivia."

I whirl around at the familiar voice. Mr. Wilder. Nate's father. His mother next to him, a grease-stained brown paper bag in her hands.

"Mr. and Mrs. Wilder. How are you?" I extricate myself from the picnic bench and stand. My heart flutters. I'd been wanting to talk to the Wilders since Nate left but had decided against it.

If Nate wanted me to know where he was, he would have called. Period. End of story. The fact that he didn't tells me all I need to know.

Until now.

Now that I see the Wilders, now that the answer to the question—where is Nate?—is right in front of me, I desperately want to know. Where *is* Nate?

His mother pulls me into a light hug. "Chuck told me you two were back," she says in my ear. She steps back and gives me a warm smile. "That's so wonderful."

"Thank you. That means a lot." I smile back and wait for them to mention the obvious and the only thing that tethers us together. Nate.

Mrs. Wilder holds up the paper bag. "I guess we'd better get this food home."

"Wait," I stammer. "I don't mean to pry but—" I pause. "Do you know where Nate is?"

Mrs. Wilder's brow furrows. "You haven't heard from him?"

No. I want to scream the word. NO. The man I loved, or thought I did, stepped out of my life with no explanation. What I'd thought was a break turned into a forever goodbye, for me and for Lucas.

"He didn't," I say simply.

"He's—" she starts, but Mr. Wilder puts a hand over hers.

He whispers something, intending for me not to hear, but I get the gist of it. That wherever Nate is, it's not for them to say. He angles his head toward me. "He's fine."

"But where is he?" I press.

"We barely speak to him," Mrs. Wilder amends. "He's busy. But he's fine." She shifts the bag of food from one hand to the other. "Thank you for asking about him."

They turn away and I immediately step after them. I want the information about where Nate is so viscerally now that it almost hurts. I open my mouth to call out, then snap it shut. I'm the girl who hauled their son away to New York and then ignored him. For all I know, they think I used him to help with Lucas. To them, I might even be the reason he's not here, in Greenwillow. The Wilders have every reason not to like me. Not to trust me. They certainly have no reason to tell me something that Nate didn't think I was fit to know.

They get into the car, and Mr. Wilder pulls out into the road. I lift a hand toward them in a small gesture of goodbye.

The Nate door.

I need to close it once and for all.

CHAPTER 80

NATE

Day 89.

I look around my bedroom. Sparsely decorated with a bed and a dresser, a threadbare throw rug on the floor. The space is bare bones but made up for by floor to ceiling windows which line the entire room. Outside are the Colorado Rocky Mountains and a big blue sky which seems to have a different, brighter hue than anywhere else I've ever been.

I go into my bathroom and look into the mirror. "I forgive you," I say out loud. I feel less ridiculous saying it now than I did on day one. But forgiveness is the essence of where I am, where I have been, and I'm following all the rules.

Dr. Alan had mentioned a forgiveness retreat when I first saw him as a patient years ago. I'd scoffed at the idea and instead entrenched myself in my own brilliant solution: guilting my way into feeling better. If I felt bad enough, if I kept myself down enough, it would make up for the accident. It hasn't worked. Clearly. When things went south with Olivia, I reached out Dr. Alan, and he suggested the retreat again. "It sounds hell-ish," I told him.

"And it's not hellish to live in the grip of your guilt every day?"

He was right.

So I'm here. I've been here. Cut off from the world per house rules. I've been working at the forgiveness thing. And it's getting better. But today? Today will be the hardest thing I've ever done. And I'm dreading it.

I shower, dress, and eat my usual egg, clementine, and rye toast in the dining room, my favorite part of the lodge. Floor-to-ceiling windows like those in my room give a picturesque view of the mountains and fields and nearby stream. The ceiling is lined with thick beams and giant rustic chandeliers. Thick, oak circular tables with cushiony chairs are scattered throughout the expansive space.

I finish breakfast and take a walking meditation on the wooded path which encircles the lodge. The walk reminds me of the ones I used to take with Lucas around Monroe Pond in Greenwillow. It's more majestic here, obviously, but the routine of it, the connection with nature, gives me that same feeling of peace. I repeat the mantra in my head as I walk:

I let go of the past to move forward.

I let go of the past to move forward.

I let go of the past to move forward.

I'm not self-conscious about this one because, unlike the mirror meditation, I say it internally. And it is helpful. Everything has been. The mediations, the deep breathing, the speakers, the journaling. Just being away, no phone, no interruptions. The therapy has been brutal, but necessary, and I can now think about Mark Carney, about the accident, without completely shutting down emotionally.

Until now.

I reach the lodge after the walk and check my watch. It's less than an hour until they come. Mark Carney's family.

The therapists here emphasized the importance of my

apology to the family in the form of a letter. I was instructed to write all the things I was sorry about and have thought about for the past nearly three years. So I did. I wrote the letter. I asked for forgiveness. I told Mark's family how sorry I was.

I was never meant to send it. The exercise was just to take pen to paper and write what I would say in person if I had the chance. But I found Mrs. Carney's address online, still in the same house in Pittsburgh that they lived in at the time of the accident. In a fit of bravery or stupidity or I don't know what, I mailed the letter with the return address right here, my name, one I'm sure is permanently imprinted on their minds as theirs is in my own, front and center. I never thought I'd hear from them.

But they wrote back. The yellow envelope sat unopened on my dresser for a week. I'd pick it up and hold it in my hand, afraid of the contents inside—of the hate and the vitriol the response had to contain—and set it back down. In a fit of anxiousness, I threw out the card but its presence in my trash was akin to Edgar Allen Poe's telltale heart, unnerving me, sitting there, unseen proof of what I'd done. I finally gave the unopened card to Tristan, head of the program, to read and dispose of. "If there's anything I need to know, tell me," I said. "Otherwise, just get rid of it."

I didn't hear anything about the card in a week. I didn't ask and Tristan didn't bring it up. Until yesterday. Surprise. Tristan informed me that the Carney family was dropping their daughter off at college and coming here to see me on the way. Today. "They want to come," he told me. "I think it will be healing for you."

Healing? There's nothing healing about looking directly into the eyes of the people whose husband and father you stole. I'm sure about that. But the whole trip was already set in motion before I could object. And how could I anyway? I indirectly asked for this meeting by writing the letter, and if the Carney family needs to confront me, I need to take it. It's the least I can do.

I return to my room, lie on my bed, and check my watch again. Twenty-five minutes.

Twenty minutes, fifteen, ten, five.

With five minutes to go until the meeting, a knock sounds on my door. I leap off the bed and swing it open. Tristan holds up a hand. Maybe the family is a no-show?

"Are you ready?"

My heart dives deep into my chest. "Not at all."

He puts a hand on my shoulder. "You got this, Nate."

I straighten my shirt and follow Tristan down the hall. We're meeting in the study, a homey room with cozy furniture, piles of books, and a fireplace. It's a place in the lodge that normally gives me comfort, but not today. My hands shake; my stomach roils. There's an ache in the back of my throat and my body feels heavy, encased in a thick layer of dread. I feel every movement I'm making, every sense heightened.

I wish Tristan would say something. Then he does, but I don't quite hear him through my blood rushing, my heart beating, the amplified sound of everything around me.

We reach the closed door to the study and stand outside of it. I'm out of my body, seeing my physical self in front of the door. Tristan pushes it open, and I step inside.

All three of them are there. Sarah, Mikaela, and Jay. Wife, daughter, son. They look different from the picture of them in the newspaper, the vacation beach shot that has been imprinted in my mind since the accident. Not suntanned and touched up. Real.

"Nate," Sarah says.

I nod, unable to interpret her tone.

"Do you want to sit?" Tristan asks and I move to a seat next to Jay, across from Sarah and Mikaela, both on the couch.

Tristan sits on the window seat, in my line of vision. I'm grateful for that.

I look from Sarah, to Mikaela, to Jay. "I'm sorry," I blurt. "I'm so sorry."

"We know," Mikaela says. I remember from the paper that she was seventeen years old. She's twenty now. Probably in college. "We read the letter."

"Yeah." I shake my head. "I'm sorry if it opened old wounds. I was just supposed to write—"

"Thank you for sending it," Sarah interrupts. "Reading your words gave me closure I didn't know I needed." She shuts her eyes, opens them. "Mark was a wonderful husband and father. But he wasn't perfect. He'd be the first to admit that." She gives a small shake of her head.

I exhale.

"We loved him, but he wasn't the flawless soul you wrote about, and he would want you to know that." She fiddles with her ring. "But I'll be honest. After it happened, I had trouble accepting the accident, accepting that Mark was gone. It was such a shock for all of us."

She pauses. Mikaela and Jay lean forward, assenting to her words with their body language.

"I'm okay now." Sarah gestures to Mikaela and Jay. "We're all okay, but it's been a hard road. I don't want to pretend it wasn't. And I villainized you, imagined you as a stuck-up, medical school-bound kid recklessly driving drunk. Over time, I didn't think about you as much—time heals all wounds and all that— but when I did think of you, that's the image I held. The spoiled, uncaring teenager who shattered my life, who took away my Mark."

I drop my gaze to the floor.

"Until I read your letter."

Sarah steps off the couch, gives my leg a pat, and sits back down. "I've spoken to Tristan and some of the workers here.

You are not who I made you out to be. You're a good young man, and you deserve to have a future. The guilt you have been holding on to is something no one should have to endure. So I, we," she gestures to her children, "came here to let you know that we forgive you." She stands up. "And we hope you will forgive yourself."

I swallow, staring, not quite comprehending. "But—"

"Nate," she says firmly, in a tone a mother would use, "there are no buts here. We forgive you. And we want you to forgive yourself. Mark would want that too. Imperfect as he was, he was kind, and he would hate the idea that his death cost not only his life but yours." She holds out her arms.

I don't deserve this. This phrase repeats itself in my mind as I get up and move into Sarah's arms. *I don't deserve this. I don't deserve this. I don't deserve this.* She envelops me and pulls me tight, and I smell her perfume, feel the realness of her, so different from the image I've had in my mind. *I don't deserve this. We forgive you. I don't deserve this. We forgive you.* The competing thoughts cycle through me and the guilt loosens. She lets go and Mikaela hugs me, then Jay. No hate. No vitriol. *We forgive you. We forgive you. We forgive you.*

I step back, my face wet with tears. "Thank you," I whisper. "Thank you so much."

"I understand," Sarah says with a nod toward Tristan, "that you have a ton of potential." She smiles. "Use it for good."

CHAPTER 81

LUCAS
Burning news!!!!
Nate is here.
At the house.

I mean, I've already been so happy to be back in Greenwillow. My room, my house, the animals. Avery. It's all been great. But I've missed Nate. Missed our pond walks. Missed his music. Missed his voice and the time we spent together.

And now he's here! In the driveway! With flowers. For Olivia, probably.

Does Oliva know he's coming? Probably not. She's great about telling me things, sometimes too much, you know, like I get it already. I doubt she'd keep something like this—like Nate coming back—to herself. No way.

I move to the front door and Nate smiles at me through the glass. He pushes it open, steps inside, and he hugs me tight. "Lucas," he says, "I've missed you." I've missed you too, I think but don't say, and I pull at his arm and lead him back into the house. Once we get into the family room, he pulls a Nemo-themed Rubik's cube from the gift bag and hands it to me. "I thought you might like this," he says.

"Lu? Is someone here?" Olivia calls. Her feet sound on the stairs, hurried. She's probably worried there's an intruder here, or a kidnapper. Even though we're back in Greenwillow, she's been somewhat paranoid since the Krispy Kreme incident.

She rounds the corner at the bottom of the staircase, and I feel like a little kid, like I've got a big surprise that I can't wait to give. She'll be thrilled to see Nate. She loves Nate. Just like I do. My heart pounds. Her feet sound on the landing. Wait until you see who's here, Olivia. Just wait.

She rounds the corner and looks in Nate's direction. She stares at him for the longest time, like he's a ghost. And the expression on her face? It is most definitely not thrilled.

CHAPTER 82

OLIVIA

Nate. It's Nate. Standing in the foyer. The man I've agonized over, pined over, thought about more than any other man I'd ever met. The one I've spent the past six months missing. When Nate first left, I'd imagined that if I saw him, I'd crash into his chest with a giant hug, inhale his scent, kiss his lips. Take in all his Nateness in a happy whirlwind of relief.

Seeing him now? I'm angry.

"Hey."

I lift a hand.

"I got you flowers." He thrusts a bouquet in my direction.

Flowers. He's gone for six months with no contact, and he gets me flowers? "Really, Nate? Flowers." I take the bouquet, and my eyes track toward Lucas, next to Nate and clearly delighted. I blow out a breath and walk toward the kitchen. They both follow me. "Water? Coffee?" I ask. "Not sure what you're drinking these days."

"Water's good," he says and slides into a seat at the table. Lucas does the same.

I put the flowers in water and take down glasses.

"So you moved back here," he says finally. "My parents told me."

I slide a water glass in front of him, a second in front of Lucas. I don't sit but lean against the counter, arms crossed. "I'm glad you've been in touch with *your parents*," I say.

"I'm sorry." He pulls his wallet from his back pocket and retrieves a laptop sticker from inside. It depicts an owl with the caption: "Be "hoo" you are." He lays it on the table.

I stare at it, then angle my head up and meet his eyes. I know Lucas is here and that he's happy to see Nate, all forgiven in his mind, it seems, but that's not me. I'm angry. The flowers were bad enough but the owl sticker. It's like waving a red flag in front of a bull.

"First the flowers and now this sticker. Boy, Nate. It's almost like you didn't disappear for six months. Like I didn't text you and call you and think that maybe you were hurt or even dead. It wasn't like I was constantly worried and had to track your well-being through cryptic comments from your parents or anything."

"We were broken up," he says flatly. "I didn't think I needed to check in."

"Not every day, but never? Not once in six months." I shift my posture. "I was going to get used to partnership. You were going to find your path. It was never meant to be a goodbye and have a nice life." I shake my head. "Do you have any idea how many times I tried to call you?"

Lucas, in the middle of the kind of tension he hates, scrapes back his chair and leaves the room. His feet sound on the stairs and the door to his room slams shut. As bad as I feel for losing my temper on Nate in front of him, and as much as I want to reel things in right now, I can't. I'm too in the grip of my anger.

I step to the table, swipe the owl sticker off it, and hold it up.

"But don't worry, Nate, this owl sticker? It makes up for everything."

"Olivia." He stands and takes the sticker from my hand. "Do you have any idea how much I've thought of you over the past months? I picked up this sticker because I thought it would make you laugh, and I really love your laugh. I have a whole box of things like this in my car. Coffee that I thought you could drink in the morning. Chocolates with caramel. A scarf that matches your eyes. Perfume that reminds me of how you smell. Oversized hoodies with fuzz on the inside. Plants that can't be killed, even if you never have time to water them. Owl earrings."

A lump lodges in my throat. Otis saunters in and makes a beeline toward Nate. He bends down and scratches his chin. "Hey, buddy."

He looks up. "It seemed pathetic to bring in the box and even the flowers, so I just have this stupid sticker." He throws it on the table. "Obviously, I know a sticker or even the box doesn't make up for disappearing, but I thought it might break the ice." He crosses his legs, leaning against the counter. "You haven't even bothered to ask me where I've been, Olivia."

"You caught me off guard. You knew you were coming here. I didn't."

He nods. "Fair."

"I do want to know where you've been," I say. "Of course, I do."

"I've been at a forgiveness retreat," he says.

I repeat the words in my mind, and my heart expands as I take in their meaning. A forgiveness retreat. Of all the places I'd imagined Nate being, that had never occurred to me, but it's exactly what he needed. Time to finally slay the guilt that had riddled him for years. "Oh, Nate," I gush. "That's good. That's really good."

"Thanks."

"Why didn't you tell me?"

He blows out a breath. "I didn't think I would stay. The whole time I was going there, I was thinking, no way, no way am I doing this. But when I got there" he shrugs, "something changed."

I lean forward, still not understanding why a forgiveness retreat would be something he'd keep a secret. "But you still didn't tell me. Even when you decided to stay, you didn't call. I would have supported you. You know that."

"I do. I know." He pauses. "But I was in such a dark place, Liv. We'd broken up, my path to medical school was shot, and I had no idea what I wanted to do with my life. I just felt wrong." He drops his gaze to the table. "I told my parents, figuring anyone worried about me would ask them. It was the best I could do at that moment." He lifts his face and meets my eyes. "You deserved better. I'm sorry."

I turn his explanation over in my mind. I'd been too busy with the Jupiter Rowan case and with chasing down partnership to realize Nate had been in that bad of a place. I put my hand over his, rub my thumb over his knuckle.

"How was it. The retreat?"

He nods. "I met the Carneys."

I shift, placing the name. "The Carneys? Mark's family?"

"Yes." He shares about the meeting in detail, and I give a silent thanks to Sarah Carney and her children for their kindness. Nate's voice has a different tone. Still regretful, but not hopeless. "Sarah made me promise to do something good with my life," he says. "I have some ideas about that. And you," he gestures toward me, "you worked so hard to be a partner. What happened?"

I tell him all of it. How I set Lucas up with therapy to fill every minute. How I worked constantly to keep up with the partnership obligations. I tell him that Lucas disappeared in Times Square and how everyone from Greenwillow came to help. I share my conversation with Marjorie and about how his uncle Chuck stepped in to help me navigate the criminal process. I tell him about my realization that the kind of law I was doing was no longer what I wanted. That New York no longer felt like home.

"So you're here. For good?"

"For good," I tell him. "It's home."

CHAPTER 83

NATE
It's Sunday dinner at Jenny and Rod's with the usual crew, which now, a month after I returned from the retreat, includes Olivia. We're around a dining room table full of heaping plates of haphazard food and scattered wine glasses. The atmosphere is happy loud, multiple streams of conversation taking place at once. Carly telling a funny dating story about a guy that showed up in a cow onesie, Rod complaining about the Steelers and all else Pittsburgh sports. It's normal and fun and I don't want to drop my bomb, if it is that. I don't know anymore.

"So I've decided," I say loudly. As soon as I do, Olivia grabs my hand under the table and gives it a quick squeeze. My family *should* support this idea, but it's not what they, really my Dad, wanted for me, so I don't know.

Mom shovels a bite of meatloaf into her mouth and swallows. "Decided what, dear?"

"What I'm going to do with the rest of my life."

All conversation stops in an instant. The sounds of utensils scraping and ice cubes rattling cease. The atmosphere is so still, everyone so quiet, it feels almost like we're frozen in place at the table.

Dad nods in my direction. I have no idea if it's a nod of support, but I internalize it as one, which is enough to get me started. "This may disappoint some of you," I start, then shake my head. No. This news is not disappointing.

"It might," I continue, "but it shouldn't." I swallow. "I'm not going to pursue medical school. I lost passion for that a while ago; I just couldn't get myself to admit it. What I'm going to do instead"—I pause and Olivia rests her hand on my thigh—"is go back to school. I'm going to become an autism program special- ist. I didn't fully believe in the program at Lucas's New York school, but it did have components I think would be beneficial for a lot of students with ASD. I'm not sure of the path I'll need to take to get there, but it's my goal to work with school districts on implementing some innovative programming for autism without losing the kindness and familiarity these kids need." I blow out a breath. "That's it in a nutshell. I'm still working out the details."

No one speaks. And as much as I've told myself I didn't care about anyone's approval, in the silent seconds that follow my announcement, I realize that I do. I may not need approval, but I very much want it.

Finally, Olivia lifts her glass. "To Nate and his exciting new venture."

Her toast uncorks what I assume was a latent reaction. Glasses clink. Mom reaches across the table and squeezes my hand. Carly shoots out of her chair and hugs me. The mood, at least in my head, has shifted, and my heart lifts along with it. I would have proceeded with my plan regardless, but the affirma- tion of my family warms me—icing on the cake.

I shift my gaze to Dad, fully expecting he's part of it all, his glass in the air along with the others. But his wine remains flat on the table. And he's unmoving in his chair, head swung down, fingers pinched around either side of the bridge of his nose like he's in pain. Maybe he is. Maybe he can't let go of the idea of Dr. Nathan Wilder.

Irritation cascades through me, well on its way to anger. Everyone else is excited for me. Why can't he be? It's my life, not his, and I'm excited about this. "Dad," I prompt, ready to have it out with him right here and right now if that's what it takes.

He lifts his head and the second he does, I see it in his face. Not anger or disappointment, but pride and love. He wipes a sliver of tears from his cheek. "I'm proud of you, son," he says, his voice breaking. "What a difference you'll make to those future kids." He pushes out his chair and moves directly behind me, one hand on my shoulder, the other holding a glass of wine. "Nate," he says, and though there are a dozen people in the room, it feels like it's just the two of us. "I'm so proud of the hard work you've put in the past months to get to a point where you can see a path forward with hope. I can only imagine how lucky those future students will be to have you at the helm, working to make sure they have the best opportunities for rich and expressive lives. This career choice is perfect for you. Congratulations." He holds up a glass. "To Nate."

"To Nate," my family echoes back.

I field questions the rest of the dinner, but unlike the awful intervention all those months ago, I'm not on the defensive. And no one is worried about me. The conversation is good and while I don't have everything figured out yet, I do have a framework to work within.

Olivia stays by my side, her hand occasionally brushing my leg or my arm. I love that she's here, that she's next to me, that we're a thing again. Resuming our relationship hadn't been an easy road. As happy as she'd been that I'd gone to the forgiveness retreat, she'd been angry at me for "disappearing off the face of the earth," and I don't blame her for that. But we've slowly eased back to where we were before, stronger now. She's no longer torn between two lives, and I'm no longer paralyzed by guilt. Weird, and I'll never say this to Olivia, but I think the time apart without contact made us closer. Not that I shouldn't have called—I know I was wrong—but in the end we both figured out what we needed to do without worrying about the other. We needed that.

At the end of the night, I find Olivia standing with Lucas and Carly in the foyer.

"Carly and I are going to see Wicked on Broadway," Liv announces. "And to look at apartments." She squeezes Carly's shoulder. "I just know she's going to get that Manhattan job."

Carly beams. "I would love it."

"Me too," Olivia says. "It's a great city." She swings her head toward Lucas. "But don't worry, Lu. No more New York for you."

I swear Lucas smiles, just the tiniest bit. He and I are happy to let Carly fill Olivia's New York fix. Neither of us have a need to go back there. At least not anytime soon.

Olivia puts her hand on the door. "Ready to go home, guys?" she asks, and I smile. Because home is now the three of us.

CHAPTER 84

O LIVIA
To-dos

1. Plan birthday party for Lucas
2. Increase volunteer hours at legal clinic
3. Finish Impact 100 application for Include
4. Sign up for cooking class with Fab Five
5. Organize Mom and sister New York day

"Okay, coming out," Nate calls from the massive bathroom of our hotel room.

"Ready out here too." I snap my laptop and to-dos shut.

Nate and Lucas emerge from the bathroom in the tuxedos we rented for Ellie's wedding. I rise from the hotel desk chair, my heart surging at the sight of them. Lucas, tall with slicked back hair, in clothes he probably hates but is wearing anyway for me and for his cousin Ellie. And Nate. God. Nate with his happy blue eyes and sweet, lopsided grin. He fills out the tuxedo like an undercover superhero. "You guys look amazing," I gush.

"You"—Nate barrels toward me and grabs my hands—"are

stunning." His eyes sweep down my body. "Jeez, Olivia. Was this the dress you said made you look like Casper the ghost on prom night?" He shakes his head. "If it is, Casper's date is one lucky guy."

My cheeks flush and I catch a mirrored glimpse of myself in the off-white gown. It's full-length and fitted satin, a slit up the side to the middle of my thigh. After alternations, the dress bears no resemblance to the tent-like structure I'd tried on all those months ago. My skin is now less pale, sun-touched from spending some time each day outside. It's glowing too. Or I am. Things have been good.

Nate kisses my cheek. "Let's get you to the church."

The hotel, in downtown Wycoff where I'd lived with Mom, Adam, and the twins for the bulk of my childhood, is down the block from the church. I walk, Lucas on one side and Nate on the other. Once in the church, Lucas and Nate take a seat in the back next to Shelby's girlfriend, Greta. Greta and Shelby's "big reveal" about their long-time, secret relationship is new. Mom has been supportive, which surprised me, given her traditional leanings. I'd like to think that her growing relationship with Lucas—she does things with us periodically now—warmed her to the idea that not every person or every relationship needs to fit into the same box.

I leave the three of them and move to the hall where I'm to meet Ellie, Mom, and the others. I push open the door. Ellie is wearing a dress with a tight, beaded bodice, a tulle flared skirt, and a long train. Mom's fooling with the veil, and the other bridesmaids mill around, several holding perfect circular flower bouquets.

Ellie's face splits into a smile. "Liv. Hooray."

I'm not sure my presence has ever been met with the word "hooray" and I smile. "You look like a celebrity." I squeeze her hand and give an air kiss.

I talk to the other bridesmaids, feeling a part of the group in a way that used to feel foreign. I'm part of numerous groups now. The Fab Five. Nate's family. The twins and Mom. Include caregivers. The local bar. I rarely think about my Bennett Connor "family," my tenure with them seeming to belong to an entirely different woman.

After a bit, Mom, self-appointed wedding planner, claps her hands. "It's time," she says. We move through the halls to the vestibule; the groomsmen and Adam are already there. One of the groomsmen walks Mom to her seat and Pachelbel's Canon in D rings out from the giant organ in front. Each bridesmaid pairs off with a groomsman, each set walking in the slow manner Mom demonstrated during yesterday's rehearsal.

At my turn, I stand at the end of the aisle and link my arms with Brian, a tall redhead who was one of Hunter's best friends in high school. Tessa, Jared, and Suzanne, having bonded with the twins during the awful Krispy Kreme night and in later trips to Greenwillow, wave from a pew. Sloane and Beau Cushing smile at me as I pass, the former in a stunning bohemian dress, the latter wearing a standard tux. My eyes scan over relatives and old neighbors I'd dismissed over the years. I'm glad to see them now, each carrying with them tiny bits of my childhood.

I reach the front few pews and spy the two broad-shoul-dered men sitting side by side. Nate twists his head around and throws me a smile so genuine that my heart catches. Our eyes meet and I feel it. Home.

EPILOGUE

L
UCAS

Eighteen months later

It's Christmastime and very early in the morning. Avery and I, along with the Fab Five, stand in front of the Rockefeller tree in New York. The lights are still stunning and while I still love it, I'm more interested in Avery's reaction. I look at her look at the tree and she looks just as surprised as I did that first time. I'm glad. She's here because of me. Because I asked her.

Yup. Me. I asked her, and she said yes. A simple thing, but wow. WOW. This is an actual date. Our first, I'd say, though we have been hanging out a lot.

Anyway, how? How did I ask Avery to come to New York? And how did she answer? Well—wait for it—we can both type. Right?!?

Nate, as part of his masters, is doing massive research on facilitated communication and the rapid prompting method, both of which teach nonverbal autistic individuals like me and Avery to type. Both methods get a fair amount of hate in the science and some autistic communities, according to Nate. He said some facilitators got so excited that they spoke for the autistic students. If you ask me, I don't think those people meant to do that. But whether they meant to or not *doesn't mean the methods never work. They work for me. And Avery. And lots of other people as far as I understand. I get that it's not for everyone and it doesn't work for everyone, but I say, let us try. Why not? When it works, it's a game changer.*

Anyway, Nate taught me and Avery and a few others at Include as part of his study. It's been hard because it requires more than just knowing how to spell—that I can do—but also muscle coordination, which is harder. But I was motivated, and I worked at it, and though typing takes FOREVER, the end result is, well, life-changing. Case in point: me and Avery here in front of the tree I'd wanted to take her to ever since I saw it.

Avery pushes my shoulder, and I glance toward her. She looks pretty in a blue coat and hat, cheeks pink from the cold. Blue is her favorite color, I now know. Along with other things. She likes chocolate ice cream. And the beach. She follows the Pittsburgh Pirates, something I do too now, for her. She hates to be hot, she likes Ms. Caddell, and her favorite movie is Mary Poppins. *She watches that on a loop, like I do with* Back to the Future *and* Finding Nemo. *I find out more about Avery every time we get together. Real things. I can't tell you how awesome that's been.*

She holds her iPad up in my direction and I read the words. HER words. "The tree is pretty."

I smile and take the time to write back, fingers poking at the singular letters on my iPad. Poke. Poke. Poke. Takes forever, like I said. I hold up my own device when I'm done. "I knew you would like it."

She smiles.

I'm feeling pretty good about things, if I'm honest. Now that I can type, I can go back to school and learn the way I was supposed to, all along. Not the easy stuff like in Ms. Caddell's class and not the mostly too advanced classes at ACE. And who knows what will happen then? I definitely want a job. Maybe teaching, like Nate. Or law, like Olivia. Or something else. I don't know yet. But the possibilities are there now, where they weren't before.

Avery puts her hand on top of mine. I let out a breath and smile. Broken body and all, my life right now is beautiful.

THE END

AFTERWORD

Dear Readers,

Thank you for reading *Home!* Of all my books, this one was the most difficult to write and took me the longest. I think this was in part because of the inclusion of a non-verbal autistic character, Lucas. It was important for me that Lucas be non-verbal because, in my reading, most fiction characters with Autism Spectrum Disorder are high functioning. Since an individual with high functioning autism will have a vastly different experience than one who is non-verbal, I wanted to give the latter a voice. My original idea was to include vignettes at the start of each chapter - little scenes which would show Lucas interacting, or not interacting, with the other characters and the world around him. As much as I liked these small glimpses, the ultimate effect was that they showed how Lucas's ASD impacted others, not how *he* felt.

At the time, I was working with a phenomenal book coach, Hend Hegazi. She asked why I was afraid to give Lucas a viewpoint. I said that I didn't want to give him a voice because he was non-verbal and I didn't know what he would be thinking.

And duh! Isn't that the exact reason I wanted to include him to begin with? To try to understand his thinking?

With this in mind and in addition to other research, I read several books written by non-verbal individuals with ASD who learned to type. These book include *Why I Jump* by Naoki Higashida, *Ido in Autismland* by Ido Kedar, *In Two Worlds* by Ido Kedar, and *Carly's Voice* by Arthur Fleischman. Using the collective knowledge about the inner thoughts and experiences of those with non-verbal ASD from these brave authors, I began to write in Lucas's words. I don't presume that what Lucas thinks or experiences is typical of every individual with ASD, but I was happy to give him the voice he would not have in real life.

A second challenge was creating a plot arc for Lucas. The other point-of-view characters in the book, Olivia and Nate, have clear goals and can act to make them happen, or not. But because Lucas cannot communicate beyond the basics and because he has substantial needs, he has no real agency over his life circumstances. If you have read the book, you'll have seen that he gets a happily-ever-after, but much of the story happens *to* him without his input. This was a challenge, but I ultimately decided his lack of control is a relevant theme as it reflects the reality of many with ASD.

The final challenge was writing about autism itself. Having close friends with an autistic child, I was a witness to some of the more difficult challenges in navigating ASD. Every individual diagnosed with this disorder presents unique needs and I wanted to be sensitive to the fact that caring for Lucas, who is not violent and fairly amenable, may not be the experience of all caregivers. While this is not stated in the book directly, I want to acknowledge that fact here.

Finally, thank you for reading *Home*. I hope you found meaning in the stories of Olivia, Nate, and Lucas. I appreciate you.

Love, Leanne

ACKNOWLEDGMENTS

For and foremost, I thank Terri and Mike Grant. These close friends raised a wonderful son, Dylan, with ASD to whom this book is also dedicated. Terri was instrumental as a beta reader and her insights made the book much better.

Thank you to Hend Hegazi, the book coach who encouraged me to include what I call "the Lucas chapters." Hend helped me through a time where I was discouraged with writing and almost gave up and opened a toy store (for real!).

Thank you to Nanette Littlestone for proofreading *Home*. Proofreading is a weakness of mine and having a professional like Nanette read over my work was a gift.

Thank you to Jena Collins, the amazing artist who designs all of my covers. I look forward to working with Jena every time I finish a book. The book cover design process truly is the icing on the cake and the cover for *Home* is my favorite yet.

Thank you to Wendy Stetson, Katie Treese, Kevin Treese, and Maria Imbalzano for giving input on the early drafts of this book.

Thank you to the Clinton Presbyterian book club ladies for giving input on the back cover blurb and the cover.

And last but not least, thank you to my husband, Jake Treese. He has always been my biggest supporter and cheerleader and I couldn't be luckier to have him in my corner. If he's my only fan, it's enough.

ABOUT THE AUTHOR

 Leanne Treese is an award-winning and bestselling author of women's fiction and romance. Her books have each independently been described as having "all the feels." When she's not writing, Leanne loves running, forcing her family to play board games (Settlers of Catan anyone?), and spoiling her beloved dogs. Leanne's favorite locations include her backyard, the Jersey shore, and anywhere that sells books or coffee, preferably both. A lifelong learner, Leanne's dream life would include going back to college and majoring in everything. More about Leanne and her books can be found on her website: www.leannetreese.com.

AMAZON BESTSELLER

FOR FANS OF JODI PICOULT

"*Mother of the Accused* is a master class in how to keep the reader engaged." Sheila Athens, author of *Neena Lee is Seeing Things*

"Well developed and full of heart. A great book discussion choice!" @lovemybooks2020

After the tragic death of her husband, Meredith Morgan spends a decade raising their son, Zach, alone. On the verge of Zach's graduation from high school, Meredith moves in with her fiancé, Dr. Reed Edwards, excited to begin a new chapter. But, when Zach is accused of sexually assaulting the daughter of a prominent lawyer, Meredith's life spins out of control. Reed's ex-wife does not want their daughters in the same house as Zach; Meredith's best friend distances herself and her sons from the fray. Only childhood friend and lawyer, Peter Flynn, remains by Meredith's side.

As Peter and Meredith team up to prove Zach's version of the events, long buried feelings resurface, complicating an already difficult circumstance. Meanwhile, evidence mounts against Zach and Meredith faces the ever-increasing likelihood her son is guilty. Struggling to cope with the idea of Zach behind bars, Meredith learns just how far a mother will go to protect her own.